Sheila O'Flanagan's books, including *Someone Special*, *Bad Behaviour* and *Yours, Faithfully*, have been huge bestsellers in the UK and Ireland; they are all available from Headline Review. Prior to taking the decision to write full time, Sheila pursued a very successful career in banking and finance. In her spare time she plays competitive badminton and is currently a director of the Irish Sports Council.

By Sheila O'Flanagan and available from
Headline Review

Sheila O'Flanagan

The Perfect Man

headline
review

First published in 2009
by HEADLINE REVIEW
An imprint of HEADLINE PUBLISHING GROUP

First published in paperback in 2010
by HEADLINE REVIEW
An imprint of HEADLINE PUBLISHING GROUP

1

ISBN 978 0 7553 4395 9 (A-format)
ISBN 978 0 7553 4381 2 (B-format)

Typeset in Galliard by Palimpsest Book Production Limited,
Grangemouth, Stirlingshire
Printed and bound in Great Britain by
Clays Ltd, St Ives plc

Headline's policy is to use papers that are natural, renewable and
recyclable products and made from wood grown in
sustainable forests. The logging and manufacturing processes
are expected to conform to the environmental
regulations of the country of origin.

HEADLINE PUBLISHING GROUP
An Hachette UK Company
338 Euston Road
London NW1 3BH

www.headline.co.uk
www.hachette.co.uk

Acknowledgements

Writing a novel in which one of the main characters is also a writer was trickier than any of my other books, mainly because I was afraid that people might think that it might be autobiographical. But I promise you, it's not. Unlike Britt, I always wanted to write, and I am still ecstatic each time a book makes it into print. (Also, she's far more glamorous than me!) She does, however, have a supportive team behind her and so do I. So I'd like to thank, as always:

Carole Blake, my agent, on whom Meredith is not based but who does share her love of shoes . . .

Marion Donaldson, my endlessly patient editor

Everyone who looks after my books around the world

My family who are still my greatest champions

Colm for everything else

Thanks also to Kate Rist of P&O Cruises who didn't realise that she was giving me the inspiration for *The Perfect Man*.

Special thanks to the charming Commodore Steve Burgoine and his lovely wife Kathy who were so warm and welcoming and gave me lots of great information. Also to Sophie,

Rosie and Digi. And thank you, too, to Gill, Philip and Benjamin for being such good fun.

Extra thanks to Kay, Anne, Philip, Stephen and Lauren for the wonderful day in Spain, with particular thanks to Philip for driving around the mountains – another evening of inspiration.

And to my readers, a million thanks from the bottom of my heart for buying my books and being so generous with your time in sharing your thoughts with me. I'm always thrilled and delighted to hear from you. You can get in touch with me through my website: www.sheilaoflanagan.net where you'll also find a link to my Facebook fan page, and you can follow me on Twitter: @sheilaoflanagan.

Chapter 1

Position: Barbados.
Weather: fine and dry. Wind: south-easterly force 4.
Temperature: 26°. Barometric pressure: 1014.9mb.

'There's a calypso band on the quayside.' Mia leaned further over the ship's rail and peered into the dusky light below before straightening up again and turning to face her sister. 'I think they're supposed to be serenading us.' She pushed her tawny curls out of sparkling green eyes that danced with amusement. 'I've never been serenaded before.'

'Neither have I,' admitted Britt. Her glance flickered to the band and then back across the docks and towards the yellow and white lights that were beginning to dot the landscape beyond. 'I guess serenading is a little bit old-fashioned these days.'

'Wouldn't it be wonderful, though,' said Mia, 'if a guy actually did that? Stood underneath your window in the moonlight, a single rose in his hand, and sang about ever-lasting love. It'd be so romantic, don't you think?'

'Any guy hanging around beneath my window warbling in the middle of the night would find himself in police custody pretty damn quick,' Britt told her decisively. 'I don't want my beauty sleep interrupted by a karaoke reject, thanks very much. Anyway, it would probably just be a diversionary tactic on his part to distract me while his burglar mate nipped in around the back and made off with the TV or something.'

'Britt McDonagh!' Mia's tone was one of scandalised humour. 'How can you say something like that? You of all people!'

'Of all people?' said Britt drily. 'Of all people, I'm clearly the most qualified on board this ship to say what is totally cheesy when it comes to romantic gestures. And someone mangling "Nessun Dorma" or "Three Times a Lady" outside my two-bed terraced would be fighting for the number one spot.' She shuddered suddenly. 'I have a horrible feeling that this entire voyage is going to be full of cheesy moments, and I really and truly am beginning to think that it was a mistake to even consider it.'

A worried expression crossed Mia's face. 'Don't say that,' she protested. 'It's the trip of a lifetime. You know it is.'

'No it bloody isn't,' responded Britt. 'I can tell you here and now that if I was picking my trip of a lifetime, spending the best part of a fortnight on this floating love palace wouldn't be it.'

'Oh, come on.' Mia used her most persuasive tone. 'It's fantastic. You know it is. And you know that we're going to have a great time, too. How can we not?'

Britt said nothing, but turned from the rail and sat

down on one of the comfortable deckchairs. Mia's eyes followed her anxiously. It wouldn't do, she told herself, for Britt to start having doubts about the trip again. She thought her sister had already dealt with all that. Mia knew that Britt wasn't exactly thrilled about her role on the journey ahead of them, but she'd been hoping that her sister had managed to convince herself that everything was going to be OK.

Mia herself was perfectly prepared to concede that joining the exclusive MV *Aphrodite* for its romance-laden Valentine Cruise was probably not exactly the voyage either of them would have booked as the trip of a lifetime – even if they'd had the appropriate boyfriend to take with them and thus could be part of the whole loved-up experience – but the fact was that they were still going to spend almost two weeks sailing in tropical seas on board one of the world's most exclusive cruise liners, which had to be a good thing.

And it was because of Britt that they were staying in the amazing suite with its private balcony as (almost) pampered passengers and not prepping food in the galley or sluicing out the loos as would have been far more likely – at least in Mia's case – otherwise. So it absolutely wouldn't do for Britt to get an attack of nerves again now, and it was Mia's job to make sure that she didn't. The only problem was that Mia wasn't entirely sure she was qualified to carry it out.

Earlier on, when they'd first boarded the *Aphrodite* (smaller than the average cruise ship because it was supposed to offer passengers a more intimate at-sea experience, but still enormous in her eyes), Mia had remarked that she could see why the brochures billed it as the holiday of a lifetime. And Britt had looked at her with a suddenly stern expression on her heart-shaped face and reminded her that neither of them was there on holiday, they were there to work. And that she wasn't to forget it.

How could she forget it? thought Mia, pushing her river of curls out of her face again. Britt reminded her of it often enough. But though she might want to call it work, surely a fortnight of island-hopping – even if you did have to spend half of it delivering workshops and lectures in Britt's case, or making sure everything was exactly right for her perfectionist sister in Mia's – was a million times better than spending it in Dublin in what had turned out to be the wettest February on record. And despite the fact that Mia herself hadn't been in the gloom of Dublin but had been working in Spain, where it was dry although not yet particularly warm, at the time the call from Britt had come, the carrot of a trip that meant travelling from the Caribbean to the Pacific and calling in to Guatemala (where she'd first met Alejo) was too good to pass up no matter how many times she asked herself whether she was doing the right thing by going. She concentrated on the calypso band in their brightly coloured shirts and white shorts on the quayside below, and very firmly pushed Alejo out of her mind. She wanted to visit Guatemala again because she'd spent a wonderful few months there four years ago and because she'd loved the country and its people. She didn't want it to be some kind of homage to her foolish past. Or to Alejo. She couldn't exactly forget the past, of course, but perhaps she could use this opportunity to put it into context. Visiting Guatemala, she assured herself, would bring closure to that time in her life. It needed closure. She sighed imperceptibly. Being ruthlessly honest with herself, despite what she knew she *needed*, she wasn't exactly sure that she *wanted* closure on it at all.

A motorised buggy, precariously piled with a mountain of luggage, zipped along the quay and stopped at the side of the ship where the bags were placed on a ramp leading into its hold. Two ship's officers paced up and down alongside. Mia's eyes followed them as they oversaw operations, and she couldn't help thinking that crisp white uniforms had a lot to recommend them. She whistled the theme tune to *An Officer and a Gentleman* under her breath. She'd been a toddler when the movie was released but it had been one of her mum's favourites, and due to the number of times she and Paula had watched it together, it had become one of Mia's favourites too. She'd always agreed with her mum that nobody could look as good in a white uniform as Richard Gere. But now she conceded that she might be wrong. The young officer shepherding the final passengers towards the gangway appeared, even from a distance, very hunky indeed. She wondered fleetingly if the ship's crew were allowed to get into the spirit of the Valentine Cruise. She liked the idea of being romanced by a man in uniform, even if he didn't have a calypso band to serenade her.

She closed her eyes for a moment and allowed herself to think of being swept off her feet by an officer. Then she opened them again and told herself not to be so bloody silly. Whatever else was on the cards for the next two weeks, Valentine Cruise or not, it certainly wasn't romance. At least not personally. Any romantic moments that came her way would be entirely due to the job she was there to do. Besides, she wasn't in the market for being swept off her feet. She'd learned her lesson the hard way.

The final passengers began to board the ship, stopping at the bottom of the gangway to have their photographs taken in the pink and gold light of the sunset by the pretty young ship's photographer, who was making sure that they looked happy and excited despite the fact that it had been a long day and most of them were exhausted. She'd just removed her camera from around her neck and begun to walk towards a group of her colleagues when one more passenger strode swiftly across the quayside, hesitated very briefly and then, before she had the chance to take his photograph, hurried up the gangway, leaving her standing looking after him in consternation, her camera in her hands.

The photographer hadn't been there when Britt and Mia had arrived and so neither of them had had their embarkation photos taken. They'd caught a scheduled flight that had left London early that morning rather than travelling on the Blue Lagoon Cruise Company's chartered plane later in the day. Their earlier departure had meant they'd boarded the ship before anyone else and before the photographer had taken up her position at the gangway. Mia supposed that it was a good thing they hadn't had to pose for a photo with a massive cut-out heart as a backdrop.

She was pretty certain she couldn't have persuaded Britt to agree to it anyhow.

The scheduled flight had been courtesy of the cruise company and at the insistence of Britt's needle-sharp agent, Meredith, who had originally intended to accompany Britt on the trip and for whom 'economy' was an unknown word. And although Mia was as excited as anything about the cruise ahead of them and had to keep reminding herself that it was real and that she was actually here, she couldn't help feeling deep down that it might have been better for everyone concerned if Meredith had been able to come as planned. As it was, she had to keep telling herself that on this voyage she wasn't Britt's hopeless younger sister. She was her assistant, her paid assistant, and so a professional person. She also had to remember – hugely difficult though it might be – that her sister wasn't plain old Bridget McDonagh any more. She was Brigitte Martin, author of *The Perfect Man*, the heartbreaking romantic novel that had spent the last six months at the top of the international bestseller lists and was now about to be a major motion picture starring two Oscar winners and an Oscar nominee.

As a result Britt (somewhat unbelievably in Mia's opinion, given that her sister was probably the least romantic person she'd ever known and had, after all, divorced her husband after less than a year of marriage) was now seen as a kind of authority on love and romance as well as being an award-winning novelist, and was in massive demand to appear on talk shows and at literary events to discuss the nature of love and talk about her life as the writer of the most romantic book of the year. This demand, Mia knew, escalated every time Britt said no to appearing on anything. And Britt said no quite a lot, which Mia was certain drove Meredith to despair. Mia – who loved chat shows and eagerly watched them all so that she could keep up with the latest showbiz gossip – couldn't quite understand how Britt could keep refusing to appear on them. Mia loved Jonathan Ross and Ryan Tubridy and even Podge and Rodge's anarchic show, but Britt insisted that she had no intention of discussing her life with anyone or being mocked by two wooden puppets on television. Eventually, however, she'd caved in and appeared on the *Late Late* on RTÉ, but that was only because Paula had been horrified at the idea of her daughter refusing to appear on the nation's longest-running chat show and had badgered Britt incessantly until she'd finally given in. Paula could wear Britt down more effectively than Meredith. She wanted the trip up to Dublin, she told Britt firmly, and she wouldn't be denied a great night out just because Britt was being silly about it. Paula had eventually triumphed and afterwards had raved to Mia about the evening, saying that Britt had been amazing and brilliant and an absolute natural. She'd sent Mia a DVD of the show and Mia had been astonished to see that Paula was absolutely right.

The most amazing thing of all, Mia thought, was the transformation of her sister's fashion look from the black linen suit and white silk blouse ensembles that she'd almost invariably worn over the past ten years to the astonishingly pretty woman with sleek curls and a colourful dress who was laughing and joking with the audience. It had been a long time since Mia had seen Britt laugh and joke like that, and it had made her think that writing the book might have been a turning point in her sister's life. But it hadn't. Paula had told her that once the programme was over, Britt refused to hang around and chat with the celebs but insisted that she was tired and wanted to go home, where she'd immediately removed the make-up and brushed the curls out of her hair. And, Paula had added, Britt had said that the whole thing had been a huge strain and that she hoped she'd never have to do it again.

It was typical of Britt, Mia thought, that she'd managed to be so successful on the show even though she hadn't wanted to do it. She knew that in the same circumstances she herself would have been tongue-tied and useless. Britt, though, was annoyingly good at most things – especially things she didn't like doing. She'd once told Mia that it was easy to be good at stuff you enjoyed. Being good at stuff you hated was a much greater challenge. (Mia had been doing her maths homework at the time and it hadn't been going particularly well. Unlike Britt, she was terrible at doing things she hated!)

Britt, however, was also obstinate and much to Meredith's disgust still turned down many of the publicity opportunities that her agent and her publicist presented to her, regardless of how good she might have been at them. ('I can't spend my life telling people how to find the right man,' she would protest. 'Sooner or later someone's going to notice that I don't have one myself and they'll ask me questions that I am absolutely not prepared to answer.')

9

Given that Britt had had to be strong-armed into agreeing to the cruise, Mia kept reminding herself that she had to be like Meredith and treat her as the amazing success she was instead of simply her irritating older sister, so that her stint on *Aphrodite* would be a total triumph. She wasn't entirely confident in her own ability to do that, and the more she thought about it, the more she felt that agreeing to step into Meredith's high-heeled Louboutin shoes was a very bad idea indeed.

Although she was accustomed to acknowledging Britt as one of life's constant successes, Mia had spent most of her life doing her best to put her in her place rather than pandering to her. She'd been the one to put spiders in Britt's bed when they were small, or hide her schoolbooks to get her into trouble, or rob the last of her favourite perfume just to hear her rant and rage. She was used to provoking Britt at every available opportunity, if only to shake her out of her complacent self-satisfaction at always getting top marks at school as well as being the teacher's pet.

When she'd been much younger, Mia had been utterly convinced that she must have been adopted as a baby, because she couldn't understand how she could possibly be related to somebody as overachieving as Britt. (Especially a blond-haired, blue-eyed, pouty-lipped overachiever.) It seemed impossible to her that the same people who'd produced such a wonderful daughter the first time around could've messed it up so spectacularly with her. It made much more sense to think that Paula and Gerry had taken her in after she'd been abandoned by her own mother.

In her teens, Mia had decided that she was actually the daughter of a (slightly plump) Russian princess whose family had been made destitute during the Revolution and who'd had to give up their children in the hope of a better life for them. It had taken a long time for her to accept the evidence of her own birth certificate and finally admit that she was actually Paula and Gerry's natural child. (She'd never forgiven them for bequeathing the slightly plump gene to her and not Britt.)

She knew that Britt was serenely unaware that her sister envied her her self-possession, her brains and her ability to say no to second helpings of Paula's chocolate fudge cake every Sunday. Britt was totally focused and had a relentless determination to succeed in whatever she chose to do. She was also amazingly disciplined, and that, Mia knew, was something that all novelists were supposed to be, so perhaps it made sense that she'd suddenly, though unexpectedly in the eyes of everyone who knew her, written the book of the year.

In fact, the only time that Britt's famous self-discipline had snapped was when she'd married Ralph. Mia often thought that a little less discipline over other things and a little more discipline over Ralph would have been a lot better for her sister, although she kept that thought strictly to herself. Because after Ralph, Britt had changed utterly – from a warm person with flashes of icy reason to an icy person with flashes of warmth. And that was why Mia had been so utterly astonished when Britt's book had been hailed as a romantic masterpiece. As far as Mia was concerned, Ralph had killed off Britt's romantic gene.

And in all honesty, despite *The Perfect Man*, she hadn't seen any sign of it in her sister since.

So she'd been stunned when Britt had phoned and asked her about joining her on board the *Aphrodite*, and thrown into a total quandary about what to do.

'Are you absolutely sure you want *me* along?' she'd asked doubtfully when Britt had called her out of the blue and put the proposal to her. 'Not that I wouldn't love to come and everything,' she added hastily, 'but I would've thought that someone from your publishers might be better at this sort of thing than me.'

'I have to share a cabin,' Britt said with a hint of panic in her voice. 'I can't do that with someone I don't know. It would've been OK with Meredith, I'm used to her by now and I can cope.'

Britt wasn't good at sharing. She liked her own space. When they'd been younger and had been invited to sleepovers in friends' houses, or when Paula had asked them if they'd like friends to stay with them, Britt had always refused because she preferred to sleep on her own.

She must be in a real state, Mia thought as she listened to her sister give the lowdown on the cruise, to ask me to come with her even as a standby. She's neat and I'm messy and I know it drives her bonkers.

'Can you do it or not?' Britt had sounded agitated but imperious.

'It sounds great, and thanks for asking, but I can't really leave Allegra,' said Mia, who was wrestling with the desire to see how the other half lived (after all, there wasn't a chance in hell that she'd ever be able to afford a top-of-the-range cruise herself in normal circumstances) against the knowledge that she had a three-year-old daughter to worry about. Britt could ultimately look after herself. Allegra couldn't.

'It's only for a fortnight,' said Britt. 'She'll be fine. And I'll pay you, of course. Mum told me that you'd lost your job at the town council.'

Mia gritted her teeth and wished that her mother wasn't such a damn blabbermouth.

'Only because it's seasonal,' she said. 'Sierra Bonita is a growing place and the council arranges a lot of English lessons for its employees. I'm a good teacher and they said that they'd take me back in a few weeks.'

'Perfect so,' said Britt. 'In the meantime you can help me and I can help you.'

'I . . .'

'Please. I really need you.'

It was rare that Britt ever asked for help, and Mia hadn't heard her sound so anxious in years. She glanced at her petite dark-haired daughter, with her button nose and rosebud mouth, who was playing with her doll on the tiled verandah outside their house on the hillside, and tightened her grip on the phone.

'I really can't,' she said regretfully. 'It's a long time to leave Allie and there's no one I can leave her with.'

'Don't be daft,' Britt retorted. 'What about James and Sarah? Didn't they visit you last year? Allegra knows them. Besides, she'll have a great time with Barney and Luke. They're all around the same age.'

Mia didn't correct her. Barney was eight and Luke was

six, and that was a huge difference. But then Britt was clueless about kids; she'd been the only one on their road not to do babysitting to earn pocket money when they were teenagers. She'd said that she found children too annoying and not worth the money.

'I'd have to bring her back to Ireland,' said Mia doubtfully. 'And it's a year since she's seen them so she might not remember them and perhaps she'd feel abandoned.'

'She won't feel abandoned,' said Britt. 'And it would be good for her, don't you think, to mix with other children?'

'She mixes fine with other children.' Mia had bristled slightly at the implication that there was something amiss in Allegra's life.

'Ask James,' said Britt urgently. 'I bet he and Sarah would be delighted to have her.'

Mia wasn't so sure about that, but she was wrong.

'She rang me already,' said her brother when Mia phoned him later that night to tell him about Britt's request. 'Aren't you the lucky one! She's never asked me to go anywhere with her, even though I'm sure I could be a great bodyguard.'

'Yeah, right.' Mia was teasing. It was well known in their family that James was a gentle giant who ran a mile at the first sign of trouble. 'I'd probably be a better bodyguard than you.'

'So that's why she asked you!'

'I'm surprised,' admitted Mia. 'We haven't really talked in ages.'

'She hasn't "talked" to anyone in ages,' James reminded her. 'You know the way she is these days.'

'The way she's been for years,' said Mia.

'It's not her fault.' James stuck up for Britt. 'She was really hurt by the marriage-we're-not-allowed-to-mention.'

'For crying out loud, it was years ago!' exclaimed Mia. 'You'd imagine she'd be over it by now.'

'I don't know which bit she isn't over,' said James. 'The fact that she got divorced, or the fact that marrying Ralph was a mistake in the first place.'

Mia giggled. 'She hates making mistakes.'

'And this was her biggest ever.'

'She'd have been better off getting her nose bloodied in a few hopeless relationships when she was at school,' Mia told him. 'But you know what she was like. Holding out for the perfect person from the start.'

'Absolutely the wrong way to go about it,' agreed James. 'How in God's name did she manage to write this book when she's so bloody hopeless about men? Has she even gone out with anyone since Ralph?'

'I haven't a clue. She doesn't fill me in on the state of her love life. And as for the book – would you read a love story written by someone who probably hasn't been shagged in a decade?'

James laughed. 'I read thrillers,' he said. 'So no. But I can't help wondering what on earth her readers think when they meet her and she bites their heads off.'

'I think that's why she needs someone with her on the cruise,' said Mia. 'Apparently her agent knows when she's had enough of pretending to be fluffy and nice, and hustles her away before she cracks and allows her true nature to erupt. I'm supposed to do that as well as make sure everything's organised for her.'

'It could be fun,' James told her. 'It's a cruise in the Caribbean, for heaven's sake.'

'I'm sure it'll be wonderful,' agreed Mia. 'At least for the other passengers! But I just don't know what to do. On the one hand, I'd so love to go on the cruise. On the other, it's with Britt, and I can't reconcile the Britt I know with this romance person she's supposed to be. On the one hand, she's paying me. On the other . . . Oh, James, I can't leave Allegra. I'll miss her like crazy and she'll hate me for ever.'

'Of course she won't hate you for ever,' said James. 'Don't be silly, Mia. I know you'll miss her, but it's not that long really. Besides, Sarah would love to have her to stay. I think our testosterone-laden environment gets a bit much for her sometimes.'

'I haven't decided yet,' said Mia. 'Oh, why on earth did her stupid agent fall off her stupid horse! If the woman had stayed on the damn animal, Britt would've gone off quite happily without me.'

'Maybe it will be good for the two of you to go away together,' said James seriously. 'You know, be girlie.'

'You're joking, aren't you? I do love her, but she's such hard work and there's no chance of us being girlie together. Anyway . . .'

'Anyway what?'

'She always makes me feel so bloody inadequate,' admitted Mia. 'I mean, there she was with the glittering career and getting her name in the papers before, and now here she is with another glittering career and being on the telly; and it's not like I ever wanted it or anything, but I know she's going to give me the "you too could be brilliant if you put your mind to it" lecture. She always bloody does!'

James laughed. 'It's hard work having her in the family,' he agreed. 'But she's a decent soul really.'

Mia groaned. 'She means well. But she can be so patronising sometimes. And whenever she is, I want to scream at her that her husband left her after a few months and so she's not successful in everything she does. But her marriage is the elephant in the room, isn't it? We can't discuss it. Oh, no! *She* can criticise us till the cows come home, but nobody can talk about her massive divorce.'

'Maybe you shouldn't go if you're going to be like that about it,' agreed James. 'You'll kill each other.'

'I know . . . Hold on a sec!' Mia catapulted across the verandah and just managed to catch the empty terracotta pot that Allegra had almost pushed from its plinth on to the tiles below. 'That's bold,' she told her daughter. 'Really bold. I told you not to touch it.'

Allegra stared at her mutinously from her dark brown eyes and then sat on the steps with her back towards her mother, indicating her annoyance.

'All the same, you could do with a break.' James's voice came over the phone again. 'You've been on your own with her for over three years, Mia. You haven't had any holidays. You deserve one.'

To Mia's horror, she felt her eyes fill with tears.

'I don't need a holiday.' She swallowed hard before she spoke. 'And I'm perfectly fine.'

'You don't need to do it all on your own all the time,' said James gently. 'It's only a fortnight. I know it seems like a long time, but it'll go really quickly. And we'll look after Allegra for you. We won't let her miss you.'

'Of course she'll miss me!'

'She'll be fine with us,' James promised, 'honestly.'

Mia leaned against the whitewashed wall and stared across the lush green valley towards the thin blue strip on the horizon that was the Mediterranean Sea. She lived in one of the most beautiful places in the world, with its glorious climate and wonderful people. But sometimes she felt trapped. And sometimes she was very lonely.

'Come and stay with us for a few days before you leave,' suggested James. 'That'll give Allegra time to settle in with us.'

'I'll think about it,' said Mia. 'I'll think very hard.'

In the end, she'd decided to go.

I'm so lucky really, she reminded herself when she arrived in Dublin with Allegra in tow and Sarah met them at the airport, wrapping her arms around them and saying how lovely it was to see them. I have the most fantastic family. I must get them to visit me more often.

Although Allegra had met her two cousins when they'd visited Spain the previous year, Mia had worried that she might feel shy now, but within minutes she had thrown herself into the game they were playing and before long she was chattering away to them in Spanglish, the mixture of Spanish and English she spoke with Mia.

'She can talk quite well now,' Mia assured Sarah. 'In both languages. She understands English perfectly, especially things like "no" and "put that down" and "what the hell d'you think you're doing?"'

Sarah laughed. 'She's an absolute pet,' she told Mia. 'We're really looking forward to having her here.'

'She hasn't been away from me before,' said Mia anxiously. 'She might get upset.'

'You've recorded those video clips for her,' said Sarah. 'You can call her every day. Don't you worry. She'll be fine.'

Yes, thought Mia a couple of days later as she headed over to London to meet up with Britt, who had been on a publicity junket, Allegra might be fine. But what about me? Blissful though it was to walk through an airport without having to worry about whether she'd brought enough wipes, or Tig-Tag doll, or her daughter's favourite apple juice, she felt as though part of herself was missing. As she pressed the button for the lift, a surge of loneliness took hold of her, so intense that she almost gasped out loud. She swallowed hard and blinked away the tears that had unexpectedly flooded her eyes. She didn't want to turn into a foolish, possessive mother who couldn't bear to be parted from her child for an instant. It would be good for Allie to spend some time with the boys. She muttered the words out loud to convince herself. But she only succeeded in feeling guilty again.

She was meeting Britt at the exclusive boutique hotel in Paddington where her sister was staying during her time in London. Despite her loathing of publicity, Britt had given in to Meredith's insistence that, as *The Perfect Man* had been nominated for its third award of the year, she had an obligation to everyone who'd gone out and bought it to give something of herself back. Besides, Meredith had said, even though you say you hate being interviewed, you come across really well. Britt had opened her mouth to disagree but in the end she'd nodded. Mia had been startled to see her sister's picture on the front of a TV listings magazine at the train station, promising that she was going to give her top five tips for landing the man of your dreams. It all sounded impossibly glamorous, and a far cry from her world of running after Allegra or struggling to teach English to exhausted town officials who would much rather be at home with their families. It was exciting, if nerve-racking, to think that she was going to be part of it.

Mia got the Heathrow Express into London, grateful that the hotel wasn't far from the station because her suitcase was ridiculously heavy. She'd tried to go light on the packing, but her head had been filled with ideas about dressing up for dinner in the evenings and she'd got into a complete panic about what she might need to wear. Consequently she'd put just about everything she possessed into the case. She'd had to pay a hefty excess baggage charge because of the weight and was wondering what Britt would say if she tried to claim it back as a business expense.

The hotel where her sister was staying was relentlessly modern, with black marble floors, snow-white walls and minimalist black leather furniture, only occasionally relieved by a single pillar-box-red plant. The bedrooms were black-and-white minimalist too. Britt had enthused about them. Mia hated them. She would have preferred some comfortable sofas and colourful cushions, even though she did quite like the enormous marbled black-and-white bathroom with its toasty underfloor heating, huge shower area and super-sized warm towels.

'I always stay here,' said Britt, who'd placed her hands on each of Mia's shoulders and pecked her lightly on the cheek when she'd opened the door, so that Mia hadn't, as she'd intended, hugged her in return. 'It's comfortable.'

'But not very homely,' observed Mia, wondering where the wardrobes were and then realising there was a white panel on the wall that slid back to reveal a built-in unit.

'I like it.'

'It's your style all right,' said Mia. She looked at Britt. 'Your old style. You look the same as always. I thought you'd have changed completely. I was expecting you to look like Brigitte.'

Britt grinned, and suddenly Mia felt better about everything. Britt's grin was always unexpectedly wicked, hinting at a sense of humour buried deep beneath her cool and calm exterior, if she'd only let it come to the surface. Unfortunately, in the last few years, she hardly ever had.

'I'm two different people,' she told Mia. 'When I'm doing book things I'm Brigitte. But the rest of the time I'm the sister you know and love.' She looked quizzically at Mia. 'Do you prefer Brigitte?'

Mia stared at her sister, uncertain of what to say. Right now Britt was herself – tall and leggy, with her straight fudge-blond hair loosely pinned up at the back of her head. She was wearing stone-washed jeans and a soft lilac V-necked jumper. A small white-gold pendant hung around her throat, the tiny diamond in the centre glittering under the bedroom lights. As always, because she hated towering over people, her shoes were flat.

It was a completely different look to her *Late Late* appearance, and indeed the last time Mia had seen her on a UK morning TV interview, which she'd watched on the internet. Britt had been even more over the top then, with her vivid eye make-up, long lashes and bright pink lip gloss. Her top was silk, her skirt long and floaty, her pink shoes high-heeled. (The heels, in fact, were skyscraper high, and golden. Mia noticed that the presenter didn't stand up when Britt joined him.)

Britt had smiled a lot during the interview, and even flirted with the presenter – at that point Mia had been utterly flabbergasted, because she'd never known Britt to flirt with anyone in her life – not even Ralph. She'd watched the download twice, and it was only on the second viewing that she realised that Britt's smile didn't reach her eyes and that when the presenter touched her on the shoulder, her sister edged away.

'I'm not sure Brigitte is really you,' she said eventually. 'But this hotel certainly is.'

'I know you'd prefer chintzy cushions and drapes,' Britt teased. 'But I really do like this stuff. That's why they put me up here. If I expressed a preference for flowers and flounces, they'd do that too.'

Mia looked at her in wonder. 'Do they do everything you want?'

'At the moment they do,' said Britt, in an offhand way. 'I'm their big money-spinner this year. In a year's time they'll probably have found someone new and more exciting and I'll be yesterday's news, but at the moment they're making a fortune out of *The Perfect Man*, especially since the movie deal and the awards.'

'Glad that some man is good for something,' said Mia.

'In general I made a lot of money from them,' said Britt, and Mia laughed. Britt's real career – the one she'd been so successful in before the publication of *The Perfect Man* – was as a lawyer specialising in high-profile divorce cases. She nearly always represented the woman and she nearly always won them excellent settlements. Mia knew that Britt's legal career had been very important to her. But, she thought, how much better fun it must be to write about true love than deal with messy divorces.

'Our flight is at eleven in the morning,' Britt told her as Mia began to unzip her case. 'So you don't need to unpack anything.'

'Just getting my nightie and stuff,' Mia told her. 'And . . .' she waved a book at her, 'my copy of *The Perfect Man*.'

It was a new copy with an airport price tag on it. Britt frowned.

'I sent signed copies to everyone as soon as it came out,' she said. 'I sent one to you too.'

Mia looked at her apologetically. 'I got it. But you know me and books. I was never much of a reader. And before I got around to reading the copy you sent . . . well, it accidentally ended up in a swimming pool. Sorry.'

'You mean you haven't read it at all yet?' Britt's eyes opened wide.

'I read it in Spanish,' Mia assured her. 'But I want to

read it in English. I know I can speak the language but I don't read it so well and I guess I didn't quite – quite get it.'

'You mean you didn't like it?'

'It's not that,' said Mia hastily. 'I didn't get every word of it, though.'

'I understand,' said Britt. 'It's fine.'

But Mia had known, from the sudden tightness in her sister's voice, that actually it wasn't.

She read *The Perfect Man* on the flight to Barbados. She hadn't entirely told the truth about the fate of the copy that Britt had sent her. Its immersion in her neighbour's swimming pool hadn't been accidental at all. On the day the book had arrived she'd been tired, up all night because Allegra had developed a worrying cough, and so she'd been quite unable to sleep. She'd also managed to puncture a tyre on her ancient third-hand jeep driving her daughter to the doctor that morning which meant that she'd turned up at the clinic looking haggard and wan. The only up side was that Allegra had improved with every passing minute and by the time they eventually got home again she'd run around the house like a mad thing, broken Mia's favourite vase, used up her only decent lipstick on herself, 'to make me feel better', and generally driven her mother demented. So when the postman arrived with the book and Mia saw the 'International Bestseller' blazed across the front of it and Britt's gorgeous, carefree face smiling at her from the back, she'd actually lost her temper completely and flung it over the terrace balcony, watching it sail in a wide arc through the air before landing with a splash in Carmen Colange's pool halfway down the hillside. Carmen rented out the house for a good part of the year and Mia had known that there were tourists staying in it. So she hadn't gone to retrieve her sodden signed copy but had eventually bought the Spanish translation in the tiny bookshop in Sierra Bonita a few weeks later. Naturally she hadn't told Britt this at the time – all she'd actually done was to send her a text thanking her for the lovely book. And even when she'd got around to reading the Spanish version her heart hadn't been in it; she'd simply skimmed through it to get the gist of the story.

Now, relaxed and comfortable in the business-class seats, she couldn't believe she'd ever skimmed through the book. Every so often, as she turned the pages, she glanced at her sister, but Britt was engrossed in the in-flight movies and didn't return her look. When Mia finally finished it, just twenty minutes before they landed, she cleared her throat and sniffed. Britt glanced at her.

'So did you get it this time?' she asked.

'Oh yes.' Mia cleared her throat again. 'I suppose . . . when I read it in Spanish I was all caught up with Allegra and stuff and I didn't . . . didn't appreciate it. But it's wonderful, Britt, it really is. It's warm and lovely and . . .'

'No need to go overboard,' said Britt dismissively. 'As you said yourself, you're not really into books.'

'I know, but . . .'

'So you don't have to pretend just for me.'

'I'm not pretending!' cried Mia. 'It's great. It's just . . . I never would have expected it from you.'

'Oh?' Britt looked at her enquiringly. 'And why's that?'

'Because . . . because it's just gorgeous!' she cried. 'It's so utterly, utterly romantic. And uplifting. It's so . . . so unlike you.'

Britt made a face. 'It's fiction.'

'Yes, but . . .'

'And it wasn't meant to be romantic.'

'What, then?'

'It was just about a man,' said Britt.

'The most amazing man ever.' Mia's tone was heartfelt.

'Which is why it's fiction.'

'Don't be like that,' said Mia. 'Admit that you've rediscovered your softer side.'

'There wasn't anything there for me to rediscover,' said Britt.

'I know that you were never the most romantic girl in the world,' conceded Mia. 'But it's nice to see that your heart hasn't been completely hardened over the years.'

'My heart is the same as it always was,' Britt told her. 'And my feelings about romance haven't changed one single bit.'

Mia glanced at her. Britt's face was taut. And Mia knew that it was time to drop the subject of true love for the time being.

Now, at the quayside in Barbados, six thousand miles away from the minimalist London hotel, she turned to look at her sister again. Britt had stretched out on one of the balcony's teak loungers, a faraway expression in her indigo-blue eyes.

How is it, Mia wondered, that our lives have turned out to be such polar opposites? How is it that she's always been so astonishingly successful, but the only success in my life has been Allegra? Not that most people would consider being a single mum an entirely successful thing in the first place. How can she be so cool and calm about her achievements, while all of my life has been about being hot and bothered about my failures? And what in God's name are the chances of me managing to look after her the way she needs to be looked after on this trip when I haven't a clue what to do?

'Why don't we head down to the sail-away party?' she suggested suddenly as she glanced at her watch. 'It's happening beside the pool. And there's free champagne.'

'We're not here to go to parties and knock back free booze,' Britt told her firmly. 'We're here to work.'

'Bridget Marie McDonagh!' Mia sounded incredulous. 'I know you've always been a total workaholic, but what kind of work could you possibly expect to do tonight? It's been a long day and you deserve some time off. Besides, your first session isn't until the day after tomorrow. Now, maybe I'm sadly lacking in work ethic myself, but all the same, I don't think going to the sail-away party is some terrible waste of our time. You might get to meet some of the passengers.'

Britt looked horrified. 'I don't want to meet the passengers,' she said.

'That's what you're here for,' Mia told her. 'To meet them and be nice to them and talk to them about *luuurve*.'

'Oh, please!'

'Are you saying that whenever you meet anyone you're going to be rude and nasty?' asked Mia.

'Of course not. But I'd rather not bother.'

Mia regarded her sternly. 'I'm here to bolster your image,' she said. 'You can't avoid everyone all of the time.'

'I know, but . . .'

'They won't recognise you now anyway,' said Mia. 'You don't look anything like your photos.'

Brigitte's publicity photo was one of her in what Mia mentally described as her 'full metal jacket' look with the curled hair and extravagant make-up that made her seem like a total stranger.

Britt shrugged with impatience. 'I'm not worried about being recognised,' she said. 'I'm completely different when I'm Brigitte. But I'm here as Brigitte, so I don't want to talk to anyone when I'm not.'

'Oh, for heaven's sake!' Mia was exasperated. 'Don't tell me you're not going to step outside the cabin unless your hair is perfect and you're plastered with slap. That's ridiculous. You don't have to turn yourself into another person to walk around the ship. You're not Dolly Parton, you know.'

'Be sensible,' retorted Britt.

'Be yourself! Nobody will give a toss what you look like,' said Mia.

'People expect me to be a certain sort of person because of the book,' Britt told her patiently. 'They think I'm warm and caring and romantic, and I'm not. You know I'm not. They'll be very disappointed when they realise that I'm a grumpy cow. You're here to stop them finding that out.'

Mia looked at her thoughtfully. 'You're not . . . gushy,' she conceded finally. 'But you can be warm and caring when you want to be; you're not always a grumpy cow.'

Britt raised an eyebrow at her. 'I thought that's what you and James used to call me.'

'Years ago.' Mia blushed. 'When you were studying for your law exams and wouldn't talk to us.'

'You called me that at school too,' Britt reminded her.

'OK, OK. But I didn't actually mean it.'

'It's fine,' said Britt. 'I know I can be moody and grumpy. I just don't want to be that way with the passengers.'

'You're not as bad as you try to make out,' said Mia. 'I know there's a caring person buried underneath the moody exterior.' She looked at Britt curiously. 'So who *do* you care about these days?'

'My clients,' replied Britt.

Mia exhaled sharply. 'You're being deliberately tough,' she said.

'Not really.' Britt shrugged. 'I'm a single girl. I'm a divorce lawyer. I live on my own. I don't even have a cat! I don't need to be warm and caring.'

'Let me earn my keep, in that case,' said Mia after a moment in which she wrestled with the desire to hit Britt over the head. 'If someone tries to talk to you and you can't be nice, I'll tell them that you're jet-lagged.'

Britt smiled faintly. 'I guess that's as good an excuse as any.'

'So come on, we're going to the party and we'll have a good time, and nobody is even going to notice you because they'll be far too excited about their holiday and probably jet-lagged themselves.'

'I suppose you're right,' agreed Britt in resignation.

'I accept it's not your thing,' Mia acknowledged. 'But it's mine. And you'll be with me so you don't have to mingle. You'll have a good time and nobody will bother you. I promise.'

And before Britt had time to raise any more objections, Mia had hustled her through the cabin and out of the door.

Chapter 2

Position: MV Aphrodite.
Weather: fine and dry. Wind: south-easterly force 4.
Temperature: 25°. Barometric pressure: 1014.8mb.

Britt had forgotten how impossibly enthusiastic Mia
was. She'd forgotten, in the months since she'd last
seen her sister, that Mia always wanted to see the best in
things; that despite any setbacks in her life she believed
that things happened for a reason and that the reason was
always a good one.

Paula, their mother, had told her that when Mia broke
the news that she was pregnant and that there was apparently no future with the father of her child, she'd been
optimistic and cheerful and told them that it didn't matter
anyway, that she knew the baby would be welcomed and
that it would be raised in an atmosphere of warmth and
love.

She'd been equally optimistic and cheerful when she'd
told Britt herself. Britt had wondered whether her sister
was totally naïve or whether she was simply putting a brave

face on things. But when she'd tried to ask her about the father, Mia had shrugged her shoulders and said that he wasn't in the equation and that her plan was to be as good a mother as she could be so that she would make up for the less than ideal situation the baby would be in.

'I always believed that two parents made more sense for a child,' she had said calmly. 'But that doesn't mean that I won't do my best for my baby and make sure that she feels loved and wanted.'

'*Do* you want it?' Britt had asked curiously, not minding that Mia had flushed with annoyance.

'Of course. And she's not an *it* any more. My baby is a girl.'

'You don't think that having any baby, girl or boy, will mess up your life?'

'Any more than it already is?' Mia had laughed at that. 'At least from your point of view.'

Well, Britt thought, maybe having Allegra hadn't messed up Mia's life. But it was damn hard to tell. Ever since she'd left school, her sister's lifestyle had been chaotic and unplanned as she drifted from job to job, from country to country and, it seemed, from unsuitable man to unsuitable man. (Although the unsuitable men had always been around. Even at school Mia had gone out with an array of boys Britt disapproved of because they were slackers and loafers.) Paula had once said that her younger daughter had a short attention span, and Britt agreed with her. Mia was always looking for something, someone or somewhere new. But not in the same way as Britt herself. Britt looked for new things to advance her career. Mia wanted new things just for the experience. Well, Britt thought, she'd certainly found that with Allegra. Britt couldn't imagine how difficult an experience raising a child on your own would be. And she absolutely couldn't imagine Mia as a mother. She thought her sister far too disorganised for that. But Paula said that Mia was doing a great job in bringing Allegra up by herself, especially considering that she was doing it in Sierra Bonita, away from everyone she knew. Although why . . . and then Paula would rant about Mia's decision to move to Spain, which, she said, was utterly ridiculous, didn't Britt agree? Britt was always non-committal in her answer, never wanting to take sides, but deep down thinking that their mother was probably right and that Mia was being silly about it all.

She glanced now at her sister, who was sliding her feet into fluorescent green flip-flops decorated with lemon-yellow beads. She still didn't know what impulse had made her ask Mia to come with her on this trip. It wasn't as though the two of them were close any more. It wasn't as though she even thought that Mia would be that good as her assistant. But she'd panicked about the idea of being on the Valentine Cruise on her own and she desperately needed someone to support her. It had been an uncharacteristic moment of weakness; now she couldn't help wondering whether it had been a good idea to ask Mia at all.

Perhaps she would have been able to cope by herself, but she certainly hadn't thought so immediately after Meredith, her agent, had called her to say that she couldn't come with her. Meredith had been devastated about it, because the whole trip had been her idea. She had once shared a flat with Blue Lagoon's head of PR, and the notion of having a writer-in-residence giving workshops and talks on romance and romantic fiction had come to her one night when she met Annie Highsmith for their semi-annual dinner-and-drinks catch-up night at the latest London hotspot (that night a restaurant entirely decorated in black and silver and so dimly lit that it was almost impossible to see what you were eating). Annie had been looking for an innovative idea to add to the Blue Lagoon entertainment package and Meredith had suggested Britt, whose debut novel was selling like hot cakes. Annie had nodded slowly, and the idea of the workshops on the Valentine Cruise had been born. After all, Meredith pointed out, people could only smooch their way through so many days before wanting something else to do. And tons of people wanted to write books. Who better to tell them about it than Brigitte Martin, author of the most talked-about book of the year. It would be a real coup for Blue Lagoon to get Brigitte (Meredith only called her Britt when they were on their own together, and even then not all of the time; it was important, she said, to keep the personal and public personalities separate). Plus, Meredith had added as she grinned at her friend, it would be lovely to go on a cruise somewhere warm in February.

Annie had laughed at that but had promised Meredith she'd give it some more thought. And then she'd come back to say that they would run with it, that they wanted Brigitte to give some writing classes and perhaps be interviewed by their cruise director in an evening event – 'A

Night of Romance with Brigitte Martin'. Did Meredith think her client would be up for it? Meredith had nodded enthusiastically and said that she was sure she would.

Britt, however, wasn't up for it at all, partly because she'd never given a writing class in her life and hadn't a clue how to do it, and partly because she thought that people on a romantic cruise would be far too busy being romantic (or at least having lots of sex) to want to write about it. As for the Night of Romance – Britt snorted and said that it would be over her dead body. Meredith, horrified at the prospect of missing out on some good publicity for Britt but even more so at missing out on the cruise, had adamantly refused to listen to her client's objections.

'Are you cracked?' she'd asked in her taut South African accent. (Meredith had come to London after graduating from university in Johannesburg, and had immediately carved out a successful career for herself so that her name commanded instant respect among the other literary agents.) 'Do you know how many writers would cut off their arm for this opportunity?' Britt rather thought that no one in their right mind would be cutting off their arm for a two-week torture-fest of so-called romance, but she said nothing because Meredith didn't give her the chance to answer; she simply said that Britt had to do it because it would be a stroll in the park for her and because it was the Caribbean in February, for God's sake, and because she, Meredith, desperately needed a bit of warm air to make up for the dull and damp winter that hadn't yet let England out of its grip. We're going on the cruise together,

Meredith had said, and it'll be fun and fabulous and you'll be a complete success and everyone on board will buy signed copies of *The Perfect Man* and what more do you want? Eh? This last in a tone that suggested that Britt would be off her rocker if she refused.

Normally nobody ever made Britt do anything she didn't want to, but somehow Meredith had managed to persuade her that giving writing classes would be good for her as a person – new strings to your bow, she had said – and Britt had found herself agreeing with her and then wondering what on earth was happening to her that she'd given in to Paula about *The Late Late Show* and now Meredith about the cruise instead of being firm and in command as she used to be at the legal firm of Clavin & Grey. Her agent had spent the next couple of months talking about how fab it was all going to be, and then, two weeks before they'd been due to depart, she'd been thrown from her horse in a riding accident and cracked a number of ribs as well as dislocating her shoulder and generally ending up black and blue as a result.

'I so want to go!' she wailed down the phone to Britt. 'I want to lie on deck and sip exotic cocktails under the sun. I want to be pampered in the spa. I want to come to your talks and revel in your brilliance. But I can't even move without crying right now.'

Britt had suggested calling the whole thing off, but Meredith told her that Blue Lagoon had already advertised her workshops on board the Valentine Cruise so there was no way she could back out of it, and that she should take someone else along as moral support (not that she really needed it, because she was an absolute superstar and she should never forget it).

Britt, with absolutely no idea of who she could possibly ask, had eventually considered going on her own, but somehow, excluding the fact that it would be stressful to have to cope by herself, it seemed a totally sad and lonely thing to do. She didn't think she'd feel sad and lonely (she actually enjoyed being on her own), but she didn't want other people thinking that she was. After all, she was supposed to be warm and wonderful. That was how anyone who'd read *The Perfect Man* expected her to be, although she knew perfectly well that the people closest to her never used those words to describe her. James and Mia had practically patented the grumpy cow expression. And Ralph, her ex-husband, had once called her a hard-hearted bitch. (Then again, she remembered ruefully, he'd also called her the love of his life. He'd soon changed his tune, though.)

She knew that she needed to have someone on the trip with her. Usually when she was at an event Meredith watched over her, making little comments to the readers who came up to speak to her so that Britt appeared to be far more chatty than she actually was. She depended on Meredith to do the warm and fuzzy stuff, and her agent was good at it. Mia was good at warm and fuzzy stuff too. Britt wasn't sure that her sister would be as organised as Meredith, but she didn't really feel as though she had many other options. And so, wondering if she'd regret it in the end, she'd eventually asked Mia to join her.

'You'd be working,' she warned her after Mia had called her back and told her that she'd do it because, as Sarah had pointed out, she couldn't possibly turn down the chance of a super holiday cruise. 'Making sure that everything is properly sorted out for me and stuff like that. I don't want to have to deal with the cruise director about the entertainment programme . . .' She stumbled over the sentence. It seemed nonsensical to her that she would be considered part of the entertainment on the cruise. She was a divorce lawyer, not an entertainer, for God's sake.

'So I'll be like Julia Roberts in *America's Sweethearts*,' said Mia. 'Running after your Catherine Zeta-Jones and pandering to your every whim. I wonder, will I get the man in the end?' She laughed.

'I've no idea what you're talking about,' said Britt (who hardly ever went to the movies). 'What I need is someone to make sure that the rooms are properly set up and that I'm in the right place at the right time and that everything runs like clockwork, as well as someone who gives off good vibes about the whole set-up.'

'Crikey, Britt, you'll be on a boat.' Mia chuckled. 'Hard to be in the wrong place at the wrong time. And how can you not give off good vibes when it all sounds so fabulous?'

'Fabulous maybe. But it still needs organisation,' said Britt firmly. 'I don't want to turn up to an empty room.'

'I doubt that'll happen,' said Mia. 'Aren't you the most famous writer in the country at the moment? Didn't the *Times* mutter about you having your finger on the pulse of What Women Want?'

Britt looked sceptical. 'People will be on holiday. Their loved-up Valentine Cruise holiday! So what they'll want is sun, sea and non-stop sex. I can't believe they'll want to come to writing lessons when they could be lying out in the sun instead. Or shagging each other senseless in their cabins.'

Mia guffawed at that.

'I have to be realistic.' Once again Britt struggled to clamp down on the feeling of panic that threatened to engulf her. 'Annie and Meredith cooked this up between them. But it's *me* that has to do it all, and it's me who'll take the blame if everything goes pear-shaped.'

And that was the thing, thought Britt. Meredith had decided that her being writer-in-residence for the cruise was a brilliant idea, but it wouldn't be Meredith who would be wrecked with embarrassment if nobody showed up to any of the writing sessions. More worryingly – Britt felt her throat constrict as she thought about it – they all seemed to think that she had some kind of wisdom to pass on to people about writing and (even worse) relationships. But the actual fact was that she hadn't. Because the truth was that the success of *The Perfect Man* had been a total fluke, and she hadn't expected anything like the fuss that had accompanied its publication. And when it came to relationships, the only thing she had to boast about was a failed marriage. Meredith had managed to gloss over her divorce in all the publicity about *The Perfect Man*, merely saying that Britt had experienced the highs and lows of being in love and that her brief marriage had given her the in-depth emotional experience necessary to make her novel so utterly moving.

Britt usually skated around the issue herself in her interviews, agreeing that relationships weren't easy and stressing the importance of romantic moments to keep the love light in your life burning. Despite what she said, though, she remained sceptical about romance. Her own experience had shown her that it was rubbish, and her career was based around dealing with people's biggest mistakes. She saw the absolute worst side of them when their so-called relationships disintegrated into bickering, dislike and sometimes downright hate. Britt knew better than to believe in Happy Ever After. It didn't exist. Nobody and nothing in the world could make her think otherwise. Not even her own book.

She still hadn't decided whether she'd given in to a deep-seated romantic impulse when she'd embarked on her own fleeting marriage, the marriage that had surprised everyone else almost as much as it had surprised her. In any event, the impulse hadn't resurfaced since. She thought now, with the benefit of being ten years older, that back then she'd just lost her senses entirely. But back then, marrying Ralph had seemed exactly the right thing to do. And so she'd allowed herself to succumb to the romance of it all as she'd stood there in her snow-white dress, pink and blue flowers in her hair, and accepted the stunned congratulations from her friends and family, all of whom were saying that they never would've thought that she'd get married so young, but all of whom told her that she and Ralph would be a perfect couple. (They'd lied, of course, she realised afterwards. They all actually thought she was cracked. They'd known, even though she hadn't, that Ralph was far too good looking and sociable for her and that she was far too serious and hard working for him. It would always have been a great romance, one of her friends had told her afterwards, but you were mad to marry him.)

But she'd been seduced. Not only by Ralph, but by the whole idea of finding someone who was fun to be with, who treated her like a princess and who made her laugh. Good qualities in a boyfriend, she admitted. But not necessarily good qualities in a husband. You needed more than fun and laughter in a marriage. (Whenever she thought this – as she had done almost every single day after they'd come back from their honeymoon – she couldn't help feeling that she was giving marriage a bad name.)

All the same, she hadn't expected to fall out of love with Ralph. She'd been sure that she would always love him just as much as she had that day when she'd first seen him on the lawns of Trinity College, his loose cotton shirt open over his jeans, showing off his tanned and toned body. She'd fallen in lust at first sight for the very first time, and when Ralph had looked up suddenly and caught her gaze, she'd felt herself go rigid with embarrassment.

But he hadn't been embarrassed at all. He'd come over to her and started to talk to her, and she discovered that he'd graduated with his degree in acting studies the same year as she'd graduated in law. She was now a trainee in a small practice in Dublin, while he was, he said, learning all about characterisation by working in a bar.

Modelling might be a better option, she'd suggested, unable to keep her eyes off his abs, and he'd laughed and said that when he was six years old he'd been the face of MishMashMallow ice cream. She'd frowned and said she didn't remember it, and he'd said that nobody remembered the ice cream but that for ages people remembered him. Although not now, he'd added, given that he was that much older.

He'd made her laugh, that was what she remembered most about him. He'd made her laugh until the day he'd made her cry. She never cried. But when it had all gone wrong with Ralph, she hadn't been able to stop.

In the end, *The Perfect Man* had been her therapy, although she'd never expected to share it with anyone else, let alone the whole world.

It was the lawyer handling her divorce who'd suggested she write as a way to come to terms with the break-up of her marriage. The irony of having to have someone to dish out advice and deal with her own divorce wasn't lost on Britt, but she'd known that it wouldn't be sensible to try to do it herself. Her best attribute when dealing with divorces and break-ups was that she was always cool and calm, even when the opposition's legal team were spoiling for a fight. She was certain that she could be cool and calm with Ralph's lawyers too, but she didn't want to take the risk of losing it in front of them. As far as she was concerned, she'd lost it by marrying Ralph in the first place. And when it came to the divorce proceedings themselves, she knew that Ralph's side would do their best to make it all seem as if it was her fault, even though it really and truly wasn't (at least she didn't think it was; it was hard to be objective about your own divorce). Which was another reason for letting somebody else handle it.

Anyway, she didn't think that it would be an advantage

for her to be arguing her own case when she'd become so successful in arguing for other women. Most spectacularly, she'd managed to increase the alimony payments to an ex-airline stewardess who had been married for less than a year by a whopping 250 per cent – thus generating head-lines in the papers saying that marriage was a great career move for women who were stuck in a rut. It didn't matter that the woman concerned had worked for a private airline and had been paid well in excess of the going rate. Or that she'd given up a very decent salary and benefits when she got married because the businessman in question had wanted her home at the same time as him. And that it was the businessman who had precipitated the divorce by begin-ning an affair with his PA as soon as he'd come home from the honeymoon. Britt had argued persuasively and succinctly for her client and had been pleased at the outcome, even though she'd hated the newspaper headlines (one of which had screamed, 'Watch Out Boys! This Woman Knows How to Get Her Hands on Your Money'). After that, she reck-oned that a hands-off approach would work better in her own situation.

She hadn't wanted anything from Ralph. She'd only wanted him out of her life for ever. She'd wanted to forget she'd ever been fooled by him into thinking that there was such a thing as true love. She'd wanted to forget that she'd been beguiled by his words and his flowers and his way of making her feel, for a short time at least, like the most important person in the whole world.

Stop it, she told herself now, making a conscious effort to relax her jaw bones and let her shoulders flop as the memories rushed back. It was a long time ago. You are over Ralph. Over the marriage. Over everything.

Thanks to *The Perfect Man*.

If thanks were really what she should be giving.

She knew that she should be happy and proud and grateful. She knew that everyone thought of her as the luckiest woman in the world. But the silly thing was that she would have preferred it if her marriage had worked out. If she hadn't had to dream up *The Perfect Man*. If she'd known him and married him already. If she'd been proved wrong in thinking that romance was bullshit.

After Sabrina, who'd been handling her case, had eventually agreed the terms of the divorce and had taken Britt to lunch in Dobbins to celebrate, they'd had a conversation quite unlike any of their previous discussions. Until then, both of them had been utterly professional with each other; Britt giving Sabrina all the relevant information about the train-wreck of her marriage, Sabrina laying down the possible outcomes with the minimum of emotion, as though none of them were part of Britt's actual life, just inconvenient details that she had to deal with.

It was when they were having coffee that Britt had sighed and said that the whole thing had rattled her confidence in everyone and everything and that she'd found it surprisingly difficult to cope.

Sabrina had looked at her client in astonishment. It was the first time Britt had ever expressed any emotion about her marriage. Sabrina had thought that her client was as cold and unemotional as everyone in legal circles said she was. And that she was more concerned about the chunk of time the divorce was taking out of her working life than anything else.

'I didn't think it mattered that much to you,' she remarked.

'Of course it matters!' Britt cried. 'It matters that I was so bloody stupid. It matters that I let my heart rule my head, as if that's any reason to marry someone!'

'A lot of people would think that's a very good reason.'

'And they'd be wrong,' said Britt savagely. 'As you should know yourself. Marriage is more than a surge of uncontrolled hormones and heart-shaped chocolates. It's a legal contract. And you have to approach it that way.'

'Nobody does,' said Sabrina.

'They should,' Britt countered. 'People like us most of all. Let's face it, in our line of business we see the need. We know how many marriages break down. And it's because it's impossible to make it work.'

'Plenty of marriages work,' Sabrina told her.

'Plenty fewer than you'd think,' retorted Britt. 'And you know why? Because we allow ourselves to get suckered in by someone who isn't worthy of us and we accept his major flaws and we put up with all sorts of crap – and why? Because we're afraid to be on our own!'

'I can't imagine that you were afraid to be on your own,' remarked Sabrina.

'Nobody wants to end up as the eccentric old dear who lives alone and robs footballs that are accidentally kicked into her garden,' said Britt. 'I thought it would be good to be part of a couple. It was stupid. I should've known better.'

Sabrina laughed. 'You were looking for perfection,' she said. 'That's impossible.'

'I was not!' cried Britt. 'I was just young and silly and thought that there was such a thing in life as a decent bloke.'

'There *are* decent blokes,' Sabrina assured her.

'Yeah, in fiction.'

'You should write your own,' said Sabrina. 'That way you can iron out all the flaws. It might be good for you – therapy, even.'

Britt had laughed. And then, months later, after she herself had had a similar lunch with a client whose marriage had broken up, she thought that Sabrina had a point. Maybe if she invented her very own perfect man, the fact that she hadn't met him in real life wouldn't matter. All the better that she wouldn't have to meet him and deal with him as a real person! He could be like the imaginary friend she'd had at school – someone who knew all there was to know about her and how she felt. Someone she could trust. And then, like Steffi, someone she could let go without consequences.

She wrote on her laptop at home, propped up in the king-sized bed she'd once shared with Ralph, her fingers flying over the keyboard as she poured her heart into her words. She'd always been considered good at writing essays and reports, both in school and later at work. But this was different. This was dealing with ideas, not facts. Yet she enjoyed allowing the ideas to unfold on to the screen in front of her. She loved escaping into her own fantasy world, the world where everything worked out how she wanted it to work out and where broken hearts could be mended. Night after night she wrote about the man she'd wanted Ralph to be. The man she'd thought he was.

The more she wrote, the more real Jack Hayes, her hero, became to her; changing from a superior version of Ralph into his own person altogether, so that in the end he *was* her perfect man. And then, feeling a million times better and much more able to face the women who turned up at her office asking about getting a divorce, she shoved the manuscript into the bottom drawer of her desk and forgot all about it, just as she'd forgotten about Steffi.

It was her personal assistant, Amie, who found it. Britt walked into the office one day, having had a very successful meeting with the opposition's legal team that meant that her client was going to get almost everything she wanted, and discovered Amie sitting at her desk, tears streaking down her face.

'I'm sorry,' her assistant sniffed. 'I was looking for information on the Hayes case and I thought you'd said you put it in your desk drawer. And I saw this folder and I assumed it was the case notes and I started to read it and I just couldn't stop.' She scrubbed at her face with a tissue. 'Where did you get this?'

Britt was so startled by the fact that she'd inadvertently used the name of one of her client's husbands for her perfect man that she didn't say anything. (Jack Hayes, she thought wildly. He's bald. And paunchy. Not like my man at all. What on earth made me do that?) And although she could see that Amie was crying, it never occurred to her that it was the book that had made her cry.

'I mean . . .' Amie sniffed again, 'it's so poignant and so moving and so . . . so real!'

'Get a grip, Amie.' Britt suddenly realised that her assistant had actually been reading her novel. 'And don't tell me you've been reading all afternoon!'

'I had to!' cried Amie. 'I had to know if Jack . . .' She sniffed again. 'He's so great. If only more men were like him.' She turned her tear-filled eyes to Britt again. 'Who wrote it?'

'It . . . it's mine,' said Britt diffidently. 'Now, Amie, I really think—'

'Yours! You – you wrote it?' Amie stared at her in disbelief. 'You did this yourself?'

'Just for fun,' said Britt. 'For something to do.'

'But it's brilliant!' cried Amie. 'It really is.'

Britt had always thought that Amie was a bit too emotional to work in law. Now she was certain.

'It was just something I did in my spare time,' she said briskly. 'Now, d'you think you can pull yourself together enough to get me the actual file on the Hayes case?'

'Yes. But listen, Britt – you've got to get that book published. Everyone will want to read it. It's, like, so amazing.'

'It's not amazing at all,' Britt said dismissively. 'It's just . . . I did it for fun, that's all. It's not that good.'

Amie looked at her defiantly. 'You're talking nonsense, Britt. It's great. Look – can I give it to my sister, Bethany?'

'Why would you want to do that?'

'Because Bethany's boyfriend's cousin is one of those literary agent people. I bet she says it's brilliant.'

'I bet she doesn't,' said Britt drily. 'No, you can't give it to one of those literary agent people. Now come on, Amie, we've work to do.'

Britt was still uncertain how she felt about the fact that Amie had totally ignored her and had, in fact, copied *The Perfect Man* anyway. She'd given it to Bethany, who gave it to Stephen, her boyfriend, who passed it on to his cousin Lily in the Clover Agency, who passed it on to Meredith. Britt didn't know any of this until Meredith rang her to say that she thought the book had great potential and she already had a number of people interested in it.

'Amie!' Britt yelled for her as soon as she'd put the phone down. 'What the hell did you think you were doing?'

Although Meredith had talked about people being 'interested' in *The Perfect Man*, Britt had taken her comments with a pinch of salt. She'd heard of aspiring authors who'd plastered their walls with rejection letters, and she was pretty confident that this was what would happen to *The Perfect Man* too, despite Meredith's optimism. So she'd been utterly stunned to learn that two different publishing houses wanted to publish it and that they were vying with each other for the privilege.

'Trevallion is the one we want,' Meredith told her. 'They're top-notch in romantic fiction.'

'My book isn't romantic fiction,' said Britt (feeling a bit weird to be talking about 'my book' when as far as she was concerned actually it was just a collection of printed A4 paper that had been sitting in her desk drawer for nearly a year). 'It's . . . well . . .'

'Unashamed romance,' said Meredith firmly. 'That's how

we're going with it. At the same time it's very strong. The emotion pulses through, which is what's so great. We might liken it to *Gone With the Wind*. It's got that epic feeling. Only shorter, of course. Maybe more *Bridges of Madison County*. And we should probably mention *Pride and Prejudice* too. It's always popular, and Jack Hayes makes Mr Darcy look positively lame.'

'But . . . but I think . . .'

In the end, it didn't matter what Britt thought. Meredith called her back to say that Trevallion were prepared to pay a hefty sum of money for *The Perfect Man*, and that they were confident that the book would be a success.

Britt spent the next couple of months feeling stunned at the whole idea, although she kept her mind on her work and didn't think too much about the imminent publication. She had other things to worry her, including two high-profile divorce cases where the protagonists were using the newspapers to wash their dirty linen in public. She was spending hours on the phone telling the women in both cases that they weren't doing themselves any favours by leaking stories to the tabloids, and that she didn't work through the media; that divorce was a personal issue. There were times during conversations with her clients when she wondered whether being a novelist might not be the better option. And then Jennifer Kitson had turned up in her office, a woman who had sacrificed everything for her husband – who had spent the past ten years frequenting lap-dancing clubs and paying for personal services – and Britt knew that fighting for women like Jennifer was why she did her job. So she pushed thoughts of the impending publication of *The Perfect Man* right out of her head and thought about Jennifer's divorce settlement instead.

Meredith was the one who had to worry about *The Perfect Man*. Meredith's job was to make everything sound brilliant and wonderful, though Britt was far too cynical to imagine that it could be as brilliant and wonderful as her agent suggested. She'd read a piece on the internet about the fact that most writers earned below the minimum wage, and even though Trevallion had paid her a surprisingly high advance, Britt knew that she couldn't depend on more money from them in the future.

So while she waited for her book to be published, she didn't really give it much thought, other than occasionally reflecting that there was a certain symmetry about the fact that it was Ralph who'd left her with a black hole of debt when he'd gone but that it was because of Ralph that she'd written the book that had given her finances such an unexpected boost.

She hoped (because it was a matter of personal pride) that *The Perfect Man* would rack up some decent sales. But the book wasn't going to change her life. No man – she'd chuckled grimly to herself at the thought – perfect or not, was ever going to change her life again.

It was astonishing how many times she could be wrong about something, she thought afterwards. Because, of course, it had changed her life completely, even though she hadn't wanted or expected it to. And that was because it had been far more successful than she or Meredith or Trevallion had ever hoped.

'It's a brilliant book,' Meredith confided at a dinner to

celebrate the fact that it was at the top of the bestseller lists and outselling its nearest rival by two to one. 'It's Jack who's the key to it all. He's so gorgeous and so hunky and he appeals to both men and women. Best of all, like I said, Jack Hayes knocks Mr Darcy into a cocked hat.'

Britt hadn't been convinced about that. Besides, she'd never understood the obsession with Mr Darcy. She'd read *Pride and Prejudice* at school and she'd enjoyed it, but she'd thought that Mr Darcy was far too moody and hugely over-rated. If it hadn't been for the multiple movies and TV series – and especially Colin Firth in the wet shirt – Britt doubted that many women would've liked him at all. She conceded that TV had probably given him his iconic moments. But as far as she was concerned, Jack Hayes was nothing like Mr Darcy. He was much more positive about life.

When that thought had popped into her head, she'd chided herself for thinking of Jack as an actual real person and for believing that any of it mattered.

It was a few weeks after publication, with the book still at the top of the bestseller lists, that Britt realised that she had to rethink her career options. Trevallion wanted her to embark on a series of publicity events (even though she'd very firmly ruled them out, there had still been a lot of newspaper articles about the divorce lawyer turned romantic bestseller); Meredith had lined up a publisher in the States who wanted her to make the trip to New York to sign the deal; and Jeffrey Clavin, the managing partner of Clavin & Grey, called her into his office to suggest that a career break might be the best thing under the circumstances.

'I have women calling me up asking for the romance lady to do their divorces,' he said irritably. 'And then I have women saying that they want anyone but the romance lady because what the hell would she know about divorce. I can't juggle things around you, Britt.'

'But I've tried to keep a low profile!' she wailed. 'I didn't use my real name, I made sure I looked completely different in the photos . . .'

'Oh, come on!' He looked at her impatiently. 'This is Dublin, for heaven's sake. Everyone knows who you are – didn't one of the tabloids do a spread all about you getting that obscene settlement for—'

'I know, I know,' she interrupted him. 'But people will forget all that after a while.'

'I don't know what's the matter with you,' he said. 'Most women would be delighted to chuck in a pressure career like this for the life of a novelist. I mean, what d'you have to do besides float around all day thinking of impossible love stories before heading off for a spot of shopping and lunch with the girls?'

'I'm not a novelist!' cried Britt. 'I'm a divorce lawyer who wrote a book. That's completely different. And I don't do shopping and lunch with the girls! Give me a break, Jeffrey.'

'Yes, well, I'm doing my best,' said Jeffrey. 'But it's very difficult right now. Look, why don't you take some time out? We'll be glad to have you when you get over this fame and fortune period.'

'Are you firing me?' she demanded.

'Of course not.' He looked guarded. 'I'm telling you

that this publicity stuff doesn't sit well with your position in the firm at the moment. I'm asking you to take unpaid leave – and don't tell me that's a hardship; you're apparently making a fortune out of your pot-boiler. When things have settled down, there'll be a place here for you again.'

Britt couldn't believe her ears. He wasn't firing her yet he wanted her to leave. But this was her job, her career! She loved the law. She loved the preciseness of it. She didn't want to be a romantic novelist. She didn't want to appear on TV shows and give people hints on how to find the perfect man. She hadn't managed to do it herself, for heaven's sake! She wanted to get back to what she did best. Handling divorces. Was that such a hard thing to do?

In the end, though, she'd given in. She agreed to take the leave. Meredith was delighted and immediately organised a whirlwind tour of European capital cities so that Britt could sign copies of *The Perfect Man* in its many different translations. Then they flew to LA to discuss the movie rights. After that, Britt went to a number of industry dinners to pick up awards for *The Perfect Man*, feeling a total fraud every time she accepted them and guilty at dashing the hopes of the other writers there – people who'd made it their career to write books instead of just getting lucky with their first effort. She realised, after talking to some of them, how unusual it was to get lucky with your first effort. How unusual it was to get lucky at all. She knew that she should feel very grateful. But all she felt was stunned at the way her life had begun to spiral out of her control. In some ways, she thought desperately, it was like being married to Ralph all over again, never knowing what was going to happen next, always worried that someone else was in charge of her decisions.

After spending months travelling and signing and reading and feeling guilty that she'd had to hand Jennifer Kitson's divorce over to one of her colleagues, Britt told Meredith that she was feeling exhausted and needed a break.

'Well, you certainly need to be thinking about that all-important second book,' agreed Meredith.

'Second book!' Britt looked at her in horror. 'No way.'

'Sweetie, you have to write a second book,' Meredith told her. 'You can't rest on your laurels for ever. Besides, you signed a contract.'

Britt looked warily at her agent. Shortly after they'd met with the people from Trevallion, Meredith had come to her with the news of the offer they were making for *The Perfect Man*. They wanted, Meredith had said, to sign her for two books. For *The Perfect Man* and whatever book Britt would write next. Britt had retorted that she wasn't going to write another book and that there was no point in signing this contract, but Meredith had said that there was no rush to produce a second book and Trevallion was giving her plenty of time but that it would be good to have something in the bag for whenever Britt decided she was ready to write again. In the end Britt had signed the contract and had opened a separate account for the portion of the advance that was for the second book. She confidently expected to be returning it to the publishing company.

'I don't want to rest on my laurels,' she told Meredith now. 'I want to get back to my life.'

'You can't do that.' Meredith's look was almost pitying. 'This *is* your life now and you owe it to yourself to use your talent and write.'

'But I don't know *what* to write,' Britt cried. 'You know that already! I'm not a writer. I'm a lawyer.'

'Both deal with pure fiction!' Meredith chuckled. 'What you need to do is, like you said, take a little time out, recharge your batteries and then get going again.'

Britt swallowed hard. She didn't know what to say.

It was a week later that Meredith called to tell her about the Blue Lagoon offer. A way of recharging and being out there all at once, the agent had said in a satisfied tone. Killing an entire flock of birds with one stone, she'd added.

And killing me too, Britt had thought darkly, even though she didn't say that to her agent at all.

Chapter 3

Position: sail-away, MV Aphrodite.
Weather: fine and dry. Wind: south-easterly force 4.
Temperature: 25°. Barometric pressure: 1014.9mb.

Despite the fact that it had been a long and tiring day for most of them, there were plenty of passengers at the sail-away party, lured to the Trident Pool by the complimentary champagne and canapés and the cheerful music of the ship's own band, which was continuing with the calypso theme. The sound of their laughter carried on the night air as Mia and Britt – having briefly got lost on their way from their cabin and somehow ended up at the wrong end of the ship – eventually found the pool area, which was decorated with brightly coloured fairy lights and a massive ice sculpture of Neptune himself.

The sisters pushed their way through the throng and accepted glasses of champagne from one of the stewards, who was dressed for the occasion in a floral shirt and white trousers; although Britt refused the slivers of crispbread with salmon that accompanied them.

'Not hungry,' she told Mia, who'd scooped up a couple.

'How can you say that?' demanded her sister, swallowing hastily and bagging another before the tray disappeared. 'It's ages since we had anything to eat and the restaurant doesn't open for another hour.'

'I'll be hungry in an hour,' Britt assured her. 'Just not now.'

'Wish I felt that way.' Mia looked mournfully down at her hips and belly. 'I'm fat enough already.'

'I like your shape,' said Britt. 'I wish I had curves.'

Mia was startled. 'You don't really.'

'I do,' said Britt. She smiled faintly. 'I think romantic novelists are supposed to be a bit curvy.'

'Why?'

'I dunno. Helps with the warm look, maybe.'

Mia giggled. 'You're mad, you know that?'

'Yup.' Britt ignored the tray of miniature vol-au-vents that was proffered in front of them as Mia took one.

'If you want curves you should eat,' she told her sister.

'Later,' promised Britt. She looked around the crowd of passengers, who were laughing and joking as they tucked into the champagne and canapés. 'What d'you reckon?' she asked. 'Is everyone part of a couple, or is there anyone who looks like they might be interested in a writing work-shop given by someone who'd much rather tell them never to get married at all?'

'You don't really think that,' said Mia.

'I bloody do.' Britt continued to assess their fellow passengers. 'Quite a lot of young people – apparently there's going to be six weddings on board, although one of them is a pair of seventy year olds.'

'Good God!' Mia looked astonished. 'I didn't think getting married at sea was that popular.'

'These days all sorts of weddings are popular,' Britt told her. 'I've handled the divorces of couples who got married in Alaska or in a hot-air balloon or underwater . . .'

Mia chuckled. 'Are you saying that the more offbeat the wedding, the more likely they'll divorce?'

'Oh, no.' Britt shook her head. 'Doesn't much matter, to tell you the truth. People just get divorced anyway.'

'So what about our six weddings?'

'Half of them will go down the tubes,' said Britt promptly.

'Cynical.'

'That's life.' Britt smiled faintly. 'I suppose there'll be a clutch of people getting engaged on this trip too. And don't forget the anniversary couples.'

'It's starting to hit home,' said Mia. 'We're the odd ones out here, aren't we?'

'And that's partly why I wasn't keen on this in the first place,' Britt told her. 'Maybe there are people who only care about the fact that they're on holiday, but I can't help feeling that we've fallen into the middle of a floating wedding fair, which is my idea of hell on earth.'

'Perhaps it won't be that bad.' Mia grimaced, then grinned at her sister. 'Maybe there'll be a few on-board divorces, which'll give you something to do. Anyway, who cares! We don't have to spend all our time wrapped up in romance. There's always the Treasure Hunt to keep us occupied.'

They'd read about the Treasure Hunt in the ship's daily

newsletter. It would begin after their visit to the private island of Espada, the newsletter informed them, and the prize would be a diamond ring valued at $5,000 from the ship's jewellery shop.

Mia's eyes had widened at that. She'd already poked her nose around the door of the jewellery shop and gazed longingly at the diamonds glinting fierily in the bright lights.

'I have to admit, the Treasure Hunt sounds exciting,' Britt conceded.

'And you never know,' said Mia wickedly. 'Perhaps there is a single gorgeous guy on board who will sweep one of us off our feet and change your ideas about love and romance for ever.'

'Somehow I seriously doubt that.' But Britt laughed.

Mia grinned at her. It was good to see her sister laugh. Mia realised that this was the first time Britt had looked truly at ease since they'd met up in London. And it was her job to make Britt feel at ease. She took a slug of her champagne. Not exactly a slam-dunk task. She doubted that Britt had ever been at ease in her entire life. There was no reason for her to start now.

'Thank you, thank you.' The band leader spoke into the mike. 'We hope to see you all again soon.'

Mia glanced at her watch. It was almost seven, and the restaurant would be opening soon. Restaurants, she corrected herself. *Aphrodite* had four of them, and unlike the bigger cruise ships, which catered for a huge number of passengers, there weren't scheduled sittings for dinner. The restaurants were open from seven to eleven and you could eat whenever you liked. The down side to this arrangement was that you couldn't reserve a table, which meant that sometimes you had to share with other people. According to the brochure (which Mia had read from cover to cover at least a dozen times before she'd left), this meant that they would meet interesting new people and forge lifelong friendships.

She didn't mind the idea of eating with people she didn't know, although she very much doubted that she'd forge friendships with any of them. But she knew that Britt wasn't very keen on the notion. Mia accepted her sister's limitations at social chit-chat and knew she was always awkward about meeting people for the first time. When they'd been children, Mia had realised that her older sister was almost cripplingly shy and hated talking to people she didn't know. Which made it all the more surprising that she'd managed to do the publicity for *The Perfect Man* without losing her cool completely. Of course, as Britt had got older, she'd overcome her shyness – her stellar success in her chosen career had helped tremendously. And when it came to her newest career, Meredith had been the one to steer her through the events and make sure that she didn't mess up. Mia wished she'd had the opportunity to talk to Britt's agent to find out how she'd managed to make her appear witty and spontaneous when everyone in the family knew that Britt didn't do anything without a massive amount of forward planning and thinking about it first.

The only time that she *had* been mad and spontaneous, it had turned out so badly that Mia perfectly understood why she was so cautious now. Mia (as well as James, Paula and Gerry) had been astounded at the fact that Britt had been swept off her feet – even by someone with Ralph's smouldering good looks and undoubted charm. Britt had been totally unaffected by the good looks and charm of the local boys when they'd been growing up in Templeogue, saying that looks weren't important and that they were all stupid and immature. (She would use their brother James as an example of stupid, immature boys, and Mia hadn't been able to defend him – poor James had been utterly hopeless until his late twenties, and both girls were in agreement that it was only because of Sarah that he'd turned into a functioning human being.) Ralph, however, had seemed anything but stupid and immature – he'd been gorgeous, with a hint of danger about him, something that had obviously turned Britt's head completely and caused her to make the biggest mistake of her life. And somehow, thought Mia, she still seemed to be paying for it.

I hope Allegra doesn't make any stupid mistakes when it comes to men, she said to herself. Not like Britt and not like me. I hope she finds the right person for her and lives happily ever after.

She felt another tug of loneliness as she thought about Allegra. She'd phoned her when they'd boarded the ship, although at that point – since Dublin was six hours ahead of them – it was close to Allegra's bedtime. Her daughter had asked her when she was coming home, and Mia had said 'soon' and felt terrible because in the eyes of a child two weeks certainly wasn't soon, it was a huge amount of time. At that moment she'd bitterly regretted agreeing to come, regretted the selfish motivation that had made her feel that she deserved a holiday, even a working holiday, and that it would be good for her to be away from Allegra for a while. It wasn't good for her and it wasn't good for Allegra and she was a terrible mother, just like people had predicted.

'Mia? You OK?' Britt looked at her curiously and Mia was horrified to realise that a tear was brimming in her eye.

'Of course,' she said rapidly. 'Fine.'

'Have I said anything to upset you?'

'No.'

'Is there a reason for you to be upset about anything?'

'No,' Mia repeated. 'I was just thinking about Allegra.'

'Are you missing her?'

'Britt! She's my daughter. She's only three. Naturally I'm missing her.'

'Of course. I understand that.'

Mia shrugged. 'I'll be fine. Allegra will be fine too.'

'I appreciate you coming,' said Britt. 'I know it was hard for you to leave her behind.'

'You're welcome.' Mia swallowed the last of her champagne and gave her sister a half-smile. She knew that Britt was making a big effort to be caring. She wondered for how long she'd be able to carry it off without cracking.

In the short time since the band had finished playing the passengers had begun to drift away from the pool, and now only a few of them remained: Mia and Britt, a group of women, a quartet of elderly men, and a younger man on his own who was leaning against the rail, a brightly coloured and apparently untasted cocktail in his hand. Mia frowned. He looked like the last passenger, the man who'd boarded as soon as the photographer had turned away. Perhaps, she thought, he was someone famous, trying to get away from it all. Maybe he was having a secret love tryst on board.

'Come on,' said Britt. 'Let's see if we can get a table in the main restaurant. We've probably left it too late.'

Mia looked at her watch again. It was still showing just before seven, and she tapped it in irritation. 'This needs a new battery,' she said. 'Or maybe I'll pick up a watch at a stall somewhere exotic. Will you be able to hack it if we have to share a table tonight?'

'I'd rather not,' said Britt honestly. 'If there isn't a free table, could we go to the café instead?'

Mia nodded. Britt was the boss after all. Besides, she was suddenly feeling very tired. And, surprisingly, not all that hungry.

The Parthenon Restaurant was almost full but, in what they regarded as a massive stroke of luck, Britt and Mia managed to nab a small round table just inside the door. It was set for three, but they reckoned nobody could possibly be on the Valentine Cruise on their own (that, remarked Mia, would be taking sad a bit too far) so they wouldn't be stuck with anyone else coming along.

'This is wonderful, isn't it?' Mia's tiredness disappeared as soon as she sat down, and she looked around her with interest. Despite its size, the restaurant was designed to feel intimate and elegant and the vast swathes of white muslin that hung from the ceiling managed to achieve that effect. The lighting was muted, the carpet a soft mink grey that gave it a hushed, unhurried atmosphere. The extravagant floral arrangements scattered around the room added colour and warmth.

'Pretty good all right,' agreed Britt.

'Thanks for asking me.' Mia looked at her happily. 'I'd never have been able to afford something like this in a billion years.'

Britt opened her mouth and closed it again. Mia felt sure that she'd been about to give her the 'if you worked hard like me' lecture but had suddenly thought better of it. She wondered whether the entire trip would be punctuated by one or the other of them biting back their unwanted words of advice to each other.

They were both sitting in silence, observing the bustle of the restaurant, when one of the stewards came over to their table and asked if they'd mind someone sharing with them.

Mia glanced at Britt, who looked uncomfortable but nevertheless said 'of course not' in a polite, if not exactly enthusiastic, way. The steward beamed at her and waved the passenger forward.

'Miss Martin and Miss McDonagh,' he said, introducing them. 'And this is Mr Tyler.'

'Leo,' the man said, extending his hand to them. 'Pleased to meet you.'

'Britt.'

'Mia.'

Mia smiled brightly at him while Britt's blue eyes regarded him seriously.

'I'm sorry if I've intruded,' said Leo.

'It's perfectly all right, and of course you haven't intruded.' Mia recognised him as the man who'd been leaning over the rail during the sail-away party. He couldn't be here on his own, she thought. He was far too attractive to be let away by himself! Not her type of guy, though. She went for the tall, dark, handsome types, and Leo (while he was certainly tall) had fair, almost white, hair which was cut very short. His eyes were brilliant blue in a symmetrical face with a strong jaw and square chin.

'I left it a bit late to come to dinner,' said Leo. 'I didn't think it would be so crowded.' He frowned. 'And I'd hoped to get a table by myself, which was unbelievably silly.'

'I don't think the *Aphrodite* is geared up for individual tables. Not on this cruise anyway,' commented Britt.

'Besides, it's nice to be sociable and meet people,' Mia said. 'So we're glad you joined us. I suppose the restaurant is particularly crowded tonight. Everyone's hungry. You can't really exist on airline food all day. Anyway, the food on board cruise ships is legendary.' Mia watched as one of the stewards walked by the table with plates of grilled yellow-fin tuna. 'My stomach is absolutely rumbling,' she added, realising that she'd reacquired her appetite.

'I'm not all that hungry,' said Leo as he opened a menu and held it in front of him, hiding his face. 'But I thought I should eat.'

Britt and Mia opened their menus too. Both of them asked for red snapper, while Leo chose steak. After the steward had walked away with their orders, they looked at each other awkwardly.

'Maybe we should tell each other about ourselves,' suggested Mia into the silence, wondering if this was going to be the first test of her skill as her sister's assistant and if she was supposed to make Britt appear to be witty and charming in front of the handsome stranger.

'Aren't you two here together?' Leo frowned. 'I thought I saw you earlier.'

'We're sisters,' Mia told him brightly.

Leo looked startled. 'Really?'

And that, thought Mia, was the usual reaction when people learned that she and Britt were related. It was the pre-programmed reaction to brilliant versus average, blonde versus brunette, thin versus – well, not fat, Mia reminded herself. Britt had called her curvy, and she supposed it was a fair enough assessment. But in a size-0-obsessed world, being curvy marked you out as someone with no willpower. Which, she had to concede, in her case was quite probably true. No willpower and no discipline, and that was why she was the assistant and Britt was the bestselling superstar. Mia had never quite been convinced by the story Britt told in her interviews about her PA being the one to send off the manuscript. She couldn't help thinking that Britt had probably planned it. She was a planning person. Mia was the one who went with the flow.

'Britt's the successful one and I'm just along for the ride,' she told Leo cheerfully, shooting a glance at her sister.

'Mia . . . honestly.' Britt looked uncomfortable.

'Well, it's true,' said Mia. She turned back to Leo. 'Britt's the writer-in-residence on the cruise.'

Leo looked at her blankly.

'Brigitte Martin,' added Mia helpfully.

Leo still looked blank.

'*The Perfect Man*,' Mia said.

'I'm sorry,' said Leo. 'I'm not a big reader. I don't think I've heard of you.'

'That's fine,' said Britt hastily. 'I wouldn't have expected you to.'

'I would!' cried Mia. 'Everyone's reading *The Perfect Man*. Even men. It's a massive bestseller and it's going to be a movie soon too.'

'Really?' Leo looked vaguely impressed.

'It's for sale in the ship's bookstore,' Mia informed him. 'At a special ten per cent discount for anyone who attends Britt's talks on how to write a mega-selling novel. You can sign on at the booking desk for her first one. It's the day after tomorrow.' She looked at her sister triumphantly, reckoning that she had lived up to her job description by plugging the book and the talk at the first available opportunity.

'I'll certainly buy it,' said Leo.

'Don't feel obliged to,' Britt told him hastily. 'It's probably not your thing.'

'How d'you know what his thing is?' asked Mia. 'He's on the Valentine Cruise, after all. There must be some romantic bones in his body.'

'It's a romantic book, then?'

'Totally,' said Mia helpfully. '*Pride and Prejudice* meets—'

'Mia! I'm sure Leo doesn't want to know all about it,' said Britt.

'He asked,' said Mia. 'I'm telling him.'

The steward appeared with their food, which (thankfully from Britt's point of view, because she was very uncomfortable talking about *The Perfect Man* to someone who hadn't heard of it or her) effectively changed the topic of conversation as they started chatting about the quality of the meal.

'I'm like a kid let loose in a theme park,' Mia told Leo as she helped herself to some baby potatoes. 'The choice is mesmerising.'

Britt's eyes wandered around the restaurant as Leo turned his attention to Mia and the food, scanning the tables, wondering – as she always did – about the people around her. Happy marriage, she said to herself, looking at the couple directly opposite. And then, as her gaze moved, she put other diners into various categories: Not Married Yet. Madly in Love – for now. Married Too Long. Edge of Divorce. Her eyes lingered on the Edge of Divorce couple. They'd managed to nab a table for two but they weren't speaking to each other. And there was something in the way that they were mentally miles apart despite being physically close together that made Britt put them into the divorce category. They were going through the motions. Perhaps this trip was an effort to salvage something. But it would be a waste of time in the end.

She remembered sitting like that with Ralph. It had been a few months after their wedding. He was hungover, having been out the night before with some of his friends, and she was trying to decide whether they'd made a mistake. Ralph had drunk too much because he hadn't got a part in a play at the Project even though he'd been absolutely certain that he was exactly right for it. He'd been so certain that he'd chucked in his job working in a city-centre bar. Britt had been annoyed with him for walking out on the job before getting the part, but she'd tried to be sympathetic.

'The trouble is,' Ralph had told her as he gazed at her from his bloodshot eyes, 'you don't do sympathy. You think it's my own fault.'

'I sympathise about the part!' she'd cried. 'I just think it was stupid to throw in the towel at the bar before you knew if you'd get it.'

'I'm not a barman,' Ralph had said. 'I'm an actor.'

She'd wanted to say that he was an actor who didn't act, but there wasn't any point in that. Everyone knew how difficult it was to break into acting. Everyone knew that talent was only part of the story. That luck played a huge role. And, she reminded herself, Ralph was gorgeous and sexy and deserving of a lead in some hot-blooded play. Or even, she thought a little more prosaically, an ad like MishMashMallow ice cream again.

She'd done her best, she really had. But a few months later it was over and people were commiserating with her and saying that it was such a shame but not to worry, sure wasn't she still young and lucky that she had loads of time to find Mr Right. (Although Britt knew that many of them had actually sympathised with Ralph too, telling him that they knew she'd be impossible to live with because she was so ambitious and so unlikely to be supportive of him when she was completely caught up in her own career.) They'd been wrong about that, she thought. She'd ended up being supportive despite herself.

She smiled absently at a comment from Leo, not really hearing him and not really caring what he was talking about. She did wonder why he was here on his own. If he actually was. Like Mia, she found that hard to believe.

But she wasn't going to ask him. She wasn't interested. Really, all she wanted to do was to go home and get back to her normal life again. And if that marked her out as an oddity on board the *Aphrodite*, she didn't really care.

Chapter 4

Position: Caribbean Sea.
Weather: fine and dry. Wind: south-easterly force 4.
Temperature: 25°. Barometric pressure: 1014.5mb.

As soon as he'd finished his main course, Leo excused himself from the table, telling Britt and Mia that he was absolutely whacked and was falling asleep on his feet. Over their concerned protests he assured them that they'd been wonderful company but that he really needed to be on his own. And he'd pushed his chair away from the table, nodded stiffly at them (feeling a bit like a character in a period play) and then taken the lift up to A deck – or Apollo, as it had been helpfully called. Leo was sure he'd be sick and tired of Greek names by the end of the cruise.

He opened the door to his cabin and walked inside. Earlier that evening, when he'd first arrived, he'd been taken aback by how big the cabin was and how luxuriously it had been furnished. He supposed he shouldn't have been surprised. After all, the trip was costing him as much as his five previous holidays put together. It had seemed appropriate when he'd booked it, of course. But totally inappropriate now.

Until the very last minute he hadn't been sure whether he'd actually board the ship. Even after the long flight from London, when he'd been deposited on the quayside with the rest of the excited and chattering holidaymakers, he'd asked himself what he was doing, why on earth he'd come. He'd considered trying to take the return flight home again. Or perhaps staying for a night or two in Barbados before departing. But then he'd looked at the *Aphrodite*, with her floodlit decks and string of white lights stretching from her funnel to the bow and to the stern, holding a promise of fun and excitement, and he'd reminded himself that, as everyone had told him, he had to move on. Although this seemed a heartless way of doing it. He wasn't heartless, no matter what some people thought these days. The idea of travelling on the *Aphrodite* was hard. Yet it had become, in his head, a symbolic thing to do. And so, after everyone else had boarded and when the pretty photographer was taking her camera from her neck, he'd almost sprinted up the gangway and into the *Aphrodite*'s elegant marble lobby.

A member of the crew, standing just inside the door and wearing the regulation crisp white uniform, asked him which cabin he was in, and when Leo had said that it was the Delphi suite, the crew member had instantly smiled at him and welcomed him on board.

'It's a pleasure to have you with us, Mr Tyler,' he said, which made Leo look at him in surprise. He hadn't expected to be greeted by name, despite the fact that the Blue Lagoon website had made a lot of the fact that every passenger was treated as a personal friend. The business part of Leo's brain wondered whether the crew member could possibly remember everyone's name or whether they were only instructed to remember the fools who had parted with a fortune for the most expensive suites. (The Delphi had been the second most expensive. The most expensive, the Oceanus, was occupied by a retired businessman and his wife who spent six months a year on board the *Aphrodite*.)

Leo didn't necessarily think that people were fools to pay for the best, but sometimes you had to accept that the best was out of your reach. It wasn't a concept he wanted to believe in. He'd never accepted that there was anything he couldn't have if he worked hard enough. And life had proven him right.

People used to say that he was lucky. Friends – especially his best friend Mike – often told him that he didn't know how lucky he was. It used to annoy Leo sometimes, because as far as he was concerned he made his own luck by working hard and putting in the hours and being in the right place at the right time. And that had brought the benefits of being someone who could, when the right occasion came along, afford to pay for the best.

Which was why he'd agreed to the Delphi suite on board the *Aphrodite* months ago, when everything in his world seemed just about perfect. On the day he'd called the cruise company, the adviser he'd spoken to had been doubtful about the availability of the suite. She'd said that one of their regular clients was considering the same two weeks as Leo. But then she'd called him back and said that the regular client had changed his dates, not wanting to be on the Valentine Cruise, and so Leo could have it.

He'd thought that was lucky. Possibly it had been the last lucky thing that had ever happened to him.

He felt his heart race in his chest and made a deliberate attempt to slow his breathing. It wasn't all about him. It hadn't been his fault. There had been other people involved. Other people he'd trusted. He had been the innocent bystander in it all. He had nothing to feel guilty about. He knew that. Logically, he should be able to deal with it. What bothered Leo was the fact that logic, something that had always been an asset of his in the past, seemed to desert him on a regular basis these days to be replaced by a whole series of unexpected and very unwelcome emotions instead.

He began to crack his knuckles, something he always did when he was stressed. He knew that it was a stress-related habit, but knowing it still didn't make him stop. He couldn't help thinking that it had been a mistake to come on this cruise, even though Mike had told him that it would be good for him. Cathartic, Mike had said, in a tone he rarely used with Leo. You need to get away, mate. It will do you good.

Leo had agreed about that. But now, in the extravagant surroundings of the Delphi suite, he couldn't help feeling that the *Aphrodite* had been the worst possible place to get away to.

'You can't beat yourself up about it for ever,' Mike had said, and Leo agreed with him about that. He wasn't really beating himself up. He was just thinking that being on the *Aphrodite* surely marked him out as callous and heartless when the truth was that he still felt the burden of guilt. Which was crazy, he thought, because if anyone should carry that particular burden, it certainly shouldn't be him.

'You've got to move on,' Mike had added helpfully.

Leo was sick of hearing those words. They were easy to say. But nobody ever told you where you should actually move on to. Until he'd come away, he'd been convinced that he *had* actually moved on. He'd been able to put it all in the mental box he kept in his head. The mental box was where he put all his wrong business decisions. Whenever something didn't work out the way he expected, he would unlock the box, put the deal inside, and lock it away again, telling himself that it was done and dusted and no point in worrying about it now. And he had done that with Vanessa and Donal too. It was just that every so often he couldn't help opening the box again and thinking about what had happened and wondering if he could have done anything differently. Behaved differently. Changed the outcome somehow. And he thought that perhaps if he hadn't been so arrogant or if he hadn't lost his temper then it might have been all right. Maybe not all right, he amended mentally, but it wouldn't have turned into the disaster that it had become.

He got up from the bed. The Delphi suite was bigger than the entire studio apartment he'd lived in when he'd left college. As well as the sleeping area, with its walk-in wardrobe, sensational bed with canopied muslin net above it, and long dresser, there was also a living area with table and chairs, a sofa, a couple of armchairs and a flat-panel TV. The bathroom was tiled in the same white marble as the ship's lobby and had a generous supply of pampering products. Leo wondered whether it was standard practice to include products for both men and women or whether the crew expected him to find a woman and bring her back to the cabin to use the Caribbean Therapy Avocado and Mango Body Scrub. What was it about fruit in their cleansing products that appealed to the opposite sex so much? he wondered. He replaced the body scrub on the shelf beside the plump navy and white towels and robes monogrammed with the Blue Lagoon logo.

Standing in the bathroom, looking at his rather pale face and tired, bloodshot eyes in the large mirror, Leo peeled off his shirt and trousers and pulled on one of the blue and white robes. He tightened the belt around it and stared at himself in the mirror again. He didn't look any better in the robe, he thought. More of a prat really, like a bloke in a shaving ad or something. Men didn't generally wear fluffy robes. Not unless women forced them. He picked up his clothes and brought them back to the bedroom, where he put them into a bag marked 'Laundry'.

A bottle of Moët was nestled in a silver ice bucket on the table in the living area. Beside the bucket was a wide-brimmed glass filled with chocolate-dipped strawberries. The champagne had been there when Leo had first been shown to the cabin but he'd ignored it. Now he walked over and took it out of the bucket, noticing that the ice had been replenished while he was at dinner. He wiped the bottle with the starched napkin, thinking that if he cared anything about this holiday he'd be very impressed with it so far.

He took the bottle and one of the flute glasses from the table with him as he opened the door to his verandah. A blast of tropical air met him, invitingly warm after the air-conditioned chill of the cabin. He stood beside the ship's rail and gazed into the darkness of the water below. It was all so weird, he thought as he eased the cork from the bottle. Weird and unexpected and . . . The cork popped noisily and sailed in an arc over the water, its splash lost in the wake of the ship. Leo flinched. According to the Blue Lagoon brochure, passengers shouldn't litter the sea. He hadn't exactly intended to litter the sea with the cork. Maybe, he thought hopefully as he poured himself a glass of champagne, maybe corks didn't count. They were natural, weren't they? Like coral. Or something.

Leo took a large gulp of champagne. He'd acquired a taste for it over the last few years, but the truth was that he preferred beer. Still, there were times when champagne made you feel as though life should be OK. You couldn't drink champagne and be miserable. Could you? He didn't feel miserable now, did he? Tired, if anything. It was getting late, and his body clock thought it was the middle of the night. He was used to working in the middle of the night, but this was different. He yawned widely and finished the glass in another gulp. He wondered if they left complimentary champagne in all their private suites. He supposed so. Complimentary champagne and complimentary strawberries and complimentary God only knew what else. To make you feel pampered and privileged just as the brochure said. Which was all very well. Only, in the end, it didn't make you feel any better inside.

He poured himself a second glass of champagne. He knew that it was a stupid thing to do because he didn't really want it, his mouth was already dry from too much alcohol and his eyes were beginning to close. But he couldn't help himself. He thought that maybe he should get blindingly drunk. He hadn't got blindingly drunk in ages. Well, not if you didn't include the night out with Mike when he'd told him about the cruise.

'You mean you didn't cancel it?' Mike looked astonished.

'I completely forgot,' said Leo. 'There were more important things on my mind. And then I saw the entry on my credit-card statement and I realised what it was.'

'Then go,' said Mike. 'Go and have a great time and shag the first woman you see.'

'I can't go.' Leo looked horrified. 'I can't even think about—'

'Of course you can,' Mike interrupted him. 'You can't put your life on hold for ever.'

This time Leo winced. 'I really don't think . . .'

'Yeah, I know. But you need to get back into gear again. You need to get out there. And the best way of doing that is by shagging someone.'

'Mike, women aren't objects just waiting to be shagged, you know.' Leo thought he sounded incredibly pompous when he said that. After all, he'd shagged a few of them in his day without worrying about it.

'I know,' said Mike. 'I do have a sensitive side. But sometimes, man or woman, it doesn't matter. You just need a bit of mindless sex.'

Leo had already thought about the mindless sex. Months

earlier, he'd gone to a Dublin nightclub, ready and willing to take home with him the first carefully made-up giggling blonde he could find so that he could (as they used to say when they were younger) ride her ragged. He was determined that it would be no-strings-attached sex, nothing more than an hour or so of pure physical pleasure (if, he thought to himself, he could even manage an hour!). But when he'd got to the club he'd bought a bottle of their overpriced champagne and drunk most of it himself, even though some gorgeous women had come over to him and suggested sharing. They'd sat down beside him, but he reckoned they'd seen the desperation in his eyes or something, because none of them had finished the drink with him, much less come back to his renovated house in Monkstown, which now felt empty and forlorn.

'It's the Valentine Cruise,' Leo reminded Mike – who didn't know about the barren evening at the nightclub. 'All the shaggable women will be there with their boyfriends. If there are any unattached females, they'll either be dried-up old bags or Ugly Bettys hoping against hope to snare someone with bad eyesight.'

'Not at all,' said Mike robustly. 'I'm sure there'll be some luscious totty lurking around in skimpy bikinis.'

'No there won't,' retorted Leo. 'It's not the sort of cruise where they'd expect to find unattached men.'

'Maybe not passengers,' said Mike wisely. 'But you know what they say about girls loving sailors. They might be there to jump on the crew.'

Leo looked at him sceptically. 'I don't think so. Besides,' he added. 'It's not a cheap-o package cruise job. This is more of your luxury superliner yacht. There won't be totty on offer, and even if there was, you know I'm not in the market for it.'

'Get a life, mate,' said Mike. 'When it's there, everyone's in the market for it. You've been on the sidelines for long enough. You've done your penance.'

'I didn't need to do penance,' said Leo sharply. 'It wasn't my fault.'

'In that case, stop acting like it was,' said Mike.

'Am I?' asked Leo. 'Still?'

'Mate, I know it was the toughest thing that ever happened to you, but you're like an effing martyr,' Mike replied. 'And it's doing my head in.'

'I'm sorry,' said Leo. 'It's just . . .'

'. . . just time for you to move on,' Mike said. 'Like I said – go and shag someone. I can't believe there won't be at least one available female just panting for you. And the luxury part means that it'll be rich totty. You know perfectly well that when some loaded young thing catches sight of you flexing your muscles beside the pool – well, you'll be in, no problem. You always are.' He winked at his friend. 'It is, of course, totally unjust that you seem to hook in the ladies without too much effort. Dunno why, myself. I'm not into blond blokes with six-pack abs, but it works for them.'

'Don't be such a fool.' Leo's tone was irritable, but he sat up straighter in the seat so that his already lean body looked leaner. 'The thing isn't pitched at people who only want to get drunk and shagged. It's supposed to be more stylish than that. It's all dress suits and designer gear.'

Mike guffawed. 'Everyone wants to get drunk and shagged,' he said. 'Especially people who've shelled out a fortune for their floating paradise.'

'Maybe.' Leo lowered his beer, allowed his body to slump again and looked blearily across the bar.

'Now *she's* shaggable,' said Mike, following his gaze to where a leggy redhead was paying for some drinks. 'And I bet you'd be in there, no problem.'

'Yeah, I could be.' Leo made another effort to sit up straight as the leggy redhead walked past them. She didn't glance in their direction at all. He abandoned his efforts. 'But I don't want to be.'

'Jeez, pal, you're in a bad way if that's the case,' Mike told him. 'You need the holiday. Anyhow, maybe you'll meet some excruciatingly rich widow who's looking for a hunky young toyboy and her eye will fall on you and she'll whisk you away to a life of ease.'

'You're sick, you know that?'

'Yeah. But I'm a good friend. I'll come with you if you like.' Mike grinned at him.

'I don't give much for our chances with the ladies if they heard we were sharing the Delphi suite,' said Leo. 'It's got a heart-shaped king-size bed.'

'Oh, right. Off that then,' said Mike hastily.

Leo laughed suddenly. 'Love to see their faces if we showed up, all the same.'

'I'm a friend, but not that much of a friend,' said Mike. 'You're on your own. But you should go and have a good time. With or without the shagging.'

*   *   *

So here I am, thought Leo. And on my very first night I've had dinner with two unattached women. Mike would be proud of me, even if I'm now in the cabin on my own clutching a bottle of champagne and getting kinda drunk. Which really is not how I want to spend my time here. He'd pored over the brochure to make sure that there was plenty to do, plenty to keep him away from the whole notion of getting plastered for a fortnight. And there was. Seeing some new places, for one thing. Leo had never been to the Caribbean before, although everyone had told him that it was a great place to chill out. Nor had he been to some of the less developed places on the itinerary, like Costa Rica and Guatemala. He thought there might be a lot to learn by visiting them. And then, of course, there were the lectures – the Blue Lagoon company prided itself on the quality of the lecturers it brought on board. One year they'd had Quentin Tarantino (or some other movie director, Leo couldn't quite remember who; not Spielberg anyhow, someone edgier) giving talks about the industry. There'd been a famous opera singer too, and a Nobel Peace Prize-winner. And on the cruise before this, *Aphrodite*'s main attraction had been a celebrity chef giving cooking lessons. (Not that Leo needed them. He prided himself on being a good cook. He liked chopping things up in the kitchen.) There had also been lectures by a former American President, which, Leo thought, truly was the top end of the market.

They were moving down the ladder somewhat for the Valentine Cruise. The keynote speaker this time was a female novelist he'd never heard of. He squeezed his eyes together and opened them again. But of course he'd already met her. She was one of the women at dinner. God, he thought, how could I have forgotten that?

She didn't meet his usual shaggability criteria, though. He liked brunettes, not blondes. And he preferred outgoing, smiling women. He didn't think the novelist was outgoing at all. She was too quiet. Unlike the girl with her, who was definitely better-looking but who would talk the hind legs off a donkey. Definitely more shaggable. If that was what he was up for.

Leo knew that the alcohol was taking control of his brain now because his thoughts were becoming increasingly in-coherent and turning towards sex. He always thought about sex when he was drunk (not that it did him much good).

Romantic novelist, he thought. That was the main draw. And a musician. Or conductor. He vaguely remembered reading something to do with a conductor in the brochure. Or was it a singer? He couldn't recall.

The ship rolled slightly and Leo stumbled on the decking. I have to get to bed, he told himself. I need to sleep.

He placed the half-empty bottle of Moët in the corner of the verandah and left the glass behind it. Somewhere in the depths of his mind he wondered if it wouldn't be a good idea to bring it inside. But he thought it would be happier in the open air. He wanted it to be happy.

The chill of the cabin nearly woke him up again. But it was momentary. He walked over to the heart-shaped bed, flopped down on the pink cover, and fell asleep straight away still wrapped in his fluffy Blue Lagoon robe.

Chapter 5

Position: Grenada.
Weather: partly cloudy, fine and dry. Wind: east-south-
easterly force 4. Temperature: 28°. Barometric pressure:
1015.9mb.

Mia woke abruptly the following morning and automatically patted the side of the bed beside her,
looking for Allegra, before she remembered that Allegra
wasn't there. The rush of loneliness enveloped her again,
along with the sharp stab of guilt. She took her mobile
from her bag, which was beside her bed, and checked for
a signal. To her surprise there was a strong one, so she
pushed back the covers and nudged open the heavy curtains
over the patio doors.

She blinked in the unexpectedly bright sunshine that
streamed through the chink, and then let herself out on
to the balcony before the light woke Britt, who was still
asleep, her face calm and untroubled, her blond hair fanned
out on the plump pillow. Mia was astonished that Britt was
still sleeping (her sister had always been an early bird), but

she supposed that she might have succumbed to jet lag as well as the large glass of Chardonnay that she'd downed at dinner the previous night.

She gasped with pleasure at the panorama in front of her. The dark green foliage of Grenada, their first stop, was jutting out of the azure sea, while its red-roofed houses tumbled down the hillside towards a crescent of golden beach. It was utterly idyllic, thought Mia. If only Allegra was here to see it with her.

She dialled James and Sarah's number. After a few seconds of echoing nothingness, she heard the burr of the phone as it rang and then Sarah's voice answering.

'Hi,' said Mia. 'It's me.'

'How are you?' exclaimed Sarah. 'Where are you? Is it gorgeous and wonderful?'

'Anchored off Grenada,' said Mia. 'And, not that I want to make you pea green with envy or anything, but yes.'

'It's tipping it down non-stop here,' Sarah told her, although her voice was cheerful. 'We're all off to Liffey Valley in a few minutes for the afternoon movie.'

'Has Allie been good?'

'A pet so far,' said Sarah. 'Will I get her for you?'

'Yes please.' Mia waited impatiently until she heard Allegra say, '*Mama?*' and then almost choked up again. '*Hola, chica,*' she said. '*¿Qué tal?*'

'*Bien,*' said Allegra.

'And are you being good for Auntie Sarah and Uncle James?'

'Yes.'

'Are you having a good time with your cousins?'

'Yes.'

'I know they love you being with them,' said Mia warmly. 'So you keep being a good little girl and do what you're told and I'll be home before you know it.'

'Really?'

'Really. But I'll ring you every single day.'

'Promise?'

'Absolutely.'

They exchanged kisses over the phone and then Mia ended the call, realising that at that moment she would have exchanged the jade green of Grenada for the emerald green of Ireland even if it was tipping it down.

'Good morning.' The door opened behind her and Britt, pulling the belt of a robe tightly around her waist, stepped outside.

'Hi.'

'Everything all right?'

'Sure.'

'This looks lovely,' said Britt.

'Gorgeous.' Mia swallowed hard and smiled at her sister. It was OK to miss Allegra, she told herself, but she didn't want to dissolve into tears every time she talked to her. She didn't want to wallow in guilt either. She'd made the decision to come with Britt for the selfish reason that she'd wanted the holiday as well as the slightly less selfish one that she really thought that Britt needed her. And leaving her daughter in the care of her brother and sister-in-law, where she knew that Allegra was in great hands, didn't make her a bad mother. She had to tell herself that twice before she almost believed it.

'So,' she said brightly. 'What d'you want to do today? Go on an excursion or maybe head to the beach?'

'I'm going to sit on the verandah and work on my talk for tomorrow,' said Britt.

'You're joking!' Mia exclaimed. 'Don't you ever stop thinking about work? You're in the Caribbean, for heaven's sake. We're moored off Grenada! How exciting is that? We could be in dreary old Dublin, but instead we're out here under the sun. So we should be having some fun and exploring the island or something.'

'As I've said to you about a million times already, I'm not here to have fun,' said Britt. 'I'm here to work. And so are you.'

'Britt, honey, work can be fun,' said Mia. 'Besides, your talk isn't until tomorrow afternoon. We've plenty of time to do whatever it is we have to do.'

'The key to success is good planning,' said Britt. 'If I get everything right beforehand, then the talks will be OK.'

'I'm sure planning is important,' agreed Mia. 'But surely the key to success is being nice to everyone who comes along.'

Britt smiled knowingly at her. 'You're the nice one, remember? I'm the taskmaster. I'm supposed to be talking to them about romance and about writing. I don't have to be nice when I'm doing that.'

'I rather think you do,' said Mia doubtfully. 'How did you get on with this before?'

'I've never done this before.' The note of panic had suddenly returned to Britt's voice. 'I've done interviews, that's all. And that's easy because someone asks you questions and all you have to do is answer them.'

'But I guess you've done some kind of talks before,' said Mia.

'Yes. Legal talks. And the key to success . . .'

'. . . is planning. Right, right, I get you,' said Mia. 'OK, what preparation do you want me to do?'

'You've got to meet with the cruise director and make sure everything will be set up properly. Make sure that there's power for my computer and that the posters are up.'

'Right.' Mia nodded. 'Anything else?'

'Book a hair appointment for me.'

'OK. And after that?'

Britt looked at her from beneath her long lashes. 'You don't have to hang around while I work,' she said. 'So if you want to go ashore after you've done the other stuff, that's fine.'

'Really?'

'Of course.'

'I do love you, you know.' Mia hugged her.

'Get off!' Britt pushed her away gently. 'I expect you to work hard.'

'I will,' promised Mia. 'And I know you're a perfectionist about everything you do and that planning is the key to everything, but are you absolutely sure you wouldn't like to come ashore too?'

Britt shook her head. 'I need to spend some time with this.'

'It seems an awful waste to—'

'Really I do,' said Britt. 'And I'll be fine. I'm going to sit here in the shade and I'll be perfectly happy.'

'Sure?'

'Certain.'

'OK.' Mia nodded. 'In that case I'm going to have a shower, then get on with the day.'

After her shower and a tropical breakfast of fruit and banana bread, Mia walked down the narrow corridor that led towards the stairs. The Hellenic beauty salon was on the top deck, and she made the appointment for Britt's hair before taking the glass lift all the way down to the spectacular marble lobby. She'd almost been waylaid by the notion of an aromatic body wrap guaranteed to knock an inch off her hips, but had decided that she could have the body wrap any time, whereas she only had today to see the island.

There was a small crowd of people gathered in the lobby, either waiting to go on organised tours or simply to go ashore. Mia asked one of the receptionists if she could speak to the cruise director, and the man behind the desk nodded and told her to wait.

Mia sat on one of the squashy comfortable chairs and watched as the other passengers left the ship. She was itching to go ashore herself and couldn't help feeling that it was a terrible waste to be sitting here instead. But, she reminded herself, it would only be for a short time and then she could head off, and she had a terrible cheek feeling fidgety about it when, if it hadn't been for Britt, she wouldn't be here at all!

'Miss McDonagh?'

She looked up. The officer standing in front of her was younger than she'd expected, with dark hair and dark eyes.

He was wearing the obligatory white uniform and he looked cool and unhurried.

'Steve Shaw,' he told her. 'Cruise director. Pleased to meet you.'

'Pleased to meet you too,' said Mia.

'Do you want to come into my office?' he asked. 'It's small but we can chat there.'

Mia followed him behind a curved wooden panel and waited while he unlocked a frosted-glass door.

'Can I get you anything?' he asked as she followed him inside. 'Tea, coffee, water?'

Mia shook her head. 'No thanks.' She sat down. The furnishings of the office were less luxurious than the rest of the ship. The carpet was a standard grey, the walls cream with a large day-planner on the one behind Steve's desk, which was covered in various folders of different colours. He picked up a blue one and opened it.

'So did you want to run through the set-up for tomorrow?'

'Yes,' said Mia. 'I'm sure everything's fine, but Br . . . Brigitte, she's a perfectionist.'

'So I heard.'

Mia looked startled.

'Our PR person sent me an email,' he explained. 'Setting out Miss Martin's requirements.'

'Requirements?' asked Mia.

'In terms of equipment and the layout of the room,' said Steve. 'And, of course, in having her book available too. But obviously there might be other requirements . . .'

'True.' Mia kept her face perfectly straight. 'Besides loads and loads of copies of her book, she needs six vases of white orchids and a large bowl of M&Ms with the blue ones taken out.'

'What!' Steve Shaw stared at her and Mia burst out laughing.

'You're making her sound like a pop star,' she said. 'She's a writer, that's all. She doesn't have requirements.'

'She's a celebrity to us,' said Steve.

'Really?' Mia looked at him in astonishment. Britt had featured in papers and magazines because of both her legal career and now the book, but celebrity was pushing it a bit.

'She's our VIP lecturer on this tour,' said Steve. 'So if she wants M&Ms with the blue ones taken out, she can have them.'

'Are you serious?' asked Mia. 'You'd actually do that for her?'

'Blue Lagoon spares no expense to keep our guests and our cultural team happy,' said Steve solemnly.

'Gosh.' Mia grinned at him. 'What will you do to keep me happy?'

'You're Miss Martin's assistant,' he told her. 'So whatever it takes.'

'I'm loving the sound of that,' she said. 'But actually it takes very little. Unlike my sister, I'm low maintenance.'

'Your sister!' Steve looked at her in astonishment, and Mia couldn't help the dart of inadequacy that she suddenly felt.

'Her less talented sister.'

'Head office told me that her agent was coming with her.'

'Oh, right. Meredith fell off her horse,' said Mia. 'So I'm the substitute. But,' she added sternly, 'I'm no pushover.'

Steve grinned. 'I didn't think you were.'

'So it's really important that the room is prepared and all her stuff set up.'

'Obviously we won't have the room ready until tomorrow because our investment adviser is giving a workshop there today, but don't worry about it, it's under control.'

'Investment adviser?' Mia looked surprised.

'There are a lot of wealthy people on board,' said Steve. 'They like to know what to do with their money when they're not spending it on cruises.'

'I could help them on the spending part of it.' Mia grinned at him. 'But I guess I'm out of my league a bit.'

'I'm sure you're not,' he said. 'You could always go along to one of his chats.'

'Maybe I'll send Britt instead.'

'Britt?'

'Miss Martin.' Mia was annoyed with herself for forgetting to call Britt by her published name when she'd made such an effort to remember earlier.

'Right.' Steve nodded.

'Anyway, you seem to be on top of everything,' she told him, getting up. 'Which means my work here is done and I can head out into the sun.'

Steve laughed. 'I thought you were here to give me a hard time.'

'Why?' asked Mia.

'You looked very fierce when you came in.'

'Did I?'

'Fierce and determined,' he said.

'That's us substitute PAs,' she told him. 'We're always fierce and determined to make sure that our employers are given the respect they deserve.'

'Don't worry,' said the cruise director. 'We'll make sure she's fine. We want things to go well. It's our Valentine Cruise after all, so we're keen to make sure that the romance element is high.'

'I think she's a bit concerned that there'll be too much actual romance going on around us for people to care about fictional romance,' confided Mia.

'She doesn't need to worry,' said Steve. 'We've already had pre-bookings for her sessions. The room holds about forty people, and twenty-five booked before the cruise. Another five signed up this morning. I expect they'll be a sell-out.'

'Goodness,' said Mia. 'I didn't think so many people would actually want to know how to fall in love or how to write about it.'

'Apparently they do,' said Steve. 'Never underestimate the power of romance.'

'I'll make sure Britt's totally up to speed,' said Mia seriously, thinking that she'd have to have a long chat with her sister and make sure that her talks were sufficiently gushy to keep the cruise director happy.

Steve smiled at her. 'All I want is for them to have a good time,' he said. 'Your sister has to do her part.'

'Don't you worry,' said Mia. 'She will. Planning is the key to success, apparently, and she's planning away like mad even as we speak.'

'Excellent news.' Steve's eyes twinkled at her and she returned his smile. He was kind of cute, she thought. And it was great that he was so easy to get on with. That would make her job a lot simpler.

She left the office and walked back into the lobby. There were still plenty of passengers wandering around, discussing what tour they were going to take. Mia had intended simply to go ashore herself and potter around, but she suddenly decided to take a tour of the island instead.

'Hurry along so that you catch up with the rest of the group,' the excursions manager told her. 'Go through the port area and you'll find bus number two. That's yours. I'll radio the driver to wait for you.'

'Thanks,' said Mia. She walked quickly to the gangway and made her way through the bustling port, jammed with the usual throng of locals trying (and sometimes succeeding) to sell T-shirts and spices to the tourists. Mia loved the noise and the hubbub and the sing-song cadences of the incessant entreaties to buy. 'On my way back,' she promised as she crossed the street to where a squadron of eight-seater buses was lined up. She looked at them a little half-heartedly. Organised tours weren't really her thing and she didn't know what had made her decide to do it. She much preferred wandering around on her own, getting the feel of a place and its people. She didn't like being lectured.

She was the last person on to the ancient and somewhat rickety bus (she didn't mind ancient buses; she'd travelled on a lot of them in the past and rather liked their basic nature) and she found herself squashed beside another passenger. It wasn't until she'd sat down and arranged her bag and run her fingers through her hair, which had frizzed up more than ever in the tropical heat, that she recognised Leo Tyler, looking cool and comfortable in a grey marl T-shirt and loose shorts, a distant expression in his eyes, which, she thought, seemed somewhat bloodshot.

'Hi.' She smiled brightly at him. 'Warm, isn't it?'

His smile barely made it to the edges of his mouth. 'We *are* in the tropics,' he said shortly.

God, she thought, he's cranky this morning. How can anyone be cranky here when it's so gorgeous?

'Okay, you folks,' said the driver as he climbed on board and pulled the door closed behind him. 'Let's get goin'.'

The bus shuddered into life as he ground the gears and lurched forward. Mia found herself catapulted sideways towards Leo.

'Sorry,' she said as she straightened up again.

Leo rubbed his left temple with his fingertips and said nothing.

Mia abandoned any attempts to engage him in conversation. If he was going to be cranky in paradise, there was nothing she could do about it.

It was hot even with the air-conditioning, so she tore a page from the brochure she'd brought with her and pleated it into a makeshift fan. She waved it in front of her nose as the bus inched its way through the narrow streets of the town, which were clogged with traffic as well as people selling fruit and vegetables and simply strolling along with apparent aimlessness.

'First stop, nutmeg factory,' said the bus driver. 'Very interesting.'

Enormous trays of nutmegs gleamed warmly in the squares of light that came through the gaps in the walls that served as windows, and Mia listened with interest as the guide explained the manual process of grading the nuts and grinding them into spice. (Factory was overstating the case, she thought afterwards as she bought some nutmeg in a hessian packet to bring home with her. It was just a big building really.)

She almost asked Leo what he thought about it when she took her seat beside him on the bus again, but he was staring out of the window with a forbidding expression on his face so she contented herself with staying silent and fanning herself vigorously with her pleated paper as they shuddered along the dusty street towards their next stop.

The verandah of cabin B45 was in the shade. This suited Britt because it meant she could see the screen of her laptop, which she'd opened and set on the round teak table in front of her. She was looking at the PowerPoint presentation that she'd done for her talk, skimming through the slides, murmuring under her breath.

When she'd first put it together a week ago she'd been happy with it. Yet somehow here, on the ship itself, it didn't quite ring true. It didn't sound convincing enough.

But, of course, she didn't know how to be convincing about love. It was one thing to be light-hearted about it in a short TV interview, and even, perhaps, be flirty with the host, but she couldn't be flippant or flirty now. She was being paid to sell passion but she was very worried that she wasn't up to the task.

What do I need here? she wondered as she flicked through the slides. More bodice-ripping maybe. More sex. But that's not the same as romance, is it? Or do people think it is? She scratched the top of her head with her little finger, a gesture that her former colleagues at Clavin & Grey knew meant she was stumped. Only she was never stumped for long at Clavin & Grey. There she could always come up with the right solution to move things forward. Now, though . . . now all she could think of was that romance made you lose your senses and do stupid things and fall for the wrong person and end up divorced and (unless you had a decent lawyer) broke.

It was all very well for a guy to give you bouquets of flowers or boxes of chocolates or even to tell you that he loved you – but that didn't actually mean he did. It just meant that you'd been conned into thinking that a romantic gesture was the same as love.

There had to be more to romance, more to falling in love, than meaningless actions. Bouquets of flowers needed to be backed up by something more. But women were so foolish about it. They believed all the hype, believed the Hollywood movies, believed the fairy tales. They even believed in *The Perfect Man*. She'd contributed to the myth that he existed by writing it. And now she was contributing to it by talking about love and romance on this damned overcrowded passion-ship when she'd much rather be getting a good divorce settlement for a client instead.

She pushed the laptop to one side, stood up and leaned on the ship's rail. Grenada, thrusting green and gold out of the aquamarine sea, looked beautiful and enticing. Meredith had been enthusiastic about calling there, saying that there was a possibility of visiting the newest, most exclusive hotel on the island for their signature tropical fruit spa treatment. Britt had been bemused as to why Meredith would want a spa treatment in a hotel when there was a top-of-the-range spa on board the *Aphrodite*, but Meredith said that the hotel was an experience and that Sienna Miller was supposed to swear by it, and what was good enough for Sienna was good enough for her. Didn't Britt think so too? Eh?

I'm so hopeless as a girl, thought Britt darkly. I couldn't care less about the tropical fruit spa and its facials. I'm not interested in slathering myself with crushed apricot and avocado and drinking hot water and lemon juice and getting my chakras balanced, whatever the hell that means. I don't believe it does the slightest bit of good anyway! She rested her chin on the rail. There must really be something wrong with me, though, to want to be back in my office at Clavin & Grey when this is such a beautiful place.

A gentle breeze wafted around her and blew her hair across her face while the tropical sun splintered the sea into shards of glittering light.

It's wrong to say I want to be back in the office, she realised, as she tucked her hair behind her ears. The office is only an excuse. I'd be delighted to be here if I was on my holidays from Clavin & Grey. I'm just . . . She shook her head slowly. I'm just out of my depth. I'm not used to that. And I don't like it very much at all.

* * *

The bus continued on its way around the island, the plastic statue of the Virgin Mary stuck to the dashboard wobbling furiously as they climbed the steep hills of the banana plantations and descended into the lush green valleys below. The sky was china blue, dotted with powder-puff clouds.

It's a pity Britt didn't come, thought Mia as they rounded a bend and the driver told them that they were going to stop for some refreshments. This is really beautiful, and a far nicer way to spend the morning than making notes for a talk that, knowing her, she's probably practised like mad already.

The refreshment stop was at an old plantation house that had been converted into a bar and restaurant. Other tour buses were parked nearby, and the passengers mingled with each other, jostling for position to take the best photos of the house and the scenery.

Mia hadn't brought her camera. She wasn't much of a photographer and she preferred to look at things rather than take snaps of them. Despite the beautiful views over the island, she was beginning to think that her original idea of wandering around the town might have been a better one. There were too many tourists swarming around an area that should have been quiet and peaceful to really appreciate it.

'Hello there. Lost your husband?'

Mia turned round and frowned slightly at the woman behind her before recognising her from their tour bus. She was, Mia reckoned, in her early fifties, wearing a wide-brimmed hat to protect her fair-skinned face from the sun (although somehow she'd already managed to get the tip of her nose burned) and matching shorts and T-shirt.

'My what?' asked Mia.

'He's at the bar having a beer,' said the woman. 'John's having one too. He's my other half. I'm Eileen. Eileen Costello.'

'Mia.' She smiled at the other woman. 'But I'm not married.'

'I make that assumption,' said Eileen. 'Which is silly these days, isn't it, because so many people don't bother getting married. I don't blame them. There's so much fun to be had as a single person.' She laughed loudly.

'I'm really sorry, but I think we've got our wires crossed somehow,' said Mia. 'I don't know why you'd think I was married at all.'

'Oh.' Eileen looked surprised. 'We thought you were with that fair-haired chap. We saw you at dinner with him last night too.'

'Coincidence,' said Mia. 'He joined me and my sister at our table, that's all.'

'How strange.' Eileen smiled slightly. 'We all thought you looked like a family and we decided that you were the one who was married to him.'

'You all?'

'My husband and my daughter and myself.'

'I'm sorry, you all got it wrong.'

'Well, you never know.' Eileen laughed. 'Valentine Cruise and all that. Cupid might yet fire that arrow and you'll have something to celebrate.'

Mia wondered how many similar comments might be made to her over the next fortnight by other smug loved-up passengers.

'And you?' she asked. 'Are you celebrating anything on the cruise?'

'Our twenty-fifth wedding anniversary,' said Eileen proudly. 'Hard to believe, sometimes, that it's been that long. I'm expecting John to buy me some very nice diamonds on board to celebrate. The jewellery shop is to die for. Of course he could always win the ring in the Treasure Hunt. That'd do just as well!' Her voice rose slightly as a weathered, marginally overweight man joined them, rearranging a red baseball cap on his bald head. A model-thin girl, with a mane of glossy nut-brown hair, wearing a short, stylish sun-dress and over-sized sunglasses, accompanied him.

'John and Pippin, this is Mia,' said Eileen. 'Pippin is my daughter,' she added proudly.

'Nice to meet you,' said Mia, wondering whether Paula or Gerry would ever have brought any of their offspring along on a wedding anniversary cruise with them, and thinking not. She was also wondering how on earth two average-looking people like John and Eileen Costello had managed to produce a daughter as exotic as Pippin. (Pippin, she wondered, where the hell had that come from?) The girl, who Mia reckoned was about twenty, had pushed her sunglasses up on to her shining hair, revealing a flawlessly made-up face and dark brown eyes.

'Mia came on the cruise with her sister,' Eileen informed them. 'Just the two of them.'

'Oh,' said John. 'We thought you were with—'

'I told her that,' said Eileen.

'So who's the man?' asked Pippin, flicking her fingers through her glossy waves and tipping her shades back over her eyes again. 'You're with him again today, aren't you?'

'No,' said Mia. 'We're sitting beside each other on the bus, that's all.'

'Hmm,' said Pippin. 'So you're not an actual couple. He's rather hunky, isn't he?'

'Actually, he's a bit of a bore,' Mia told her. 'But, hey, if you fancy him . . .'

Pippin laughed. 'He's very attractive, but I'm not sure he'd be a good career move for me just yet.'

'Pippin is a model,' said Eileen proudly.

'Ah.' Mia nodded. The full make-up, the extravagantly styled hair and the expensive sun-dress made sense now. Pippin clearly believed in being prepared at all times.

'She did the ad for that new hairspray,' said John. 'One Spritz and You're Sleek.'

'Great,' said Mia, who hadn't seen it.

'It was my best work so far,' Pippin told her.

'Great,' said Mia again.

'And I've been so busy in the last few months that Mum and Dad thought it would be nice to come away together. I do feel slightly like a gooseberry with them on their anniversary cruise, but they insisted.'

John and Eileen beamed. Mia could see their obvious pride in their stunning daughter.

'If you and your sister are on your own, you're both very welcome to join us for drinks or dinner any time,' said Eileen.

'That's very kind of you,' replied Mia.

'It would be cool to hang together sometimes,' said

Pippin. 'I don't think there are too many single girls on board.'

'That's true,' agreed Mia.

'So why did you pick this particular cruise?' asked Eileen. 'It seems odd for people on their own. It's different for Pippin because she's family.'

'It picked us,' Mia told her. 'Britt is working and I'm her assistant. So I don't have too much time for hanging around really.'

'Oh?' Pippin widened her eyes. 'Is she an entertainer? I know quite a few people on the Dublin scene these days, but I don't think I know her.'

'A writer,' Mia said. 'Brigitte Martin.'

'Really?' Eileen gasped. 'I didn't recognise her at all. I read her book. It's wonderful. We could've gone on a different cruise but we picked this ship because we heard she'd be on it.'

'Did you really?' Mia looked pleased. 'I'm sure she'd love to hear that.'

'In that case you must definitely join us for dinner some evening,' said Eileen. 'We'd just love to have you, and Pippin's read the book too, haven't you, Pips?'

'Yes.' Pippin nodded. 'It was brilliant.'

'I'll talk to her when we get back,' said Mia. 'I'm sure she'd be delighted to have dinner with you. Thanks for the invitation.'

'I would never have recognised her either.' Pippin frowned slightly. 'She doesn't look anything like her photo.'

'She's not . . . she doesn't . . .' Mia wasn't sure what to say. That her sister hated having her hair curled and wearing loads of make-up? That she didn't like the look? Which, she suddenly realised, was Pippin's own look, despite the different hair colouring.

'She's probably trying to be incognito,' said Eileen conspiratorially. 'Doesn't want to get recognised while she's on her own time.'

'Yes,' agreed Mia thankfully.

'Anyway, you just tell her any night for dinner.'

'Sure.'

'Would you mind taking our photo?' asked John.

'No problem.'

Mia took the digital camera from him.

'Not here,' John said. 'Over there. With the views across the valley. Spectacular, isn't it?'

It took a while to take the picture. John fussed about the background and the light while Pippin insisted on getting her poses just right so that her nose didn't look too big.

'I'm having a job done on it when we get home,' she told Mia. 'It's an investment in my future. I had my boobs done a few years ago. The best move I ever made.'

John was looking at the digital image on his camera.

'They'll print it off for us in the on-board photography studio,' he said. 'They can do some touch-up there too. But I like it to be as good as possible first.'

'John's a great photographer,' said Eileen. 'He goes to the photography classes on board.'

'And I'm going to the beauty seminars,' said Pippin.

'I'll be keeping tabs on Britt,' Mia told them. 'But I'm sure I'll see you around.'

'You'll see me at her writing classes,' said Eileen.

'I hope you enjoy them,' Mia said.

'I hope so too,' said Eileen. 'If I could write anything like *The Perfect Man* . . .' She sighed dreamily. 'Wonderful, isn't it?'

Mia nodded as their tour guide beckoned at them to reboard the bus. She followed behind John, Eileen and Pippin and clambered into her seat. A couple of minutes later Leo Tyler got on too. Mia stood up again so that he could squeeze into his window seat beside her.

He smiled briefly and she almost asked him if he'd enjoyed the stop, but she decided she didn't want to be snapped at again. Instead she thought about the last time she'd been in a shuddering bus, on her way to Guatemala, backpacking with a couple of college friends who were there to study the ecostructure. She'd just come along for the ride. It had all fallen into place because the manufacturing company where she'd been working as an accounts analyst since she'd left college a couple of years earlier had decided to close its Irish operation and relocate to the Far East. Mia hadn't exactly been devastated about being made redundant – accounting had never been her passion (not even an interest, really; she'd just taken the job for experience, but it was an experience she'd pretty much had enough of). So she'd decided to take a few months off and head to Central America, somewhere she'd always wanted to visit.

Paula hadn't wanted her to go. She'd told Mia that it was an unstable region and that there were all sorts of 'goings-on' there. But Mia had laughed and told her that she would be with Peter and Frank, her two pals from college, and that she'd be well protected.

Well, she thought now, they'd tried to protect her from any 'goings-on'. But they hadn't been able to protect her from herself.

The bus hit a pothole in the road and jerked her out of her memories.

'Sorry, folks,' called the driver. 'These roads ain't so good. But we'll be on the main road soon. Have you back to your lovely cruise ship in no time. Then you can chill out with a long drink.' He laughed an infectious belly-laugh, and the rest of the bus laughed too.

Despite the driver's prediction, it was nearly an hour before they were standing on the quayside again.

Mia looked up at the ship, gleaming white in the tropical sun. She narrowed her eyes against the glare as she tried to locate their cabin, and then realised that she wasn't sure which side of the ship they were on.

I'll have to sort out my port from my starboard, she thought as she boarded and took the lift up to Boreas deck. Because otherwise I'm going to get lost every single time. But not this time! She smiled as she stopped outside B45 and realised that she'd accidentally got it right first go.

The cabin was empty. Mia was both surprised and pleased at that. Surprised because she'd had the feeling that Britt was planning to spend the whole day sitting on the verandah working on her talk. Pleased because the fact that she wasn't there meant that her sister had got over her reluctance to mingle with the other passengers.

Mia slung her bag on the bed and changed out of her rather sweaty T-shirt and shorts into a cool vest-top and another pair of shorts. She was ravenously hungry. The good thing about being on the ship was that there was always food to be found somewhere. And she intended to find it!

Chapter 6

Position: MV Aphrodite.
Weather: partly cloudy, fine and dry. Wind: east-south-easterly force 3. Temperature: 28°. Barometric pressure: 1015.5mb.

Actually, Mia thought, as she made her way to the snack bar beside the Trident Pool, it would be possible to spend the entire day on board the *Aphrodite* doing nothing but eating. Before leaving the cabin she'd looked through the ship's newsletter for the day, which had listed all the dining options on board, and had come to the conclusion that if she didn't want to end the fortnight with the body shape of a beached whale, she'd have to ignore the full three-course lunches and go for the lighter options instead. She knew that she could easily pack away three courses right now because touring around the island had left her totally famished, but she felt that if she could limit her intake at lunchtime, then she could pig out at dinner, where the dessert options included both profit-eroles and tiramisu, particular weaknesses as far as her willpower was concerned. (She knew she would also have to avoid the afternoon tea and the chocolate buffet, which both sounded so gorgeous and tempting that she was already having difficulty with the idea of saying no.) But if she didn't manage to limit the calories somewhat, then all the clothes she'd brought with her for the trip would have been so much wasted excess luggage!

The poolside snack bar was crowded with people sitting underneath large cream-coloured sunshades over the café's round tables. None of them seemed to be too worried about their calorie intake as they tucked into lunch. Mia stood uncertainly to one side and scanned the café for a free table – she was beginning to think that such a thing would always be a luxury on board. Then she saw Britt sitting at one in the corner reading a book, a glass of white wine in front of her.

Mia raised her eyebrows a little at the white wine. Britt had been so businesslike about her day that Mia would have expected her to be frugally sipping mineral water and reading through her notes, but, she thought as she threaded her way through the tables, it was nice to see that her sister wasn't actually a complete workaholic after all. She went over to the table and dumped her bag on one of the chairs.

'Hi,' she said brightly. 'How's your day been?'

Britt looked up from her book, a John Grisham legal thriller.

'Not bad,' she replied. 'How was the tour?'

'The usual stuff,' admitted Mia. 'Jolting around in a bus for a while. A bit of local industry. A bit of touristy stuff. Meeting some of the passengers. Hot and sweaty. You know yourself.'

'Which is why I thought it a much better use of my time to work on tomorrow's presentation.' Britt inserted a bookmark into the Grisham and closed it.

'Presentation? I thought it was a talk,' said Mia as she sat down at the table.

'Presentation, talk, it's the same thing.'

'Not really,' argued Mia. 'A presentation is telling people things. A talk is more . . . well, chatty I guess.'

'You do your thing and let me worry about mine,' said Britt. 'Did you arrange everything with the cruise director? And organise my hair?'

'Did you ask me to?' Mia looked at her enquiringly.

'Of course I did! That's what I—'

'Chill, chill – that was the first thing I did this morning,' interrupted Mia. 'I know that by your standards I'm hope-lessly disorganised and chaotic, but I have managed to raise a daughter on my own for the past three years as well as hold down a job, so I do think that I can manage to do whatever you ask.'

'Sorry. I'm being control-freaky,' said Britt. 'It's just that I have to be sure that everything is done, and . . .'

'. . . and it will be,' finished Mia. 'Good planning, blah, blah, blah. I'm going to get something to eat. Want anything?'

'No thanks.' Britt shook her head. 'I had a salad earlier.'

Mia went to the salad bar and, feeling that she had to follow Britt's example, loaded up her plate with greenery. Then, enticed by the smell of the burgers that had just been flipped on the grill, she asked for one of them too. It's hardly overindulging, she told herself as she walked back to the table with her plate. I'm not having a bun with the burger. And I picked a low-cal dressing.

'So what's your talk, sorry, presentation going to be about?' she asked as she put her plate on the table and slid into her chair.

'It's a whole series,' replied Britt. 'It's called "Romance through the Ages. How to write your own Romantic Couple."' She twirled her wine glass around between her fingers. 'D'you know, I've come to the conclusion that most great passions are all about being horribly selfish.'

'Britt McDonagh! How can you say such a thing?'

'Think about them. Antony and Cleopatra . . . leading on to Richard Burton and Elizabeth Taylor; Edward and Mrs Simpson . . . leading on to Prince Charles and Camilla Parker Bowles; and then the fictional ones: Romeo and Juliet, Catherine and Heathcliff, Jane Eyre and Mr Rochester . . . all self-indulgent nonsense.'

Mia spluttered. 'You're going to consign every great love story into the trash-can of self-indulgent nonsense!' she exclaimed. 'They'll lynch you.'

'Well, take Antony and Cleopatra,' Britt said. 'They were both headstrong people. She was the queen of a huge country. And in the end she betrayed him because it was better for her to do that. You know he was already married, don't you? It always surprises me how many of these so-called great love stories are actually about married people having affairs.'

Mia kept her eyes fixed firmly on her food as she sliced her burger into small pieces.

'Elizabeth Taylor and Richard Burton,' continued Britt relentlessly. 'Such a big story because they actually met on the set of *Antony and Cleopatra*. But she was married already. In fact she was already a serial marrier. Everyone bangs on about it being a great romance, but basically it was just the same as someone from the office having it off with the new guy.'

'You can't possibly believe that.' Mia looked up from her plate. 'And you don't know how people feel . . .'

'People should be able to rule their feelings and not let their feelings rule them,' said Britt firmly. 'They shouldn't go around making excuses for doing the wrong thing just because they say it's "lurve".'

'You're here to make people feel romantic and passionate,' Mia told her sister. 'Not to make them feel stupid about love. I'm no expert, but I can tell you here and now that if you say that Elizabeth Taylor was just a slapper and that Cleopatra was nothing more than a betraying whore, you won't get a lot of sympathy.'

Britt laughed. 'I know, I know. It's just that I can't stand it when people get sentimental over lust.'

'You did once.' Mia knew that she was straying into very dangerous territory by talking about Britt's personal life.

'But I realised the error of my ways,' Britt said calmly. 'C'mon, Mia, you've got to admit that passion and romance are very short-lived. It takes a lot more than that to make a relationship work.'

Mia smiled slightly. 'You said that as though you meant it.'

'I do mean it,' Britt told her. 'Whereas the idea of standing up there and talking about hearts and flowers and stuff is actually quite terrifying. How can you sound sincere when . . .' She twirled the glass again and then looked up at Mia. 'I know what I should be telling them; it's just that I have to go against my instincts to do it and I don't want to make a mess of it.'

'You won't make a mess of it,' said Mia dismissively. 'You never make a mess of anything you do. Except your marriage, I guess,' she added. 'Sorry.'

'If I hadn't let myself get overwhelmed by Ralph's charm and his habit of sending me red roses, I wouldn't have got married at all,' said Britt wryly.

'Everyone gets suckered by the red roses,' agreed Mia.

'Proves my point.' Britt looked triumphant. 'Romance is bollocks really. And I'm right not to be warm and fuzzy.'

'Maybe,' Mia told her. 'But you asked me along to be your warm and fuzzy side, so please, please go with me on this one. Don't tell everyone at the talks that you think love is nothing but bullshit. They'll never forgive you.'

'We'll see,' said Britt ominously, and she finished the glass of wine.

Leo was in the cybercafé, logged on to his email account. Even though his colleague back at the private bank where he worked was looking after his clients, Leo was checking his work emails so that he could keep an eye on what was going on. Mike had told him not to bother looking at anything to do with work while he was away, but Leo couldn't help himself even though he'd deliberately left his BlackBerry at home. He'd sent a proposal for a new investment product to some of his high-net-worth clients the previous week and he couldn't help checking to see if any more of them would bite.

He noted, with a stab of satisfaction, that two of them had committed funds to the project but he managed to restrain himself from sending an email to either of them. They would have got his out-of-office message, and Peter, his colleague, would have been in touch with them already. So there was no need for him to behave like the saddo that some people thought he was.

He checked his personal account too. He'd received only two emails since boarding the *Aphrodite*. One was from Mike, asking him how the cruise was going and reminding him that part of moving on was to put himself about on board and let the totty know that he was available. The second was from his mother's sister, Aunt Sandra, instructing him to enjoy himself on the cruise, and telling him that life was too short, that misery loved company and that love came around doing something that you liked. Sandra Bishop had a wide selection of clichés for every known situation, and whenever she wanted to make a point she used them liberally. She hadn't been able to think of any when Leo had come to tell her about him and Vanessa and Donal. Even though he'd given her the minimum information, she'd looked at him with a stricken face and put her arms around him, holding him close to her and making him feel like a kid again. He'd been grateful for that. She'd been shocked too, and he felt as though she needed the comfort as much as he did. He tried to take account of how other people were feeling, but it wasn't easy when he was the one who felt both guilty and betrayed. Now, though, Sandra was at him to get on with things. That was what his mother would have wanted, she told him. She would have hated to think that his life had been ruined.

Leo didn't really know how his mother would have felt or what she would have wanted. He'd been ten years old when she'd died, and although he remembered her, she was only a vague presence in his life. His father had died last year. Leo had been sad at the time. Now he was relieved.

He glanced back at Sandra's message. 'Have a great time and enjoy every single moment,' she'd said.

He was trying, but he hadn't really enjoyed today's tour. Not because the island wasn't utterly beautiful and the warmth of the tropical breezes totally beguiling, but because his hangover (a filthy headache and a general feeling of seediness, despite the fact that he'd always believed champagne didn't leave him with any ill effects) hadn't been helped by the noisy shaking of the bus. He'd felt hemmed in too, sitting beside the chatty sister of the novelist. He thought it was freaky that he'd ended up beside her again and had shuddered when she'd tried to engage him in conversation when he felt so out of sorts. Surely, he'd said to himself as she'd boarded the bus, there were enough passengers on the damn ship not to keep bumping into the same person over and over again. He didn't want to get friendly with her. He didn't want to get friendly with anyone. And despite Mike's advice and encouragement, he certainly didn't want to get involved with any unattached women on board, no matter how suddenly desperate he might feel. So he didn't intend to get close to Mia or to the romantic novelist (what could be worse, he thought, than having a relationship with someone who probably thought that

St Valentine's Day was a wonderful idea? Maybe she even made her own cards and wrote her own soppy verses).

Nor did he want to get to know the other girl who'd spoken to him as they'd returned to the ship after the cruise and whose name he hadn't quite caught. He'd been taken aback when he'd first seen her. For a nanosecond she'd reminded him of Vanessa, with her long dark hair and languid, sensuous walk. But she was a stick-insect girl and not like Vanessa (who'd once described her own body as bootylicious) at all. Nevertheless, when she'd smiled at him and asked him if he'd had a good time, he'd seen Vanessa in her eyes and in her smile and he'd shivered involuntarily beneath the tropical sun. And when he didn't say anything in return she'd chatted away as though she hadn't noticed his silence and then said something about seeing him around sometime as she pushed her long, manicured nails through her mane of glossy hair in a gesture that was pure Vanessa.

It had squeezed Leo's heart. And he'd had to turn away quickly so that she didn't see the mixture of despair and longing that he knew must have shown on his face.

Steve Shaw was looking at the posters that the on-board printing press had produced for the talk by the romantic novelist the following day. Steve was still very sceptical about the appeal of having writers on the ship. He much preferred practical classes like art, which was always hugely popular and where the passengers amused themselves by painting their impressions of the destinations they visited and the *Aphrodite* herself. Some of them were really good, and after the classes all the paintings were displayed in the ship's art gallery. Sometimes people even bought them. It wouldn't be the same with the aspiring writers, who could hardly stick an A4 sheet up on the display wall and wait for someone else to review it!

Britt Martin was gorgeous, though. Steve looked at her picture beside an image of *The Perfect Man*. Her blue eyes peeped out sensually from behind a swirl of golden locks, and her voluptuous lips were slightly parted to show a row of white, even teeth. Steve was well versed in the ability of Photoshop to turn even the most ordinary of women into a total babe, but he reckoned that Britt Martin had a lot of natural attributes of her own.

Just as long as keeping the passengers entertained was one of them. Steve wished that he knew the woman or that he'd had the opportunity to talk to her before Annie had foisted her on the ship. He had to admit that the idea seemed like a good one, but he was still apprehensive about the following day.

'The Book Everyone is Talking About' it said at the bottom of the poster. And 'Are You the Perfect Man?'

He laughed. What chance had any man of being perfect these days? He wondered what the romantic novelist thought made a perfect man – someone macho but sensitive, he supposed. In Steve's experience, women all wanted sensitive but they didn't want too sensitive. They wanted macho but not too macho. They were impossible to please really. And someone who wrote about it, who peppered the pages with candlelit dinners and moonlight walks, would probably be the most demanding of them all.

Steve's mates often ribbed him about the opportunities available to him on board the *Aphrodite*, and Steve had to admit that there had been a couple of times when he'd broken the cruise line's very strict rule about fraternising with the passengers, but it had never been anything more than an opportunity taken in the heady atmosphere of the moonlit deck. (It was amazing the effect the moonlit deck had on the female passengers, he mused. It was like sprinkling them with some kind of potion. They felt romantic and desirable and very, very up for it, which was extremely handy if you were up for it too!)

He looked at the picture of Brigitte Martin again. Absolutely a babe, he thought. But very high maintenance, he was sure of that. The sister, however . . . Steve smiled to himself as he thought about Mia . . . well, she was more his sort of girl. He'd enjoyed talking to her earlier, and her dazzling, genuine smile was much more appealing than Brigitte's posed one for the photograph.

He put the picture to one side and looked through the rest of the cruise schedule. As well as the writing classes, there were photography workshops, make-up and beauty sessions, Scrabble and chess competitions, and a whole range of other activities, including the investment advice lectures, which were always well attended by the cruise's well-heeled passengers. But most important, from Steve's point of view, were the Treasure Hunt and the Valentine's Night Gala Ball. Anticipation of the Treasure Hunt was already whipping the passengers into a frenzy of excitement. It would take place partly on board the ship and partly on the private island where they would dock. And although the passengers had to solve the clues in a particular order, starting with the ones on the island, Steve knew from bitter experience that the rules didn't stop the more eager passengers from actively trying to find clues on board earlier. One year there had been a near disaster when a horde of people had tried to get into the galley, convinced that the third clue led them there. It had actually hinted at the art gallery. The chef had threatened to leave the ship at the next port, and it had taken all of Steve's efforts (as well as a long discussion with the captain) to placate him. Steve shivered at the memory.

This year there had been lots of announcements in the ship's newsletter telling passengers that there was no need to search the ship, that the clues would be given out during the voyage and that no item that needed to be located on board would be available before the relevant date and time. He knew that it wouldn't stop them. Not for a diamond ring worth $5,000. The well-heeled passengers on the *Aphrodite* hadn't become well heeled by passing up the opportunity to pick up a valuable asset for free when they could.

Steve shuffled the papers on his desk again. What with keeping the novelist happy and the passengers busy, he knew he'd have his work cut out on this trip. He loved his job. But sometimes it gave him indigestion.

Chapter 7

Position: at sea.
Weather: partly cloudy. Wind: easterly force 5.
Temperature: 28°. Barometric pressure: 1011.0mb.

Britt woke before Mia the following morning. She slid quietly out of bed and opened the door to the balcony, where she sat on one of the teak loungers and gazed at the candy-pink morning sky. She could see why art classes on board the ship could be so well attended; looking at the pastel colours of the early morning made her want to capture them on canvas herself. She wished she'd brought her camera outside with her but didn't want to open the cabin door again in case she woke Mia. Right now she wanted to be on her own.

It seemed to Britt that these days she wanted to spend more and more time on her own. Meredith had said that that was a good thing. It meant, she said, that Britt was getting in touch with her creative side again, looking deep inside herself for the heart of her next book. But Britt knew that it was simply because she retreated into herself

121

when she was stressed. And despite the luxury of her surroundings, she was very stressed now.

The problem, she decided as she wriggled her toes in the warmth of the tropical morning, was that everything that had happened to her over the last year had been out of her control. When it came to meeting her clients and talking about their divorces and giving them advice, she was totally on top of her brief. She knew what they needed, she knew what she wanted and she knew how to achieve it. She was used to being the one dishing out the advice and the rules. It was hard to be the one following them instead.

She didn't say this to anyone else in case they thought she was totally bonkers. They all thought her life was a glamorous whirl now – and part of it was. But as far as Britt was concerned, she was at her best when she was plotting strategies for her divorce clients, not plotting romantic fiction.

I need a strategy for myself now, she thought as she gazed out at the ever-lightening sky, the pinks gradually fading as the sun rose higher and drenched it in azure blue. I need to plot my way out of a world of love and romance and back into a world of divorce and loathing.

There really was only one way to do that. And that was to tell it like it was, to say that she thought romance was a stinking pile of manure and that there was no such thing as a happy ending. That was the talk she really wanted to give.

Twenty minutes later the door opened and Mia stepped outside, followed by a steward carrying a breakfast tray laden with fruit and croissants. The steward left the tray on the table and Mia sat opposite Britt. She poured aromatic coffee into the wide cups and picked at a croissant.

'Looking forward to strutting your stuff?' she asked.

Britt shrugged.

'D'you know your presentation off by heart?'

'More or less.'

'Is that how you do it in the courtroom?' asked Mia.

'I don't generally get to a courtroom,' Britt told her. 'Family law is different. But I always know what I'm going to say.'

Mia looked at her sister, who seemed so composed and relaxed. If it was me who was going to have to give a talk to loads of strangers, she thought, I'd be feeling sick. I wouldn't be able to nibble delicately on slices of melon and mango. Although, she conceded to herself as she helped herself to a Danish pastry, I did manage to give those English classes to the town council without making a complete fool of myself. Not sure if they learned much, though! Not sure I was tough enough on them. Britt, on the other hand, would've had them fluent in less than a month.

Mia suggested that they spend the morning lounging lazily by the pool while the *Aphrodite* made her way southwards through the Caribbean. It'll be relaxing for both of us, she told Britt, and you need to be relaxed before your talk. (Mia didn't know whether Britt did need to be relaxed – perhaps, she thought, it would be better if she was buzzy and up for it – but it seemed like a caring, PA sort of thing

123

to say.) Britt sat beside her for an hour, flicking idly through a magazine, before heading off to the hair salon to turn herself into Brigitte.

The stylist, a young French girl with huge dark eyes and a perfect complexion, smiled at her and told her that she'd read *The Perfect Man* earlier in the year and that it was the best book she'd ever read and she couldn't wait for Britt's next novel – there was a rumour that it would be about one of the characters in *The Perfect Man*, a girl called Lisette. Was it true? asked the stylist as she lathered Britt's hair. She'd liked Lisette but she'd preferred the other heroine of the book, Francesca.

'I haven't decided yet,' Britt told her, although the truth was that even if she did write a second book (which she absolutely wasn't going to do; she would have to talk to Meredith about that as soon as she got home, and she wasn't looking forward to that particular conversation), it wouldn't be about either Lisette or Francesca, two women she now thought weren't half strong or feisty enough. The thing about *The Perfect Man*, she thought as the hairdresser rinsed her hair, was that Jack Hayes was amazingly great but that the women in the book were far too passive, which helped him to look good. She should have made one of the female characters a kick-ass lawyer who wasn't going to be messed with. A person who didn't go to pieces, as Lisette had, because she'd walked in on her husband having sex with her best friend. If I was doing it all over again, thought Britt as the hairdresser twirled a lock of blond hair with the ghd, I'd have Lisette shoot the bastard and win her own defence in court.

*   *   *

'Wow.'

Mia had never seen Britt face to face in her full-on Brigitte persona before. She was gobsmacked by how amazing her sister looked in her pink silk blouse over tight cream trousers, her styled hair tumbling to her shoulders and her face carefully made up.

'Scary, huh?' Britt peered at herself in the mirror and dabbed a speck of mascara from her cheek.

'Not at all scary,' Mia told her. 'Glamorous and gorgeous. And definitely not half as scary as when you're in full legal mode and you're wearing your black suit with your hair scraped back off your face so that you look like the Wicked Witch of the West.'

'It's a much easier look,' said Britt. 'I don't know how some women do this whole make-up thing every single day. And I'm hopeless at high heels! I'll probably be even worse on them here, what with the ship moving and everything.' She looked down at her towering stilettos.

'Oh, I dunno,' said Mia. 'This is a very different you. A softer you.'

'Yeuch.' Britt looked at her watch and then adjusted her footwear. 'We'd better get going. You did check—'

'I was in the room fifteen minutes ago and there were already people waiting,' Mia assured her.

'I was going to ask if you'd checked that the projector was working,' said Britt.

'Yes,' replied Mia. 'But – far be it from me to tell you how to go about it – what the hell do you need a projector for?'

'Illustrative pictures of selfish lovers.' Britt uncapped her Juicy Tube Coral Rush and applied more of it to her already glossy lips. 'Right, let's go.'

Leo Tyler had spent the morning in the gym, pounding the treadmill and then putting in half an hour on the bikes. He'd managed to work himself into a lather of perspiration, reminding himself that the pain in his calf muscles was worth it, that being in the gym was taking him away from the overwhelming sense of being cosseted that the *Aphrodite* provided. Leo didn't really want to be cosseted. He wasn't, he told himself as he stood underneath a tepid shower, a metrosexual man. He didn't believe in facials and manicures and all that sort of stuff. He liked to be clean-shaven and to smell good, but everything else was way beyond him. And of course on the Valentine Cruise they were doing their best to entice everyone into the whole cosseting thing – offering spa days for couples with his 'n' hers treatments guaranteed (so the brochure said) to put the spring back in your step and the sparkle in your eyes.

Leo knew that the spring wasn't in his step, but he thought he was feeling better than he had a couple of days ago. His doctor, who he'd eventually visited when he realised that his nights had consisted of two choices – no sleep at all or sleep with recurring nightmares – had told him that it took time to get over traumatic events and that Leo hadn't really looked after himself during the last six months. Leo had dismissed the doctor's words and muttered something about being fed up with feeling sorry for himself and having other people feel sorry for him too.

Dr McClelland had said that nobody was feeling sorry for Leo but it had been a difficult time for him. Leo had responded that it was all over and done with, and Dr McClelland had looked at him sympathetically and told him to stop trying to be so bloody macho about it all.

'It's not a sin to cry,' he'd said, but Leo had looked at him in horror and told him that he'd gone past crying now. That if he cried it would just be because he did feel sorry for himself, no matter what anyone said. And then he'd asked the doctor to prescribe some damn sleeping tablets. Which was what the other man had eventually done, although he'd suggested to Leo that it would be good if he came back to see him in a few weeks.

Leo had been utterly dismissive of that. The way he looked at it, it was all in the past and not worth thinking about. And he wasn't going to cry any more. He'd had one day of tears. That was enough for anybody. Enough feeling sorry for himself.

It was certainly hard to feel sorry for yourself on the *Aphrodite*. How could you, when your every whim was being catered for, even if, in his case, that meant sitting alone on the cabin balcony after his gym workout with an Inspector Rebus novel to bring a bit of grimness to the sun-kissed surroundings.

He closed the Rebus and looked out at the expanse of blue sea. The cruise had originally been Vanessa's idea. It wasn't something he'd have chosen himself. He'd thought that he'd feel claustrophobic on a boat with other people, unable to avoid them, getting forced into more than a nodding acquaintance with them. But Vanessa had laughed and said that they didn't have to socialise if they didn't want to, and even if she was more fun-loving and outgoing than him, they would of course be spending a lot of time on the heart-shaped bed in the Delphi suite.

He swallowed hard, suddenly feeling sick. If things had turned out differently, he would have been on the damn cruise to spite her. But now, suddenly . . . he shivered in the warm air . . . suddenly it seemed wrong to be here at all. In the same way that being cosseted was wrong. In the same way as looking for mindless sex was wrong. And in the same way as everything about his life still seemed wrong, no matter how hard he tried.

A few days after he'd gone to the Dublin nightclub and come home alone, Karen Kennedy, one of the client ser-vices executives, had come up to him and asked him how he was doing. He'd looked at her in surprise and told her that he'd be finished with the investment report in about ten minutes. She'd smiled at him and said that she wasn't talking about work, she was talking about his head – after all, she'd said, everyone was really sorry about Vanessa. It must have been terrible, she'd told him in a voice oozing with sympathy, which had made him wonder whether she'd decided that he was on the market again and so was putting out feelers. He didn't know and he didn't feel equipped to find out. And so all he'd said, in a harsh tone that had grated even with him, was that he was sick and tired of people talking to him about Vanessa and that as far as he was concerned she was in the past, which maybe wasn't actually a bad thing, and that was the end of it.

'You don't mean that.' She'd sounded shocked, and he'd

retorted rudely that he never said things he didn't mean and that he was bloody busy and could she leave him alone.

They all did after that. He couldn't exactly blame them.

His attention was caught by a sudden movement in the sea, and he stood up and leaned against the rail. A school of dolphins was swimming a few dozen metres away, keeping pace with the ship and occasionally jumping out of the water. Their apparent pleasure in their movement was infectious. Leo realised that he was smiling as he watched them accompany the *Aphrodite* until, quite suddenly, they disappeared into the sea again.

I can't be miserable all the time, he told himself. I have to snap out of it. I have to be the person I used to be. He walked into his cabin and picked up the daily newsletter, skimming through the list of events for the day. He noticed that the romantic novelist was giving a talk in one of the conference rooms. 'Write your own romantic fiction' the advertisement said. 'Master classes by the most successful novelist of the year.' He wasn't really interested in writing romantic fiction, but he did wonder what she might have to say for herself. His memories of the first night on board, when he'd shared a table with her and her sister, were a bit fuzzy, but he remembered thinking that she was a cool, distant sort of person. Although he must have been wrong about that, because she was, according to the newsletter, a woman who had the power to get to the heart of love. Which didn't really imply cool. A pity, really, he thought. He didn't want to get to know women who had the power to get to the heart of love. He imagined that the novelist would be one of those gushing, caring women who loved everybody. He was fed up with caring women. Until he'd snapped at Karen, the women in the office had been gushing and caring, even though sometimes he knew that they were walking on eggshells around him. Now they were cool towards him, and it suited him fine.

Would he learn more about the female mind if he read the novelist's bestselling book or went along to one of her lectures? If he'd known more about women, would he have behaved differently? Would everything have turned out the way it was supposed to?

Vanessa had read romantic fiction. He'd been horrified by that, telling her that she shouldn't be wasting her time with such rubbish, that real life never turned out like any of her favourite novels. He'd been right about that, of course. But she'd laughed at him and told him that love and romance were what made the whole world go round, and that life wasn't just about a succession of deals for clients in the private bank.

He didn't want to think about Vanessa. He didn't want to think about the fact that she should have been with him now. My perfect honeymoon, she'd told him a month before she'd betrayed him. A month before his life had disintegrated around him.

Britt hesitated for a moment outside the door to the Athena Room. She could hear a low murmur of voices from within, punctuated by occasional laughter. Her hand tightened on the handle and she felt her mouth go dry. She was used to talking to groups of people. She'd done it all the time at her legal firm. But this was completely different. On those occasions, as she frequently reminded her audience, the most important thing was putting emotions to one side and concentrating on the facts. Today's talk was supposed to be the complete opposite. She'd done a lot of work to try to turn it into something that people who believed in everlasting love would relate to. And then she'd thought a lot about how she could say what she truly felt so that nobody would ever ask her to do this again.

She took a deep breath, opened the door and walked inside.

A sea of faces looked expectantly at her as she scanned the room. The posters with the covers of *The Perfect Man* (a head-and-shoulders silhouette against a burnt-orange background, a cover style along with the slightly quirky typeface that was being copied by lots of other books now) were in place, as was her laptop, which was also projecting a picture of the book cover on to the screen at the top of the room. The walls had been covered with cut-out hearts and baby Cupids, while heart-shaped red balloons on some of the tables bobbed with the movement of the ship. Individual gold boxes tied with red ribbon and containing a single chocolate were at every place. Britt thought the place looked like a bordello.

It had a capacity to hold forty people in comfort, and every seat was filled. A quick glance told Britt that, as she'd expected, she'd be talking to a mainly female audience. But there was a sprinkling of men dotted around the room too, looking earnestly at her, notebooks open in front of them. To her surprise she saw Leo Tyler among them, although he didn't have a notebook and was sitting back in his seat, gazing at the ceiling.

'Good morning,' she said, and then cleared her throat. 'I'm glad to see that you're all here and ready to go.'

There was a low murmur.

Mia slipped into the seat that had been reserved for her in a corner of the room. She saw the faintest sheen of moisture on her sister's forehead. She felt a stab of sympathy for Britt and wondered how nervous she was.

'Famous romances from history,' said Britt. 'That's where we're going to start.' She clicked on her laptop and looked at the faces in front of her. They were waiting eagerly for her to speak. She hesitated as the slideshow began. A woman in the front row opened her notebook and waited.

She glanced at the first slide, an out-of-focus picture of a man and a woman walking hand in hand along a beach. A corny stock romantic photograph. The sort that made people believe in true love.

The woman with the open notebook was looking at her expectantly.

They don't want to hear that it isn't true, thought Britt. They want to believe in it. They want to think it can all end happily ever after. Yet I don't personally know anyone it's worked out for. Well, except Sarah and James. But she's a saint to put up with my brother. They're exceptional because of her.

They were still looking intently, waiting for her to speak. She moistened her lips. Love was humiliating, that's what it was. Planning your life around another person. Believing you knew them and being shocked when you realised that you didn't. Allowing them to make you feel like a fool. Nobody could really believe in one true love. Could they?

From the corner of her eye she saw Mia looking at her anxiously and then giving her a thumbs-up sign. She took another deep breath and smiled.

'Right,' she said, allowing herself to relax slightly. 'Where would we be without romance? Today we'll look at some examples of famous love stories. And what we'll do is talk about how you could write those stories. Hopefully that'll give you inspiration about how you might write a fictional story of your own. And then in the next lectures we'll practise that.'

She was a good speaker, thought Mia, as she listened to Britt's talk. She could paint a picture with a few well-chosen words. Mia had to acknowledge that Britt's performance was very good, although she thought it lacked a certain passion. But that was understandable, given Britt's views on Antony and Cleopatra. Nevertheless, Mia was fairly confident that nobody else would believe, listening to her talking now, that Britt thought Cleopatra had only seduced Antony because it was a good idea for Egypt. Or that Elizabeth Taylor and Richard Burton were anything other than the century's most famous lovers.

'In *The Perfect Man*, Francesca's passion for Jack is unrequited,' said one of the women in the audience when Britt asked if anyone had any questions. 'Were you thinking of someone specific when you wrote it?'

'Um . . . maybe every guy who never asked me out,' said Britt.

Mia was startled by the comment. Was there an unrequited love in Britt's life? Someone after Ralph? She looked at her sister thoughtfully.

'You must have had someone special for inspiration,' suggested another woman. 'A man in your own past maybe. Have you ever been in love with someone who hasn't loved you back?'

'George Clooney,' replied Britt promptly, and the woman laughed.

'Jack's just the most wonderful character,' said a third in an enthralled, breathless voice. 'He really is the kind of man you'd want to be with. He's so strong and dependable.'

Mia recognised Eileen, the woman she'd met on the tour of Grenada. Pippin was sitting beside her, once again immaculately made up, although this time wearing a light top and the briefest of shorts so that her long, tanned legs were shown off to their very best advantage. Her huge sunglasses were still perched on top of her hair.

'I'm glad you like him,' said Britt.

'Are you sure he's not real?' asked Pippin. 'I mean, imagine finding Jack Hayes. Imagine such a man actually existing.'

'That's probably why it's fiction.' Britt smiled at her. 'He doesn't.'

'So what made you write the book?' asked another woman. 'What made you create Jack?'

Britt looked suddenly uncomfortable. 'I don't really know,' she said.

'That's not hugely helpful.' A large lady dressed in a white kaftan with white Capri pants looked sternly at Britt. 'And this workshop was labelled as telling us about writing techniques. That's what I want. Tips. My aim is to write a book that will make me as much money as yours has for you.'

Britt blushed and the rest of the room laughed.

'Is that how you see men?' a male voice piped up. 'As a way to make money by writing about them in an idealistic and unrealistic way? Making women believe in the impossible?'

Britt looked startled as she realised that it was Leo Tyler who'd spoken.

'Absolutely not,' she said firmly.

'Don't you think women are too concerned about romance and not concerned enough about love?' demanded Leo.

A number of the class turned to look at him.

'Perhaps some women are,' Britt told him.

'I mean, you're all looking for this mythical perfect man,' said Leo. 'But are any of you the perfect woman?'

'It's an interesting point,' said Britt. 'We'll have a look at that in the next session when we talk about developing the relationship between your hero and your heroine.'

'I look forward to that.' Leo sounded sceptical.

Some of the women in the group took up the theme, and Britt let them discuss it for a while before telling them that their time was up for the day and that she hoped to see them all at the next talk.

'You're not a bit like I imagined,' commented Eileen as they got up to leave. 'You're not like Lisette or Francesca and I thought you would be. You *look* a bit like Francesca, though.'

'They're very different people to me,' Britt admitted. 'And . . . when I was writing it, I was propped up in bed

135

in my PJs, so I certainly didn't look like Francesca then. She always wears silk nighties!'

'I love those girls,' Eileen gushed. 'I know they had a tough time, but it was so great when Jack stepped in. He's wonderful, he really is.'

Eileen and Pippin were the last to leave. Britt powered down her laptop and disconnected it from the projector.

'That was interesting,' said Mia. 'I enjoyed it.'

'Did you?'

'Yes.' Mia flicked through the comment sheets that everyone had filled in before they left. 'So did everyone else. But . . .' she added as she skimmed the comments, 'they do seem to want more about how to write romance.'

'I know, I know.' Britt rubbed the back of her neck. 'And that's the hardest bit. I've no idea how I wrote *The Perfect Man*. So before I came here I got loads of books and read up on how to be a writer – I think I did everything completely wrong! I didn't plan the sort of people who were going to be in the book or what would happen to them or how there'd be dramatic tension or anything. It just sort of wrote itself. And then they talk about using your experiences too . . . well, the thing is – I don't have any!'

'Britt McDonagh, that's just nonsense,' said Mia. 'First of all, you couldn't have done it wrong because the book is great. And everyone has relationship experiences. OK, so you had one bad experience. But what about all those blokes you said never asked you out?' She grinned at her. 'Who were they? I'm dying to know! And I want to know if there really was someone like Jack in your life that you're not telling me about. An unrequited love. I mean, they'd love that, they really would. It's *sooooo* romantic. The sad single state of the most romantic woman in the world.'

Britt laughed. 'There's no Jack. No unrequited love,' she said confidently. 'And I think unrequited love is probably the least romantic thing that can happen to you. It's such a waste of emotional energy. As for the rest of the talks, I'm hoping we can focus on their writing and keep it practical.'

'You don't always have to be practical,' Mia reminded her.

'I do.' Britt picked up her laptop and the notes she'd been using. 'It works just fine for me.'

Steve Shaw arrived at the Athena Room just as they were leaving.

'Miss Martin,' he said to Britt. 'Sorry we didn't get to meet earlier, but nice to see you now. How did it go?'

'She was great,' said Mia. 'And you did a fantastic job with the room too,' she added.

'Um, about the room,' said Britt. 'Would you mind awfully toning it down a bit for the next session? I was a bit overwhelmed by the hearts and the chubby little angels aiming arrows at my head.'

Steve's brown eyes were full of merriment. 'I thought you'd like it,' he said. 'I thought it would put you in the mood.'

'Quite honestly, not,' said Britt.

He looked surprised. 'Come on! Surely you romance ladies need your heart-shaped stuff to keep you on message.'

'I don't need fat Cupids to keep me on message,' Britt assured him. 'Actually, they kind of scared me. They look a bit malevolent. As though they'd quite like to get you in the eye with one of those arrows.'

Steve laughed. 'I'll see what I can do. We want to keep you as happy as possible.'

'Thanks,' she said.

'Anything else I can do to make things easier for you?'

'Everything is fine,' she told him.

'Blue Lagoon aspires to more than fine,' said Steve in mock severity. 'On every trip.'

'What does the Valentine Cruise aspire to?' she asked as she pulled her fingers through her hair in an effort to straighten her curls.

'Everything your heart desires,' said Steve.

'The diamond ring from the Treasure Hunt,' Mia told him quickly.

He laughed. 'You're not the only one with her eye on that.'

Britt suddenly laughed too. 'You've just sort of proved a point for me,' she said.

'Which is?'

'Romance is fleeting. But diamonds are, very definitely, for ever.'

When they got back to their cabin, Britt kicked off her high heels, massaged the soles of her feet and then went into the bathroom to remove her make-up. She reappeared in a swimsuit, brushing the curls out of her hair and pulling it back into a tight ponytail.

'I'm going to sit on the balcony for a while,' she told Mia.

'Why don't you come to the pool again?' asked her sister. 'It'll be nice up there and you could do with a bit of chill-out time now.'

'I need some time on my own,' said Britt. 'I might have a snooze. That'll be chilled enough for me.'

'Are you sure?' Mia looked at her doubtfully. 'I'm sure the passengers won't start asking you about *The Perfect Man*, so you don't have to be all Brigitte-y.'

'Certain,' said Britt. 'I need to be me for a while. On my own.'

Mia shrugged, changed into a swimsuit herself and pulled her beach dress over her head. 'If you want to be alone, I'll leave you,' she said. 'You know where to find me.'

'That's fine,' said Britt and pushed open the door to the balcony. 'See you later.'

There were lots of people around the Trident Pool, and Mia recognised some of them as having been at Britt's talk. Perhaps, she thought, she'd ask them about it later. But right now she was going to read.

She realised, as she settled on a lounger with the only other book she'd brought with her – a tale of backpacking through Peru – that a number of people were actually reading *The Perfect Man*. It was the weirdest thing to see them turning the pages, knowing that Britt, of all people, had the power to hold their attention in a love story.

I guess that solves the question about writing being autobiographical, she thought. In Britt's case it's so absolutely not. I think she's become even more anti-men since the damn book came out. And I know she still isn't convinced about the whole Antony and Cleopatra thing.

Not that she has to be convinced about everything, Mia reminded herself as she closed her eyes and allowed the backpacking book to fall to the ground beside her lounger. Just *sound* convincing. Which is something she's very, very good at.

It was some time later before she opened her eyes again and spotted Leo Tyler getting into the pool. She'd been surprised to see him at Britt's talk and intrigued by his harsh questions about how women perceived men. Was Leo trying to find the perfect woman? A task doomed to failure because of course, just as the perfect man didn't exist, neither did she. Nobody was perfect. Nobody could fulfil someone else's every wish and desire.

In any event, thought Mia as she watched him float on the surface, Leo, from her limited contact with him, didn't seem to have the social skills to connect with women at all. The only person who'd want to get involved with Leo Tyler would have to be as antisocial as himself. Which was why, she thought, a sudden grin breaking out on her face, Britt would be almost perfect for him. And he'd be almost perfect for her! The pair of them could spend days alone together on the balcony of a cabin, ignoring all the fun events on the ship. They could share a boring table for two at dinner. They could go to the intellectual lectures together and think uncharitable thoughts about everyone else there. They would be an utterly, utterly perfect couple.

Mia chuckled and then sighed. They were probably too alike for it to last. Their silences would become stony and their antisocial behaviour would make them bored with each other. That was the thing about perfect couples. The two people concerned were often very different. There was a quiet person and a more outgoing one. Someone thoughtful and someone more practical. And in every relationship there was one who looked after it more, who made sure that it lasted, who didn't allow small things to become major issues and threaten it.

Not that any of that had mattered with Alejo, she thought sadly. He was the love of my life but it wasn't a relationship. It wasn't anything. And one day I'll be able to accept that. Even though, back then, I thought he was my very own perfect man. The trouble for me is that nobody else has ever matched up. Nobody possibly can.

That was why Sierra Bonita, with its quiet social life, suited her so well. She wasn't into hectic socialising any more. Her big days out were spending a couple of hours at Señora Diez's hairdresser for her highlights or calling in to Cayetana's Estetica for an occasional body scrub. And although she had forged good friendships with some of the other mothers in the town, particularly Ana and Ramira, whose children played regularly with Allegra, she didn't hang out with any of the single girls or go to nightclubs or do any of the things that she'd done before Allegra. And before Alejo.

She wasn't actually looking for a man herself, of course. Alejo was still the only man in her life, even if he didn't know it. Anyhow, there weren't many men who'd be interested in going out with someone with a three-year-old daughter. Certainly not in Sierra Bonita. Mia blinked a couple of times as she thought of Allegra. She loved her, she'd never loved anyone as much in her whole life, but there was no question but that it was hard being a single mum. Harder still because she was doing it so far from home.

But she'd needed to be away, even though she knew that she was making life more difficult for herself. She'd stood firm despite the fact that Paula had been utterly horrified when Mia told her that she was moving to Spain and taking Allegra with her.

'Are you cracked?' she asked.

'No,' said Mia. 'It's something I have to do.'

'You don't have to do anything of the sort,' said Paula. 'You can live here with us. We could always do with help in the B&B.'

'I don't want to help out in the B&B,' said Mia. 'I want to get a job and bring up Allegra.'

'We'll pay you,' said Paula. 'I didn't mean that you would live here and help out and not be properly paid for it. There's plenty of work needs doing, especially during the summer.'

'I don't want to work in a B&B at all,' said Mia. 'The fact that it's yours is irrelevant.'

'And how do you expect to get a job and look after Allegra all by yourself in a strange country?' demanded Paula.

'It's hardly strange,' said Mia mildly. 'You took us to Torremolinos every year for about ten years.'

'That's completely different and you know it,' snapped Paula. 'I can't believe you're being so silly.' She stared at her daughter. 'Is this something to do with that man? Alejo? Does he live there?'

'I don't know where Alejo lives.' Mia knew that she wasn't being entirely truthful about that, but she really didn't want to get into a long, involved discussion with Paula about the father of her child. 'I want Allegra to know about her culture.'

'Oh, for heaven's sake!' Paula was exasperated. 'She's Irish. Her culture is here. And if you must live somewhere on your own you can live in Dublin.'

'Mum, I can't afford to live in Dublin!' cried Mia. 'Rental prices are crucifying and everything else is ridiculously dear! But I can afford to live in Spain. I've done some trawling around on the internet and I've found a house to rent for a few months and I have some savings and I can get work in a bar or café . . .'

'How do you know that?' demanded Paula. 'What makes you think that you'll get a job when there are probably loads of Spanish people looking for work?'

'Because Sierra Bonita has a website and they're advertising jobs,' said Mia patiently. 'Look, if it doesn't work out I'll be back. But it's something I have to do.'

Paula looked at her impatiently. 'You're so bloody stubborn,' she said. 'You don't have to do this out of some kind of penitence, you know.'

'I'm not penitent,' said Mia. 'I'm not sorry about Allegra. She's the best thing that ever happened to me.'

'So don't mess it up for her,' urged Paula. 'Don't isolate yourselves.'

'I need to do this,' Mia said. 'For her and for me.'

And so she'd gone to Sierra Bonita and loved it. She didn't want to come back to Ireland and work for her parents, but sometimes, she had to admit, she was very, very lonely. Until the last few days she hadn't quite realised how lonely she actually was.

She rubbed at her eyes. She wasn't sure whether the tears that had suddenly formed were because she was looking into the sun or because she was wondering about how the rest of her life would turn out. And if she was crying over how her life would turn out, she thought, she was being very silly. She had a good life in Spain and nothing to cry about. When she got back she'd check out the jobs in Sierra Bonita and the surrounding towns and she'd manage to get something that suited both her and Allegra. Which was the only thing that really mattered.

Chapter 8

Position: at sea.
Weather: partly cloudy. Wind: south-easterly force 3.
Temperature: 25°. Barometric pressure: 1011.1mb.

That evening, Mia persuaded Britt that she should celebrate the success of the first in her series of talks. Britt had been doubtful, saying that the talk had been OK but not exactly a resounding success because she hadn't quite managed to be as fervent as she should have; but Mia pointed out that nobody had accused Britt of being a non-loved-up fraud and that had to be counted as successful at least, a comment that made Britt smile.

'A cocktail in every bar,' Mia suggested. 'It'll be a bit of fun.'

'We'll be legless,' Britt protested. 'And given that we're swaying a bit already, that can't be a good thing.'

Mia grinned. 'If we exclude the champagne bar – though I don't like excluding champagne from my life – there are only three others,' she reminded Britt. 'The Troy, the Panorama Lounge and the Terrace Bar. That's only three cocktails. Surely you could manage that.'

'Two's my limit,' Britt said. 'It takes me much longer to recover from alcohol these days.'

'My poor, poor older sister.' Mia laughed. 'That's what happens when you reach thirty, is it?'

'Oh, listen, my capacity for drinking and getting up the next day went rapidly downhill as soon as I got into my twenties,' Britt replied. 'I've never been good with alcohol.'

'And mine disappeared after Allegra,' Mia admitted. 'But we have to let our hair down one night. Consider it our office party! And you don't have a talk for another couple of days, so that gives you plenty of time to recover.'

Britt had given in, and the sisters ordered a couple of rum punches in the Troy Bar, where a woman came up to Britt and told her that *The Perfect Man* had changed her life and made her dump her boyfriend after five years of a relationship going nowhere. Britt was taken aback and uneasy about having influenced her at all. But then the woman said that she'd met someone much, much better for her and that they were getting married on board in a couple of days' time and she'd love it if Britt came to the wedding. Britt thanked her and said that she didn't want to intrude, and the woman told her that it wouldn't be an intrusion, it would be great, and in the end Britt said that maybe she wouldn't come to the ceremony itself but perhaps she'd join them for a drink afterwards.

When the woman left, Mia grinned at her sister and asked what it was like to know that she'd changed someone's life.

'I loved it when I was getting them their divorces,' Britt replied. 'But I'm terrified by this. What if that woman had realised she loved her boyfriend after all? What if her marriage is a disaster?'

'I never realised how much you worried about stuff before,' said Mia. 'I always pegged you as being the kind of person who was full of confidence and didn't care what anyone thought. That woman looked very happy to me, so no need for you to fret. And if her marriage is a disaster, maybe you can help her with the divorce.'

Britt started to giggle then and was quite unable to stop, so Mia took her cocktail away and told her that she couldn't have any more until she got serious again.

They moved on from the Troy Bar to the Panorama Lounge, where they just had mineral water, before finally heading to the Terrace Bar and sipped mojitos under the stars.

'It's so romantic,' breathed Mia as they sat side by side and stared at the horizon, unable to tell where the sky ended and the sea began. 'You can see why people get married on board.'

'God, don't start with all that again.' Britt stirred her cocktail lazily. 'Haven't we had enough of it already today? Can't we just agree that you and I are a romance-free zone?'

'We are,' said Mia. 'Neither of us has anything to boast about on the romantic front, have we?'

'What's to boast about when it comes to men?'

'Oh, I don't know,' Mia said. 'There is something wonderful about being in love.'

Britt looked at her thoughtfully. 'Were you in love with that guy Alejo?' she asked.

'I thought I was.' Mia's reply was abrupt. 'But who knows really. All the same,' she made a determined effort to keep her voice light, 'I certainly remember what it was like being in love with Terry Boland. Remember him? From number thirteen? Blue-black hair and smouldering eyes. God, but he was attractive.'

'Smouldering eyes?' said Britt. 'He was only ten.'

'A very mature ten. He was my first kiss.' Mia grinned at her.

'You always had them lining up,' said Britt.

'My magnetic personality,' Mia told her. 'Who did you secretly want to ask you out when we were younger?'

'Lance Kelly.'

'You're joking!' Mia looked at her in amusement. 'That long streak of misery.'

'I thought he was soulful.'

Mia snorted with laughter. 'No. He was just miserable and boring.'

'I was never a good judge of men,' conceded Britt.

'Neither was I,' said Mia. 'But at least I picked the cheerful ones.'

'And do you do anything about it these days?' Britt asked her.

'Huh?'

'Well, Allegra's three. There's clearly nothing going to happen between you and her father. So in that case – and if you believe so strongly in love and romance – are you out there looking?'

'That sounds so clinical,' Mia murmured.

Britt shrugged. 'Finding someone is kind of clinical,

don't you think? If you want someone you have to be quite practical about it and, quite honestly, leave romance out of the equation.'

'Well, clinical, practical or romantic, there's no chance of me finding someone in Sierra Bonita.' Mia knew that her cheeks were flushed but she was hoping that Britt would put that down to the cocktails.

'So why are you holed up there?' asked Britt. 'Why are you hiding away in some arse-wipe little Spanish pueblo?'

'It's not an arse-wipe little town,' Mia objected. 'It's lovely. And an idyllic place to bring up a kid.'

'Oh come on,' said Britt sceptically. 'She'll be a little peasant girl.'

'She won't,' cried Mia. 'And even if she is – what's wrong with that? What's so great about big-city life?'

'You were always a bit of a culchie at heart.'

'I like the country,' said Mia. 'I like the pace.'

'It's such a waste,' said Britt. 'You could've done so much more with your life before becoming a professional mother.'

'I wondered when you'd break out and give me the "what a waste of your life" lecture. It's incredibly offensive, you know.' Mia's tone was mild but she was annoyed with her sister. 'Did they teach you that in law school?'

'It's hardly offensive to point out the truth,' said Britt.

'And what's so much better than being a great mother?' demanded Mia. 'Being a heartless lawyer?'

'I'm not heartless,' said Britt. 'I care about my clients a lot.'

'So what?' Mia said dismissively. 'They're not waiting at

home for you at night. You're not emotionally involved with them.'

'I *am* emotionally involved,' Britt told her. 'It matters to me that when their marriages are over it doesn't mess up the rest of their lives. And I'm perfectly happy that they're not waiting for me at home, thanks very much.'

'Well I think it's a bit sad.' Mia knew that she was going too far, but her tongue had been loosened by the cocktails and she couldn't help herself.

'What's sad is knowing that you've never achieved your full potential,' said Britt.

'D'you mean me?' demanded Mia.

'You're smart and clever but you never tried hard enough in school or in college.'

'I have Allegra,' Mia said. 'You have nobody. I think I have the better deal, but somehow you always try to make me feel a failure.'

'No I don't.' Britt put her glass down on the wooden table. 'And if I've ever made you feel a failure then I'm sorry.'

'I'm not saying that you shove it in my face,' Mia told her. 'I'm merely pointing out that if I ever want to look at my life and think how hopeless I am, all I have to do is think of you.'

'That's so not true!'

'It is. Because if I wasn't hopeless, if I had a fantastic job of my own, if I could turn my hand to anything just like you, I wouldn't have been able to come on this cruise, would I? I'd have had to say that I was too busy closing the mid-Atlantic merger deal or writing my next TV script or something, instead of just having to worry about who would look after my daughter.'

'Why are we fighting?' asked Britt. 'I didn't ask you here to fight.'

'I'm not fighting,' said Mia.

'It feels like it.'

'I know.' Mia sighed. 'And I should be nice and supportive and thankful for your generosity instead of bitching at you for being hard-working and mega-successful while I'm a waste of space. I'm sorry.'

There was a moment's silence between them.

'You're not a waste of space. That's just plain ridiculous,' said Britt finally. 'And telling me not to make Cleopatra seem like a whore was right.'

'Hum.'

'Have you any suggestions for my next talk?'

'Don't patronise me.'

'I'm not. I don't patronise people.'

'You're asking me because you think I can help?' Mia looked doubtful.

'Well, yes. D'you think there's something I could've done better? Something to make it more interesting?'

'Probably,' said Mia eventually, deciding to give her sister the benefit of the doubt. 'But you'll only get upset with me.'

'I won't. I promise,' said Britt seriously. 'I'm good at taking constructive criticism.'

Mia laughed suddenly. 'I've never known anyone good at taking criticism, no matter what sort it is.'

'I'll do my best not to glower,' Britt promised.

'OK, then.' Mia leaned back. 'The talk was great. Maybe it was just me because I know you, but even when you joked a bit with people it still seemed very businesslike. You didn't really have much passion for it.'

'Not passion again.' Britt groaned.

'Not that sort,' said Mia. 'Passion for the subject.'

'I can't conjure it up out of thin air.' Britt took another sip of her drink. 'I knew I shouldn't have agreed to do this. It was always going to be a disaster.'

'It's not a disaster. Besides, you *can* do it. I saw those TV interviews. You were all giggly and flirty then.'

'There were only a few of them and they didn't last long,' said Britt. 'Also, I knew the questions they were going to ask, and Meredith gave me ideas on how to answer them.'

'Jeez, I'll never watch another talk show again,' said Mia in disgust. 'I can't believe it's not spontaneous.'

'It probably is for some people,' said Britt. 'But I'm not spontaneous. I plan. That's the way I am.' She looked confidingly at Mia. 'I'd had three glasses of wine before the *Late Late*.'

Mia laughed. 'I didn't realise you got flirty when you were drunk. No wonder you didn't want more than two cocktails.'

'Very funny,' said Britt. 'But that's the truth. I could be Brigitte because I was prepared for it and because I was high on Dutch courage!'

'Does Mum know that?'

Britt chuckled. 'I doubt it. You know how she is about drink. If she thought for a second I'd been juiced up on national telly she'd never speak to me again. Successful romance novelist or not.'

'Well I guess you don't want to be drunk now either,' said Mia. 'But maybe you're a little overprepared.'

'You can never be too prepared,' objected Britt.

'How about this?' Mia looked at her in sudden excitement. 'You're passionate about law, aren't you?'

'I guess so.'

'And sometimes you get massive divorce settlements for people you don't think deserve them, don't you?'

'I never take a case I don't feel—'

'Oh, come on!' Mia interrupted her. 'There must be times when you think that some bitchy old boiler is just taking the piss.'

'Not really.'

'Never?'

'I suppose there are occasions when I don't actually like my clients very much,' admitted Britt eventually.

'And do you try any less hard to get a good result for them?' asked Mia.

'Of course not. It's my job—'

'Exactly!' Mia said triumphantly. 'It was your job to do your best no matter what you thought. And it's the exact same thing here. You think that furry teddy bears and Valentine cards are a big huge waste of time and money. But not everyone does. You seem to think that all men are bastards. Some women don't! You think that a bunch of flowers means, honey, I screwed up. But sometimes it actually means, darling, I love you. And so what you have to do is pretend that you mean it, just like you did at work.'

Britt stared at her younger sister. 'I never thought of it like that before,' she said slowly.

'That's because you're trying to think like a romantic person and you don't know how,' said Mia. 'But stick your lawyer's hat on again and use that experience.'

Britt looked at her thoughtfully. 'You might have a point.'

'Pretend you're arguing for a client when you're giving your next talk,' said Mia. 'Pretend there's a massive settlement at stake.'

'Y'know, that's clever,' said Britt slowly. 'You're really so much better at this than me.'

'And that can't be true,' Mia told her wryly. 'Otherwise it would've been me who'd written the damn book, wouldn't it?'

They went to bed after they finished the mojitos. Mia lay awake in the darkness long after Britt's steady breathing indicated that she'd fallen asleep. When, at 2 a.m., she still hadn't managed to drop off, she got up again, dressed in a pair of loose cotton trousers and a T-shirt, and let herself out of the cabin as silently as she could.

The corridor was quiet, but as she approached the Panorama Lounge she could hear the quiet hum of conversation. She didn't go into the bar but instead made her way to the promenade deck. She'd expected it to be deserted, but there were couples strolling hand in hand together or leaning over the rail gazing into the sea. The women were still dressed in their dinner clothes – floaty chiffon dresses or elegant evening wear, while the men were in tuxedos.

It had been a formal night in the Parthenon Restaurant that night, and the glamour quotient had been high. Britt and Mia hadn't bothered to dress up, choosing to eat in the casual terrace restaurant instead. Britt said that she hated dressing up. Mia had feared that even her dressiest clothes wouldn't be good enough. Looking at the man and woman closest to her now, she thought she'd made the right choice. The woman's dress was full-length in shimmering emerald-green silk that clung to her slender body. Her shoes were ankle-breakingly high and the diamonds in her ears and around her neck glittered beneath the lights of the deck.

They were a romantic couple, thought Mia. They looked the part. Whereas me and Alejo – we weren't romantic at all. I thought we were. I thought it was the most import-ant thing that had ever happened to me. But Britt was right. It wasn't romance. It was lust at first sight.

She felt her jaw clench. And yet . . . and yet . . . she had loved him. She still loved him. She'd loved him even when she'd learned about Belén. Even when she realised that he was leaving her and going home to Spain. She'd hated him and loved him and she'd never stopped hating him and loving him at the same time, and that was why there was no chance in the whole wide world that she'd go looking for someone else, because you didn't, did you, when you'd found the right person. Even if you lost him to somebody else. Or if you'd never had him in the first place.

The couples had continued to walk along the deck and Mia was alone. She sat down in one of the wooden chairs alongside the now closed Terrace Bar and drew up her legs, resting her chin on her knees.

Britt was wrong to criticise her. She had a quality of life in Sierra Bonita that would be hard to beat anywhere else. So what if she wasn't earning a heap of money or getting stressed out in a rat-race? That was a good thing, wasn't it? Besides, Allegra loved it there. It was a great place to bring up kids.

And it was only an hour and a half from Granada, which was a big city even though it was probably more steeped in history than any big city she knew. She'd spent two days there, pushing Allegra around the Alhambra palace in her stroller, lapping up the timeless beauty of the buildings and the gardens and inhaling the scent of oranges and columbine while at the same time revelling in the smiles of the women who looked at Allegra and murmured, '*Muy guapa*' under their breath. They were right. Allegra *was* pretty. She'd inherited her looks from Alejo.

She'd seen Alejo in Granada. She'd known she would eventually. He was sitting in the plaza having a beer, and he was laughing and joking with his companion, a petite woman with short black hair and dark Andalucian eyes. He was laughing and joking with Belén. Mia had pushed the buggy away as quickly as she could, sick with the realisation that she still loved him. That she would always love him.

Even now it hurt. Remembering him. Remembering the way it was in Guatemala and the way it was in Granada. Thinking to herself that she'd been foolish and naïve to fall for him in the first place, to not guess that there was another woman. To think that she'd found her perfect man.

'Are you all right?'

She lifted her head with a start and looked up at Leo Tyler. He was wearing a white dress shirt and black trousers, but somewhere along the line he'd ditched the jacket and bow tie. His blue eyes were regarding her with some concern.

'Of course I am.' She smiled brightly. 'Thanks for asking.'

'It's odd to see someone alone,' he said.

She smiled again. 'I guess so.'

'I thought perhaps you were unwell.'

She shook her head. 'No. Just enjoying the warmth of the evening air and . . . well, you know.'

'I didn't see you at dinner,' said Leo. 'Or your sister.'

'No,' said Mia. 'We went casual.'

'I'm not much into the formal stuff myself,' admitted Leo. 'But I had an invitation to the Captain's table and the food was good.'

'The food is always good.' Mia was surprised at how unexpectedly pleasant he was being. 'I bet you looked great in the tux. I like the shirt, too.'

He smiled. He was attractive when he smiled. Not her kind of attractive. But easy on the eye nonetheless, and she'd forgiven him for being rude on the Grenada trip because as they'd got off the bus at the dock he'd grimaced and muttered that he was never going to polish off an entire bottle of champagne on his own again. It had been a long time since she'd had a hangover in the sun, but she'd sympathised all the same.

'Thanks. I feel a prat dressed up, but when everyone does it it's not so bad.'

Mia smiled too. 'I know what you mean.'

'Where's your sister?' asked Leo. 'Working on her ship-board romance novel?'

This time Mia laughed. 'I'd be surprised, but you never know.'

'I'm reading her book,' Leo said. 'It's . . . different.'

'Have you cried yet?' asked Mia.

Leo's jaw tautened. 'No.'

'I defy you not to.' Mia hadn't noticed the change in his expression.

'I won't cry,' said Leo.

'Everyone does,' Mia told him.

'If you say so.'

This time she heard a tightness in his voice but she didn't say anything. She glanced to one side and saw another couple stepping out on to the promenade deck. The woman was carrying a plate that held a large slab of chocolate cake. Leo followed her gaze.

'The midnight buffet,' he told her, his voice back to normal again.

'It's gone two in the morning,' Mia protested.

'They're still serving dessert.'

'Do they ever stop with the food?' she wondered aloud.

'I don't think so,' replied Leo. 'But chocolate cake in the middle of the night isn't my thing.'

'It shouldn't be mine either,' she said gloomily, 'but I have a feeling I need to investigate it. I don't have Britt's willpower.'

'She seems to be a strong woman,' agreed Leo.

'You've no idea.' Mia grinned.

'Perhaps not. Well,' said Leo, 'I'm giving the chocolate a miss, but enjoy it.'

'Thanks,' she said. 'See you around.'

He headed aft and she watched until he'd disappeared into the night. An odd man, she thought. Unexpectedly easy-going all of a sudden. Unexpectedly warm. Although there was definitely something weird going on with him. However, she thought, still probably not right for Britt. It would be no good for Britt to think of him as perfectly cool and calm and then discover he had a soft interior and some kind of emotional issues. That would never do.

Right for me? The thought suddenly bounced into Mia's mind. Maybe I need someone like Leo. Someone calm and dependable even if, despite the moments of warmth, he's a bit remote. Someone who'll settle down with me and make me forget Alejo.

She exhaled sharply. And what chance was there of that when she had a three-year-old daughter? What man wanted to take on a ready-made family? It was asking too much of anyone. And even if she found that man, she'd still be asking too much of him because he'd have to live up to Alejo, and who could do that? It was impossible.

Mia turned towards the stairs. She hesitated, unsure of whether to go back to the cabin or check out the midnight buffet. I'll just look, she told herself as she walked towards the dining room. I don't actually need to eat anything.

Given that there was so much food available during the day, Mia couldn't believe that there were so many people clustering around the restaurant with plates and forks so late at night too. But there were, and she joined them. She loaded up her plate with profiteroles and chocolate cake and promised herself that she'd spend some time in the gym the next day to work it all off again.

'Having a nice evening, Miss McDonagh?'

For the second time that night a man's voice startled Mia. She turned around, her mouth full of profiterole.

'Mr Shaw,' she said after she'd swallowed rather too much in one go. 'Or is there a rank I should use?'

'Steve is fine, actually,' he said. 'How are you?'

She wiped cream away from the corner of her mouth. 'I'm good,' she said.

'Glad to see you're enjoying the work of our pastry chef.'

'He should be shot,' she said sternly. 'It's not a good thing leaving food out like this.'

Steve laughed. 'People would be very disappointed if he didn't. So what has you out and about on your own so late? The Romance Queen asleep, is she?'

'Out like a light,' said Mia. 'We went on a pub crawl to celebrate her doing the first talk without messing up.'

'I don't think she's the sort of person who'd mess up anything,' said Steve. 'She seems remarkably competent to me.'

'Oh, she is.'

'Is she working you to the bone?' He looked at her with amusement in his eyes.

'To be honest, no,' she admitted. 'I'm having a lovely time.'

'I'm glad to hear that,' said Steve. 'I hope you have plenty of time to enjoy *Aphrodite*, despite the fact that you're a working girl.'

'I hope so too.'

'However, I must sit down with you and talk about the questions for the Night of Romance.'

Mia nodded and licked some cream from her finger.

'Make them sensible questions,' she told him. 'She likes sensible questions.'

'Tell her to give sensible answers,' he said in return. 'Our audience will like some banter, so if she could loosen up for that, it would be good.'

'She'll be fine,' said Mia defensively. 'She's not as tough as you think.' God knows why I said that, she thought. Britt would probably prefer to be thought of as an iron maiden.

'All that matters to me is that she does what it says on the tin,' said Steve.

'I'll make sure she does,' Mia promised.

'Thank you.' Steve smiled. 'If only they all had PAs like you.'

Mia grinned at him. 'I'm only a temp.'

'Well, you're the nicest temp I've ever met,' said Steve.

'Oh.' Mia felt herself blush. It was years since she'd blushed.

'If you've any problems at all, don't hesitate to come and see me,' he added. 'I'm here to make your job easier.'

'Thanks,' said Mia.

'By the way, you've got a splodge of cream on your cheek,' Steve told her as he handed her a paper napkin.

She rubbed at her cheek, wishing she was the sort of person who didn't always end up with food on her face as well as in her stomach.

'Well, I'd better be off,' said Steve. 'Enjoy the rest of your dessert.'

'I will,' said Mia.

He was sweet, she thought. Maybe coming on to her a bit with that comment about being a nice temp? She smiled to herself. More probably he was just being kind to the sister of the big star. Perhaps he'd be a better bet for Britt than Leo Tyler, she thought suddenly. Steve had already worked out that Britt wasn't really soppy and romantic. Plus – and possibly a big bonus for anyone living with Britt – he'd be away for most of the year on cruises. So she could be left on her own for a lot of the time, which was what she liked. Steve might be Britt's perfect man after all.

But still, Mia thought with a certain sense of satisfaction as she made her way back to the cabin, both Leo and Steve talked to me tonight, not to Britt. It struck her that it was months since she'd had a relaxed conversation in English with a man. She'd forgotten that men could be fun as well as deceiving bastards who broke your heart.

Britt heard the muted click of the cabin door as Mia returned. She'd heard her leave too – she never slept soundly after alcohol, and the slightest thing woke her. She'd sat up in the bed and wondered what on earth her sister was up to, sneaking out of the cabin in the middle of the night. But according to the list of events in the ship's newsletter, she could have gone to the cinema, where movies showed throughout the night, or the relaxation rooms, which were open twenty-four hours and where they piped wellness music through the speakers . . . Britt thought that Mia

162

could do with a long stint in the relaxation rooms, given that she spent most of her days halfway up a mountain with only Allegra for company.

Britt just couldn't imagine that. She had never lived outside of the city and she knew that she never would. She liked the buzz and the bustle and the feeling of having to prove yourself over and over just to get by. She liked knowing that she was successful in her profession and that when her name was put forward as someone's lawyer the opposition would flinch and know that they were in for a hard time. She liked battling for her clients. She liked the fights.

It's funny, she said to herself, I'm still thinking like a lawyer. But I haven't handled a case in nearly a year. She lay immobile in the bed, but she was wide awake now and thinking about her former career. She hadn't kept up to date with any changes in the law over the last few months or any cases that might be useful to know about. She'd tried. She'd met some of her old colleagues for lunch, but they'd always been in a rush to get back to Clavin & Grey, whereas she wasn't in a hurry to get anywhere. And although they talked to her generally about cases they couldn't give her specifics, so it wasn't like it used to be.

In any event, it wasn't all that easy to stay in touch because she was spending so much of her time shuttling backwards and forwards across the Irish Sea or meeting her publishers in a variety of different countries. So although she could think like a lawyer, she wasn't one any more. There were times when she worried that she would never be allowed to be one again.

Being a successful lawyer was all she'd cared about after her marriage had crumbled into dust. It wasn't some kind of compensation, she often told herself, for having got it all wrong with Ralph. She didn't work long hours just to prove to herself that she'd been right. She worked because it was what she had always wanted to do.

And working made her forget that she'd been silly and naïve when she'd married him. When she'd made, as she called it in her head, her very own big mistake. After she'd told everyone that she was leaving Ralph, they'd looked at her with astonishment diluted by a certain level of knowingness. They weren't really all that surprised that the marriage hadn't worked out, although they were wrong about the reasons. She knew that. They *were* surprised, though, that she'd decided to cut her losses so quickly.

But what was the point, Britt had asked Paula when she'd come to the house to tell her, in staying in a doomed relationship? Paula had suggested that marriage was something you had to work at, that everyone found it difficult at times and it was wrong to walk out at the first sign of trouble.

'And it's wrong to have married the wrong person,' Britt had told her firmly. 'Me and Ralph are the proverbial chalk and cheese.'

'So why the hell did you marry him in the first place?' demanded Paula. 'Why the big rush?'

It was a question Britt had asked herself as soon as she realised she was living with a stranger. As soon as it dawned on her that she'd entered into a legally binding contract with someone she hardly knew. Someone she was certain she couldn't live with any longer.

'Are you asleep?' Mia whispered into the darkness.

Britt, realising that her sister must have sensed she was awake, pulled herself up in the bed.

'Where were you?' she asked.

'Couldn't sleep,' Mia told her. 'So I went for a walk, met Leo Tyler and Steve Shaw, then gorged myself on the chocolate buffet.'

'Oh.'

'Sorry if I woke you.'

'It's OK.'

'It was lovely up on deck,' Mia said as she pushed open the bathroom door. 'Very, very romantic!' She giggled.

Britt listened to the sounds of her sister brushing her teeth and closed her eyes.

Romance lasted a moment, she thought. But the truth was that misery stayed with you for much longer.

Chapter 9

Position: Espada Island.
Weather: clear skies. Wind: easterly force 4. Temperature:
28°. Barometric pressure: 1014.3mb.

B ritt and Mia both slept later than usual the following morning, only waking when a tap on the door told them that their breakfast was outside. Mia, more awake than her sister, pulled on her robe and waited while the steward set the silver tray on the table.

'Good luck with the Treasure Hunt,' he told her as he left.

The Treasure Hunt! Mia had forgotten all about it, but being reminded of it woke her more effectively than anything else.

'I think I might just lie here,' said Britt sleepily. 'You go and tramp around the island looking for coconuts or whatever it is.'

'Get up,' commanded Mia. 'We're doing this together. You and me. The McDonagh sisters as a team.'

Britt yawned and pulled the sheet over her head. 'We were never a team.'

'We are now,' said Mia. 'C'mon, get up, you lazy sod.'

When Britt had eventually hauled herself out of bed and drunk a large glass of freshly squeezed orange juice, the two of them got ready for their trip to Espada Island. It was after ten before they presented themselves at the tender. Steve Shaw, who was chatting to the pilot of the boat, grinned at them.

'I thought that perhaps you weren't going to bother,' he told them. 'You're practically the last people to leave the ship.'

'Really?' Britt was amazed.

'Absolutely. The only people left on board are the Sampsons, and they're both in their eighties. Esther Sampson told me that she had better things to do with her declining years than scrabble around in the sand looking for the shell of some long-dead creature to bring back as part of the hunt, and that she had regretfully decided that another diamond wasn't worth the effort.'

Mia laughed. 'Rich bitch. So are the clues easy or hard?'

'You'll see for yourself. Now hurry up, you're delaying the other late passenger.'

They both boarded, and Mia grinned to herself. Sitting at the back of the tender, green baseball cap pulled firmly over his eyes, was Leo Tyler.

'Well hello there,' she said as she sat down in the seat in front of him. 'How are you this morning?'

'Fine,' he said. 'Did you stay up late?'

'I was already up late,' said Mia. 'But I have to confess that I did call in to the buffet. So I guess if we need to do a lot of searching on the island, I'm the person to do it. I have to work off about a thousand calories.'

'You snored, by the way,' remarked Britt.

'I did not!'

'You did. Kept me awake for hours. That's why I was so sleepy this morning. So no more late-night chocolate buffets on top of mojitos for you.'

Mia stuck her tongue out at her sister.

'Stop,' said Britt. 'Leo will think we're behaving like children.'

'I feel kind of childish today,' said Mia. 'Sort of light-hearted and holidayish.'

'I suppose we're entitled to a day off,' Britt conceded.

'A day off! Maybe you're finally starting to chill out,' said Mia. 'Oh, wow, isn't that just beautiful?' She pushed her hair out of her face and stared straight ahead of her.

The island shimmered in the morning light. It was long and narrow and almost entirely green, with a wide strip of perfect white sand in its semicircular turquoise bay. A huge pelican sat on the post of the sun-bleached wooden jetty, where officers of the ship, in regulation white, waited for them.

'Welcome to Espada Island.' One of the officers smiled at them as they pulled up beside the jetty. 'We hope you have a lovely time here and that you're successful in the Treasure Hunt.' He handed Mia a gold-coloured envelope. 'The clues are inside.'

'We need two envelopes,' Mia told him. 'Leo's not with us.'

'Mia!' Britt frowned at her.

'Well he's not,' Mia pointed out. 'It's one entry per cabin, and Leo's in a different cabin. I'm sure he wants to win the ring for himself. Besides, he might be exceptionally brilliant and not need any help.'

'I'm not exceptionally brilliant,' said Leo. 'Nor do I want the ring, thanks.'

'They'd probably give you cufflinks if you prefer,' Mia told him. 'But you could always hang on to the diamond ring! You never know when you might want one.' She smiled wickedly at him, but Leo said nothing, and Mia recognised the same tautness in his face as she'd seen the previous evening. 'Or you could sell it,' she added mildly.

Britt nudged her sister. 'Leave the man alone,' she said. 'If he wants to avoid what's probably going to be a stampede for clues, that's entirely his business.' She looked at Leo. 'We're sorry,' she said. 'What you do is entirely your own affair.'

'Yes, but Leo, you absolutely have to take part in the Treasure Hunt,' said Mia. 'It'd be such a waste if you didn't.'

'Leave it, Mia,' said Britt, who'd also noticed the tension in Leo's face. 'Let's hit the beach and look at the clues.'

She strode along the jetty, her long legs already a light golden brown. Mia hesitated for a moment, then followed her.

The beach was already crowded with passengers from the *Aphrodite*, and it took them some time to find a couple of unoccupied loungers, which they then dragged into the shade of a palm tree.

'You made me look stupid in front of Leo,' complained Mia as they dropped their bags on the loungers. 'Talking to me like I was a kid.'

'The man didn't want to do the Treasure Hunt,' said Britt. 'You were making him feel uncomfortable.'

'No I wasn't.' Mia adjusted her sunglasses. 'I like Leo. We had a long chat on deck last night. He's lovely even if he is a bit standoffish. I think he's shy, actually. I wouldn't make him feel uncomfortable.'

'Whatever,' said Britt dismissively.

Mia opened her mouth to retaliate, then closed it again. There was no point in arguing with Britt because Britt always won arguments. Mia couldn't remember a single time her sister had come off worse in any of them, even when she was clearly in the wrong. She had this uncanny ability to turn things around so that no matter how righteous you felt, by the time Britt had finished with you, you weren't a bit confident of your own position.

'Go on then,' she said resignedly. 'Open the envelope and tell us what we have to do. We're obviously way behind.' She waved towards the beach, where other passengers from the ship were either walking briskly up and down, reading their sheets of paper and gesticulating wildly, or huddled beneath palm trees, deep in animated conversation.

'Ten clues to solve,' said Britt when she'd taken out the card. 'And five items to collect.' She frowned. 'I can't believe they're asking us to take stuff from the island. What about their eco-credentials?'

'They won't want us to bring back anything important,' said Mia. 'Probably not even anything indigenous to the island. Which is a hint in itself, don't you think?'

'You're probably right . . . and I know what the first thing is anyway,' Britt told her. '"Bring back a tender moment."

Don't you think that might be the ticket we needed to board the tender that brought us here?'

'There you go!' cried Mia, her annoyance with her sister forgotten. 'I knew you had the brains for this.'

They worked their way through the clues, Britt analysing them forensically and Mia making wild guesses but both of them usually coming up with the same answer.

'I'm going to get a drink,' said Britt when they'd worked out as many as they could and had collected most of the scavenger items. 'It might help my brain to start working again.' She walked to the bar the ship's crew had set up near the jetty.

Mia picked up the list of clues and looked at it, although she was finding it hard to concentrate in such an idyllic location.

'Here.' Britt returned with a fruit drink. 'I thought you might be thirsty too.'

'Thanks.'

'And the answer to that question about Gentleman's Relish is Officer Pickles,' said Britt.

'Huh?'

'The guy beside the bar.' Britt pointed to where one of the *Aphrodite*'s officers was standing, watching the bar staff, his white cap placed firmly on his shaven head. 'His name is Officer Pickles.'

Mia giggled. 'Are you sure?'

'Absolutely. That only leaves one.'

'"It may be in the name of justice, or just in my name. The name is what we seek."' Mia read from the sheet of paper again. It made no sense to her whatsoever.

'The sword of justice, perhaps?' Britt wondered. 'But I don't see any swords here. Or anything that even looks like a sword.'

'Maybe it's nothing to do with swords. Maybe it's all about justice,' said Mia. 'Is it some kind of legal term?'

'Even if it is, that still doesn't make sense,' said Britt. 'Anyone should be able to solve the clues. Not just someone with legal knowledge.'

'I guess so.' Mia lay back on the lounger and decided that she'd held her own on the clue-solving and that this was just one too far. 'Oh well, we think we have most of them right. I'm sure that's enough.'

Britt looked at her sternly. 'There'll be people who've got them all right. Plus having collected the scavenger items. There always are on things like this.'

Mia looked up at Britt and shielded her eyes from the dazzling sun. 'Do you regularly go on treasure hunts?'

'No, but it's like a pub quiz,' said Britt. 'There are people who turn up at them regularly and get all the questions right and win the top prize, so that the table who just about scrounged a few people together will always lose.'

'I don't think anyone came on *Aphrodite* just to win the prize.'

'Mia, sweetie, the ring is worth five thousand dollars. They might not have come specifically to win it, but I'm sure they're plenty serious enough about it. And we should be too.'

'I'm serious about it all right, but I'm not going to let it ruin my day. You wander off and see if you can find a starfish,' said Mia. 'That's the last of the scavenger items, isn't it? Though it seems very strange that they're looking for an actual starfish.'

'Of course!' Britt struck her forehead with the palm of her hand. 'They're not looking for a starfish. They're looking for a starfish emblem. And they're on the cocktail sticks!' She grabbed the juice drink she'd given Mia and took the stick out of it. 'See?'

'Clever-clogs strikes again,' said Mia, but she smiled at her sister. 'Tell you what, I'll think about this other clue if you let me close my eyes.'

'Sure.' Britt got up from the lounger and dusted the fine sand from her beach dress. 'I'll go for a walk and think about it myself.'

Leo Tyler had caved in and asked for a copy of the Treasure Hunt clues. He was sitting on his lounger looking at the list but not actually reading the clues. Obviously there was no way he was trying to win a diamond ring. He had one of those nestling in a navy blue box at home, and it had cost him considerably more than the one on offer from Blue Lagoon. Vanessa's mother had been the one to return it to him. He felt sick as he thought about it.

He still sometimes felt physically sick when he thought of Vanessa and how life could change for ever in an instant. And how much longer it took to live with that change. He'd woken up one morning feeling happy. He'd gone to bed frozen with despair. And he wondered sometimes whether he would ever unfreeze again.

He stared out at the aquamarine sea as it lapped languidly

against the shore. The passengers who had either solved the Treasure Hunt clues or had given up on it altogether were splashing around, laughing and joking with each other as the warm water sparkled in the light of the sun.

We should have been here together, thought Leo. That was how it was supposed to be. I thought we were perfect for each other. But I was kidding myself.

A woman sidestepped a beach ball as it hurtled in the wrong direction. She picked it up and threw it back into the water, her lithe, delicately tanned body perfectly set off by the white bathing suit she was wearing. Leo recognised Britt Martin again. The Romantic Fiction Queen. People had been talking about her while they'd waited for the talk to begin the other day. They'd all said that *The Perfect Man* had made them cry. No book had ever made Leo cry.

He'd expected the talk to be about the failure of men on the romantic and emotional front. He'd expected a bit of a rant about how hopeless they were as a sex. And despite having thought, following dinner with Britt and Mia, that the novelist was a bit on the frosty side, he'd expected her to thaw considerably when talking about love. She hadn't been cool about it. But she hadn't been half as gushing as he'd imagined either. And in the end the talk had been very practical, although from his point of view it hadn't made him understand women any better.

She was attractive, thought Leo. Different today with her hair slicked back and without all the make-up she'd been wearing at her talk. She looked better this way, less artificial and, he thought, less uncomfortable too.

He wondered if it was hard work being romantic all the time. He supposed that even a woman might get tired of it.

Britt glanced in his direction and their eyes met. He felt a little embarrassed at having been caught staring at her. She smiled slightly at him and began to walk towards him.

'Hi,' she said as she trudged through the deep white sand a few feet away from his lounger. 'Gosh, that's hard on the calf muscles.'

'Want to sit down and rest?' He was surprised at himself for suggesting it.

'Thanks.' She perched on the edge of an adjacent sunbed.

'Did you solve all the clues?' he asked.

'Are you cracked?' She smiled. 'They're very difficult. Have you given in and decided to do it anyway?'

'Not for the prize,' he said. 'For the satisfaction.'

'How are you getting on?' she asked.

'Can't get number three.'

'The sword one.' She made a face. 'We haven't got that either.'

'Oh well.' He couldn't think of anything else to say. Talking to Britt embarrassed him even though he wasn't sure why. Maybe it was the fact that she made a living writing about love. Or perhaps, he thought, it was the knowledge that she'd written about sex in *The Perfect Man* – a descriptive page of erotic action that had taken him totally by surprise. He'd been flicking through the book before reading it and (how did it happen like that? he wondered; it wasn't deliberate on his part) he'd stopped at the scene in which some guy called Jack was putting himself in the frame with a woman called Francesca. It seemed as though Jack was (in the eyes of Francesca, and clearly in Britt's eyes too) a skilled, sensitive lover. He was certainly getting the desired results with Francesca.

Leo wondered how women rated men as skilled and sensitive. And, he added to himself, if skill came with practice, did women actually want men to be all that skilled in the first place? After all, if it was their first time together and he was super-skilled, she'd be bound to think about who he might have practised the moves with. And how often.

It was never as easy as in books, thought Leo. Which was why he didn't normally read mushy tripe like that. He liked books about ancient history himself. There was a lot of sex in them but it wasn't caught up with anything other than the act itself. Ancient civilisations had better things to do than psychoanalyse a physical performance.

'I'd better get back to my sister,' said Britt when they'd sat beside each other for almost five minutes without exchanging another word. 'She's supposed to be mulling over that clue.'

'Of course. See you around.'

All the same, Leo thought as he watched her walk up the beach, I bet the romantic novelist would be good in bed. It'd be part of her skill set. Surely?

'I see you were getting close to Mr Tyler,' said Mia as Britt returned. Her green eyes danced with merriment. 'You'd make a lovely couple. I've thought that more than once.' She looked coyly at her sister. 'Both of you seem to be the strong, silent type. Although I think he thaws more often than you.'

'Don't be daft,' said Britt dismissively. 'You're the one who met him on deck in the moonlight.' She narrowed her eyes against the sun. 'Given that he does seem to be on his own and that he's clearly loaded enough to afford a suite on the *Aphrodite*, maybe he's someone you should consider.'

'Britt McDonagh!' Mia cried. 'I'm certainly not considering people, as you put it. And cute though Leo Tyler might be, he's not my type.'

Britt laughed, an easy, genuine laugh. 'That's what women always say in books. And that's when they fall for the romantic hero despite themselves.'

'Not me,' said Mia firmly. 'Besides . . .' She glanced back down the beach. 'He's now in conversation with our high-maintenance celebrity model. I think that as the only unattached male passenger, he's clearly fair game to all of us!'

Britt turned on the sunbed. Mia was right. Leo was talking to Pippin Costello, who was wearing a bright red slashed swimsuit that showed off her designer boobs and long, long legs. Her hair was tied back today and her face shaded by a large straw coolie hat in matching red.

'Maybe she's his type,' said Britt drily. 'Maybe women with enhanced chests and tinkly laughs are always the right type for a man.'

Not a good career move, my arse! thought Mia as she watched Pippin touch Leo lightly on the arm and then gesture towards the ship. She's totally into him.

'Any luck on the clue?' Britt turned away from observing Leo and Pippin and took up the Treasure Hunt list again.

'No.' Mia frowned. 'I was looking around to see if anything reminded me of a sword, but . . .'

'I think it might be the *name* of a sword they want,' said Britt thoughtfully. 'Though the only one I know is Excalibur.'

'Oh!' Suddenly Mia's cheeks were pink. 'Espada. That's the answer.'

'Espada? The island?' Britt looked at her questioningly. 'Why would they want the name of the island?'

'Because it means sword in Spanish,' said Mia in excitement. 'I just wasn't thinking straight. But when you do think about it, that's exactly what the island looks like. It's long and narrow and this part could be the curvy handle.'

'Bingo!'

Mia thought she saw a glint of respect in Britt's eyes and she laughed with pleasure.

'So, the ring is in the bag,' she said. 'We've answered the clues and we've got the scavenger items and we totally rock! Go, Team McDonagh!'

Britt laughed too.

And Leo Tyler, as he walked up the beach with Pippin, saw them high-five each other in the sand.

'Have you read her book?' asked Pippin, who had observed him looking at the McDonagh sisters.

He shrugged. 'Dipped into it.'

'Everyone says it's heartbreaking,' Pippin told him. 'I don't know about that. It's good, of course. Not as good as they're making out, though. I guess the Jack Hayes guy is hunky and great, but I prefer my men a bit more real.'

Leo smiled suddenly. 'Until you find one and try to change him.'

Pippin laughed. 'I guess so. But hopefully not too much.'

'That'd be a first.'

'I like my men to be men,' said Pippin.

'I'm glad you know your own mind.'

'I do. I have my career and my own stuff. A man should have his career and his own stuff too.'

Vanessa had complained about his career. That it took up too much of their time. That it mattered to him more than hers did. She was right on both counts. But it hadn't mattered more than her. Regardless of what she obviously thought.

'Come on.' Pippin suddenly took him by the hand. 'Too much thinking, not enough doing. Time for a swim!'

'I'm not—' But Leo wasn't able to finish his sentence as she hauled him into the sparkling water and tugged him downwards into the sea.

Chapter 10

Position: Curaçao, Netherlands Antilles.
Weather: partly cloudy, passing tropical showers. Wind:
north-easterly force 2. Temperature: 28°. Barometric
pressure: 1012.7mb.

The following morning they arrived in Curaçao, an island
where dolly-mixture-coloured houses surrounded the
port and where the Dutch colonial architecture reminded
Mia of the month she'd spent in Amsterdam. Although it
had been a lot colder in Amsterdam. She'd been there in
January, when the weather was freezing and people wrapped
in thermal jackets were skating on open-air ice-rinks. Here
they were strolling around the streets in bright shorts and
sleeveless T-shirts.

Because Curaçao was the most commercial and developed of all of the islands they'd visited so far, they
decided to go shopping, splitting up when they crossed
over the wobbly bridge that led to the port town of
Willemstad and arranging to meet again for coffee in one
of the pavement cafés later.

Mia hadn't shopped in ages, and she enjoyed strolling around the stores, gazing wistfully at the merchandise in some of the designer outlets but actually buying from the quirkier boutiques. She selected a smiling Caribbean doll for Allegra (Mia loved the cheerful doll, but her daughter was currently going through a very destructive phase and so she wondered how long it would actually last), as well as a canary-yellow T-shirt and matching shorts. She'd bought her daughter a tee in Grenada too, and her aim was to bring her one from every port they visited.

She arrived early at the cute waterside café with its checked tablecloths and brightly coloured sunshades, and ordered herself a freshly squeezed fruit juice while she waited for Britt to arrive. Then, because it was evening at home, she made her daily phone call to Allegra, who sounded, as always, happy and contented.

Mia wasn't sure how she felt about this. She certainly hadn't wanted Allegra to feel abandoned or unloved while she was away, but her daughter chatted incomprehensibly for a minute before finishing the phone call by dropping the phone and shouting at one of her cousins to wait, she was coming.

Mia knew that she should be happy that Allegra was enjoying her time with the boys, but the nagging thought had come to her that perhaps she wouldn't want to come home again. After all, playing with Luke and Barney and having access to a Nintendo Wii and generally having a good time would make Sierra Bonita seem tame and boring by comparison. They didn't even have satellite TV there, for heaven's sake! And there were no other children to play with near their house, which was only a kilometre away from the town as the crow flew, but about five kilometres away by car along the twisty switchback mountain roads with their heart-stopping drops to the valley below that had so terrified Mia when she'd first come to live there.

It hadn't bothered Allegra before. She was happy to go to the town's *guardería infantil* in the mornings, come home for her siesta and play with Mia at night. But would she be lonely when they went home? Was it right for her to live as she did with her daughter? Was it fair?

Mia sighed deeply and sucked juice through the straw. She'd thought that she was a good mother, that being a mother had been the one real success of her life, but now she wasn't sure.

'Hi.' Britt, looking slightly hot and bothered, her vest top damp with perspiration, dumped a collection of carrier bags on the table. 'Am I late?'

Mia shook her head. 'I'm early,' she said. 'All shopped out.'

'What did you buy?'

'Nothing exciting. But some nice things for Allegra.' Mia showed her sister her purchases while Britt ordered a juice for herself and another one for Mia and fanned herself with a beer mat.

'They're pretty,' said Britt as she pushed her sunglasses on to her head. 'Those shorts are so cute. Hard to believe that we were once that small ourselves.'

'She might not be that small when we get back,' said Mia. 'She's growing at a phenomenal rate. This is a size bigger than she normally wears.'

'I suppose you get through a lot of clothes for kids.' Britt's tone implied that she was only just realising that they grew.

'Yup. But the great thing about where we live is that there isn't that whole designer oneupmanship going on,' said Mia. 'At least not among the kids. The teenagers are a different ballgame; the style there is cutting edge.'

'Meredith is always banging on at me about upgrading my wardrobe,' remarked Britt. 'Whenever I go to one of those damn dinners, she checks what I'm wearing and moans that I should get something gorgeous from Stella.'

Mia laughed. 'It's not my idea of the way to spend money, but if you can afford it, why not?'

'It's not me,' Britt said. 'I'm not a glamorous person at heart. It's like the hair and the lip gloss and the whole Brigitte persona thing. All totally different to how I really am.'

'A different part of you, but part of you all the same. What's wrong with buying nice stuff if you can afford it? OK, the whole Brigitte thing is a bit over the top, but a touch of glamour suits you.'

'I'm the world's worst shopper,' Britt said. 'Clothes bore me to tears. I spend my money on useful things like top-of-the-range vacuum cleaners and stuff.'

Mia looked at her shrewdly. 'You know what's wrong with you?'

'What?'

'You've got Mum's Catholic guilt and Dad's Protestant work ethic. You don't like spending money foolishly because you think it's sinful, and you think that the devil makes work for idle hands.'

Britt burst out laughing. 'You've got a point,' she admitted. 'However, just to prove that it's not only vacuum cleaners that do it for me . . .' She rummaged around in the bags and retrieved a small striped package tied with a black ribbon. 'I got you something frivolous.'

'What? When?'

'While I was shopping.'

'Why?'

'There doesn't have to be a why,' said Britt. 'It's just a gift.'

'OK, well, thanks.' Mia began to undo the ribbon. 'I just wondered what made you . . .' She looked at the box before opening it. 'Britt . . .'

'It's a present. Something small, that's all. You said you needed one.'

Mia opened the box and looked at the Tag Heuer watch inside.

'Britt McDonagh! This is an expensive watch. It's not frivolous at all. There's absolutely no need . . .'

'It's sensible as well as frivolous,' Britt told her. 'You needed a new watch. This is a duty-free island. The stuff is cheaper here. So why not?'

Mia stared at her. Britt's sudden generosity astounded her. Her sister had been a frugal hoarder of pocket money when they were smaller, always having a secret stash for emergencies, even though there were never any emergencies that needed it. Even when her legal career had taken off she still hadn't seemed to spend money on luxuries.

'It's lovely, but . . .'

'Consider it a bonus,' said Britt.

'For what?'

'For helping with the talk the other day. For your advice afterwards. And for helping me this evening with tomorrow's.'

'We're working this evening?'

'Absolutely,' said Britt. 'So it's not really a present. It's overtime.'

A sudden squall of hot tropical rain descended as they approached the *Aphrodite*, and they sprinted up the gangway before they got totally drenched.

'Actually, I have another task for you,' said Britt when they got to the cabin and Mia was towel-drying her hair, which had turned frizzier than ever in the rain. 'Could you stop by the music appreciation talk at four o'clock?'

'Why?' Mia stopped rubbing her hair and looked at Britt quizzically.

'I want to know what it's like,' she explained. 'You could make notes.'

'On music appreciation?' Mia looked confused.

'No, on how he does it,' said Britt. 'On how he makes it interesting. If he does.'

'Why don't you go yourself?' Mia tugged a brush through her hair.

'Because I don't want to be seen at it,' said Britt. 'People might wonder why I was there.'

'They might think it's because you're interested in music,' said Mia mildly.

'Or that I'm looking for hints.'

'You are!'

'But I don't want them to know that.'

Mia looked at her in exasperation. 'You're the weirdest person, Britt McDonagh.'

'Just do it, would you?'

'All right. But if it's all about jazz, I'll beat you up later. You know I can't stand jazz.'

It was, in fact, about the music of Chopin and Tchaikovsky. Mia was quite surprised to realise that she recognised a lot of the sonatas and symphonies, never having considered herself a classical music buff before. It probably wasn't entirely cultured to recognise them from TV ads, she admitted to herself, but at least she was able to look knowledgeable.

The lecturer, Aaron Sachs, had been a conductor with a number of orchestras and was completely on top of his subject. Mia noticed that he didn't have the stern but slightly hunted expression that Britt had worn all during her talk and that he interacted easily with the passengers. He played lots of music and gave them plenty of time to talk to him and each other about it, and Mia was surprised when the hour was up.

'Nice to see you here,' said Eileen, who had waved at her as she'd walked in. 'He's wonderful, isn't he?'

Mia glanced at the conductor. He was, she had to admit, very dashing and very much how she would have imagined a conductor to be. He had arrived at the lecture in a dress suit, which gave him an air of gravitas accentuated by his mane of silver-grey hair and his steely blue eyes.

'He knows his stuff.'

'I have all of the recordings from when he was with the Philharmonic,' said Eileen. 'I even went to a performance in New York before he retired.'

'Goodness, you're a real fan.'

'That's what's so great about the Blue Lagoon cruises,' confided Eileen. 'You get to meet talented people you've admired and you can talk to them.'

'Are you coming to Britt . . . Brigitte's talk tomorrow?'

'Of course. I just love her work. I'm hoping that she's going to give us a lot more writing tips, though. I've lived a very interesting life, you see, and I'm sure it'll make a fantastic book.'

'Wow. Good for you,' said Mia.

'Yes, I was quite a goer before I met John,' said Eileen. 'He doesn't know the half of it.'

'He will if you write about it.'

'I'll do it as a novel,' said Eileen. 'He'll never guess.'

'Right.' Mia wasn't so sure about that.

'Anyway, tell your sister I'll be bringing along my book for signing tomorrow,' said Eileen. 'D'you know if they give a discount in the ship's bookshop?'

'Ten per cent. It's a good deal,' said Mia quickly. As Britt's assistant she felt it important to get her as many sales as possible.

'I thought I'd buy some as presents and get them signed,' said Eileen. 'I can hand them out to friends during the year. Save me having to worry about birthdays for the next few months.'

'Great idea.'

'Well, got to run. I'm meeting Pippin in the spa in twenty minutes. We're having the complete body exfoliation.'

Mia left the lecture room and walked back through the cybercafé towards the stairs. Leo Tyler was hunched over one of the screens. She almost said hello to him, but something in the way he was sitting made her pass him by. He didn't look as though he wanted to be disturbed.

Leo was looking at back issues of the Irish newspapers online. He did this every so often, unable to stop himself even though he knew that it was a pointless exercise that left him feeling sick and shaking. But sometimes he had to read the reports again to make it real in his head. He knew that it had happened. He just found it hard to accept that it had.

It had been reported differently in different newspapers. The *Irish Times* simply recorded the facts in a small column on the right-hand side of the paper, and the truth was that you'd miss it unless you were reading every single item in the paper. The header over the four-line story simply read: *Couple killed in car crash.*

The *Independent* had a similar story and an identical headline but accompanied by a photograph that drew your attention to it. It would have been difficult not to notice the photo of the car, although the car itself was almost unrecognisable as anything other than tangled metal. It was clear, however, that nobody inside could have survived what had obviously been a truly dreadful accident.

The tabloids had run with the photographs and had given half a page to the story, which was headlined: *Couple perish in horror smash.*

Leo felt the familiar waves of nausea rise up inside him as he looked at the photograph. He didn't need to look at it; every image in it was etched into his brain.

'I'll fucking kill you,' he'd yelled at Donal that night. 'I'll fucking kill the pair of you.'

But Donal had killed both of them instead.

'Characterisation is very important in a novel,' said Britt out loud. 'Readers have to empathise with your characters.'

'I empathised with Jack all right,' remarked Mia, who was listening as Britt rehearsed her talk. 'But Lisette was a wimpy cow and it took me a while to like her.'

'She was a bit weak all right,' admitted Britt. 'The thing is, though . . .' she looked at her notes and frowned, 'I wasn't thinking of whether anyone would like Jack or Francesca or Lisette when I wrote the book. I wasn't thinking of having readers empathise with anyone. I just wrote it, and that silly assistant of mine sent it to her literary friend.'

'Really?' Mia admitted to Britt that despite the newspaper stories of how Amie had sent off the manuscript, she'd always assumed that her efficient sister had actually sussed out the best agent for the job herself.

'Are you cracked?' asked Britt. 'I had no intention of having it published.'

'You must be the only writer in the world who kept a hidden manuscript so,' said Mia with amusement. 'I thought that the desks of agents and publishers were groaning beneath the weight of the stuff they get every day.'

'So I've heard,' agreed Britt. 'I just didn't intend to add mine to the pile. It's all Amie's fault.'

'Bet you're glad she did.'

Britt sighed. 'I should be. I know I should be. But . . .'

'Oh, come on.' Mia looked at her sceptically. 'You have to pretend to be modest and everything when you're out and about, but you always want to succeed.'

'At law,' Britt said. 'This wasn't in my plan at all. And although I admit that once it was published I wanted *The Perfect Man* to do well, I'm really struggling with this whole novelist thing.'

'Weirder and weirder,' remarked Mia. 'But you do want to succeed at the talks. I know that. And it would be better if you were . . .' She hesitated.

'If I was what?'

'Less . . . perfect.'

'Less perfect!'

'In yourself,' said Mia uneasily. 'I know I said to pretend that you were arguing a case in court. But perhaps that's not a good idea. Because now you're coming across as someone who's trying to win an argument. Who's just arguing for the sake of arguing even though you don't believe in it.'

'It doesn't matter if I don't believe it as long as they do,' said Britt.

'Of course it does,' retorted Mia. 'You don't want to be a fraud, do you?'

'I already am a bloody fraud!' cried Britt.

'Well, you have to make yourself appear not to be,' said Mia desperately.

'I'm tired of trying to live up to other people's ideas of how I should be!' cried Britt. 'I'm not cut out for it.'

'Aaron Sachs made you feel as though you were part of something with him,' said Mia. 'You can do that too, I know you can.'

'Part of what?' demanded Britt. 'Part of telling people that they can find true love and live happily ever after when two out of three marriages go down the pan? When their so-called perfect man will probably turn out to be the complete opposite of who they think? When he'll go off and sleep with someone else given half a chance? Is that what you want me to be part of?'

Mia looked at her in complete silence. There were tears in Britt's eyes.

'Are you all right?' she asked as she watched her sister fight them.

'Of course I am.' Britt turned away from her. 'I guess this is something I do get passionate about. The wrong thing for this trip, obviously.'

'I'm sorry,' said Mia. 'I wasn't trying to upset you.'

'I'm not upset.'

'You seem upset to me. And what you're saying . . . if you truly believe that all men are like that, then I feel sorry for you.'

'I don't need you to feel sorry for me,' said Britt curtly.

Mia knew that she'd said the wrong thing. 'Let's get back to your talk,' she suggested. 'You're very good and really professional but you don't . . . sparkle. I think people want you to sparkle.'

'I'm not sparkly.'

'You are. You know you are. All you have to do is enjoy yourself. I can't understand why you don't. Why you have to keep yourself distanced from everyone and everything as though it's all kind of beneath you.'

'That's what you think?' said Britt.

'Well . . .'

Britt snapped her laptop closed. 'I've had it with this,' she said abruptly. 'I'm going to talk to Steve Shaw. I can't do it and I won't do it. It was stupid of me to think I ever could.' She glanced at her watch. 'An hour before we sail. I'm sure they can put us off the boat and we can get a flight home from Curaçao.'

'Britt! Are you mental?'

'No, I'm not.' Britt stood up. 'You can start packing. I've had enough. We're leaving.'

'Britt, for heaven's sake. You were fine. I'm just trying—'

But she didn't finish the sentence, because Britt had walked out of the cabin, and if the door hadn't been on a soft-closing mechanism, it would have slammed behind her.

She had to wait outside Steve Shaw's office for fifteen minutes before he appeared. She'd told the girl at reception that it was an urgent matter and that Steve had to meet her regardless of whatever he was doing at the moment. Tiffany Johnson, who'd read *The Perfect Man* and who'd seen Britt on TV, was astonished at how forceful the apparently sweet author was.

'He's with the theatre group,' she explained. 'He shouldn't really be disturbed.'

'I need him here right away,' said Britt, and her tone made Tiffany pick up the phone and call him.

He looked flustered when he arrived, the theatre being four decks up and at the opposite end of the ship, but he smiled at Britt and invited her into his office.

Like Mia, she was surprised at how plainly it was decorated in comparison to the public areas of the ship. He waved her into the seat opposite his desk.

'What's the problem?' he asked as he pulled a blue folder from the pile on the desk and looked at her. The folder was captioned 'Lead Speaker' and then, in smaller lettering, 'Brigitte Martin'. It reminded her of the folders that she used to have piled on her desk at Clavin & Grey.

'Miss Martin?' He looked at her enquiringly.

It had been so much easier being at Clavin & Grey. She could be herself, Britt McDonagh, with her unflappable reputation, who knew family law back to front. Who knew everything there was to know about family law, in fact. Who was never badly prepared for a case. Who was known for taking no shit from anyone. Where no one needed her to be sparkly, just competent.

Steve Shaw wanted to tell the woman in front of him that he was a busy man and that he had better things to do than being summoned to his office by someone who apparently didn't have a reason for dragging him here in the first place. But everyone on the *Aphrodite* had been warned to be nice to Miss Martin, who was the darling of the book trade and whose presence on board was (according to the PR department) a real coup for the ship because she was notoriously reticent about appearing on anything. A coup it might have been, but he'd sensed, during their brief conversation following her first workshop, that she didn't really want to be there. And the other day, on her way to Espada Island, he'd still got the impression that she wasn't entirely happy.

It was his job to make everyone on board the *Aphrodite* happy. Even ditzy romantic novelists who thought they knew what made the perfect man. He wondered who her perfect man might be. He felt quite sorry for the chap.

'How can I help you?' he asked.

Britt had never allowed herself to fail at anything to do with her career before. She'd never failed her exams, never failed her clients, never failed the company. If she allowed herself to fail now . . . but this – this wasn't a career, it was a diversion.

She'd thought about telling it like she really believed it was so that everyone would hate her, but she hadn't been able to do that. Nevertheless, she knew that she hadn't been good enough. Mia had seen that her heart wasn't in it. Mia had been able to spot the difference between her and Aaron Sachs. So anyone else would be able to spot it too. She wasn't the real deal. She never would be.

Steve Shaw was frowning now. Britt sensed that he didn't really like her. She knew that he thought she was a light-weight. A silly woman. She could see it in his eyes in the same way as she'd seen it in the eyes of some of her opponents in the past. They'd been very, very wrong. And most of them had regretted underestimating her.

'I hate to seem impatient, Miss Martin, but I'm very busy today.' Steve's smile was fixed on to his face.

It would be the first time I've failed at anything, Britt

thought. And then she reminded herself that it wouldn't be – she'd failed horribly at her marriage too. So she had form in failure. She wasn't as great as she liked to think.

'Miss Martin?'

He probably feels as though I was imposed on him, she realised. He didn't have anything to do with me getting here; it was all Meredith and that girl from the publicity department, Annie. Maybe he had someone else in mind, someone he thought would be much better equipped to talk to the well-heeled passengers of the *Aphrodite*. Someone who could get into the spirit of the Valentine Cruise too and not complain about his efforts with the hearts and flowers and fat little Cupids all around the room.

I've been up my own backside about it. I don't blame him for not liking me. I haven't made myself very likeable.

'Miss Martin?'

After she'd walked away from her marriage, Britt had sworn that she was never going to walk away from anything ever again. Which was why at work she'd always put her every effort into ensuring that her clients got the very best outcome. She never gave up. People said that about her. Even when the going got tough, she never gave up. Britt McDonagh won't let you down. It was a common quote in the office. But if she walked away now, she'd be letting down lots of people: Meredith (so what? Meredith had made a lot of money out of her); Annie, the PR person who'd booked her (she'd get over it, wouldn't she?); Mia (not that Mia had anything to complain about; she'd had a few lovely days on board the ship and she'd probably be happy to get back to Allegra); Steve Shaw (who'd tried to be nice, he really had; she'd feel bad about leaving him in the lurch); the people who'd booked the talks (oh well, there were plenty of other things for them to do); herself. If she walked away now, she'd be letting herself down most of all. She'd be saying that she was the sort of person who would only try at the things she wanted to do. At easy things. And she'd never been that sort of person before. She'd always tried hardest when the stakes were highest. When the task ahead was difficult.

Steve was managing to keep his face pleasant, but she could sense his irritation.

Was it right to give up just because this was so much harder than anything she'd done before? Was it right to throw his entertainment schedule into complete disarray just because she was struggling? Was she really a quitter? Whenever she thought about the failure of her marriage, she felt terrible. That hadn't been entirely her fault. But if she allowed herself to fail now, there'd be nobody else she could blame.

'I'm sorry.' Britt stood up. 'I had some questions I wanted to ask you, but I've just realised that it doesn't matter.'

'Excuse me?' He looked at her in astonishment.

'About the talk tomorrow. I had some questions but . . . I've resolved them myself.'

'You told Tiffany that it was extremely urgent and that it couldn't wait.' Steve hadn't meant to snap at her, but he knew he sounded snappy all the same.

'I know.' She looked at him contritely. 'And I know you're thinking that I'm a silly woman . . .'

'No, no,' he said unconvincingly.

'. . . but I was concerned about some things earlier and I'm not now.'

'Well, I'm glad if seeing my face has allayed your concerns,' he said drily. 'But if there's nothing else . . .' He stood up too.

She smiled.

It was a lovely smile, Steve thought suddenly. It changed her completely. When she smiled, you could think that maybe she did know something about life and love after all.

'I really am sorry. I . . . I had an attack of nerves.'

She was surprised at herself. She'd never in her life before admitted to being nervous about anything.

'Nerves!'

'Yes.'

'Miss Martin, you have no need to be nervous. As far as our cultural activities are concerned, you're our star turn.'

'That's why I had an attack of nerves,' she said.

'Oh.'

'I've never done anything quite like this before. And I was going through my talk for tomorrow and I thought it was complete bullshit and I'd be wasting everyone's time, and so I decided that it would be better just to leave the ship here and forget about it.'

Steve looked aghast.

'But of course that would be letting everyone down and I don't do that, and I'm sorry – I didn't mean to waffle on like this to you . . .' She picked up her bag. 'I'm sure you're tremendously busy and I've taken up enough of your time.'

'That's OK.' His voice was warmer than it had been. 'Everyone gets nervous.'

'Not me,' said Britt.

'Is it something to do with *Aphrodite*?' asked Steve. 'Can we makes things easier for you in any way, perhaps?'

She shook her head. 'It's something to do with me,' she told him. 'And it's only me who can fix it. But I'm fine now, I promise.'

She smiled again.

Jeez, thought Steve. That smile transforms her.

'Well, if there's anything we can do. Or I can do . . .'

'Not at all.' Her tone was suddenly brisk. 'I'm over it. Forget I ever came here.' She opened the door. 'But thanks for your time.'

She closed the door behind her and Steve exhaled slowly. It was five minutes before he left and returned to the theatre.

'Well?' Mia was standing between the two single beds, a locked suitcase perched on each of them. 'What's the story? Will they send someone for the cases?'

'We're staying,' said Britt.

'Huh?' Mia stared at her.

'You heard me. I changed my mind. We're staying. So you can unpack those bags again.'

'You're sure about that?' Mia looked at her enquiringly. 'You won't change your mind back?'

'No,' said Britt.

'And – are we OK?' asked Mia. 'You and me?'

'In what way?'

'What I said? I honestly didn't mean . . .'

'We're fine,' said Britt. 'You're just doing your job. Trying to point things out to me. It's what a good assistant should do.'

'And a good sister too,' said Mia cheerfully, as she unlocked the cases and began hanging clothes in the wardrobes once more.

Chapter 11

Position: at sea.
Weather: partly cloudy. Wind: easterly force 5.
Temperature: 27°. Barometric pressure: 1011.2mb.

Breakfast the following morning was delivered along with the golden envelope containing the next set of clues for the Treasure Hunt. The results would be announced at the Valentine Ball on St Valentine's Night itself, which was the second-last night of the cruise.

'I know you're so not into it, but it's exciting, isn't it?' said Mia as she slit open the envelope. 'What if some guy gets the ring and proposes to his girlfriend in front of everyone!'

Britt shuddered.

'Aw, come on!' Mia looked at her mischievously. 'Don't tell me you wouldn't love it.'

'Are you insane?' asked Britt. 'It's my idea of the wedding proposal from hell.'

'What would be your ideal?' Mia poured coffee as she skimmed through the clues.

Britt shrugged. 'Not to be asked at all.'

Mia looked at her over the sheet of paper. 'You don't have to be like this all the time,' she said mildly.

'It's true,' said Britt. 'I don't want to get married again.'

'So you made a mistake,' agreed Mia. 'But what if you meet someone?'

'You only meet someone if you let yourself get sucked into the whole thing,' said Britt. 'And so, no chance. And before you say anything else, I am perfectly, absolutely one hundred per cent happy with that.'

'OK, OK,' said Mia. 'Right. I'll stop talking about it.' She put the list of clues on the desk. 'I think I'll go looking for the scavenger items.'

'What happens if you win the ring?' Britt looked at her in amusement. 'Will you go down on one knee and ask the Captain to marry you?'

Mia laughed. 'If anyone is sick of romance I'm sure he must be, what with all those on-board weddings,' she said. 'There was another one yesterday, I saw them when I went for my walk around the promenade deck. No,' she added, 'if I win the ring . . . well, it's *we* who'll win it, isn't it? The prize goes to the cabin, after all.'

'On the basis that I'll have no use for it, you can certainly have it,' said Britt.

'In which case, I'll sell it,' said Mia promptly. 'That'll keep me and Allegra happy for a few more months.'

Britt stared at her. 'Are you broke?' she asked.

'Of course not,' replied Mia quickly. 'Just not . . . not rich.'

'But to sell it . . .'

'Hey, listen.' Mia grinned. 'I don't have anyone I want to share it with either. So it'd be a waste. Far better to have the cash.'

Britt frowned as Mia picked up the clue list again. But she didn't say another word.

Mia had expected Britt to spend the morning going through her notes for the talk later in the afternoon, but instead Britt said that she was going to lie out in the sun until her noon hair appointment. Mia, who was feeling restless and not in the mood to lie about, said that she was going to pick up all the scavenger items on today's Treasure Hunt list.

'You can work out the rest of the clues,' she said to Britt, 'while I do the donkey work.'

Britt, eyes closed, waved at her, and Mia trotted along the promenade deck, where many of the other passengers had the same idea in mind. According to the newsletter, there was an ample supply of each item needed, but the cryptic references to them meant that sometimes people were looking for the wrong thing. Mia realised that most of the items were easily found, and she wandered around quite happily picking up *Aphrodite*-logoed goodies throughout the ship.

She bumped into Eileen and John in the café, where they were both drinking creamy lattes and where Eileen was tucking into a slice of chocolate toffee cake.

'I know it's sinful,' said Eileen as she wiped crumbs from her lips. 'But it's so gorgeous I can't help myself. Pippin is disgusted with me. I've put on four pounds in the last few days and I'm starting a strict regime tomorrow.'

'I'm sure I've put on weight too,' admitted Mia. 'But I don't think there's any point in me going on any strict regime until I get off this floating food palace.'

'They're doing a detox programme in the spa,' Eileen told her. 'My aim is to be back to my usual weight less a couple of pounds by the time we get to Acapulco.'

'I'm making no promises to myself,' said Mia as she took one of the café's menus, an item for the scavenger hunt. 'However, if they do a last-day emergency slim-down I might book in.'

'They probably do,' said Eileen.

'I'll ask. Oh, and by the way, Britt said she'd be happy to sign as many books as you like.'

'That's great,' said Eileen. 'I'll stock up so.'

Mia waved at them and continued through the ship, past the photo gallery where the ship's photographer displayed the photographs she'd taken after the formal dinner. The walls of the gallery were crammed with the smiling, slightly sunburned faces of men in tuxedos and women in evening dress. Also displayed were the photographs that had been taken as they arrived at Espada Island. Mia spotted one of herself and Britt, standing on the jetty. Britt looked leggy and elegant in her white sun-dress. While I . . . Mia grimaced . . . I really must learn to do elegant, at least occasionally. My top and shorts might be comfortable but they're not exactly glam, and I make a shocking contrast with the romantic novelist.

And a shocking contrast with Pippin Costello too! (Her modelling name was simply Pippin, Mia had discovered – she'd gone online in the cybercafé and Googled her and followed the link to a tabloid caption, 'What a Pippin!', beside a picture of her in a sexy camisole, her enhanced boobs spilling out of the top.) She looked absolutely amazing standing on the jetty, her swimsuit covered by a multicoloured sarong, one hip slightly forward, making her look even taller and thinner than in real life.

She also spotted Leo Tyler's photograph. He looked uncomfortable posing for the camera, even though the photographer was really good at making everyone appear relaxed and happy. Leo clearly wasn't someone who liked getting his photograph taken, no matter how at ease the photographer tried to make him feel.

She pushed open the door leading to the starboard side of the ship. The air outside was, as always, warmer than the air inside, but the breeze was delightfully refreshing. I can see why people do this, she thought as she allowed air to blow around her face. It feels so damn decadent and carefree. I can see why they like the pampering and the luxury and the feeling of everything being so perfect.

But it's not real life, is it? she murmured to herself. In real life the sun doesn't always shine and the breeze isn't always warm and if you want something you have to do it for yourself. And I'm not the sort of person who can take time off to wander around the Caribbean on cruise ships, whether I look elegant and gorgeous or not.

Before I had Allegra, then I could wander around. Then I *did* wander around! And despite the fact that it was never elegant and gorgeous, it was always great fun. I only had to think about myself and look after myself and I never had to worry about setting a good example or being a good mother. Of course, getting up the duff was hardly setting a good example to anyone, was it? Even if, for a few short hours, it was the most magical thing that ever happened to me.

She rested her elbows on the polished teak of the rail and stared across the sea to the horizon.

She'd got pregnant in Antigua Guatemala. The idea hadn't even occurred to her at first because she'd been having such a great time in the ancient, laid-back city. And then quite suddenly she'd realised that she'd missed two periods. She did sometimes miss one, especially when she was in a new country. But she'd never missed two. Once she'd realised it was possible, she'd bought a pregnancy test. She hadn't really expected it to be positive. In fact she'd half thought of not bothering to take it, having almost convinced herself that the missed periods were due to having caught a bug shortly after arriving in the country, which had left her feeling tired and run down for a while. But when she had – then she'd realised that she was carrying a part of Alejo inside her and that it would be their child, and she suddenly knew what people were talking about when they said that pregnancy could be the very best thing that ever happened to you. She'd wanted to rush out and tell Alejo straight away, but he was off on his trip into the countryside; he was a geologist studying the area around the country's incredible active volcanoes. And so she didn't get to tell him that night because he was spending it away from the cobbled streets and crooked houses and she was on her own, hugging the knowledge close to her.

She went to Riki's bar that evening and salsaed with

Jimmy and Per-Henrik and Clarissa and Vivi and everyone else in the group she was with, but even though she was having fun, it suddenly seemed very juvenile to dance around the tables or down bottles of beer in one go. (She'd told them that she was having a day off from beer and they'd nodded at her, because none of them were heavy drinkers; the atmosphere was far more important to them than the alcohol.) She'd even started singing, she remembered, despite the fact that she hadn't a note in her head and that she'd been unceremoniously dumped from the school choir when Miss McAdams realised it was Mia's voice that was totally wrecking their rendition of 'Panis Angelicus'.

She'd waited for him with such excitement, counting the hours until she could share the news. She'd been scared too of how he might react. But deep down she'd been convinced that he would want their baby. After all, she'd told herself over and over as she'd lain in the narrow bed in the hotel and looked at the moon through the grilles of the window, he loves me and I love him. We're perfect for each other.

We're going to be together for ever.

What a fool I was, she thought now as the breeze, suddenly stronger, whipped a strand of hair across her face and into her eyes, making them sting with tears. I really should have known better.

Because even then I knew that nothing in life is for ever.

There were no Cupids or hearts in the lecture room. Steve Shaw had heeded Britt's request and had removed the fussiest cut-outs. But he'd inflated some more heart-shaped balloons (they were, after all, items for the scavenger hunt), which bobbed merrily at each table.

The men had arrived early and, once again, were sitting with notebooks open in front of them, serious expressions on their faces. The large woman in the kaftan, whose name was Antoinette Bond, also had a notebook open in front of her. In fact, given that today's talk was entitled 'Write Your Perfect Hero', there were a lot of open notebooks and a lot of expectant faces.

Britt and Mia arrived a minute before the talk was due to start. Britt's Brigitte Martin curls tumbled around her face. Her make-up was youthful and light, and today she was wearing a filmy blue dress that clung to her slim body. Mia thought that she looked absolutely stunning, and had considered changing out of her own strappy top and Bermuda shorts into something more sophisticated so that she looked like a professional PA. But she didn't have anything filmy and gorgeous to substitute for them, and besides, she hadn't gone for the detox treatment in the spa, so there would have been rather too much of her for anything filmy to cling to.

It's totally unfair that Britt doesn't have to work at it, she thought. And it's hard not to be jealous of someone who has everything. Even if she is my sister. She slid into her seat while Britt stood at the top of the room and smiled at everyone.

'I do hope you're having a good time on the *Aphrodite*,' she told them. 'Isn't she the most romantic ship in the world?'

Mia opened her eyes in surprise. That hadn't been part of the rehearsal of the talk that Britt had done the previous day.

'I can't help having these moments where I think of Kate Winslet in *Titanic*,' added Britt. 'Though at least we can be fairly confident that we won't hit an iceberg.'

'Now that was a romantic movie,' agreed a woman called Jessica Walton, who'd seen it half a dozen times and still regularly played the soundtrack (much to the irritation of her next-door neighbour, who detested Celine Dion).

'What made it romantic?' asked Britt.

'Leonardo DiCaprio,' said Eileen promptly.

'The doomed nature of the story,' offered Jeremy Smith, the most studious-looking of the men.

'The forbidden love between them,' said Antoinette Bond.

'Probably a mixture of all of those things,' agreed Britt. 'Do you think that all true romances have some obstacles to overcome first?'

This was a much better talk, decided Mia. Britt sounded far more confident, but more than that, she was relaxed with the people who'd come along, laughing and joking with them in a way Mia had never seen her manage before. And they were responding to her, offering more thoughts and ideas than at the previous talk, chatting to her as though they knew her.

Britt and Jacqueline Smith – an intense woman with short black hair and a perpetually aggressive expression – were debating the notion that all the best heroes were tall, dark and handsome when Leo Tyler walked into the room.

'Sorry I'm late,' he said as he looked around for somewhere to sit.

'We're a bit short of seats,' Britt told him. 'But you can take mine and drag it to the side if you like. I'm walking around so I don't need it.'

Leo nodded and pulled the chair so that he was sitting next to Mia. She shot him a small smile and he smiled back at her.

'My absolute favourite hero is Mr Darcy,' said Antoinette. 'He can't be bettered.'

Britt didn't give her own opinion on Mr Darcy, but suggested a few other heroes instead.

'Oh, not Mr Rochester!' she groaned as someone proposed the hero from *Jane Eyre*. 'He locked his wife in the attic, for heaven's sake. I always thought he should have been arrested for cruelty and attempted bigamy. I was devastated when Jane married him and I'm convinced she would have wanted a divorce eventually.'

'Do you want all your heroes to be perfect?' asked Leo.

'Absolutely not,' said Britt. 'Everyone has a flaw.'

'Even your perfect man?' asked Antoinette.

'Jack Hayes has plenty of flaws,' said Britt. 'But he's a good person at heart. I think all of us are prepared to accept flaws once we know that we're loved.' She cleared her throat.

'Who's your personal favourite?' asked Jacqueline.

Britt considered the question while Mia looked at her with interest. Despite Britt's opinion, she was a Mr Darcy fan herself. And she'd loved Mark Darcy in *Bridget Jones's Diary*, too! She liked those strong, silent types. She'd thought Alejo was one of them.

'To be honest . . .' Britt looked a little embarrassed, 'I'm not really a hero person. But when I was about twelve I got a copy of *The Scarlet Pimpernel* out of the library, and I did like the bit where Sir Percy kisses the steps his wife walked on, even though she thinks he hates her.'

'That's carrying things a bit far,' said Eileen.

'He was madly in love with her,' explained Britt. 'But he didn't trust her because he thought she'd betrayed friends to the guillotine.'

'No chance of my husband ever kissing anything I walked on,' remarked a woman at the back of the room. 'We're here to celebrate our tenth wedding anniversary, and so far the most romantic thing he's done is come to the beach with me. He hates the beach, though, so actually from his point of view he's being incredibly nice.'

Britt laughed. 'Some men aren't cut out for romance.' She looked around at the men in the room. 'What d'you think, guys? Are women fools to want it?'

'They don't know what they want.' Jeremy spoke first. 'They want us to give up our seats on the bus or the train, but if we do, they think we're patronising them.'

'That's not true,' Mia piped up. 'I love it when someone lets me sit down on the train!'

'They expect us to second-guess their moods,' said the man sitting beside Jeremy, whose name was Robbie. 'You know, when you're in a bad mood and we ask what's wrong and you say, nothing.'

Everyone laughed. Britt recalled the scene in *The Perfect Man* where Jack Hayes asked that very question. But he'd known what was wrong. He always did. That was why he was perfect.

'You want us to be successful,' said Leo Tyler. 'But when we work hard to achieve that success, you complain that we're never around. And you look for someone else.'

His tone was bitter, and Britt glanced at him with concern. She'd worked really hard to keep the talk light and fun, and she didn't want Leo dragging it down into some kind of serious debate.

'Which is more important?' she asked, thinking on her feet. 'Money or love?'

And Leo's comment was lost in the flurry of answers she received.

Five minutes before the end of the session, Steve Shaw slipped into the room. He'd heard the laughter from outside as he'd walked past and he wanted to see how things were going.

'Well, I don't know about true love,' Brigitte Martin was saying, her blue eyes twinkling, 'but there's nothing like a first date to put a spring in your step. Now, what I want you to do for the next session is write a short piece – five hundred words or so – describing your perfect hero. Or guys, if you prefer, your perfect heroine. If you leave them at the desk in the lobby marked for my attention, I'll have them all read before the next session and we'll talk through them then. Thank you.'

There was a brief round of applause, which made Britt's cheeks redden. She smiled at them all again, though suddenly looking more awkward than she had only a few moments earlier.

Steve Shaw walked up to her.

'That seems to have been very successful,' he said.

'Thank you.'

'So . . . no need for the nerves, then?'

She smiled ruefully. 'Always a need for the nerves. I don't like doing this.'

He looked astonished. 'Why?'

'I'm not comfortable with it.'

'You seemed perfectly comfortable with it to me,' he said.

'That's thanks to Mia.'

'Not really,' Mia protested.

'For sure,' said Britt. 'It's because of her that I made myself think that romance was the most important concept in the world, and talked as though I believed it.'

Steve laughed. 'You don't?'

Mia grinned at him. 'My darling sister thinks it's the biggest con in the history of the universe,' she informed him cheerfully. 'When it comes to romantic gestures, her cynicism knows no bounds.'

'I don't believe that for a second,' said Steve.

'I write fiction.' Britt grinned. 'You can believe whatever you like.'

'I read your book.' Leo Tyler had waited for her outside the room. 'All that one true love stuff – it's all nonsense, you know that, don't you?'

Britt knew that if Leo had made that comment a day earlier she would have agreed with him. But she was buoyed up by the enthusiasm of the people at today's talk and she wasn't in the mood to have her work criticised, especially by a man who seemed to have a chip on his shoulder. Besides, *The Perfect Man* hadn't been about one true love. It had been about finding love. And so she told him that a million or so readers obviously didn't agree with him.

'They're deluded,' said Leo. 'Real life doesn't work out like that book.'

'Nobody said it does,' Britt told him. 'But that doesn't mean you can't enjoy the idea.'

'I can't enjoy anything unless it's grounded in fact,' said Leo.

'In that case, why on earth are you coming to talks about writing fiction?'

'I thought it might give me an insight into the female mind,' said Leo. 'And it did. It showed me that generally speaking it's a bird's nest of incoherent, fanciful notions, which only confirms my suspicions.'

'I don't think my ideas are incoherent,' said Britt. 'Idealistic, maybe. But there's nothing wrong with setting the bar high.'

'Women set it so damn high that it's impossible to reach,' said Leo.

'You know,' she said slowly, 'I think most of us set it far too low. And we allow the wrong man to skip over it and into our hearts and our lives and we live to regret it.'

'Bullshit! What actually happens is that as soon as a woman gets into a relationship, she tries to change the guy to suit her, and when he doesn't change, she starts complaining about the useless man she has.'

'Spare me,' retorted Britt. 'What *really* happens is that

women change their lives for men who won't compromise an inch.'

'How would you know?' demanded Leo. 'You probably sit at home thinking your romantic thoughts and waiting for Mr Right to come along and improve your life.'

'You're unbelievable!' cried Britt. 'I don't sit around and I rarely have romantic thoughts because they were well and truly crushed out of me by my ex-husband! Anyway, don't you dare lecture me about waiting for Mr Right. It's no wonder you're on this cruise alone. No girl could put up with you for more than five minutes.'

'I'd rather be alone than stuck with someone whose head is in the clouds. And your husband is probably ex because no one could live up to your unrealistic ideals,' returned Leo. 'I pity the poor man. I really do!'

Britt's eyes flashed with fury.

'I'm sorry that you seem to dislike women so much,' she said through clenched teeth. 'And even though I know from bitter personal experience that men can be complete and utter shits, that doesn't mean that I tar them all with the same brush. Which is just as well, or I'd think that you were the rudest, most ignorant male I'd ever met in my entire life. And given that I've met a lot, that's putting you at the top of a very tall heap!'

Then she turned on her heel and strode down the corridor, Mia, stunned into silence, following behind her.

Chapter 12

Position: Panama Canal, Panama.
Weather: partly cloudy. Wind: light airs. Temperature:
30°. Barometric pressure: 1010.1mb.

When his alarm clock went off the following morning – early, because it was the day that the cruise ship was scheduled to enter the first of the three locks that would take them through the Panama Canal – Leo's first thought wasn't of the journey at all but of the harsh words he'd exchanged with Brigitte Martin after her talk the previous day. He was annoyed that he was thinking about it, because he'd been pleased that finally something other than romance had been given the status of most exciting day on board and had been eagerly awaiting the Panama transit. But it was being overshadowed by his uneasiness about their argument.

Of course she'd deserved a bit of a hard time, peddling her nonsensical ideas about heroes and heroines to gullible people. She knew it was nonsense too – she was divorced, for heaven's sake. (And no, he didn't blame the poor guy, whoever he was. It must have been hell waking up every morning to someone whose standards were utterly unattainable.)

Still, perhaps it had been a bit much to attack her in the way he had, especially the personal jibe about her husband. That hadn't been fair. Perhaps he'd been a bit harsh about her book too which, loath though he was to admit it, was actually quite moving, even if it was ridiculously idealistic.

Nevertheless, she was used to criticism, he told himself as he drained his cup and realised that they were approaching the first lock. She probably hadn't given it a second thought. He was the one being soft centred. Which was not in his game plan for the rest of his life at all.

Britt had also set her alarm to go off early, but she'd actually woken up about fifteen minutes before it. Her thoughts too had turned to the clash with Leo. She hadn't particularly expected him to like *The Perfect Man* (although thousands of men apparently did), but she'd been taken aback by his obvious disillusionment about love and women in general. She'd always thought that she was the most cynical person in the universe when it came to romance. Yet Leo was far, far worse. And she had been hurt when he'd told her that he sympathised with Ralph. It wasn't that people in the past hadn't sympathised with him (even though none of them knew the intimate details of their relationship), but it was a bit much when people who didn't know him at all were on his side!

She was still thinking about Leo when the alarm began

to ring and she reached out quickly to silence it. Then she pushed all thoughts of their argument firmly out of her mind as she wrapped her robe around her and walked out on to the balcony.

The ship was at the beginning of the locks and the entire area was a hive of activity as the vessel prepared to make the first stage of its transit.

'Mia,' she called. 'This is just amazing. Come out!'

Mia pushed back the covers, reflecting that when she was first up she always tiptoed around the cabin so as not to wake her sister. But Britt had clattered around the place, clearly determined to get her up. Maybe that was the difference between them. When Britt was absorbed in something, she expected everyone else to be enthusiastic too, but Mia never expected other people to share her interests.

When she stepped on to the balcony, Mia gasped. The sides of the *Aphrodite* were mere inches away from the walls of the lock and she could see the ship rising along with the water level.

'I hope our captain knows what he's doing,' she said edgily. 'We're awfully close to those walls!'

'I presume he didn't get to be a captain by ramming his ship into locks,' Britt told her. 'But goodness, I didn't realise it was going to be such a tight fit.' She leaned further over the rail. Ahead of them, and through the lock, she could see the stern of the vessel that had passed through before them.

'Isn't it amazing, though?' she said. 'And not just the canal – everything!'

Mia had to agree. All the places they'd stopped at until now had been delightfully tropical in a picture-postcard kind of way. But the green mountains of Panama, emerging from the swirling early-morning mist, were majestic and awe-inspiring.

A knock at the cabin door was followed by their steward with the usual breakfast tray of fruit and croissants.

'Fantastic, isn't it?' he said as he put the tray on their table.

'Amazing.'

'I do this trip every year,' said the steward. 'But every time is just as exciting. When we go through the Miraflores locks, there'll be lots of people waiting to see us because it has a visitor centre there. They wave and cheer as we go through.'

'Cool. I've always wanted to be the centre of attention,' said Mia happily.

'The photographers will get off the ship later and take photographs,' the steward told her. 'And you'll need to find yours for the Treasure Hunt.' He winked broadly at them as he handed them an envelope with the day's clues. 'Also,' he added, 'keep your cameras ready for the lakes. You can see crocs there.'

'You're joking.' Mia's eyes widened.

'No,' he said. 'Real crocs. Big fat mamas. The lake is about forty miles wide and there are lots of small islands on it. The crocs sunbathe on them.'

'Sunbathing crocodiles! You're kidding me.' Britt laughed. 'Any other wildlife we should look out for?'

'There are lectures all day on the ship about everything

to do with the canal and the area around it,' the steward said. 'You should go if you're interested. They're in the Panorama Lounge.'

Spurred on by thoughts of crocodiles and treasure, the sisters ate their breakfast quickly. Then they got dressed and made their way to the crowded promenade deck, from where they could get a better view of proceedings.

While the big ship negotiated the lock, every passenger was on deck watching intently. But as it entered the lake, they filtered off to various pursuits. It was hot and humid on the still water, and the cooling sea breezes that had been with them for the journey until now had disappeared. The tops of trees that had grown long before the man-made lake had flooded the area poked incongruously through the water, used as perches by the many birds that swooped through the sky, which was still covered by a thin layer of high cloud.

'I'm going to sit here and listen to my iPod for a while,' said Mia. 'And I'll go through the Treasure Hunt clues while I'm at it. I have the info leaflet and I'm sure that'll give me the answers to most of them.'

'You don't mind if I leave you, then?' asked Britt. 'They're showing a DVD in the Panorama Lounge about the construction of the canal, and I thought I'd go and watch.'

'You're a freak, Britt McDonagh,' said Mia. 'You studied ancient history, you work in law, you wrote a book about love, and now you're interested in mechanics.'

'I prefer to think of myself as well rounded.' Britt grinned at her.

'Um. Yeah. Still freaky,' Mia told her. 'But off you go and be mechanical! Take the other copy of the clues with you so's you can answer them if a specialised nugget of information comes your way.'

Britt nodded at her and wandered slowly to the lounge. The Panorama was the *Aphrodite*'s biggest bar, with comfortable leather tub chairs and low glass tables dotted around the room. But its main feature was the wraparound windows that gave an impressive 360-degree view. Many of the passengers had already bagged themselves window seats and were gazing outside, while another cluster stood beside a cut-out model of the canal and listened to a dark-haired man – Miguel Hernandez, according to his name tag – explain exactly how the locks worked. Britt nodded in recognition at people who had been at her talks. Leo Tyler was standing at the edge of the group, intent on the model of the lock and not looking around him.

'Captain Henderson has transited the canal half a dozen times in each direction.' Steve Shaw was standing beside Miguel and answered a question from a passenger. 'So there's no real danger that he'll make a mess of it. And, of course, the canal company employees make sure that the ship maintains the correct position in the locks.'

'Has anyone ever swum through it?' Britt asked suddenly.

Steve looked up and smiled at her. 'Miss Martin,' he said. 'How nice to see you here. I hope you're enjoying our transit. Actually, yes, a number of people have swum the canal, but obviously the canal authority doesn't like it. Shipping has priority and there are health and safety reasons why you wouldn't want to swim it.'

'What sort?' asked a burly man wearing a T-shirt with a logo from the Mexican city of Acapulco on the front. (Britt and Mia had remarked one evening that there was a lot of one upmanship on the T-shirt front, generated by people wearing shirts from places that the cruise ship hadn't yet been, and so proclaiming themselves as seasoned travellers or repeat passengers.)

'Well, the water for one thing,' said Steve. 'This is a tropical area and there's a chance of picking up something nasty. So you'd want to have some typhoid injections, for example. And perhaps have taken malaria tablets too. A guy called Albert Oshiver did the swim in twenty-nine hours back in 1962. A lot fewer ships in the way then, though. Mind you, he still had to pay a toll.'

'Do we?' asked Leo.

'Pay a toll?' Steve nodded. 'A ship like ours, the charge is over two hundred and fifty thousand dollars.'

'I suppose that's added to our fare,' said one of the female passengers, a stick-thin woman draped in gold jewellery.

'Just as well we don't ask you for it on the day,' said Steve cheerfully.

Miguel Hernandez told them that he was going to play the DVD about the original construction of the canal, and the passengers settled into their seats. Leo indicated the chair beside Britt.

'Do you mind if I sit here?' he asked.

She glanced at him warily. 'You can sit wherever you like,' she said, returning her look to the screen.

'Um. Yes. I . . . I wanted to apologise to you,' he said

awkwardly. 'After your talk. I was way out of line when I spoke to you.'

Britt was surprised. She hadn't expected an apology from Leo. She didn't think he was the sort of man to make them.

'No apology necessary. You're perfectly entitled to hate my book, and I'm sure you have your reasons for thinking the way you do about everything else.' Britt spoke quietly as she continued to watch the screen, which was showing jerky black-and-white newsreel of the early construction work.

'As I'm sure you have your reasons for thinking that I'm at the top of your heap of men who are complete bastards. I'm sorry you seem to know so many!'

She glanced at him again, but he was facing the screen.

'I don't think all men are bastards,' she said softly. 'But I've met a few.'

'And I don't think all women are conniving and betraying, either,' said Leo.

'But you've met a few?' This time she turned around to look at him properly.

'I'm sure we've all . . .' He shrugged. 'It's not important. I know the difference between fiction and real life. I guess I was just pissed off at the fact that in fiction things always work out.'

'Not always.'

'They did in your book.'

'Depends on your point of view.'

'It worked out the way I wanted,' admitted Leo.

'I hope that's a good thing.'

'Jack's a real hero,' said Leo. 'But that's just bullshit.'

'We all have to have heroes,' said Britt.

'I hate the fact that you think there can be a perfect anyone,' said Leo.

'I honestly don't,' she said. 'But people can be perfect for each other. Everyone on the ship wants to believe that.'

'That's because they're under the cosh of this bloody Valentine Cruise,' said Leo.

'Why did you come on it,' she asked, 'if it's not your thing?'

'It wasn't my idea.' His face was grim.

'Wouldn't have been my choice either,' she said, but he was staring straight ahead, looking intently at the screen. She realised that he didn't want to talk any more. She glanced at him again and thought, quite suddenly, that he should be her ideal hero, what with his mistrust of anything to do with romance. And then she laughed at herself for even considering it.

When the DVD ended and Miguel had answered some more questions about the canal, Leo turned to Britt again.

'Even though you say you don't need an apology for yesterday, I really am sorry,' he said. 'And to be honest, I actually enjoyed the book despite your perfect hero guy.'

'Thank you,' she said. 'If I offended you . . .' she grinned suddenly, 'or if he offended you in any way, I apologise too.'

'OK. That's cleared up then.' He looked at her awkwardly for a moment and then nodded briefly. 'See you around.'

'See you.'

She watched as he walked along the deck. As he reached

the stairs, he looked back at her and smiled briefly before turning away again.

She felt a sudden hollow feeling in the pit of her stomach. For a split second the expression in his eyes had reminded her of the way Ralph had first looked at her that day in Trinity College. And she felt now exactly as she had done then. As though she had just seen the most important man in the world. She swallowed hard and then turned away abruptly to stare out over the lake.

But she didn't see the glint of the sun on the still water. Nor did she see the tropical foliage of the islands within the lake. All she could see was a picture of herself, standing beside Ralph. And all she could think of was how she'd fallen in love with him. For no other reason than the fact that he'd smiled at her just like that. It was the single craziest thing that had ever happened to her, and it had led to the single craziest thing she'd ever done in her life.

Nowadays she thought she'd had some kind of brain-storm. That she'd lost complete control of her senses. She couldn't understand, when she thought back on it, why she'd wanted to marry him, why she simply hadn't moved in with him instead so that she could have moved out again without any hassle. But she'd wanted him. And she'd wanted him to be hers.

'We'll be perfect together,' he'd said to her on the night he had proposed in a stylish and ridiculously expensive restaurant, the ring brought to her on a dessert plate by a smiling waiter who had accompanied it with a bottle of champagne. For the briefest of moments she'd wondered what on earth would happen if she turned Ralph down, but of course she hadn't wanted to turn him down; why would she, when his proposal was so wonderful and great and made her feel like all those princesses in the stories Paula used to read to them when they were children? And so she'd said yes and they'd got married and it had all gone downhill from there.

Mia had solved half of the twenty clues on the list by the time she went to the lunchtime buffet. Even though she got there early, there were already plenty of people waiting for them to start serving.

We're like locusts, thought Mia. A hint of food and we're there straight away. And the funny thing is . . . she grabbed a plate and napkin and joined the queue that had begun to form . . . I'm absolutely starving again! I had a great breakfast a few hours ago, but I'm ravenous now. And I really can't say that it's being out in the fresh air that's doing it, because it's so hot and sticky today. She brushed a drop of perspiration from her forehead with the back of her hand. No, I have to admit to myself that I'm totally devoid of willpower when it comes to the food on board. Tomorrow, she added mentally, tomorrow I'll start that detox thingy in the spa!

'Hello there.' Eileen and John Costello joined her in the queue. 'Having a good time?'

She nodded. 'It was very exciting going through the lock, wasn't it?'

'Though this bit isn't much,' said John.

'Oh, I don't know.' Mia looked across the lake towards the jade-green mountains as they swept down to the water. 'I think it's spectacular. Sort of primeval, really.'

'For a while,' agreed Eileen. 'But we're spending hours on this lake.'

'Have you seen any crocs yet?'

Eileen looked startled, and Mia told her what the steward had said.

'We must look out for them!' John looked enthusiastic. 'I might win the prize for the best photo of the trip if I get a good one of a croc.'

'I'm going for the diamond ring myself!' Mia laughed.

'Are you doing well on the Treasure Hunt?' asked Eileen. 'The clues are very difficult.'

'Well, I'm managing some of them,' said Mia. 'And of course Britt is getting others.'

'And where is our famous author?' Eileen looked around her. 'I have to make an arrangement with her to sign the books for me.'

'She's gone to one of the lectures. But if you give me the books, I'll get her to sign them for you, no problem.'

'Oh, I'll wait till I see her. She's fearsomely studious behind that lovely warm exterior, isn't she?' asked Eileen. 'You must be totally intimidated by her.'

'Well . . .'

'After all, she's so beautiful and so talented! It doesn't seem fair, does it?'

Mia blinked rapidly. 'No,' she said uncomfortably. 'It doesn't. But Britt's very . . .' Very what? she wondered. Very kind? Very nice? Very modest? Very difficult could be a more appropriate expression, she thought, and instantly felt bad about it. Britt had been doing her best over the last few days to be warm and generous and easy to get along with. And in fact she *had* been easy to get on with. Most of the time.

'Very motivated,' she finished. 'She's a perfectionist.' Which was definitely true.

'I wish I had her talent. I bet you do too,' said Eileen.

'Ah, I'm grand,' Mia told her easily. 'I have plenty of talents of my own!'

Although, she thought, as she brought her food to a table for two, unless it's eating for Ireland, I'm really not sure what on earth they are.

They saw the crocodiles later in the day. Britt had arrived for lunch just as Mia was about to dig into an enormous slice of blueberry pie. She'd obviously given off 'do not disturb' signals while she ate, because although there were plenty of people milling around for lunch, nobody asked if they could share her table. Which was why Britt was able to drop down into the empty seat beside her.

'Did you have an interesting morning?' Mia asked, realising that she was feeling peeved at her sister simply because Eileen had been so effusive about her, triggering memories of the times in school when the teachers had wondered why she couldn't be a bit more like Britt and pay attention in class. She'd harboured dark thoughts about her older sister then, wishing that just for once she'd fail an exam or forget to do her homework so that there would be a chink in her perfect armour. And although she'd lost the niggling resentment of her childhood, she knew that it still surfaced, as it had today, from time to time when someone praised Britt too much. I'm a horrible person, she thought, pushing the pie to one side. And I shouldn't eat this. It'll just make me a horrible fat person.

Britt, conscious of a certain strain in Mia's tone, simply replied that everything to do with the transit was interesting.

'Did you get answers to any of the clues?'

'D'you know, I forgot all about that,' said Britt contritely. She hadn't been able to concentrate on anything with the unexpected emotions that Leo's smile had ignited in her and the subsequent thoughts of Ralph crowding her head, but she wasn't going to say that to Mia, who was looking at her hopefully.

And why wouldn't you forget about it? Mia was thinking as she looked at her sister. Sure, haven't you got enough money to buy the ring in the first place? It doesn't mean anything to you. She was utterly disgusted at herself for the thought but quite unable to stop herself thinking it.

'I'm sorry,' said Britt. 'I was caught up in the presentation, and then Leo . . .'

'Leo what?' Mia looked at her quizzically, her irritation forgotten. She'd been taken aback by the spat between her sister and the normally taciturn Leo and afterwards had suggested that Britt might want to apologise to him. Britt had looked at her as though she was cracked and told her that apologising to dickheads wasn't in her life plan and that if anyone should be saying sorry it was Leo himself, the arrogant shit. Mia hadn't known what to say after that. 'Leo what?' she repeated.

'Oh, he apologised,' said Britt shortly. She took the list out of her white canvas bag and skimmed through it. 'They answered that one! And that!' She filled in the information about the toll for the ship and the name of the person who'd swum the canal in 1962, and she also filled in the name of the first ship to have passed through it.

'How did Leo apologise?' asked Mia.

'By saying sorry, of course.' Britt shrugged and looked at the list again. 'So we're only left with the country that uses the canal most. And the names of two of the Panama Canal Authority tugboats.'

'What made him do that?'

'Huh?'

'Apologise. What made him?'

'I presume he realised that he'd been unbelievably rude.'

'You were a bit rude yourself.'

'I apologised too,' said Britt. 'You were right, I was a touch out of turn. Just as well you're here to keep me on the straight and narrow. Maybe we'll find the tugboats at the next lock.'

'Britt!' Mia was swamped by a desire to know what had happened with Leo. Britt was being suspiciously casual about it, and Mia couldn't help feeling that there was more to it than that.

'Nothing else.' Britt put down the clues and looked at Mia. 'He apologised. I accepted. I apologised. After all, he's a passenger and I'm sort of employed on this trip, so I thought I'd better be nice. He accepted my apology too. So all is well.'

'Did he—'

'What's with all these questions?' Britt interrupted her impatiently. 'We were both perfectly pleasant to each other, that's all. Give it a rest, for heaven's sake.'

'All right,' said Mia after a moment in which Britt picked

up and studied the sandwich menu as though she'd never seen it before.

When Britt was finished eating, Mia closed the paper she'd been reading and smiled at her.

'Want to go and look for tugboats?'

They didn't see any tugboats, but it was then they saw the two crocodiles basking lazily in the sun, which had by now burned away the earlier haze.

'Mobile handbags,' murmured Britt as she watched one flick its tail and then move with surprising speed into the water.

'They sure are ugly!'

'I think they're magnificent.'

Both girls turned around to see Leo, who was looking at the crocs through a pair of binoculars.

'Not as magnificent as a lovely bag,' said Mia.

'You can't mean that.' Leo looked scandalised.

'Well, no, to be honest,' she admitted. 'I've never had a crocodile-skin anything in my life.'

'I wouldn't want to,' Leo said.

'Are you coming to dinner tonight?' asked Mia suddenly. 'We've decided to do the whole formal thing.'

'Oh, I don't know.' Leo let the binoculars hang around his neck. 'I'm not really into it, and—'

'Neither am I,' Mia assured him. 'I'm probably going to be a huge failure in the formal stakes. I don't do elegant and gorgeous and my dress isn't really up to scratch, but I'm giving it a try tonight. So should you. Otherwise that tux will go to waste.'

Leo looked hesitant.

'Oh do!' cried Mia. She glanced at Britt and then back at Leo. 'Look, why don't we all go to dinner together? Make the dresses and the tux worthwhile.'

Britt frowned at Mia. 'I don't—'

'We could meet in the Troy Bar first and eat around seven thirty,' suggested Mia before Britt could finish her sentence.

'Leo might have his own plans,' said Britt.

'I . . .' Leo shrugged. 'I hadn't thought about it either way, to be honest.'

'You surely don't want to eat alone?' Mia asked.

'Would you stop trying to organise people?' said Britt.

'It's my job to be an organiser on this trip,' said Mia. 'That's what you told me, Britt. So that's what I'm doing. And I'm asking Leo to join us because it would be nice to have someone else to talk to besides ourselves every evening. And because I'd like you to, of course,' she added hastily as she looked at Leo.

'I didn't realise I was boring you so much,' said Britt drily.

'You're not,' said Mia. 'But . . .'

'OK,' Leo said. 'The bar at seven. See you then.' And he strode across the deck.

'What was all that about?' Britt demanded. 'Practically forcing him to agree to join us?'

'He's on his own,' Mia said. 'I thought it was a nice thing to do.'

'Yes, but . . .'

'But what? You said he apologised to you and you

apologised to him. We're all slightly out of it on this ship. And I think he's lonely.' She looked at Britt challengingly.

'But . . . Oh, it's nothing. I'm going for a walk around the deck.'

And Mia was left staring after her as Britt began striding in the opposite direction to the one that Leo Tyler had taken.

Chapter 13

Position: at sea.
Weather: partly cloudy. Wind: north-westerly force 2.
Temperature: 29°. Barometric pressure: 1010.5mb.

In the end, though, it wasn't dinner for three.

Mia and Britt met Leo in the Troy Bar, which was already crowded with people having pre-dinner drinks. The bar was glittering and buzzy, the music from the piano barely audible over the hum of excited conversation, while the ship's photographer was busy taking portrait shots of glammed-up passengers beside the elaborate floral arrangement at the bottom of the winding glass staircase.

Because of the fact that it was a formal evening, Britt had gone to the hairdresser's again and was in her full-on Brigitte look. She was glad to discover that seeing Leo this time didn't send her stomach churning. It had obviously been a one-off reminder of Ralph. (Not, she argued to herself, that reminders of Ralph should really do anything other than make it churn in rage!)

'You look like a completely different person when your hair is like that,' he observed as he handed her a cocktail.

'Yeah, I know.'

'It's nice. But it suits you better straight,' said Leo, which made both Britt and Mia look at him in surprise.

'Why don't you both pose for a photo?' suggested Mia brightly.

'Are you mad?' asked Britt. 'No thanks.'

Leo shook his head too.

It would have been a glamorous photo, thought Mia. Leo looked very distinguished in his tux and Britt, no matter how much she might dislike getting dolled up, was extremely elegant in her silver-grey dress edged with sequins, perfectly matching shoes on her dainty feet. She had told Mia, as they'd got ready earlier, that it was her most expensive dress, the one she'd bought for the last awards dinner, when Meredith had told her that glamour was essential. Mia herself had chosen her favourite purple chiffon, which suited her colouring but wasn't as obviously expensive as Britt's. Probably much more comfortable, she told herself as she watched her sister adjust the sequinned straps of her dress, while Leo looked past her towards the photographer.

Mia frowned. Something had happened between Britt and Leo, she was certain of it. She didn't know what and she didn't know whether it mattered. But she'd never seen her sister looking so ill at ease, not even at her workshops.

After their cocktails they made their way to the restaurant. It too was more crowded than usual and they frowned at the lack of available tables.

'Mia!' Eileen Costello, seated at a large round table near the window, waved to her. 'Come and join us. You're very welcome.'

Mia looked doubtfully between Britt and Leo.

'There aren't any other free tables at the moment. Not for two or three, anyway,' said Britt as she rapidly scanned the room. 'We can leave it if you like.'

'Do you mind where we sit?' Britt asked Leo.

'Well . . .'

'Leo!' Pippin stood up beside her mother. 'Over here.'

'We can't really refuse to join them,' said Leo.

'In that case . . .' Mia led them to Eileen's table. As well as Eileen, John and Pippin there was another couple at the table, who Eileen introduced as Judy and Hector. 'They were the first couple married on board this trip,' said Eileen proudly.

'It was wonderful,' said Judy, a woman in her late thirties. 'Captain Henderson was lovely.'

'Judy, I know you haven't been to the lectures because you're far too busy.' Eileen beamed at her. 'But this is the lovely Brigitte Martin. You know. The author.'

'I read your book,' said Judy. 'It was brilliant.'

'Thank you.'

'And her sister Mia,' added Eileen. 'And this wonderful gentleman is Leo. He's on his own on this trip so we're doing our best to keep him from feeling lonely.'

Leo shook hands with Judy and Hector.

'We thought they were all the one family at first,' said Eileen as they all sat down. 'But they said no.'

'Which is a good thing really.' Pippin beamed at Leo, showing her perfectly capped dazzling white teeth.

'Good evening, ladies and gentlemen.' Their steward arrived and the conversation turned to the dinner menu.

As soon as they had finished ordering, Eileen began to talk about famous people she'd met – *other* famous people, she said with a sideways smile at Britt. She was on first-name terms with a well-known Dublin newsreader as well as a radio presenter and a celebrity chef. 'But you're the sweetest of them all,' she said triumphantly to Britt.

Britt smiled politely and rearranged her cutlery while Mia stifled a fit of the giggles and then mouthed, 'Sweet! You!' at her. Eileen was being particularly silly tonight, showing off in front of Hector and Judy and generally dominating the dinner table, while Pippin occasionally interrupted her and added stories about the Dublin social scene as well as her ambitions about her future career.

'I'm thinking of writing a book myself,' she informed Britt. 'As part of building up my profile. That's why I've been coming to your talks. They're very useful.'

'I'm glad to hear that,' Britt replied. 'What are you going to write?'

'Fiction,' said Pippin. 'Well, why not? You've made me realise how easy it could be. Of course my real aim is to get into TV and maybe even the movies. I'd love to have my own perfume and clothes line as well. But that'll take time.'

'Writing a book will take time too,' Britt told her.

'Sure, but I can do it whenever I've got a spare moment,' said Pippin cheerfully.

'And have you decided what it's going to be about?' asked Mia.

'I thought perhaps it could be about a model who meets a gorgeous stranger on a cruise liner,' Pippin replied.

'I suppose you've got lots of inspiration here,' said Britt.

'Absolutely!' Pippin beamed at Leo again.

'I hope you meet a gorgeous stranger, in that case,' he said, and everyone laughed. Leo himself didn't look entirely at ease, even though he smiled at Pippin. Was he interested in her? Mia wondered. It was hard to tell. Leo was a difficult man to read. Which was why she'd thought, early on, that he and Britt were made for each other. Which was why she'd been so intrigued by whatever had passed between them. Clearly, though, it hadn't been that important. Neither of them had spoken to each other during the meal at all. So perhaps he would be a lot happier with the delectable Pippin.

'What made you decide to get married on board the ship?' Mia asked Judy during a momentary lull in the conversation.

'Second marriage for me,' said Judy. 'I'd done the big white wedding thing before and I didn't want to do it again. This worked just fine.'

'We wanted to make it a day just for us,' said Hector. He smiled at his wife. 'And it was.'

'So!' cried Eileen. 'A toast to Judy and Hector.'

'Judy and Hector,' repeated everyone obediently as they raised their glasses to the newly-weds.

'*A toast to Britt and Ralph! The bride and groom.*'

She remembered her father making it and she remembered everyone raising their glasses and she remembered thinking that her life had changed for ever and that she was the luckiest person in the whole world. She'd found her perfect man and she'd married him and nobody could be happier than she was that night. She remembered the fact that she'd had those thoughts and that there hadn't been a hint of irony in them; that she'd really and truly believed them.

She remembered, too, Ralph's speech. It had been the most wonderful speech she'd ever heard in her life. He'd called her his one true love and the light that lit up his world, and his voice, deep and rich, had held the guests spellbound. For the voice alone, Britt had thought, he was worth marrying. She could have listened to him for hours.

After their divorce she'd actually counted the number of hours they'd lived together as man and wife. Five thousand nine hundred and twenty-eight. Give or take an hour or two. About five thousand seven hundred and sixty too many.

'*A toast to Mia and Alejo!*'

Per-Henrik had made it sometime before Alejo had left them for his trip to the volcanoes. Mia closed her eyes as the memory flooded back. They'd been toasted for doing a very dirty tango together in the bar. It had been noisy and raunchy and the crowd had clapped their approval as they'd moved across the wooden floor. She remembered the desire that had surged through her then, her hot body pressed close to Alejo's. She remembered thinking that she wanted the moment to last for ever. She remembered thinking that she was in love and that it was the most wonderful feeling in the world.

'*A toast to Vanessa and Leo.*'

Donal had proposed the toast the day they'd announced their engagement. Actually it was a few days later, Leo corrected himself; they'd had a party then, because Vanessa loved parties. She'd worked in PR and she was forever looking out for spectacular ideas for celebrations. It was because the engagement party had been so massive that Leo had broached the subject of something a little more low-key for the wedding. But Vanessa had laughed at him and told him that a girl's wedding day was the most high-key thing she'd ever do in her life and that hers would be no different. And for the honeymoon, she'd said, she had the perfect plan.

It was a lifetime ago, he thought. It was hard to believe that he was the same person who'd kissed the back of her smooth neck and lain beside her in their double bed, and who'd loved her more than anyone else in the whole world. And who hadn't realised that loving her simply wasn't enough.

'Hey, over there!' Eileen clicked her fingers so that Britt, Mia and Leo all snapped out of their daydreams.

'I'm sorry,' said Mia, tucking in to her chicken terrine. 'I guess I was thinking how lucky you are, Hector and Judy.'

'I know we are,' said Judy. 'I didn't think I'd ever find someone like Heck. Especially after my first attempt at being married. I made such a bad choice! But it's great to find the right person. Don't you think?' She turned to Britt and smiled.

'Absolutely.' Britt nodded but kept her eyes on her plate.

'So is there anyone in your life, Leo?' asked Pippin brightly.

'Not right now.' His face flushed.

'This is the time and the place,' she told him. 'Gorgeous cruise ship. Nights under the stars . . .'

'I can't imagine anyone meets their future partner on a cruise,' said Leo. 'So it won't work in your novel.'

'We actually met on a cruise,' said Judy. 'That's also part of the reason we got married on the *Aphrodite*.'

'Oh?' Leo looked defeated.

'Yes. On this ship. The year before last.'

'How romantic!' sighed Mia, while Britt groaned softly beside her.

Judy grinned. 'Isn't it? Although it wasn't the Valentine Cruise that time. Still, we thought it would be nice to celebrate this way.'

'It's all so lovely!' Eileen smiled at them all. 'And you never do know when love will strike. Do you, Mia? Brigitte? Leo? Pippin?'

'I think we do,' said Britt. 'At least in my case, and in Mia's, I think we can safely say that we absolutely do.'

'Maybe you'll change your mind before the cruise is over, Leo,' said Pippin cheerfully. 'Maybe you'll find someone after all.'

'I can't . . .' Leo looked up at her. Her eyes were sparkling and her smile dimpled her smooth cheeks. She reminded him of Vanessa before it had all gone so terribly wrong. How she'd once looked at him. He swallowed hard. 'It's a long shot,' he said finally. 'I don't think I'm looking for anyone.'

'Oh, everyone's looking,' Pippin told him. 'They just don't always admit it.' And she smiled again as she refilled his glass from the wine bottle in the centre of the table.

After dinner, the Costellos said they were going to the theatre to watch the nightly show.

Pippin linked her arm in Leo's and told him that he had to come, it would be great, but he said he wasn't mad about the singer and so he'd give the show a miss and no doubt he'd see Pippin and her parents later on.

Pippin squeezed his arm and said that she hoped so; they'd probably come back to the Panorama and hopefully they'd see him there. Once again he was reminded of Vanessa and the way she used to organise him, and the way he liked her to organise him because he wasn't good at being social.

After the Costellos had headed to the theatre, Mia suggested that she, Britt and Leo have a drink in the Terrace Bar.

'It's so nice there at night,' she said. 'It makes me feel glamorous and elegant in a *Titanic* sort of way.'

Britt laughed and Leo smiled.

'Terrace it is so,' said Mia. 'Let's go.'

It was enchanting, thought Britt, as they sat at a table outside the bar, if moonlit nights overlooking the vast expanse of the Pacific Ocean was the sort of setting that enchanted you. Actually, it was impossible to feel totally cynical about it, she conceded, because it truly was lovely.

Mia and Leo were talking about the transit through the canal, Leo sounding more animated than Britt had ever heard him before.

Why is he on his own here? she wondered. She could perfectly understand why a single person would decide to go on a cruise – there was so much to do and so many people to meet that you wouldn't have to be alone unless you chose to be – but this particular cruise wasn't one for the singleton. And why, she asked herself, her mind wandering off in another direction, did the term singleton seem to apply only to women? Why did it also sound slightly sad and lonely? There wasn't really an equivalent word for men. Bachelor was old fashioned, and anyway sounded more carefree than lonely. And of course rich single men were still seen as a good catch.

Was Leo a good catch? She'd thought he was well off because of the Delphi suite, but somehow he didn't strike her as fabulously wealthy. In her experience, fabulously wealthy men usually let you know about it sooner rather than later. (Unless they were fighting a divorce settlement, in which case they liked to pretend to be impoverished. Although they were never very good at it. Being poor wasn't alpha enough for a wealthy man.) So maybe Leo wasn't rolling in it but still had enough to be able to bag the second most expensive suite on the ship. Comfortably off, she decided. But lonely? That was harder to decide. Why was he on the Valentine Cruise by himself? Her thoughts returned to her original question. Some kind of pilgrimage, she thought suddenly. Maybe in honour of a girlfriend. Perhaps he'd come on this cruise before with someone who'd meant something to him, only now . . .

'. . . don't you think?' Mia's question startled her out of her daydream, and Britt looked at her in irritation. She'd been enjoying thinking up a story for Leo, making up a life for him.

'Don't I think what?' she asked.

'That getting married on board is quite a good idea if you don't want the whole big white wedding palaver?'

'You're talking about weddings?' Britt looked at her sister and Leo incredulously.

'Yes,' said Mia. 'We were saying how sweet Judy and Hector were and how this was a good idea for them.'

'I suppose so,' said Britt.

'You seem remarkably uninterested in all the weddings, for someone who makes a living writing about them,' said Leo.

'There isn't a wedding in *The Perfect Man*,' Britt pointed out.

'True,' conceded Leo.

'Getting married is so often the end of a good romance,' Britt told him, a sudden mischievous look on her face. 'In more ways than one.'

'Do you think so?'

'She's got lots of experience,' said Mia. She leaned forward to put her glass on the teak table, and then shrieked as she misjudged it and ended up with half a mojito on her lap. 'Bloody hell!'

'Are you all right?' asked Britt.

'I'm fine,' said Mia. 'But my posh frock is ruined.' She stood up. 'I'll go and change,' she told them. 'If I get down to the cabin now, I might get it into tonight's laundry.'

'Hang on until I finish this and I'll go with you.' Britt indicated her own drink.

'Oh, don't rush it,' said Mia. 'I'll be back later. You stay there.' And before Britt could protest, she headed back towards their cabin.

After she'd gone, Britt and Leo sat in silence. Britt realised that she hadn't contributed very much to the earlier conversation and now she was trying to think of something interesting to say. She was also a little embarrassed about the fact that she'd been making up stories about Leo's life and his reason for being on board the *Aphrodite*. Embarrassed too at how her stomach had fluttered at the sight of him earlier, though thankfully it had now stopped and she was glad that she seemed to have got over whatever had sparked it in the first place.

Maybe his reason for coming on the cruise had been to find someone. After all, he'd spent far too much time staring at Pippin Costello than was really necessary all during dinner. But then it had been hard not to. Pippin had been wearing a gold lamé dress slashed to the navel as well as gold sandals and a selection of gold jewellery, and her hair had been piled high on her head in a tottering beehive. Britt had thought the whole thing way over the top, but obviously from Leo's point of view it had its attractions.

Although what would I know about attractive looks? she

asked herself. After all, I'm the romantic novelist who doesn't do romance. How would I know what attracts a man? It's not as though my life has been littered with conquests. There's been no one of consequence since Ralph. A few awful dates with men who bored me to tears, that's all. How pathetic can I be?

She squeezed her eyes shut, then opened them again. Not pathetic at all, she reminded herself. Perfectly rational, in fact. There was no point in trying to find someone serious. All relationships were ultimately doomed to failure.

The sound of laughter floating on the night air brought her back to the present, and once again she felt the need to say something – anything – to the man beside her.

'Have you—'

'Are you—'

They both broke the silence at the same time.

'You first,' said Leo.

'I was just going to ask if you've ever been on a cruise before,' said Britt. 'It's a kind of lame question, though.'

Leo shook his head. 'Not really my thing. Though it's certainly a good way of getting to see a lot of places.'

'What made you come?'

'It was arranged a long time ago,' he said.

She desperately wanted to ask him more but was afraid of becoming too personal with him. She'd seen how little he wanted to answer questions at dinner and she didn't want to make him feel uncomfortable. She was surprised at her own sudden interest, and wondered whether his actual story would be more or less interesting than the story she'd been making up about him in her head.

'And what were you going to ask me?'

He looked a little surprised, as though he'd expected her to question him more, but he answered her all the same.

'Oh, just whether you were enjoying giving the lectures.'

She laughed. 'Not really. It's not *my* thing.'

'So why did you agree to do it?'

'I was persuaded,' she said grimly. 'My bloody agent organised it.'

'Somehow I can't see you being the sort of person who gets persuaded very easily,' said Leo.

'On this occasion I was,' she said. 'But fortunately Mia came with me and she's looking after me.'

He smiled. 'I like Mia. She's a very easy person to get to know, isn't she?'

Britt was conscious of a sudden spurt of jealousy at Leo's words, which shocked her. She'd never been jealous of Mia before, although she'd always envied her easy relationships with other people.

'Mia's certainly outgoing,' she said. 'That's why I asked her to join me.'

'And you're not?' He looked at her curiously.

'What d'you think?'

'You seem OK to me,' he said. 'You're good at the talks.'

'That's a relief,' she told him. 'I'm terrified when I'm doing them. But Mia was great at advising me.'

'It seems the wrong way around,' said Leo suddenly.

'Sorry?'

'You'd think that Mia was the novelist. She's more . . . more . . .'

'Warm and fuzzy,' supplied Britt.

'Yes. I suppose so. And more like someone who believes in the romance stuff, too. Whereas you . . .'

'I what?'

'Despite saying that you're terrified at the workshops, you strike me as someone who's very self-assured. Someone . . . Well, if Jack Hayes turned up on your doorstep, you'd probably send him away with a flea in his ear.'

Not really, thought Britt. I was in love with Jack when I wrote him. If he came along I'd fall into his arms. And it wouldn't have to be Jack. Maybe just someone who understood me. Or maybe not, she corrected herself quickly. Because I don't need someone to understand me. And why should anyone? Half the time I don't even understand myself.

'Hi, you guys!' Mia returned wearing a pair of shorts and a long T-shirt and sat down beside them again. 'Hope you haven't been sitting in total silence in my absence. I've noticed that neither of you are chatterboxes.'

'We talked,' said Leo.

'A bit,' added Britt.

'About what?' asked Mia.

'Nothing much,' said Britt.

'No.' Leo stood up. 'Well, thanks for your company tonight, ladies. I'm sure I'll see you around.'

He walked towards the stairs and Mia turned to her sister.

'Did you row with him again?' she demanded.

'No,' said Britt.

'Well, what's the matter . . . ? Oh!'

'Oh, what?'

'Did I interrupt? Were you and he . . . ?'

'Don't be so bloody silly,' retorted Britt as she swirled the mint around in her cocktail. 'Sometimes you can get the wrong end of the stick completely.'

'Another mojito?' asked Mia as a waiter went by.

'No,' said Britt. 'I think I'll go to bed.'

'Whatever you like,' said Mia, who'd been looking forward to another cocktail but knew better than to push her sister when she was in a very strange mood indeed.

Chapter 14

Position: at sea.
Weather: partly cloudy, fine. Wind: southerly force 3.
Temperature: 29°. Barometric pressure: 1011.00mb.

Crossing from the Atlantic to the Pacific Ocean had marked the halfway stage of the journey. Until then the days had been noted in the minds of the passengers as 'days until Panama'. Now they were talking about days until they docked in Acapulco. It was fortunate, Mia said to Britt as they were getting ready for her final talk, that there was still the result of the Treasure Hunt and the Valentine Night Gala Ball to look forward to.

'And our rain-forest walk tomorrow and the trip to Guatemala,' Britt reminded her. 'There's plenty of things going on. Oh, and my bloody Night of Romance thing with Steve Shaw, too.'

Mia grinned at her. 'He'll go easy on you. I rather think he's smitten by you. He's been *soooo* polite lately.'

Britt smiled. 'It's ever since the day I confessed to nerves. I think he's still terrified that I might jump ship or something and that'd be a total disaster for him. So he's being extra nice to me.'

'I think he fancies you, to be honest,' said Mia. She looked archly at her sister. 'So does Leo Tyler.'

'Mia McDonagh!' Britt's face flamed. 'Neither of them fancy me, as you put it. Steve is doing his job, and Leo . . .'

'Yes?'

'If Leo Tyler is interested in anyone at all, it's you. He said that you're easy to know.'

'He was just being polite and showing an interest,' said Mia. 'I like Leo too, but I don't fancy him.'

'Why not?' asked Britt. 'He's attractive and friendly. I'd've thought he was exactly right for you. You have great conversations together, whereas when I'm with him I can't think of a thing to say.'

'Have you suddenly become Brigitte the Matchmaker?' asked Mia in amusement. 'That's so unlike you! Maybe the Valentine Cruise has worked its romantic magic on you after all.'

'Don't be silly,' said Britt. 'I think Leo would be a good catch for you. I'm sure I caught him staring at you over dinner last night.'

'A good catch!' Mia guffawed. 'I'm not in the market for a good catch. He may have glanced my way from time to time, but he was staring at the ample charms of Pippin a great deal more often. Although that was probably only from sheer amazement that she was attempting to carry off Helen of Troy meets Jordan.'

'That's true,' said Britt. 'But it doesn't take away from the fact that—'

'Would you ever put a sock in it!' exclaimed Mia.

'Why aren't you interested?' asked Britt. 'Don't you think it would be good for Allegra to have a father?'

'She does have a father,' Mia told her shortly.

'A biological father,' agreed Britt. 'But – hello – he isn't here, is he?'

'You know nothing about it. And I am not, absolutely not, going to discuss this with you any further.'

'Oh, for heaven's sake!'

Mia opened her mouth and then closed it again. 'No,' she said.

'No?'

'I know you. You want to sort out my life. But you're not living it, so don't think for a second that you know what's best for me.'

'I never—'

'Britt, honey, you always think you know best for everyone.'

'That's not fair!' said Britt as mildly as she could, even though she was peeved with Mia. 'I admit that sometimes I think that people could do more with their lives . . .'

'Um, hello. Like me, you mean?'

'Well don't you think you could have done better if you hadn't got pregnant by a guy who didn't want to know?'

The moment the words were out of her mouth, Britt regretted them. She saw the hurt expression on Mia's face and wished she'd held her tongue. But it was too late.

'You have no idea about me and Alejo,' said Mia tightly. 'None. So don't think that you do. And getting pregnant might have been a mistake, but I'll tell you this, Britt McDonagh, Allegra is the most wonderful, wonderful daughter anyone could wish for and I don't for one second regret the fact that she's part of my life. And if we had a poll right here and now about which of the two of us is happier, I'd say it's me by a streak!'

'Oh, come on . . .'

'Oh, come on nothing.' Mia looked at her hotly. 'I love my life and I love my daughter, whereas you – you could have a great life, but all you've done since we came on board the ship is whinge about how difficult it all is and how you hate everything and everybody and how miserable you are. And so what I'm saying is that you might be the most successful novelist of our time or whatever crap it is they say about you, but you're a sad loser when it comes to life.'

'I admit that I've been anxious about it,' said Britt. 'I let you know how I felt because you were here to support me. I didn't realise that what I was actually doing was baring my soul and allowing you to think that I'm a hopeless case with no life skills whatsoever.'

'You said it, not me!'

'Great.' Britt's eyes flashed with anger. 'I ask you along to be my assistant, but basically you think you're better than me.'

'I didn't realise I was here to be humble,' returned Mia. 'I thought I was here to help you out, not to be a constant reminder to you that hard work pays off and that if you don't keep your nose to the grindstone you'll end up a sad slacker like me.'

'That is so not true!' exclaimed Britt. 'I asked you to come because I wanted you—'

'You asked me because your bloody agent fell off her bloody horse!' interrupted Mia. 'I'm the last resort, remember? I'm here to make you feel good and me feel inadequate.'

Britt looked at her in frustration. 'People are responsible for their own feelings,' she said. 'For how they deal with them. Even you.' She gathered up her things. 'I've got to get to the Athena Room. You don't have to come this time. I'm sure there are plenty of other things you'd rather be doing than listening to your pain-in-the-arse, patronising, too-clever-for-her-own-good older sister talk to people she doesn't know about things she knows absolutely nothing about.'

Steve Shaw had decided to come to Britt's final workshop. At first he'd resented her being foisted on him, but ever since her visit to his office when she'd confessed to being nervous, he'd felt unexpectedly protective towards her. He wanted to go to the workshop and make sure that everything was exactly as she'd requested.

She strode into the room, an array of brightly coloured bracelets jangling on her arm as she smoothed back her luxuriant golden curls. Her eyes seemed bluer than ever, her lips a glossy coral pink and her skin smooth and sunkissed. She looked confident and happy.

Nobody would ever have guessed that a few days ago she'd wanted to leave the ship. That she'd doubted her ability to carry on. He couldn't believe it himself. Maybe the nerves had been uncharacteristic for her, he thought. Maybe Brigitte Martin's life was normally a whirl of happy events, which had infused her writing and made *The Perfect Man* so successful.

Love. Romance. Togetherness. Joy. Happiness. Fulfilment. Heartache. Tears. He looked at the words on the handout she passed around the room. Standard romantic fare, he thought. He wondered how many people got more love and romance than heartache and tears.

'This is for later,' she told them. 'I want you to write a story with six out of those eight words in it. You can make it as long or as short as you like. I really enjoyed the pieces you did the other day. Some of them were very strong.'

And she's off again, thought Mia, who had followed her to the room despite Britt's assertion that she didn't have to, and despite the fact that she was still shaking with anger. She didn't want to give Britt the opportunity of saying, at some point, that she hadn't lived up to her end of the deal. She wanted to be able to tell her that she'd worked hard and done everything that she was supposed to do, including making notes on how well each workshop went, even though this was the last one. Just as well, she thought. The strain of togetherness was becoming too much for both of them.

Mia watched Britt sparkle as she spoke. There had been a massive transformation between her first session and this one. She was confident and funny, and the group hung on her every word. She was absolutely Brigitte Martin and not Britt McDonagh. So, wondered Mia, is it simply that she's still thinking of romance as a case to be argued? Or does she suddenly believe what she's saying?

Mia doubted that. Britt had a hard heart. After she'd left Ralph she'd simply said that it was never going to work out and she didn't want to discuss it because there was nothing to be gained by pointless talking. She'd never gone in for long, girlie chats where boyfriends and relationships were dissected, and she hadn't started after Ralph either. Mia simply couldn't understand how her older sister could remain so self-composed when anyone else would have been devastated. She had an ability to switch off her emotions that Mia pitied and envied in equal measure.

She might not like what she's doing now either, thought Mia, but she's doing it very well all the same. It's hard to believe she was so angry such a short time ago, when she's being so charming now. Charming enough that everyone else here thinks she is sweet and lovely and a believer in happy ever after.

Mia glanced around the room. Everyone was listening to Britt, hanging on her every word. It was utterly ridiculous. They were listening to the most cynical woman on the ship. Yet many of them were scribbling furiously as she spoke about characterisation and emotion. No wonder Britt had been so damn successful in her legal career, Mia thought bitterly. She could make anyone believe anything.

Her gaze rested on Leo Tyler, who was watching Britt attentively. Once again he wasn't taking any notes (Mia didn't think he'd even bothered to bring a pen with him), but he was clearly engrossed in what she was saying. There had been a chemistry between them the other night, she was sure of it. And yet Britt had dismissed the notion very firmly. Maybe, thought Mia, I felt the wrong sort of chemistry. Maybe Leo had seen through her and had said something to that effect. And perhaps now he was actually thinking about Pippin Costello, who was also at the talk and who was writing rapidly in her *Aphrodite* notebook with its picture of the cruise ship on the front. Mia knew that she might have been wrong about Leo and Britt, but she certainly wasn't wrong about Leo and Pippin.

All the same – he told Britt he liked me. Mia smiled to herself at the thought. It was nice to think that a man liked her, nice to bathe in the glow of knowing that someone had noticed her. She knew that since Allegra's birth she had become the invisible woman. A mother. Totally defined by the fact that everywhere she went, her child came along too. In Sierra Bonita everyone knew her as *La madre de Allegra*. Allegra's mother. Hardly anyone called her by her name.

Do I mind about that? Mia asked herself. Do I care that every second of my life is dictated by Allegra? Because even when she isn't physically with me, I'm always thinking about her, always planning my day around her.

She smiled to herself. She didn't really mind, because as far as she was concerned, she was happy being a mother. She didn't need any other identity right now.

'On behalf of Blue Lagoon Cruises, and most especially the *Aphrodite* cultural team, I'd like to thank Miss Martin for her series of very informative talks.'

Steve Shaw had stood up when Britt had finished her workshop and walked to the front of the room. 'We hope they've encouraged the writer in you to come to the fore. And I want to remind you that I'll be in conversation with

Miss Martin on the evening of the thirteenth, when we'll learn more about her and her life and how she wrote her fabulous book. I'm sure you'll all find it very interesting.'

There was a round of applause, and people began filing out of the room.

'D'you want me to bring your stuff back to the cabin?' Mia asked Britt.

Her sister shook her head. 'I can do it.'

'It's my job. It's why I'm here.'

'Hi, Brigitte.' Steve Shaw, who'd been talking to the other passengers, interrupted them. 'The Captain wondered if you and your sister would like to join his table for dinner tonight.'

'Oh.' Britt didn't know what to say. She couldn't refuse the invitation, but she wasn't at all keen on the idea of sitting through dinner trying to be polite when she was still scalding with rage at Mia (a rage made worse by the fact that she'd had to bottle it for the duration of her talk).

'Who'll be there?' asked Mia.

'Captain Henderson himself, obviously, and two of our newly married couples,' replied Steve. 'Mr and Mrs O'Neill and Mr and Mrs Chisholm. Unfortunately I can't be there myself, but perhaps you'd like to join me tomorrow evening? We do need to chat about your Night of Romance interview.'

Mia, without looking at Britt, said that they'd be delighted to join Captain Henderson.

'And me too, I hope,' said Steve. 'No other passengers at that one.' He looked at Britt as he spoke, and Mia was conscious of a dart of jealousy. She'd thought that she got on with Steve, that he liked her better than Britt. Which was very childish of her. Especially as her chameleon sister had somehow managed to get him on her side. He was looking at Britt now as though the only thing in the world that mattered to him was that she came to dinner.

'Of course,' said Britt.

'Mia?' Steve turned to her. 'You'll come too?'

Mia shook her head. She didn't feel like playing goose-berry to Steve and Britt.

'I'm sorry,' she said. 'I've booked a spa treatment for tomorrow night. But it doesn't matter. You guys can discuss the interview together.'

Britt looked startled and glanced at her sister, who ignored her.

'I thought . . . well . . . does the Calypso sound OK?' Steve turned back to Britt.

The Calypso was the smallest, most intimate restaurant on board. Yup, thought Mia, he's interested, and I would've been surplus to requirements.

'Lovely,' Britt said.

'Great.' Steve smiled at her, then looked at Mia. 'You sure you wouldn't like to change your spa treatment?'

He's so good at making you feel wanted, she thought. Much better at the whole caring thing than Britt.

'No,' she said. 'But thanks anyway.'

'See you later then.' He nodded at both of them and left the room.

Mia always found it difficult to stay annoyed for long, no matter how angry she was, but Britt was much better at it, and the sisters hardly spoke until they were getting ready for dinner with the Captain that evening.

'It'll probably be desperately boring,' said Britt as she fastened a gold chain around her neck. 'All those newly married couples.'

'You are such a pain!' cried Mia. 'You're utterly determined to be a killjoy, aren't you? It's no wonder your marriage broke up. Poor Ralph never stood a chance.'

Poor Ralph! Britt took a deep breath and then released it very slowly. Everyone had said *poor Ralph* when she'd left. Everyone had assumed it was her fault because she was difficult. She wasn't that difficult! She'd been in love with him, after all. She'd tried very hard not to be difficult with Ralph.

She was still thinking about him even as she and Mia sat down at the big round table with Captain Henderson and he introduced them to the other guests. She could still feel the knot in her stomach that thinking of him gave her. That was why she tried never to think of him. Even ten years on, it still had the power to hurt her.

The first two weeks – their honeymoon at the Italian lakes – had been beyond wonderful. They'd stayed in the most perfect of hotels, a renovated palace on the shores of Lake Garda, and had sipped Chianti on the terrace every night before going to the restaurant to eat amazing food. They'd gone for long walks along pine-scented country roads and boat rides across the cool water of the lake, and it had been the best two weeks of Britt's life. Italy suited Ralph; his dark good looks accentuated by his tan made him seem as though he belonged. After they'd gone on a trip to Milan and he'd bought designer jeans, a cashmere jumper and a pair of soft leather shoes, it was impossible to tell him apart from the local men. He flirted like them too, and at night, in their bedroom, he would whisper to her in an Italian accent, telling her that she was his *bella donna* and that he adored her.

She didn't want the honeymoon to end. She'd never been happier in her life, and as she put the key in the door of her house in Ringsend and Ralph suddenly lifted her up to carry her over the threshold, she told herself that the best was yet to come.

On the first evening after their return, when she got in from work, she was greeted by him wearing a tuxedo and white shirt, a linen napkin over his arm. The aroma of Italian cooking wafted from the kitchen.

'*Ciao, bellissima,*' he said in his Italian accent. 'I'm Antonio, your waiter for tonight. What can I get you?'

She laughed, even though she was stressed because it had been a particularly busy day and she'd had to bring home some papers to go through that night.

'Whatever's on the menu,' she told him, slipping her jacket from her shoulders and putting her briefcase on the floor.

'Ah . . .' He smiled at her. 'That would be me, then. And you.' And he led her out of the hallway and into the bedroom without a second glance to the kitchen.

They'd made love and Ralph had stayed in the character of the Italian waiter the whole time, telling her that she was his favourite customer even though she was a bit hard to please. He said he was going to find the exact right way to please her and suddenly he was doing things to her that he'd never done before.

'Don't worry, *bella*,' he told her when she gasped involuntarily. 'I know what you like on our menu. I know what you want for dessert.'

Afterwards she was exhausted and fell asleep beside him. When she woke up at eleven, his arms were wrapped around her, and since she didn't want to disturb him, she never got around to dealing with the legal papers she'd brought home.

The following day when she got in, he was dressed in a doctor's white coat with a stethoscope hanging around his neck.

'Ah!' he cried as she walked into the kitchen (he hadn't cooked, but there were some dirty dishes piled in the sink). 'My favourite patient. I need to bring you to my special consulting rooms today to do a thorough examination.'

'Maybe later,' she told him. 'I'm whacked. We had a conference this afternoon and it went on and on and—'

'You're tense.' He stood behind her and massaged her shoulders. 'But Dr Ralph knows how to fix that.' His hands crept around to the front of her body and cupped her breasts beneath the silk blouse she was wearing. 'Oh yes. Dr Ralph will sort you out for sure.'

Afterwards, while he slept, she slid from his arms and tiptoed to the living room. She was halfway through the work she'd brought home when he joined her, pushing it from the coffee table to the floor and telling her not to bother about boring stuff like that. Then he made love to her again.

Britt had enjoyed making love to Ralph before they were married. But it had always been Ralph she'd made love to. Since they'd come home from Italy, he'd been a different person every time. She didn't want to make love to different people. She wanted Ralph. But he told her that it was more exciting this way and that she should be glad he was making an effort. It was important, he said, to keep things fresh and interesting.

Over the next few weeks, as well as the waiter and the doctor, he became a fireman and a mechanic and a businessman (and even once a member of the Chippendales, his chest waxed and wearing a gold lamé thong), always ready to give her what she wanted. The trouble was that Britt didn't want him to be those people. Sometimes all she wanted was to sit down in front of the TV with a cup of coffee and a Danish pastry. She knew this was shockingly boring, and she worried that there was something wrong with her, because surely she should be flattered by the amount of time and attention Ralph was putting into their sex life, but she couldn't help herself. She hadn't thought that sex would be such an effort. And then some of the characters he played . . . Well, he'd been a teacher once and it had all been very predictable, because he'd told her that she'd been a naughty girl and he was going to have to punish her and it had actually hurt. She'd protested then and he'd apologised, but he hadn't come near her for the rest of the week.

On the Monday of their fourth week home, the sixth of their married life, she was especially late getting back from work and had a pounding headache because of a meeting that had overrun and the difficulty of trying to negotiate a settlement between two people who had apparently decided that their divorce was a pissing contest and that settling was the last thing either of them wanted. Britt had simply been at the meeting to take notes, but she hadn't been able to help getting involved.

'Wouldn't it just be better to agree on this and then walk away and start a new life?' she'd asked the wife as the woman dug her heels in about who should get their (admittedly gorgeous and outrageously expensive) set of Louis Vuitton luggage. But the woman had been utterly intractable, saying that the luggage had sentimental value far in excess of its monetary worth. Britt had sighed at that. She hated it when people got hung up on sentimental value. Later, when she was dealing with cases herself, she always tried to get her clients to quantify sentimental value in legal fees.

Anyway, the woman hadn't yet made the necessary leap to make her think of settling, and Britt had left the office tired, frazzled and short tempered. When she walked into the house, Ralph was wearing a policeman's uniform and was dangling a pair of pink plastic handcuffs from his fingers.

'Oh God, not tonight,' she said the minute she saw him. 'I truly have had a pig of a day and I'm not in form for your play-acting.'

'Are you the narky solicitor we've been told to watch out for?' demanded Ralph, opening the handcuffs. 'The girl on the run from the man who loves her?'

Sometimes she wondered whether if she'd dealt with

that moment differently, her marriage would have been saved. She knew deep down that the answer was probably no, and yet a tiny nugget of doubt always lingered. If she'd spoken to him differently, if she'd been less dismissive . . . She hadn't intended to be quite so brutal, but it had been a truly horrible day. Maybe if she'd been nicer it would have lasted longer, she told herself, but it would've gone down the tubes in the end.

She'd looked at Ralph and told him that she didn't want to play games, she wanted to be on her own for a while and why couldn't he understand that? She'd said that she was tired of coming home just to be jumped on by a succession of idiot men in ridiculous uniforms or gold lamé thongs and that she hadn't realised that being married to him would turn her into an extra in a porn movie. And then (unforgivably, she knew) she'd added that of course the way his career was going at the moment, porn movies were probably the best he was likely to get, and did he really think that hanging out all day at home or in Starbucks with his mates was going to lead to any kind of job? Finally – just to put the boot in – she'd said that as she was the sole money-earner in the house, she'd appreciate it if he didn't waste all of it on bottles of outrageously expensive wine and marinated olives, especially when they hardly ever got around to food and drink.

He'd stared at her for a full minute without saying anything, then grabbed her by the wrists and snapped the handcuffs closed around them.

'Oh for God's sake, Ralph.' She was furious with him now. 'Don't be such a child.'

'You bitch,' he said as she stood in front of him in her tailored suit, her wrists cuffed in front of her. 'I've done everything for you. Everything.'

'You've treated me like a whore, is what you've done,' she retorted. 'I feel as though I've slept with more men in the last month than any woman would in her whole life.'

'I was making it exciting for us,' he said. 'For you. You told me when we were going out that you needed excitement. I was giving it to you. It was only acting.'

'Yes, well, now I need a coffee, not acting,' she snapped. 'Let me out of these stupid cuffs.'

But he simply glared at her, picked up his mobile phone from the table, and walked out of the house.

For a few minutes Britt couldn't quite believe that he'd actually gone out. She expected him to come back (perhaps this time in the guise of a fellow prisoner or something) and undo the cuffs. But he didn't. She flexed her wrists. The cuffs didn't hurt, but they were locked tight. She gritted her teeth. Her headache worsened.

'Are you enjoying the *Aphrodite*?' Captain Henderson asked her, bringing her back to reality.

'Absolutely.' Britt nodded. 'It's wonderful. And everybody's been great to us. We're having a fantastic time.'

Liar, thought Mia.

'My cruise director tells me the talks have been great,' said the Captain.

'That's good,' said Britt. 'I'm glad people have enjoyed them.'

'We're all going to the Night of Romance,' said Tamara
O'Neill. 'We can't wait.'

'I'd have thought you'd have been getting enough
romance of your own,' said Britt. 'After all, you're only
just married!'

'Every little helps to keep the spark alive.' Tamara's hazel
eyes danced wickedly. 'Don't you think, Tony?' She turned
to her husband, a dark-haired man with the build of a
rugby player.

'Whatever you say,' he told her. 'I'm just here for the
beer.'

'And that's the difference between men and women,'
said Britt brightly. 'We look for the beautiful things in life,
but they're happy with beer.'

She's good at this despite herself, thought Mia. No
wonder she's a brilliant lawyer. No wonder she writes
fiction.

It took Britt nearly an hour to free herself from the pink
handcuffs. She managed to break the link chain between
them, but the safety catch that should have released them
didn't work. Eventually (she couldn't believe she was actually sitting in her house doing this) she managed to open
them using a hairgrip. She threw them into the rubbish
bin, popped two paracetamol tablets for her headache, made
herself a strong coffee, and took out the work she'd brought
home with her.

It was after midnight before Ralph returned, no longer
wearing the policeman's uniform but dressed instead in

jeans and a T-shirt. Britt wondered where he'd been and whose clothes he was wearing.

'Ah, my little criminal,' he said as he walked into the living room. 'Oh – look, you escaped. Now that's a really bad, bad thing.'

'Fuck off, Ralph,' she said shortly.

'Is that any sort of way to talk to a man who's taken your words to heart?' he asked.

'What d'you mean?'

'I've got a job,' he said.

'Oh?' She looked at him warily. 'A part? In a play?'

'No,' he told her. 'You wanted some more money coming into the house. So I got a job as a barman.'

'Oh,' she said again.

'But I don't mind. I can observe people,' he told her. 'I can add characters to my repertoire. It will be worthwhile. And it'll mean you're not the only one paying the way.'

'Ralph, I never intended . . .'

'Sure you did,' he said. 'You never do anything without intending it.'

After dinner, Mia suggested going to the theatre and watching one of the shows, but Britt said that she didn't feel like it, that she'd probably go back to the cabin. Mia said she'd rather like to see the show, and Britt, her head stuck somewhere between her past quarrels with Ralph and her present one with Mia, replied that she wasn't stopping her and that she could do what she liked. So Mia headed off to the theatre while Britt, not really wanting to be alone with her thoughts, decided instead to wander around the ship.

She called into the casino for the first time (it consisted mainly of slot machines, which she hated, so she didn't stay there for long); then she stopped off at the art gallery and tried to make sense of a painting entitled *sun shower*, which consisted of lots of yellow lines. She walked around the shopping mall and bought a silk cardigan, for no particular reason other than she wanted to spend some money, and then she went to the Troy Bar, where she ordered a glass of wine and picked at the saucer of cashew nuts that the steward had placed in front of her. When more people came into the bar she took the drink out on deck and sat on one of the sun loungers beside the Trident Pool, staring out at the night sky, which was brightened both by the ship's lights and by the occasional flash of lightning from a storm in the west. She wasn't able to keep the old memories from joining her. She knew there was no point in trying to push them away.

Britt knew that her marriage had ended the night Ralph had snapped the handcuffs on her. She knew that he wasn't the man she'd thought and that she wasn't the right person for him. She didn't blame him. She blamed herself. She wasn't sexy enough for him and she wasn't carefree enough for him. She just didn't quite know how she was going to tell him.

She'd worked herself up to it, but then he got the acting job, a small part in a play at the Project. She didn't want to talk about divorce when he was so happy. Anyway, she didn't see him very much because he was always at rehearsals. And then one day she came home early and found him in the arms of one of the actresses.

She knew that he was lying when he said it was a rehearsal. He was dressed as a fireman, after all.

Mia enjoyed the show but felt guilty about having left Britt on her own, even though, as she reminded herself, she was a grown woman who spent most of her time on her own anyway. But she knew that she hadn't helped Britt's mood by allowing herself to get under her sister's skin.

She made her way back to the cabin, resolving to be nice to Britt. But Britt wasn't there and Mia was surprised. It was nearly midnight, and although her sister was a night owl, she preferred sitting in a corner reading a book to socialising.

Maybe, thought Mia, she's hooked up with Leo Tyler after all. Maybe she's realised that he is actually interested in her (well, maybe he is, maybe he isn't, but we're on the ship of romance, so let's give him the benefit of the doubt). Perhaps at this very moment she's having sensational sex with Leo in the Delphi suite. There had been a scene in *The Perfect Man* where Jack and Francesca had been making love out of doors that had been truly erotic. Mia had wondered then whether Britt was writing from experience. Because if she was, it revealed a whole new side to her nature that Mia wouldn't have expected.

She shuddered. Britt and Leo – Britt and anyone – wasn't the kind of thought she wanted in her head. Besides, she acknowledged, she knew that wasn't what was happening.

If Leo was bonking anyone it was precocious Pippin, and the sad fact of the matter was that there wasn't a snowball's chance in hell of Britt bonking anyone on board the *Aphrodite*.

She left the cabin again and headed towards the Panorama Lounge. There was no sign of Britt there, but Leo Tyler was sitting with the Costello family, and Pippin was beaming her wide smile at him while her hand rested gently on his shoulder.

Britt probably wasn't in any of the bars, thought Mia. It was more likely that she was in the library or the cyber-café. But she wasn't. Nor was she on the promenade deck or at the pool or in any of the public places Mia looked.

She could be with Sexy Steve, thought Mia. In his cabin. After all, Steve had made his intentions fairly clear. But somehow she didn't think Britt was with him. And she was getting ever so slightly worried. It wasn't that she thought Britt could actually have fallen overboard or anything (could she?), but she wanted to know where she was.

She poked her head around the door of the champagne bar. Steve was talking to the pianist, whose music was soft and rippling and very seductive.

'Hello,' he said. 'How was dinner with the Captain?'

'Lovely,' said Mia automatically. 'You haven't seen Britt, have you?'

Steve shook his head.

'I seem to have lost her,' said Mia. 'I know that there's loads of places she could be, but . . .'

Steve frowned. 'Have you a reason to be worried about her?'

'Not at all,' said Mia. 'Except that we argued a bit today. Nothing really important, but she wasn't in a good mood and I feel bad about it and I'm . . .' she shrugged, 'being silly, I know.'

'Want me to help you look?'

Mia nodded.

'Come on then.' Steve smiled sympathetically. 'I know all of the hidey-holes on the *Aphrodite*. But let's check your cabin first.'

Ralph had played the part of the suitor and the lover and the husband. But, thought Britt, she hadn't really been his girlfriend or his fiancée or his wife. She'd been a prop.

He tried to play the part of the errant husband too – he admitted that his fling with Cherise had been wrong, but in the same breath he told Britt that it wasn't surprising given the way she made him feel. The way she wouldn't participate in their lovemaking. In fact, he told her, he was beginning to wonder if she had issues in that particular department because she was particularly strait-laced about it, wasn't she?

'There's nothing strait-laced about not wanting to be handcuffed or shagged by a man in a gold lamé thong,' she protested. 'And there's nothing strait-laced about not liking things that hurt, either.'

He laughed derisively.

'Is your actress friend any different?' she demanded, and he laughed and said that she certainly was – hadn't Britt seen that with her own eyes?

She couldn't believe she'd been so stupid. She couldn't

believe he'd been equally stupid by wanting to marry her, but then he'd been living in some kind of fantasy world of his own. She told him she wanted a divorce. He said she was a hard-hearted bitch who only looked out for herself. He'd gone out and hadn't come back. She'd sat in her bedroom alone and cried.

'You think she wanted to be somewhere private?' said Steve as he and Mia stood on the deserted balcony of cabin B45.

'She's a very private person,' said Mia.

'Really?'

'Yes.'

'And yet she's doing a very public thing in being on *Aphrodite*.'

'She didn't want to.' Mia smiled weakly at him. 'She was talked into it by her agent, apparently. If Britt had her way, she'd spend her life sitting in a room full of dusty legal tomes.'

'Really?'

'Oh yes.' Mia nodded. 'The law is her passion.'

'I never would've guessed that. She seemed passionate enough this afternoon.'

'She's pretending she's arguing a case.'

'You're joking?'

'Nope.' Mia looked at him anxiously as they walked back into the cabin. 'I know that I'm probably getting into a heap about nothing, but . . .'

'We've still to go up to the top deck,' said Steve. 'It's usually deserted at night because it's only the spa and fitness areas and you can't access them from the outside.'

'Which probably makes it ideal for Britt,' agreed Mia. 'I didn't think of there.'

'OK,' said Steve. 'Let's go.'

Money was always the issue when it came to divorce settlements. Money was often the issue in bringing marriages to the brink of divorce in the first place. And money played a part in Britt and Ralph's separation too.

She sometimes thought that it was the money aspect that had stung her the most, and that was why, later, she was able to sympathise with and understand the women who came into her office angry about the break-up of their marriages and worried about their financial future.

Britt didn't worry about her financial future at first. After all, they hadn't been married long and they didn't have any children. But a few weeks after Ralph had left the house (and that had been a struggle in itself; he said that she was the one pushing for a divorce and she should be the one to leave), she went online to buy some books from Amazon and her credit card was rejected. She re-entered the information carefully but the card was rejected again. She logged on to her credit card account and called up the latest balance. Then she looked at it in horror.

It was five hundred euros over her already generous credit limit. The last entry was a fee for exceeding the limit. But all the entries before it were for shops in and around Dublin or for items from eBay that she knew she hadn't bought. She felt herself begin to tremble. She hadn't bought clothes in Louis Copeland or Brown Thomas but she could guess that Ralph had. Ralph, who loved expensive suits and good tailoring, would quite happily have spent money in the gents' department of the exclusive Brown Thomas or bought a bespoke suit at Louis Copeland. And he could easily have charged it to her, because his card was also on her account.

When she'd met him first, his account was with a different provider and, he told her, was permanently close to its limit. A shockingly low limit, he'd added, because his income was so precarious. But when he got work he was often paid well and had plenty of money. So it was really annoying to have a mere thousand euros to play with. Britt had nodded understandingly and told him to apply for a card on her account, which would give him access to her limit. He'd kissed her on the lips and told her that she'd just made him a very happy man, but that she wasn't to worry, he wouldn't abuse it and would give her the money every month for whatever he owed.

A month ago he'd owed just under a thousand on it. Now her card was over the limit and it was his fault.

She'd phoned him in a total rage and he'd laughed and suggested that if she was all that worried, she could sue him. After all, he said, you'll get a discount on the fees. But the thing was, she'd never be able to prove that he'd spent all the money; the account was in her name, not his, and it would be very difficult to get out of the debt.

'I don't have that sort of money,' she cried a couple of days later when she rang him to rant at him again. 'You have to pay me back.'

'I'll call around later,' he said.

And he did. He came to the house dressed in the clothes

he'd bought on their honeymoon, carrying a bunch of roses, and took her in his arms before she'd had half an opportunity to push him away, and he kissed her and told her that he was truly sorry for everything, that she was the only woman in his life.

And then he made love to her, as Ralph, not as anyone else, and she moaned softly beneath him and whispered that she was sorry about everything too.

'So,' she said, 'can we work this out after all? Can we get our marriage back on track? Will you make payments on the credit card?'

'I might have,' he said, 'if you hadn't dragged it into the conversation so quickly. But the truth is, my darling, you're more worried about owing the money than losing me. And so what I'm sorry for is having married you in the first place.'

He got off the bed and zipped up his jeans and then rolled his T-shirt over his head, and she'd realised that he was acting again. And that she'd been utterly taken in by his performance.

She leaned over the rail on *Aphrodite*'s top deck. She'd been so silly about him, and so silly afterwards. She'd started paying off her credit card and she'd taken on more work at the office and she'd done her very best to put Ralph Jones out of her mind. Only, of course, she thought about him every time she realised that she was still paying for his Louis Copeland suits, and she thought about him again later when his solicitor had contacted her and told her that he was looking for half of the value of the marital home.

'Mia, she hasn't fallen overboard,' Steve told her as they took the lift up to the Hellenic deck. 'I just know she hasn't.'

'And I know she hasn't too, but I'd still like to see her,' said Mia. 'She . . . well, she gets upset so rarely that I can't help thinking her way of dealing with it might be much worse than anyone else's.'

'You know you're overreacting.'

'That doesn't mean it's not the right reaction all the same.'

Steve put his arm around her shoulders and hugged her. Mia looked at him in surprise.

'Don't worry,' he said.

She liked the feeling of his arm around her. She liked feeling protected.

Sometimes Britt thought that he was right. That it was the money that upset her most of all. And that scared her, because it made her think that she hadn't really loved him, even though there was still a hollow feeling in the pit of her stomach whenever she thought about the very first day she'd seen him. And she ached with the need to be held in his arms while he kissed the top of her head as he'd done so often in the past. She might have been partly to blame for the breakdown of her marriage, she admitted, but at least she'd really been in love. Ralph had been in love with the idea of being in love. She just happened to be the wrong person at the right time.

So when it came to the divorce, she was just like every

other woman who'd ever walked into Clavin & Grey, and she'd wanted to fight to keep everything that was hers and to demand he repay her all the money she'd spent in the short time he was with her and in the months afterwards. Sabrina had told her that the money wasn't the most important thing. And she'd said that it was, that she wanted them to tell him that he was nothing without her and that he'd betrayed her trust and that he owed her big time. When she'd finished speaking, she'd looked at Sabrina's impassive face and realised that she'd completely turned into a client. And so she'd allowed the other woman to thrash out a settlement that placed a monetary value on the work that Ralph had done in the home ('supporting Britt's career', his legal team had called it), and then, after a bit of haggling, they'd come to an agreement and the divorce had been finalised and she was a free woman.

'It's just a pity it takes so damn long in this country,' she'd said afterwards. 'All that time before I could apply and all the time afterwards . . . I feel as though Ralph and I have only just split up, even though it's been years!'

'Good years for you, though,' Sabrina had said, and Britt had only been able to agree. Because after they'd separated she'd worked harder than ever to be the best at what she did and she'd risen like a meteor within the firm, and she'd been ecstatic about it.

She wondered if Ralph had read *The Perfect Man*. She wondered if he would see in Jack the complete opposite of himself. Someone who never acted. Someone who was scrupulously fair and completely honest. Someone that any girl would be proud to know and love.

She felt a lump in her throat and she loosened the chiffon scarf she'd been wearing around her neck. I am not going to cry, she whispered under her breath. I've done all my crying for Ralph and for me and I've long since got over it. It's just this damn boat and its lurve themes playing havoc with my head again. She ran her fingers through her hair, and the breeze tugged at her scarf and whipped it into the night sky. She leaned across the rail to catch it, but it was just out of reach, and she cried out with annoyance because it was the only scarf she possessed and it went with nearly all her evening outfits.

'Britt!'

The shriek startled her so much that she dropped the glass of wine she was still holding in her left hand. She spun around and saw Mia and Steve Shaw as they stepped out of the doorway.

'What on earth's the matter?' she demanded. 'You've made me lose my scarf.' She looked out towards the horizon, but the wisp of cream fabric had already disappeared from view.

'Your scarf?' Mia looked confused, and then realised what Britt was talking about. 'Oh. Your scarf.'

'What's wrong?' asked Britt.

'Mia was anxious about you,' said Steve.

'Anxious? Why?'

'I didn't know where you were,' said Mia.

'I went to the bar,' said Britt. 'Chilled out. Like you're always telling me to. Then I came up here for a bit of peace and quiet.'

'I'm glad you're all right, Miss Martin,' said Steve. 'It's not a good idea to have too much to drink on board.'

'I didn't have too much to drink,' protested Britt. 'I had a glass of wine, that's all. And I hadn't even finished it.' She picked up the cracked wine glass from where it had rolled on the deck and put it on one of the low tables before frowning at Steve. 'I don't know why you're here, either.'

'I asked him to help me look for you,' said Mia. 'I was afraid . . . Well, you hear about people falling overboard.'

'For heaven's sake!' Britt looked at her impatiently. 'I'm not a child. You don't have to look after me.'

'I thought that was why I was here,' said Mia.

'Oh God, not all that again! You didn't need to call in the cavalry. I don't need looking after. I can look after myself.'

She'd said that to Ralph once, Britt remembered. When she'd had a touch of a cold and he'd brought her hot whiskeys and clove drops. He'd told her that he wanted to look after her, but she'd felt suffocated by him. I push people away, thought Britt, even when they want to help. Why do I do that?

'Mia couldn't help being a little worried,' said Steve. 'I was happy to help her find you and put her mind at rest.' He looked down at Mia, who was standing beside him. 'You OK now?'

She nodded. 'Thanks.'

'You're welcome,' said Steve.

'Sorry,' said Britt abruptly. 'I didn't mean to . . . Sorry.'

'I'll be off,' said Steve, glancing between the two of them. 'Take care, both of you.'

'Right,' said Mia. 'Thanks again, Steve. You were great.'

He smiled at her and then disappeared down the stairway to the deck below.

The two sisters looked at each other.

'You weren't really worried, were you?' asked Britt.

'Just a little.'

'I'm the most sensible person in the world,' Britt told her.

'Even sensible people can do silly things from time to time,' said Mia.

'Like arguing with their sisters who are only trying to help?'

'That sort of thing,' agreed Mia.

'I'm sorry about earlier,' said Britt. 'I didn't mean to pick on you and I really don't try to make you feel a particular way. I don't want you to think that I . . .' She shook her head. 'I know you're different from me. I just thought that your life would be . . . better.'

'My life is just the way I want it.'

Britt laughed shortly. 'Do you pity me?'

'Of course not.'

'Do you envy me?'

'No.'

'Do you resent me?'

'No.'

'What then?'

'I think you're someone who's not content in her own skin,' said Mia. 'But the truth is, Britt, I don't know what sort of skin you have.'

'I guess I'm not very sure of that either,' said Britt.

'Come on.' Mia linked her arm in her sister's. 'Let's have a nightcap. Let's go to the champagne bar and toast the fact that no matter what happens in the future, we're here now and it's very lovely and we're very lucky.'

Britt nodded slowly. 'Meredith always says things look better after a glass of champagne.'

'I know you won't like to hear this,' said Mia as they walked towards the stairway together, 'but Meredith sounds like she could be my kind of gal.'

Chapter 15

Position: Puntarenas, Costa Rica.
Weather: fine. Wind: southerly force 3. Temperature:
28°. Barometric pressure: 1011.1mb.

'I'm *so* not convinced that this was a good idea.' Britt
sprayed some more mosquito repellent on her legs. 'It
sounded OK on paper, but in reality . . .'

Mia giggled. 'Would you stop putting that stuff on yourself?' she demanded. 'That's the third time you've applied
it and we're still not even off the bus! No flying insect has
a chance of feasting on you. If it attempts a landing it'll
just skid off your slippery legs.'

'Very funny,' said Britt as she rubbed the film of spray
into her ankles. 'But *you* don't swell up like some alien life
form after a bite.'

'I guess not.' Mia watched her sister in amusement. 'You
don't half whiff, though. So stay downwind of me.'

'I'll do my best. Ouch!' The last as the bus bumped off
the narrow potted road on to an even narrower one. 'Can
I also add that I know you're into this whole backpacking

wildlife experience, but on mature consideration I doubt very much that it's my thing?'

'It's fun,' said Mia. 'And you'll be walking through an actual rain forest.'

'I know. I'm just finally beginning to think that maybe I'm the kind of person who's more suited to walking through Grafton Street.'

'Material girl.'

'Don't care.'

They'd been on the bus for nearly an hour as it made its way through the lush green Costa Rican countryside. Britt had been astonished at how fertile the country was, and when they'd stopped at a particularly beautiful spot with views sweeping down towards the sea, she couldn't help comparing it to west Cork, where they'd holidayed as children with Paula and Gerry. The patchwork of greens and yellows was the same, as was the biscuit-coloured sand and deep blue of the ocean. Half a world away and yet I could be in Ireland, she thought. Except, perhaps, for the fact that it's a good deal hotter here than it ever is in west Cork.

She yawned suddenly. It had been an early start that morning and she was still tired from the night before. After they'd got back to the cabin, she and Mia had sat outside on their balcony for almost an hour in a companionable silence broken only by the occasional remark about how tranquil it was.

She felt relaxed as well as tired today. More relaxed in herself (although, she thought, that was probably due to the fact that her talks were finished and she only had the dreaded Night of Romance to negotiate), and more relaxed in Mia's company too. Peace has broken out between us, she decided. And that's not a bad thing.

The driver put the bus into a lower gear and the engine groaned as they climbed higher into the mountains. Britt tried not to look down. She was already wondering about the wisdom of agreeing to a trip that would have her walking across rope bridges in the forest. She didn't mind heights once she had something solid to hold on to but, as far as she was concerned, a rope bridge didn't come under the heading of solid. However, Mia – who'd done a rainforest walk before – had assured her that it was a piece of cake. Perfectly safe, she'd told her, and the bridges are well maintained, so you don't have to worry about Indiana Jones moments.

Eventually their bus and the two others in their convoy (the rain-forest trip being the most popular by far) pulled to a halt at the entrance to the forest walk. The passengers spilled out into the dusty parking area, stretching their arms over their heads and rubbing their backs. Britt spotted Leo Tyler, who had been on the bus ahead of them, and Pippin Costello, who'd been on the one behind. Pippin looked as though she was about to take part in an Amazonian-themed fashion shoot, in her skimpy Kate Moss shorts and an emerald-green vest teamed with a pair of green Converse boots. I'd be afraid of showing that much skin, thought Britt. Far too enticing for the mozzies! The thought of the insects made her itch again, and she took out her spray.

Their guide, Manolo, shepherded them together and gave them heavy walking sticks to help them on the trails.

'It can be slippery,' he warned. 'So please watch your footing.'

'This is so exciting,' said Mia. 'Let's go!'

Britt took a firm grip of her stick and followed the crowd into the dark green of the rain forest, straining to hear Manolo as he talked about the ecology of the region and its environmental importance.

'Ants.' He held up his hand and they stopped. 'See their trail?'

The group watched the army of tiny creatures tramping industriously across the path, carrying pieces of leaves with them. Actually, thought Britt, they're not that small. Quite big, in fact. Really enormous for ants. She scratched her ankle.

'Oh, and look!' exclaimed Mia. 'A hummingbird.'

They gazed in fascination at the ruby-throated bird hovering beside a nearby flower. When it darted away, the group followed the guide deeper into the forest.

'It seems so dark and so silent,' said Mia as they stepped over another scurrying line of ants, 'yet it's positively teeming with life. Isn't it terrible to think that people are actually destroying forests like this every day?'

Britt nodded. It was impossible to believe that swathes of forest were being cut down. The idea of bringing chainsaws and machinery into places like this was shameful.

'Our first bridge,' said Manolo. 'It's very safe, I promise you.'

Britt swallowed hard. She wasn't looking forward to this at all, and the sight of the short rope bridge didn't inspire her with confidence. It seemed to be swaying quite a lot, and, of course, it was suspended over a deep chasm in the forest . . . She felt her mouth go dry. It was scary. She didn't feel she could do it.

'You'll be fine,' said Mia beside her. 'And it's beyond brilliant.'

Britt wouldn't have gone as far as that, but she managed to successfully negotiate the bridge, even though she kept her eyes half closed the entire time. Pippin stepped off it a couple of seconds behind her.

'I'm not sure I can do that again.' Pippin's eyes were wide. 'I don't like heights. And I'm allergic to some of the greenery.'

'Why are you here so?' asked Mia.

'Well, because of my charity.' Pippin smiled knowingly. 'I'm patron of an environmental group at home. It's good credentials. Shows my caring side. They'll send pics of me and a bit about my love of nature and stuff into the papers. Highlights their concerns and gives me a bit of profile.'

'And *do* you love nature?' enquired Mia.

'I have a dog at home,' replied Pippin. 'He's cute. And I adore flowers. I make sure to buy them fresh every single day. Plus I guess it's important to have rain forests and stuff because of global warming. But I'm not into snakes and vultures or things like that.'

Britt laughed. 'Neither am I.'

'There are more than two hundred species of birds here,' Manolo told them. 'Beautiful as well as deadly. Lots of animals too.'

'And there's a particularly tasty piece of wildlife,' murmured Pippin as Leo Tyler stepped off the bridge and walked a little way up the path.

'You think?' Britt shielded her eyes from the glare of the sun.

'Oh yes,' Pippin said. 'I like the strong, silent type. It's rather strange, don't you think, that such a hunky man is travelling on his own. I Googled him in the cybercafé, but I didn't get any hits on his name.'

'Did you?' Britt looked at her in surprise. 'I'd never have thought of . . . I'm sure he has his reasons for being on his own.'

'I'm hoping that one of them is snaring a gorgeous young thing like me.' Pippin giggled. 'Always providing that it's worth getting snared.' She walked after Leo.

Mia grinned and turned to Britt. 'So much for her not wanting to get involved with a man because of her career,' she remarked. 'Who d'you think is snaring who in that scenario?'

'Good question,' said Britt, tightening her grip on her stick as they moved forward again.

It was hot in the forest and the air was still so that the excited chatter of the group seemed to come from every direction. Every so often an unexpected rustle in the foliage made Britt recoil, especially as Mia kept telling her that it was probably some kind of armadillo. Or maybe just a wild pig, she added helpfully, which made Britt shudder.

'My green credentials aren't up to much,' she remarked as she scratched her legs again. 'I like the idea of nature, but getting back to it just brings me out in a rash.'

'You've been suckered into the high life,' Mia told her. 'How on earth will you manage when they get you on to *I'm a Celebrity . . . Get Me Out of Here*?'

Britt shuddered. 'My worst nightmare. For a whole heap of reasons.'

'I'm hoping to get on to that someday,' said Pippin, who had stopped beside them as they looked down over a gorge in the forest. (Both Britt and Pippin stood back from the edge, but Mia was peering happily into the chasm below.) 'It would be so wonderful for my career.'

'Nothing in the world could make me eat insects,' Britt said. 'I think the whole thing is beyond disgusting.'

'I bet they don't actually eat them,' said Pippin confidently. 'But even if they do – well, think about it – you can make millions just for swallowing one.'

'There are some things that money wouldn't make me do,' said Britt. 'And swallowing anything with six legs or more is one of them.'

'It's easy for you,' Pippin told her. 'You've made it. But I'm still working on it.'

'And if they could see you now, they'd probably print the picture,' said Britt lightly. 'Glamour model does the rain forest.'

'I don't do glamour modelling,' said Pippin stiffly.

'I meant modelling as a glamorous thing,' Britt corrected herself.

'Huh.' Pippin narrowed her eyes. 'Everyone knows that glamour modelling is very different. I don't do topless shots. I never have. And don't you dare say otherwise.' She glanced over at Leo. 'Or I'll sue you.'

'I'm sure Britt didn't mean that you had,' said Mia hastily. 'No need to get in a heap about it.'

Pippin moved away from them and towards Leo again, and the sisters exchanged glances.

'She's making a definite play,' said Mia.

'She's not his type,' said Britt.

'Oh, really?' Mia's eyes danced with fun. 'And who is?'

'I don't know,' said Britt. 'But not her. She's all wrong for him.'

'There speaks the romantic novelist,' said Mia, and just managed to dodge Britt's good-natured swipe at her before they set off again.

Leo liked the rain forest. He liked the stillness of it and the way it seemed to envelop him, immersing him in a whole new world populated and run by plants and animals, where people were mere guests. He enjoyed walking on the dried-mud trails, watching out for insects or sprawling tree roots, and knowing that there was a fine line between wilderness and civilisation.

Now, a little behind the main group and not feeling the need to catch up and listen to Manolo's commentary, he felt more at peace with himself than he had at any time in the last nine months. Am I suddenly accepting what happened? he wondered. Coming to terms with it, as Aunt Sandra would say. Or moving on, as Mick would put it.

He looked at the group in front of him, identifying Pippin, Mia and Britt as they picked their way along the trail. He wondered whether he would have noticed the fact that Pippin was stunning, Britt elegant and Mia pretty if Vanessa had been with him. Would he have even noticed them at all? But the fact that I have, he told himself, must surely mean that I am actually moving on. That I have begun to put it all behind me.

Whenever he thought of that night, the images were still crystal clear in his head. He only had to close his eyes for a moment and he was there again, putting his key in the door of Donal's house, walking into the hallway, turning on the light and then realising that his brother was at home after all.

'Why didn't you call me?' he asked as he strode into the living room. 'I didn't realise you were back.' And then his voice had trailed off because Vanessa was sitting on the sofa, looking at him with wide, worried eyes. He was surprised at that. Surprised at the half-empty bottle of wine on the coffee table, surprised at the sight of Vanessa's high-heeled shoes upturned in the middle of the floor, and very surprised that Vanessa was in the house with Donal. How did she know he was here, Leo asked himself, when I didn't?

As he stood there, she got up from the sofa and put on the shoes.

'What's the story?' he asked. Still surprised. Still puzzled. But still in love with her. 'Why are you here? And,' he turned to Donal, 'you're supposed to be in London. I came by because I wanted to borrow . . .' His voice trailed off as he suddenly read the expression on Donal's face. And on Vanessa's.

'You've got to be kidding me,' he said slowly. 'You have absolutely got to be kidding me.'

'Leo, I'm sorry.' It was Vanessa who spoke first. Rapidly, urgently, her words spilling out of her mouth. 'I didn't mean this to happen.'

'Mean what to happen?'

'Can we sit down and talk about this like adults?' asked Donal.

Leo stared at him. 'Talk about what?'

'Oh, Leo . . .' Vanessa's voice quavered.

'We have to talk about it,' said Donal. 'And I'm sorry.'

'You and her?' Leo still couldn't really comprehend it. 'You and her? My brother and my fiancée?'

'It just happened.' Vanessa was crying now. 'We didn't realise at first. We never wanted to hurt you. We—'

'How long?' demanded Leo.

'A few weeks,' said Donal.

'You're my *brother*,' said Leo. 'I trusted you. When I told you to keep an eye on her while I was away last month, I didn't mean you were to jump into bed with her.'

'Look, Leo—'

'You disgust me.' Leo could feel the rage coursing through his veins. 'A few weeks! You could have told me straight away. If that was what you wanted – both of you . . . I don't believe it.'

'We couldn't believe it ourselves,' said Vanessa. 'That's why—'

'I don't want to hear it,' said Leo. 'You're my family, Donal. *Family*. And you . . . you . . .'

'I think I should go,' said Vanessa. She picked up her bag from beside the sofa. 'I'll call you, Leo. We need to talk. But not tonight.'

'Right. Run away,' said Leo bitterly. 'That's always been the way for you, hasn't it?'

'Don't talk to her like that.' Donal, taller than Leo by a couple of inches, faced his brother. 'It's not her fault.'

'No?' said Leo hotly. 'I suppose you jumped on her and she didn't know how to resist.'

'I won't hit you because I know you're upset,' said Donal. 'But don't you ever say anything like that again.'

'Donal, please . . . I'm going.' Vanessa edged towards the door.

'I'll drive you home,' said Donal. 'And then I'll come back here and we'll talk, Leo.'

'You needn't bother,' Leo told him. 'I won't be here. I'm not going to sit around and wait for you to feed me stories about not meaning to fall in love and all that bullshit.'

'We'll go.' Donal put his arm around Vanessa, and Leo flinched.

'You bastard!' he shouted as Donal walked out the door. 'I'll fucking kill you. I'll fucking kill the pair of you.'

It was nearly two hours later that the police arrived at the house and told Leo that they were both dead.

He looked up. The group had got further ahead of him and he walked quickly to catch up. He was thinking of Donal now, thinking of how his brother would have liked to have been here; how Donal had said that the cruise sounded a great idea because it would combine Vanessa's love of being pampered with Leo's love of going to new places. Donal had been pleased and excited for him when he'd told him that he was going to marry Vanessa. His brother had clapped him on the back and told him that she was a great girl and that he was delighted for him.

And yet somehow Vanessa had stopped being his girl and started, clandestinely, being Donal's. But what Leo didn't know, what he'd never know, was what the two of them had planned. To tell him? To carry on the affair? Even after they got married? Leo was wrecked with not knowing. Not knowing why or when or how. Not knowing whether it was Vanessa who'd grown away from him or Donal who'd taken her away. Not knowing what it was that Donal had that he hadn't. Or for how long Vanessa had been unhappy with him. And he didn't know whether she would have married him if Donal hadn't come along, and if so whether their marriage would have been a sham.

Lastly, in the list of not knowing, he had no idea whether her family knew anything about it either. When he met Janet Calelly, Vanessa's mother, she said nothing about any relationship her daughter might have had with his brother, but simply crumpled in his arms, crying that she'd lost her precious daughter and she'd never get over it. Vanessa's father hadn't asked why Vanessa was in the car with Donal. He'd looked at Leo brokenly and said that he was sorry; Leo had lost two people, Johnny Calelly said. It must be very hard for him.

So Leo himself didn't say anything about Donal and Vanessa and allowed people, when they had made the assumption, to think that his brother and his fiancée had been going out to the shops or the off-licence or some other undefined place together while Leo waited for them at Donal's house. The police had asked him questions about Donal and Vanessa and Leo was sure that they guessed more than they talked about; but in the end, the bottom line was that Donal had, for whatever reason, gone through an amber light in Terenure village, had then swerved to avoid a car that had jumped the lights at the intersection, and had ended up planted into the wall of the building opposite. Despite the half-empty wine bottle, his blood-alcohol level had been below the legal limit and so wasn't considered a factor in the accident. The police had wanted to know whether Donal was a habitual amber gambler, and Leo had said no, that his brother was normally a safe driver. Which was the truth. Which meant, as far as Leo was concerned, that Donal had gone through the lights because he was upset, and he was upset because Leo had arrived unexpectedly at his house and found him and Vanessa together. And because he knew that he couldn't talk to Leo there and then. And because Vanessa wanted to go home.

And so, Leo wondered, whose fault was the accident? His, for screaming after them that he'd kill them? Vanessa's, for wanting to leave? Donal's, for careless driving? Nobody's fault and everybody's fault, and the only good thing about it, Leo often told himself, was that nobody else had been injured. Nobody else had been killed.

But in dying like that, Donal had ripped Leo's dreams and hopes apart. Donal had been Leo's only sibling. He had no other close relatives, Aunt Sandra being the only person on his mother's side of the family he kept in touch with. He'd been looking forward to being part of Vanessa's family. He liked her parents and her brothers and sisters. And he'd looked forward to having children with her too. All of that had gone. A year ago he'd had everything, or the promise of everything. Now he had nothing.

And it still hurt every single second of every single day.

* * *

'Bloody hell!' Britt yelped as she stood in the middle of the last rope bridge and swatted the side of her face. 'I've been bitten.'

The bridge swayed and she stumbled, grabbing hold of the rope and holding on to it as tightly as she could.

'Are you OK?' Leo, standing behind her, held on to her arm with his free hand. The other was holding his walking stick.

'No,' she muttered. And then looked at him from an eye she could already feel swelling up. 'Well, yes and no.' She could feel her sudden panic beginning to abate. 'I felt something bite me. On my face! It's the only place I didn't spray with mozzie-killer. And then I thought I was going to fall.'

'You won't fall,' said Leo. 'It's perfectly safe.'

'Yeah, yeah,' said Britt darkly. 'I want to believe that.'

'It is,' Leo assured her. 'D'you want me to jump up and down to prove it?'

'God, no,' she said hastily. 'At least not until I'm safely on the other side.'

He smiled and she took her hand away from her face.

'Oh,' he said. 'That looks nasty.'

'Little shits,' she said. 'One piece of spray-free skin and they go for it.'

'I have one of those clicker things that you apply to a bite,' he said. 'Let's get off this bridge and I'll treat it for you.'

'Thank you.' Britt followed him to the other side, where Mia, who'd crossed earlier, was waiting for them.

'What's the matter?' she asked.

'Bitten,' said Britt succinctly.

'How on earth . . . ?'

'Mozzie magnet,' said Britt.

Leo took the clicker out of his pocket. 'D'you want to do this yourself?' he asked. 'Or will I?'

'I can manage,' said Britt. She took the clicker and began to feel the side of her face close to her eye. 'Flipping heck. I must look like Rocky.'

'Close,' agreed Mia. 'Not there, you'll miss it!'

'Let me.' Leo took the clicker and applied it to Britt's bite.

She realised suddenly that he was close to her and holding her face in the way that Ralph used to hold it before he kissed her. But her stomach wasn't doing the crazy somersault it had done before and her heart was only beating rapidly from the shock of the sting. Yet the touch of his fingers on her cheeks was gentle, reminding her that it was a long time since anyone had touched her cheeks for any reason at all.

'It's sort of working,' she conceded as he put the clicker away.

'Call into the infirmary when we get back on board,' he advised. 'I'm sure they have some antihistamines.'

'Why me?' muttered Britt. 'I was so careful. And now I'll look like a hag on my Night of Romance.'

'*Your* Night of Romance.' Mia chuckled. 'Oh, how you've changed.'

'*The* Night of Romance,' amended Britt as her fingers continued to explore her swollen face. 'I hate mozzies. I really do.'

'Hey, Britt, you OK?' Pippin Costello jumped from the

rope bridge. Somehow, despite the fact that the ground was flat, she stumbled as she landed, ending up sprawled on the ground, shrieking loudly.

The rest of the group, who'd partly dispersed along the pathway, turned at her cries and Manolo came hurrying back.

'I'm fine, I'm fine,' said Pippin as Leo, abandoning Britt, helped her to her feet. 'I'm sorry, I was silly. I didn't take your advice to watch where I was going, Manolo. But Leo here picked me up.' She clung to Leo's arm.

'Are you all right now?' asked Manolo.

'Absolutely,' said Pippin. She tested her ankle and winced, looking up at Leo with tear-filled eyes. 'I will be, anyhow. But d'you think you could help me back to the bus?'

'Of course,' said Leo solicitously, his attention now completely diverted from Britt. 'Lean on my arm.'

'I will help you,' said Manolo.

'No, I'm fine,' said Pippin. 'Leo's doing great by himself.'

'But will he be able to escape her clutches?' asked Mia as she and Britt followed along behind them.

'And would he want to?' asked Britt as she applied, too late, some repellent spray to her face.

It was early evening before they got back to the ship. In their cabin, Britt examined her face, sighing as she looked at the ugly bump just above her eye.

'It's not as itchy since they put that stuff on it in the infirmary,' she conceded. 'But boy is it ugly.' And then she spun around towards Mia. 'I can't go to dinner looking like this!'

'Why?' asked Mia. 'Do you think it matters to Steve?'

'I don't care whether it matters or not. I'm not going to sit in a dining room with an eye the size of a golfball,' she said. 'Why don't you go instead?'

'Because he asked you,' said Mia.

'He asked both of us so's he could talk about the Night of Romance.' Britt looked curiously at Mia. 'And you said you had a spa thingy on. I forgot about that.'

Mia looked embarrassed. 'That was just an excuse.'

'Why?'

'Because I thought he really wanted to take you to dinner.'

'Are you crazy?'

'No,' said Mia defensively. 'He probably wanted to wine you and dine you and tell you what a great person you were. And I thought I'd be a gooseberry, so . . .'

'You're talking utter nonsense,' Britt told her. 'I'm going to cancel, so if you haven't got a spa treatment booked, you might as well get wined and dined yourself.'

'Yes, but—'

'Oh, look, go and have a nice dinner with a nice man,' said Britt impatiently.

'I'm out of practice at dinners with nice men,' said Mia.

'It's not exactly a date,' Britt reminded her. 'It's to talk about the Night of Romance. So I'm ordering you to go as my PA.'

Mia shrugged helplessly while Britt picked up the guest services booklet and found Steve's phone extension. He answered on the first ring and she explained that she couldn't come to dinner looking like a troll. 'But Mia is free,' she added blithely. 'Her spa treatment is for another day, so you can talk to her about the interview instead.'

'You're on,' she said to Mia as she replaced the receiver. 'Calypso. Seven thirty. Don't be late.'

Mia didn't know why she was feeling so apprehensive about dinner with Steve. Britt was right. It wasn't a date. And yet there was something exciting about meeting a man for dinner for the first time in years. And something exciting in particular about meeting Steve, who had been good to her throughout the trip and who hadn't laughed when she'd panicked about Britt.

He was already at the table, looking dashing and handsome in his white uniform, when she walked into the Calypso. He's incredibly sexy, she thought. Even if I'm not at all interested in meeting incredibly sexy men. And then she laughed to herself, because, of course, it was the uniform that made Steve appear sexy. Although . . . She smiled at him as he pulled out the chair for her to sit down . . . he was attractive too.

'I'm really sorry it's just me,' said Mia as she sat down. 'But Britt didn't want to come out with her face the way it is.'

'I'm delighted you're here,' said Steve. 'Rotten luck for Britt to be bitten, though.'

'I'm sure it'll have gone down by tomorrow,' Mia said. 'She's hoping so anyway, because she's not looking forward to the Night of Romance otherwise.'

'You mean she was looking forward to it before?' Steve grinned knowingly at Mia.

'Well, no,' Mia agreed. 'But she's trying.'

'She did a great job on the talks,' said Steve. 'The comment sheets kept getting better each time.'

'That's Britt for you.' Mia took a bread roll from the silver basket on the table and began to butter it. 'Everything she does turns to gold.'

'Really?'

'More or less.' Mia explained about Britt's legal career and her sudden thrust into the world of publishing. 'She somehow manages to succeed without even trying.' She shrugged. 'It can get irritating from time to time.'

'It probably seems that way, but in my experience, people who don't appear to make any effort are usually trying very hard,' said Steve. 'She strikes me as being a workaholic.'

'You're right,' agreed Mia. 'She's not really your take-time-out-to-smell-the-roses girl. Her personal mantra is that planning is the key to success.'

'Sounds about right,' said Steve. 'So, besides the mozzies, how was your trip today?'

He was easy to talk to, thought Mia as she recounted stories of the rain forest. He listened and asked questions and generally made her feel as though he was really interested in what she had to say. She kept having to remind herself that it was his job to be interested.

'. . . of course I'm looking forward to Guatemala the most,' she said. 'I lived there for a while.'

'Really?'

She told him about her time there (omitting references to Alejo), realising as she spoke that Alejo wasn't the only reason she'd loved living there; that she truly had enjoyed the country and the people.

'I went on the trip to Antigua Guatemala on our last voyage,' Steve said. 'It was very picturesque but I don't think I would've been able to stay there for months.'

'I probably wouldn't now,' admitted Mia. 'It's a young person's place.'

Steve grinned. 'And you're ancient, of course.'

'You know what I mean,' she said severely. 'It's a no-strings sort of town.'

'And do you have strings?' asked Steve.

She didn't know what made her tell him about Allegra. She hadn't intended to, but she couldn't help herself. It seemed like ages since she'd talked properly about her daughter. She didn't with Britt, who, no matter how hard she tried, simply looked bored whenever her niece was mentioned.

'Have you a photo of her?' Steve asked.

'Of course.' Mia smiled. 'But I'm sure you don't want to see it.'

'Why wouldn't I?' He put his knife and fork down on his plate. 'I have six nieces and three nephews and I love 'em all.'

'Really?' Mia looked surprised. 'I wouldn't have thought . . .'

'There you go,' he said good-naturedly, 'stereotyping all men.'

'I'm not. But usually guys aren't interested in photos.' She opened her bag and took out the slim wallet containing photos of Allegra that she took everywhere with her. 'Here she is.'

'She's very pretty,' said Steve as he flicked through it. 'You're lucky.'

'See, that's what I reckon,' Mia told him. 'But most people don't think that way about single mothers.'

'Oh, I don't know . . .'

'People think you're either stupid or selfish,' said Mia. 'Or possibly both.'

'Surely not.'

She shrugged. 'Maybe not everyone. But I know Britt thinks I was daft to get pregnant. And it is kind of selfish bringing a child into the world with only one parent . . .' Her voice trailed off.

'My dad died when I was two,' said Steve. 'My mum brought me and my four brothers and sisters up by herself. She was a single parent and she did a great job.'

'I think people differentiate between widowed and divorced parents and single mums,' said Mia.

'They're wrong,' said Steve. 'A good mother is always a good mother.'

'Thanks.' She felt tears sting the back of her eyes and she swallowed hard. She hadn't expected her dinner with Steve to touch on her personal life. She hadn't expected him to be so warm and interested either. And it was nice to sit in the restaurant as part of a couple, even if he was the cruise director and it was his job to be there, and listen to him pay her compliments. She hadn't had dinner with a man since before Allegra was born. Since before Guatemala, because she'd never even gone out to dinner with Alejo; it had all been a rush and a fizz of passion and sex, and drinks in Riki's bar.

302

God, she thought, I was a fool about him.

'Are you all right?' asked Steve, breaking the silence that had settled on them.

'Of course,' she replied quickly. 'I was just thinking that we needed to get on with talking about Britt's Night of Romance.'

'Ah, yes.' He grinned at her. 'You're working on board. Just like me. We can't lounge around like the rest of the passengers.'

She laughed. He might be paid to be here, she thought, but he does a really good job of it all the same.

Chapter 16

Position: at sea.
Weather: fine and clear. Wind: easterly force 5.
Temperature: 28°. Barometric pressure: 1011.0mb.

Britt was panicking about her interview with Steve Shaw. She was panicking because despite the fact that Mia had come back from dinner with a list of the type of questions he was going to ask ('Though not the actual questions,' she had said. 'He doesn't want you to rehearse the answers'), she had a horror of suddenly freezing on stage, forgetting what he'd asked her and being totally unable to answer. Or she was afraid he'd ask her questions she wouldn't actually know the answers to, questions she'd managed to bluff her way through in the talks, like 'How do you write a book?', which she always felt was so difficult to give an intelligent reply to, even though it should have been simple.

She was also panicked about the fact that her eye was still swollen, and despite the best efforts of the girls in the Hellenic spa, she had the look of someone who, in a mad anti-ageing session, had had collagen injected into the wrong part of her face.

'It's not that bad,' Mia reassured her. 'You're just self-conscious about it.'

'So would you be if you had a large lump on the south-west of your forehead!'

'I suppose that's a kind of writer's poetic licence, is it?' asked Mia. 'It's a small bump.'

'It looks awful.'

'I never realised how vain you were before.'

Britt turned away from the mirror and faced her sister. 'I'm not vain.'

'You're being incredibly vain,' said Mia. 'You're going to be on stage, for heaven's sake. People won't be able to see your mozzie bite. So get real and stop having a mickey fit over something so silly.'

'You're right,' Britt agreed, although she peered into the mirror again. 'It's displacement activity really. Worrying about the bump stops me worrying about the interview.'

'Why are you worried about that?' demanded Mia. 'If you're all that concerned, you can get plastered before-hand just like you did for the *Late Late*.'

Britt shuddered. 'I don't think so,' she said. 'I saw the DVD afterwards and it was embarrassing.'

'I saw the DVD too. I just thought you were acting perky, which was a bit out of character for you back then all right.'

'I don't do perky now!'

'Yes you do,' Mia said. 'You've been getting perkier by the day.'

'You think?' Britt chuckled. 'Maybe it's just the cumulative effect of the mojitos.'

'Maybe.' Mia laughed. 'Or maybe it's just that actually you can be quite fun when you put your mind to it.'

'You told me I was whingey,' protested Britt. 'And miserable.'

'True,' Mia agreed. 'But also fun.'

'That's the first time anyone's ever called me fun before,' said Britt. 'I was thinking about it one day when you were off at the pool and I was sitting on the balcony. When we were kids, everyone thought you were fun and I was a bit moody. And I guess that's how I'll always see myself. If I was writing a lonely hearts ad, I wouldn't be able to put in that I had a good sense of humour.'

Mia shook her head. 'Of course you would.'

'Seriously, no.' Britt was quite determined. 'I haven't. I don't find lots of things funny. I think life is kind of hard. So many people get a raw deal – not just my divorce women, but women who get beaten up and women who are left to look after families on their own . . .'

'I look after a family on my own and I don't think I've been given a raw deal,' Mia said. 'I think I've been blessed.'

'I never thought of you as a family,' Britt said slowly. 'I guess I just thought of you as Mia and Allegra.'

'A family.'

'I'm worse than useless.' Britt sat down abruptly on the bed. 'I'm supposed to know everything and I know nothing.'

'At least you've learned to fake it,' Mia said. 'Now come on, your public is waiting.'

* * *

It was impossible to see the bump on Britt's face from the auditorium. In fact, her golden curls effectively hid it as she sat in the comfortable green armchair that had been placed on stage opposite Steve Shaw. The audience saw a woman in a sky-blue dress and matching shoes sitting back in the chair looking relaxed. Britt saw nothing but the bright stage lights in her eyes.

How do actors do it? she wondered. How did Ralph do it?

He had done it, after all. Shortly after their divorce had become final, she'd seen his name on the cast list for a production of *The Importance of Being Earnest* at the Gate. He played Dr Chasuble, and according to the critic who'd reviewed the opening night, had been a perfect fit for the part.

She'd gone to see the play on her own and stared up at the stage, knowing that it was Ralph who was up there but not seeing him, seeing only the character he was playing. And she suddenly realised that her ex-husband was a good actor and that the critic had been absolutely right.

A good actor, she thought. And a brilliant boyfriend. But a crap husband. I did the right thing. And it made me a better divorce lawyer, too.

'. . . and so,' asked Steve as the interview drew to a close, 'what you're saying is that romance is very important but talking to each other is worth more.'

'I think so,' Britt replied, her voice clear and confident. 'I think we all have different dreams, inner dreams, and sometimes they're really private and important to us. But when we're with someone, when we want to share our lives with them, then we have to share our dreams too.'

The audience applauded and Britt, who'd somehow forgotten that they were there at all, was startled by the sound.

'On that note,' Steve said, 'I want to thank the lovely Brigitte Martin for sharing her life and her experiences with us tonight and remind you that her wonderful novel is still for sale in the ship's bookstore. Additionally, all night, the *Aphrodite*'s special cocktail is the Romantic Rum – it's served in our commemorative cocktail glass, which you can keep.'

The audience applauded again, the lights dimmed and they filed out of the auditorium while Steve escorted Britt off stage.

'You were amazing,' he said. 'Great interview.'

'Thanks.' She sighed with relief. 'You asked good questions.'

'Mia helped me with them.'

'She knows me too well!'

'She's very smart,' said Steve.

'I know.' Britt smiled as Mia came towards them. 'What did you think?'

'You know you're just wanting me to say great,' teased Mia. 'It was fantastic. Everyone loved it. They were all saying nice things as they left.'

'Good.'

'So now . . .' Mia grinned at her, 'you're free to do whatever you like on board. Are you going to take your own advice and smell the roses, grab your opportunities and reach for the stars, et cetera, et cetera?'

'Not just yet,' replied Britt. 'I'm going to have a Romantic Rum and something to eat. I couldn't touch anything earlier, but I'm absolutely starving now.'

They went to the café for food and then afterwards to the Panorama Lounge, where some of the passengers came up to Britt and told her that they'd really enjoyed the evening of romance, and her book too. Leo Tyler came into the bar with Pippin Costello, and Mia nudged Britt.

'They're looking very much the couple these days,' she said.

Britt shrugged and said nothing.

'The *Aphrodite*'s very own romance,' said Mia. 'Maybe they'll be on a promo brochure for this cruise next year.'

'Maybe,' said Britt. 'But being part of a couple will hardly enhance her career in modelling, will it?'

'She's probably thinking that anyone who can afford to stay in the Delphi suite can afford to keep her in fake boobs and short skirts,' remarked Mia.

Britt smiled. 'You're being a bit harsh on her.'

'Realistic,' said Mia. 'You used to be realistic. I hope all this romance hasn't turned your head.'

'No.' Britt sipped the Romantic Rum she'd felt obliged to order. (It was actually gorgeous, she thought. Very moreish.) 'But just because she knows what she wants doesn't mean we should be judgemental.'

'Aw, come on, Britt! She's a bimbo.'

'She's clearly smart enough to see a good thing and latch on to it,' agreed Britt.

Mia grinned. 'You think Leo is a good thing?'

'Hey, anyone who can afford to stay on his own on this floating barge of lurve is obviously a good thing,' said Britt. 'But I still don't think she's the right girl for him in the long run.'

'The thing is, everyone thinks it's a totally glamorous job, but it's bloody hard work,' Pippin was telling Leo as she stirred her Romantic Rum with a cocktail stick. 'Let's face it, walking through St Stephen's Green on a frosty December morning wearing a leopard-print bikini isn't most people's idea of fun.'

'I can imagine,' said Leo. 'What d'you do about goose pimples?'

'Wrap up warm beforehand,' said Pippin. She shook her head so that her luxuriant hair cascaded around her face. 'And afterwards.'

She talked about work in the same way as Vanessa, thought Leo. She liked the limelight, she liked buzzy parties and being at the cutting edge. When he'd been with Vanessa he'd liked those things too. Although he'd sometimes told her that they were shallow and frivolous.

'Of course they are,' she'd said, her dark eyes dancing with fun. 'But we all need shallow and frivolous in our lives. It would be desperately boring if it was only about hard work.'

Leo's life before Vanessa had been about hard work. Not just work, he used to tell her; he played five-a-side soccer with his colleagues from the bank every Thursday evening, and he met Mike for a few pints at least twice a month. So he didn't spend his time totally wrapped up in his job.

Vanessa had laughed at that, pointing out that the five-a-side was followed by an informal meeting, on the basis that when they went for a drink afterwards they invariably talked about the boring, boring world of international banking; and that Mike was his best friend, so meeting him twice a month was hardly pushing the boat out. Leo had replied that most of his evenings were taken up with entertaining clients of the bank, and that was totally social, but Vanessa had shaken her head and told him that he was a blind fool who cared more about work than he did about her, but that she loved him.

When did she stop loving him? wondered Leo. She must have stopped because otherwise she wouldn't have turned to Donal. So when? And why? Because I wasn't frivolous enough for her? Spontaneous enough? She said that sometimes. But was it really the reason?

'Oh!' He'd been holding the blue plastic cocktail stick between his fingers and suddenly it snapped. He put the two halves down on the table in front of him.

'Are you tense about something?' asked Pippin.

'Not really,' he replied.

'You should go for the stress-busting massage in the spa,' she told him. 'Mum and I went the other day. It's magic. You feel like you're floating on air afterwards.'

Vanessa had loved spas, remembered Leo. She regularly booked weekends away at places like Monart and Inchedoney with her friends. 'It's my reward to myself,' she told him. 'For working hard.'

My reward to myself was buying the house in Monkstown, thought Leo, with its sliver of a view of the sea from the top bedroom window. It was an old house and he'd spent a lot of money renovating it. He'd been halfway through it when he'd met Vanessa, and she'd taken over supervising the work when they'd got engaged. The job still wasn't finished, although the main bedroom, with its six-foot four-poster bed and antique furniture, was magnificent, while the kitchen was modern but not too minimalist.

'You look tired.' Pippin suddenly leaned towards him and touched him very gently on the face. 'You shouldn't look tired.'

'I didn't sleep well last night,' he confessed.

'I've slept like a top every night,' she told him. 'But I think that's because I was totally exhausted before we came. I'm glad my parents asked me along, but I'm very, very glad I met you, because I don't want to be intruding on them all the time.'

He smiled at her. 'That's thoughtful of you.'

'It is their anniversary after all,' she said. 'Can you imagine – twenty-five years with the one person?'

'If it's the right person . . .'

'That's what I'm hoping,' she told him. 'To find the right person and to spend my life with him.'

'Are you?' he asked.

'Of course.' She looked at him seriously. 'I know that my career is important to me, but what's a million times more important is finding someone to love. And someone who loves you back.'

'What if you meet him and then someone better comes along?' asked Leo.

Pippin frowned. 'You have to work at a relationship,' she said. 'My mum always says that. And you should never think that someone better has come along because you shouldn't get into that situation.'

'So you're a loyal sort of person?'

'Absolutely,' she said.

'That's a good thing,' Leo said slowly. 'A really good thing.'

Pippin smiled her wide smile. 'Faithfulness is underrated these days,' she said. 'But I know that when I meet the right person I'll be with him for ever.'

And she touched him gently on the cheek again.

'They're looking pretty loved up now,' observed Mia.

Britt watched as Pippin rested her head on Leo's shoulder. Her stomach did the weird somersault thing again and she wondered if actually what was wrong with her was simply overeating. Certainly there was no need for her stomach to go into freefall at the sight of Leo Tyler. Who was, after all, with the most beautiful woman on board.

It must have been a relationship that crashed and burned that brought him here, she decided. Perhaps, despite his views on women and love, he'd come on the cruise to find someone new. Because the truth was that men weren't good alone. Many of them preferred to be in a difficult marriage than no marriage at all. The statistics showed that most divorces were initiated by women. In the case of Clavin & Grey, seventy-five per cent of her clients were women who wanted to divorce their husbands. She knew that many of them were still alone a year later, whereas most of the husbands had found someone else.

Men need women more than women need men, she thought. And yet we're the ones who agonise the most about our relationships. I wonder why that is.

Ralph had found someone new. The actress that Britt had seen him with hadn't been a long-term prospect and she knew, from occasional awkward encounters with their few mutual friends, that there had been a string of others after her. But there was a woman now and she'd been in his life for the past two years. Britt had heard they were engaged, although she wasn't sure if that was rumour or fact. She wondered whether Ralph acted out his fantasies for her. And whether she enjoyed them.

'Do you want to go for a walk on the promenade deck?' asked Pippin as she drained her soda water. (Pippin only allowed herself one alcoholic drink every two days. The cruise was proving very difficult in terms of sticking to her normally very strict diet.)

'Yes, why not.' Leo stood up and the two of them left the lounge.

There was something undeniably restful about standing beside the ship's rail looking out across the ocean, he thought. And something deeply satisfying about having someone to share the moment with.

He could feel the warmth of Pippin's bare arm against his, and smell the fragrance of the perfume she wore. A lighter one than Vanessa's, he thought, but not entirely dissimilar.

She's a nice girl, he thought. Ambitious, but not in the single-minded way Vanessa was. And caring. She's always asking me how I'm feeling. Vanessa didn't do that. Vanessa just told me how *she* was feeling. But maybe I didn't always listen. If I get the chance in future, I'll listen.

Pippin moved closer to him and he put his arm around her. Her face was touching his. Her floral scent was very beautiful. He turned towards her. He wanted to kiss her. He wanted to feel his lips on a woman's lips again.

It wouldn't be mindless sex with Pippin, he told himself. He cared about her. And she obviously cared about him. She'd come on to him enough. With Vanessa, at the start, he'd done all the running – from the moment he'd met her at a PR function organised by his bank. Somewhere deep in his heart, he'd always felt that he loved Vanessa more than she loved him. Well, he'd been right about that, hadn't he? But with Pippin . . . He turned towards her and she smiled at him. He hadn't had to run after Pippin. He didn't love her more than she loved him. He wasn't sure that he loved her at all yet. But maybe he would. Because she was the right sort of person to love.

He kissed her.

They were still kissing when Britt and Mia walked by, unnoticed, a couple of minutes later.

'And so romance blossomed on board,' said Mia gleefully as they let themselves into their cabin. 'I wouldn't have put money on it on the first day, but I guess if you lock healthy men and women up on a boat, something's got to give sooner or later.'

'I expect you're right.' Britt dropped her bag on the bed. 'I'm surprised, though.'

'So am I,' Mia said. 'I still think he had a thing for you, sis, if only you'd encouraged him.'

'He said *you* were nice, remember?' Britt slid her earrings from her ears. 'You. Not me. So if there was a thing . . .'

Mia shook her head. 'He's too cool for me,' she said. 'I thought maybe even too cool for you! But not too cool for Pippin, it seems.'

'Holiday romance,' said Britt. She put the earrings on the dresser. 'At least I hope so. Otherwise I can't help feeling she'll break his heart.'

Pippin looked at her watch. 'It's getting late,' she said. 'I think I'll head off to bed. I'm in cabin E22,' she added. 'Not the most luxurious, I know. But obviously Mum and Dad have the decent one, it being their anniversary after all.'

'Where are they?' he asked.

'On B deck. Not as flashy as you.' She grinned. 'A suite of your very own!'

Leo shrugged. 'In the end, it's just somewhere to put your head.'

'You can't say that,' protested Pippin. 'I saw the suites in the brochure. You could live in them.'

'I guess you're right,' Leo acknowledged. 'There's a business mogul who spends half a year in the Oceanus suite.'

'Maybe at some point in my life . . .' Pippin sounded envious.

'Would you really want to spend six months on a ship?'

'Perhaps not,' she admitted. 'But I can't believe we'll be docking in Acapulco soon. The time is flying by.'

'That's true,' said Leo. 'So, are you and your parents having a good time?'

'Absolutely,' Pippin replied. 'They're already talking about doing it again next year. Are you enjoying it?'

Leo thought for a moment before answering. 'More than I thought,' he said finally. But not as much as I should be, he added to himself. Not as much as if it had been my honeymoon.

'You look better,' she told him.

'Huh?'

'Than at the start. Then you were pale and tired looking. Now you're tanned and you look great!' She grinned at him.

'I feel better.' He was surprised to realise it was true.

'Of course you do,' Pippin said. 'Why wouldn't you?'

Why wouldn't I? thought Leo as he pulled her towards him again.

Chapter 17

Position: Puerto Quetzal, Guatemala.
Weather: fine and clear. Wind: easterly force 2.
Temperature: 32°. Barometric pressure: 1012.3mb.

Mia was awake before the *Aphrodite* docked at Puerto Quetzal. She hadn't been able to sleep, knowing that in a few hours she would be back in the country where she'd met Alejo and where Allegra had been conceived. It seemed right to her to return, as though she could find something in the old city that would tell her she'd done the right thing, and was still doing the right thing. And maybe something that would tell her how to keep doing it.

She'd already showered and dressed by the time the ship had berthed at the dock. Mia had never been to Puerto Quetzal before, but she knew that it was a popular stopping-off point for cruise ships, as well as being the country's major industrial port. There was evidence of the industry in the large cranes and freight on the quayside. She was sure there'd be something for the tourists too.

But she wasn't a tourist. She wasn't looking to buy knitted caps or other souvenir trinkets. She was going on the organised trip to Antigua Guatemala, the old city where she'd lived, but she wasn't going to get involved in any of the touristy things that might have been organised for them. She was going to have a drink at Riki's or one of the other bars and cafés that she and Alejo and Peter and Frank and the others had frequented; maybe she'd go to the house where she'd rented a room . . . she wasn't sure yet. Her plan was to retrace her past so that she could put her present into perspective.

Britt came out on to the balcony and surveyed their surroundings. She didn't think the port was very pretty either.

'But the country is,' promised Mia.

'I've decided to come with you to Antigua Guatemala,' Britt told her. 'I know I said I was going to stay on board, but I thought that maybe there'd be a beach here . . . It'd be better fun going with you.'

Mia hesitated.

'Unless you'd rather go alone?'

'I don't mind if you come,' said Mia diffidently. 'Though I'm not planning to stick with the tour exactly.'

'What then?'

'Visit places I used to go. That sort of thing.'

'Will you have time?'

'Sure. It's a small enough place. But I think you'd prefer to do the tour, to be honest. What I want to do is very boring.'

'Might help me to understand you better.'

'You understand me well enough.'

'You'd rather I didn't come,' said Britt.

'No. No – do come.' Mia turned and smiled at her. 'You can choose to go down memory lane with me or hang out with the rest of the crowd. I don't mind.'

'Great,' said Britt. 'It'll be fun.'

It was ironic, Mia thought, that the one day in the entire cruise on which she felt edgy and uncertain was the day that Britt had decided would be their fun day. Britt had originally talked about going on the tour to the Mayan ruins and leaving Mia to her own devices, but that tour had been booked out, which was why she'd then elected to stay on board the ship. Mia would have preferred to be on her own, yet she didn't want to burst Britt's bubble of spontaneity and sisterhood. All the same, it was inconvenient that she'd embraced it at a time when Mia herself was feeling completely on edge.

'Bring your fleece,' Mia advised as they gathered up their belongings before heading for the tour bus. 'It's cooler there than at the coast and it can get chilly in the shade.'

'Really?'

As always, it had been warm and humid on the balcony of the cabin, and Britt looked surprised at Mia's instructions.

'Honestly,' Mia assured her. 'You'll be thanking me later.'

So Britt took with her the royal-blue fleece that had been sitting in the suitcase ever since London.

The bus drive was long, but the sight of the country's volcanoes on the horizon awed all of the passengers, especially when their guide pointed out that the wisp of cloud over one of them was in fact smoke.

'They're still active,' Mia told Britt, who was staring at the perfectly shaped volcano. 'Agua, which is only about ten kilometres from La Antigua, has been inactive for a long time, though it does sometimes spew out mud and stuff, but Fuego blows its top every so often. They're part of the Ring of Fire.'

'Ring of Fire?' Britt looked puzzled.

'Volcanoes around the Pacific Ocean,' Mia explained. 'It's like a necklace from South America through Central and North America on one side and then down through Asia and Oceania on the other. Mount Fuji, in Japan, is part of it.'

'I didn't know that,' said Britt. 'I didn't know you were so interested in volcanoes either.'

'I came here with geologists.' Mia gazed out of the bus window. 'I picked it up. There are thirty-three volcanoes in Guatemala alone, so you meet a fair few volcanologists wandering around the place.'

'Not my idea of a fun job,' said Britt, 'but I can see it might appeal to some people.'

'Mmm.' Mia nodded. 'Perhaps if I'd done like you said and swotted more at school, I might have gone down that road.'

'You think?'

'Well, probably not,' Mia conceded. 'You have to be good at writing reports as well as the more interesting stuff like climbing into craters, so maybe it's not for me.'

The bus turned a corner and began climbing higher into the hills.

'Every single time we've been on a tour we've ended

up creaking our way through the mountains,' said Britt as the driver dropped the gears and the bus lurched forward. 'Maybe Meredith's idea of lying around getting pampered all day wasn't so bad after all.'

'You could've stayed on board,' Mia reminded her.

'Didn't want to,' said Britt. 'You're right – we're here and we should see as much as we can.'

It was another thirty minutes before they reached the old city, and Mia bit her lip as the memories flooded back. There was the street where she'd first stayed. The bar where she used to meet Alejo and the other guys on the volcano project. The restaurant where they'd shared tortilla . . . She was seeing these things while the guide was pointing out the cathedral and the small but beautiful square known as Central Park, and then finally the restaurant where they were booked in for lunch.

'It's a touristy one,' Mia told Britt. 'They do dancing and stuff too. You'll enjoy it.'

'You're not coming?'

'I want to have a wander,' Mia said. 'And the places I want to go to aren't hugely interesting. So you should enjoy yourself and I'll meet you back at the bus in an hour and a half or so. I'll haul you off to less touristy places then if you like.'

'I'm not that pushed about lunch with the masses. I'll come with you.'

'Would you mind awfully if I did this on my own?'

Britt looked at her. She understood wanting to be on your own. She wasn't going to force the issue. So she told Mia that it was perfectly all right, and then followed the guide through the wrought-iron gates into the courtyard of the restaurant while her sister turned down the street and walked back towards the park.

When Mia had first arrived here, she'd felt as though she'd stepped back in time. Antigua Guatemala, or La Antigua as it was often called, was a colonial city, built by the Spanish conquistadores and almost perfectly preserved. The houses were small, usually single storeyed, and painted in bright colours, so that the pinks and oranges glowed in the light of the sun; the streets were narrow and cobbled, and overlooking it all was the imposing Volcan de Agua, the Volcano of Water. Mia had felt, on her first day, as though Clint Eastwood could ride into town at any moment, wearing a poncho and tilting his cowboy hat against the blinding sun, ready to be on the side of truth, justice and the little guy. (He would, of course, have had to compete with the tour buses, bicycles and cars that also filled the streets, but Mia tried to filter them out and see the city as it would be without them.)

On the day she arrived, it had only taken her a few minutes to find the hostel where she'd already booked herself a bed for a few nights. After she'd dumped her bag she'd met up with Peter and Frank, who'd arrived two weeks earlier for the eco-conference they were attending. They'd all gone to a bar, had a few beers, laughed and joked together, and she'd felt glad that she'd come here. The town had a bohemian feel to it; it was a relaxed and informal place where she felt she could fit in. Internet cafés stood side by side with craft shops and old bars, and sometimes Mia felt as though she was living in a moving postcard.

While Frank and Peter were doing their eco-thing, she'd booked herself some one-to-one Spanish lessons with a local woman, Josefina, a petite beauty with a sense of fun who'd spent a couple of years in America before returning home. Mia then offered to give English lessons to anyone Josefina knew, and before long she had a number of pupils and was enjoying herself.

She'd met Alejo in the cathedral, a white building with an ornate façade, which, although somewhat shaken and stirred by earthquakes and other natural events, was still very impressive.

Mia wasn't a particularly religious person (Gerry and Paula, having come from two separate branches of the Christian faith, hadn't wanted to impose beliefs on their children), but she liked the heavy silences and the ornate statuary of old churches. She'd gone into the cathedral to look around, not to pray, but as she was leaving she noticed a man kneeling towards the back, his head bowed. It was unusual to see men who weren't elderly in Irish churches these days, although she supposed it might be different in other countries. As she walked towards him, her leather sandals clicking off the floor, he looked up and his eyes met hers.

Dark, dark eyes in an olive-skinned face. Black hair. A jawline so sharp, it was almost like a line drawing. But strong. And when he smiled at her, suddenly soft. She felt herself blush. She hadn't intended to look at him – to stare, really, which was what she'd been doing as she walked down the aisle. She dropped her own eyes downwards and hurried outside, where old women and young children were bustling by and where she finally sat down under a tree in the park.

The sun was warm through the dappled leaves, but the breeze cooled her down. She touched her cheeks, which were still hot. There had been something about the eye contact with the man in the church that had affected her in a totally unaccustomed way. Now she was hot and bothered, embarrassed but not sure exactly why.

'*Hola*.' He stood in front of her, a slight smile on his face.

'I . . . Hello. *Hola*,' she said.

'American?' he asked. 'English?'

She shook her head. 'Irish.'

His smile broadened. 'Dublin,' he said. 'I have visited there. A nice city.'

Everyone in the whole world seemed to have visited Dublin, Mia thought. She was always meeting people who'd been to her home city.

He sat down beside her. 'Alejo,' he said.

'Mia.'

'I should have guessed Irish,' he told her, touching her tawny curls. 'This is a good Irish colour. Red hair.'

She laughed. 'My hair isn't red!'

'No?'

'When I was much smaller,' she admitted, 'it was carrot-coloured. But now it's much darker.'

'I like it.'

'Me too,' she confessed. 'And you? Where are you from?'

He looked more European than Guatemalan, but she couldn't be sure.

'Granada,' he told her. 'Spain.'

'I haven't been there,' she said. 'But one day.'

'I hope so,' he said. 'It's a lovely city.'

'So Dublin is nice but Granada is lovely?' she teased.

'*Claro*,' he said. 'When you come, you will think so too.'

It was funny, she thought – though not amusing funny . . . funny in that whole life-can-be-amazing way – how they were talking about cities and yet she was thinking about him. Specifically she was thinking about making love to him. She'd never thought that way before about a guy she'd just met. She'd seen men, of course, sized them up, wondered what they'd be like . . . but she'd never pictured in her head, sitting in front of them, what they'd be like stretched out naked on the bed beside her.

She shivered.

'Cold?'

'The breeze,' she said.

'You need something?' He took the fawn jumper that had been draped loosely over his white shirt and around his shoulders and hung it around her bare ones instead. His fingers touched the skin of her arms. It was as though she had been jolted by a million volts.

'Thank you.' She sat beside him for a moment, trying to figure out what was happening to her. She'd heard about this instant attraction, but she'd never believed in it. Not like this. Not like something that drove every single thought from your head other than the fact that you wanted to make love to this person right here and right now.

Make love! She dragged her mind back from whatever primeval pond she'd allowed it to enter. They wouldn't be making love. They'd be having sex. She had to get some kind of grip on herself.

'I've got to go.' She stood up abruptly so that her pretty knitted bag fell from the wooden bench and spilled its contents on to the ground. 'Oh crap!'

'Don't worry.' He bent down and began picking up bits and pieces – her lip gloss, her spare pair of sunglasses, a pen that she'd robbed from the last hotel she'd stayed in.

'You're in a hurry to leave me,' he said.

'I – I've things to do.'

He looked disappointed. 'Perhaps a drink? Later? Riki's?'

'I don't know. I'm meeting friends later.'

'OK.' His smile drooped slightly in defeat. 'Perhaps I'll see you around sometime.'

'Perhaps,' she said as she returned his jumper and scuttled out of the park towards the hostel.

Peter told her that he'd booked a table at the Helas Taverna, next door to Riki's, for dinner. There'd be five of them: Mia, himself, Frank, plus Per-Henrik (another eco-conference attendee) and his girlfriend Vivi. They could, if there was room, go into the bar later and listen to the music. Mia nodded, but all she could think of was whether there was any possible chance Alejo would be there.

She spent much longer than usual getting ready to go out, steaming the creases from her indigo silk dress over the bath and sacrificing comfort for style by wearing her flimsy sandals with the kitten heels that she could never keep on her feet. She swapped her plain silver earrings for blue stone ones that dangled from her ears, wore the matching necklace that had been at the bottom of her ruck-sack for months, and then swirled blusher on her cheeks and dabbed gloss on her lips.

'*Muy guapa, chica!*' said the receptionist when she came downstairs to wait for the others. Peter and Frank whistled at her, and she giggled and told them that once in a while it was nice to dress up a little. Vivi, who was wearing a pretty sun-dress and bolero jacket, nodded and agreed that sometimes girls had to be girls.

Mia still couldn't remember a single thing she ate that night. All she could remember was later, squeezing into the bar and almost immediately seeing him there, leaning unselfconsciously against a wall. At first he didn't notice her, and then he did and he smiled. And Mia knew that she was completely and utterly in love with someone whose surname she didn't even know.

The touristy stuff was over and the group had been given an hour to wander around the city on their own. The tour bus had parked in the main square and Britt walked down the street in that direction. She wondered where Mia had gone for her sentimental journey. She knew that her sister had loved her time in Antigua Guatemala, but Britt had a feeling that this had more to do with that shit Alejo than with the place itself.

The guide had told them that the city was a UNESCO Heritage Site, and Britt could easily see why. But she simply couldn't imagine staying here for more than a few days. It was too laid-back and disorganised for her. Which, she supposed, was why it was perfect for Mia.

Her sister wasn't at the bus. Britt looked at her watch. She was a little early for their rendezvous, so she sat down on one of the benches under the trees and waited for Mia to show up.

Not in love, of course, Mia told herself as she sat on the edge of Alejo's bed in a small but extremely comfortable hotel at the edge of the city. Not in love, because I know nothing about him and so how can I possibly be in love? But I'm in something and I can't get out of it because I have to sleep with him, I just have to.

'*Querida*,' he whispered, and she slid the indigo dress from her shoulders so that it fell straight on to the polished marble floor.

Britt was glad that Mia had made her bring a fleece, because there was a cool breeze in the park. In the full glare of the sun it was pleasant, but in the shade it was nice to have something warm around your shoulders. She looked at her watch again and decided to go for a stroll before coming back to meet Mia. She didn't need a guided tour really. The city itself was the attraction, not individual buildings. She understood that.

He was her perfect man. He had opened her heart to a whole new meaning of love and of passion. All the guys she'd gone out with before – in school, in college, and when she'd worked for the accountancy company – all those guys were nothing in comparison with him. They were boys, children. They had no idea what it took to give her pleasure, to make her feel like the only woman on earth. Alejo did that every single day. She could think only of him. No matter where she was or what she was doing, Alejo was constantly in her mind. She thought about when she'd see him again, when they'd next be together in the wide bed of his hotel room. Nothing else mattered. Nobody else mattered. Alejo was the only person in her universe.

'You'd want to be careful.' It was Frank who'd warned her. 'You're cutting out all your friends and all the people who care about you. We don't see you any more.'

'It's only been a few weeks.' Her eyes, bright from having spent two hours with Alejo that morning, shone in her tanned face. 'You know what it's like when you fall in love with someone.'

'Yeah. I do,' said Frank. 'But it's different for men. We don't get consumed by it like girls.'

'You haven't met the right girl yet.' Mia smiled at him. 'I hadn't met the right man before now.'

'Don't do anything stupid,' said Frank, which, Mia thought, was a very silly thing to say. There was nothing she could do with Alejo that would be anything other than wonderful. But she did realise that Frank was right about one thing: she'd hardly seen any of her friends since meeting Alejo, and that was wrong. So she asked Alejo to meet her along with them at the bar that night, and although he was reluctant at first, he came along and got on well with Frank and Peter and Per-Henrik and Vivi and all the other people who had become part of their group.

'He's very, very sexy,' Vivi murmured as they sat and

listened to the guitarist play one evening. 'I'd jump his bones myself given half the chance.'

'Too late,' responded Mia. 'They're well and truly jumped already.'

Britt was bored. It was all very well for Mia to go on a sentimental journey, she thought, but her sister could at least have had the decency to get to their rendezvous point on time. It was so typical of her. Drifting along on her cloud of emotion, forgetting that she had made commitments.

She looked at her watch. Fifteen minutes after the time they'd agreed. Mia was probably in a trance in front of some run-down pueblo house, thinking how much nicer it all was than the corporate lifestyle she could have had if she'd stuck with her accountancy career.

Britt sighed. She knew Mia hadn't been cut out for accountancy. But was she really cut out to be a single mother either?

Mia hadn't expected to be a single mother. She'd been sure of herself and sure of him. They both liked the same things, both had the same way of looking at life.

Because he worked with a group who were studying the country's volcanoes, Alejo would spend some days in the city and others camped out on the mountainside. He told her he used to be happiest on the mountainside, but these days he didn't like it as much as before. He missed her, he said. He hated being apart from her.

When they were in town together, he would sometimes

smile at the little girls hurrying with their mamas or their grandmamas to the shops, full of self-importance; or the boys playing football on the streets and shouting with enthusiasm every time they scored a goal. He would laugh at their enthusiasm and say that kids lifted your spirits.

He made her think that he would like to have their child.

He made her think that everything would be all right.

Britt decided to go for a walk. She was fed up sitting and she wanted to see inside the cathedral, which was facing the central park. The original buildings had been damaged by a number of earthquakes but the whitewashed façade looked very beautiful in the sunlight, although it reminded Britt more of an ornate Mexican town hall than a traditional cathedral building.

She walked slowly up the central aisle, absorbing the atmosphere of peace that she always felt in churches, even if, like this one, they were crowded with tourists.

Alejo wasn't due back for another week, during which time Mia allowed herself to imagine what it would be like to live with him, to be a parent to their child with him and to marry him. She hadn't decided in what order any of these things would happen, but she didn't really care. Well, she wanted to live with him above everything, she admitted. But after that, married or unmarried, she didn't care.

He wanted children. He'd told her that the night before he left, as he kissed the sensitive area just below her belly button.

'Lots of children,' he'd said. 'Boys and girls. A whole troupe.'

She'd laughed at him then and made him kiss her even lower.

The day before he was expected back, she met Peter and Frank and the gang in one of their favourite bars, just across the street from Alejo's hotel. There were ten in the group that evening, including Christian, one of the geologists who worked with Alejo. Mia had only met him once before, very briefly, but she remembered his Nordic blond hair and blue eyes. There was a woman sitting beside him who she didn't know at all, very petite and very pretty, with short black hair and dark brown eyes.

There was a sudden silence as she sat down at the table and smiled at everyone.

'Don't mind me,' she said. 'Keep on yapping away. You were very animated about something before I arrived.'

'Nothing important,' said Vivi, her eyes flickering between Mia and the dark-haired woman. 'Um – Mia, do you know Christian?'

'Of course.' Mia smiled at him.

'And this is Belén,' said Christian, indicating the woman beside him. 'Alejo's wife.'

Mia felt her heart pound in her ears and a sudden tremor in her stomach. She could feel the heat of Vivi's eyes on her. She stared unblinkingly at Belén.

'Hello,' said Alejo's wife. 'I'm happy to meet you. I'm sorry. I do not speak English well.'

Mia couldn't speak herself. She continued to stare at Belén.

'Belén arrived today,' said Vivi quickly. 'She wanted to surprise Alejo.'

'Surprise him?' Mia found her voice.

'It is my birthday tomorrow,' explained Belén. 'We always are together on my birthday.'

'Oh.' Mia knew that she wasn't capable of stringing more than a couple of words together.

'It's great that you're here,' Christian said to Belén. 'We missed you.'

'We met Belén in Spain,' explained Tommy, one of Christian's friends. 'When we were working in Granada.'

'Oh.'

'So, Mia.' Peter smiled at her supportively. 'Are you hungry?'

Mia said nothing.

'I'm just going to the bathroom before we order,' said Vivi. 'Mia, d'you want to come too?'

'What is it about ladies?' demanded Tommy. 'Always going to the bathroom together.'

Mia nodded at Vivi and the two of them walked through the stone-flagged restaurant to the tiny bathroom at the back.

'Are you all right?' asked Vivi.

Mia was shaking now. She couldn't believe what she'd heard. A part of her still wanted to think that it was all some kind of mistake. Alejo wouldn't have done this to her. He loved her. He'd told her that a thousand times. She'd believed him. There'd been no reason not to.

'She just turned up at the hotel apparently,' said Vivi. 'Nobody was expecting her.'

'Has anyone . . . said anything?' Mia turned tear-filled eyes to Vivi, who shook her head. 'I can't believe it,' she whispered. 'How could he do this to me?'

'I don't know,' said Vivi. 'I liked him. I thought he was a bit full of himself but I liked him.'

'I loved him.' An enormous tear toppled down Mia's cheek. 'I loved him, and . . .' She leaned her head against the wall. She loved him and she'd thought he loved her. But it had all been a sham. She barely made it to the cubicle before she threw up for the first time since she'd done the pregnancy test.

There were local people in the cathedral too, kneeling at the pews and praying. Britt often wondered why people prayed. Why they thought it did any good when the world was such a difficult place. Prayer didn't stop wars or famines or diseases. Praying didn't get you the job you wanted or the winning lotto numbers or the phone call you'd been waiting for. Praying was a waste of time. If I was the creator, thought Britt, I'd have done a much better job of it in the first place. And people would know whether their prayers to me were worthwhile or not.

Most of the local women in the church were wearing headscarves or mantillas. It was the red-brown hues of Mia's curls that marked her out as different.

Alejo had called at the hostel two days later. She'd been lying on her bed when she heard his distinctive knock at the door. She briefly thought about ignoring it, but that would've been silly. So she got up from the bed and pulled a brush through her tangled hair before going to answer it.

'Mia.' His almost black eyes were full of regret. 'I'm so, so sorry this happened.'

'Sorry what happened?' Mia's voice was rasping. 'Sorry you got married? Or sorry I found out?'

'Mia, listen to me, please.'

So she listened to him. And then she slammed the wooden door closed in his face.

'Mia. I've been waiting for ages.' Britt's whisper managed to convey her annoyance. 'You said you'd meet me half an hour ago.'

'I'm sorry.' Mia looked up at her sister. 'I lost track of the time.'

Britt stared at her. Her face was pale and there were tear tracks running down her cheeks.

'What's the matter?' she asked.

Mia shook her head slowly but didn't speak.

'For heaven's sake, Mia! Something's wrong. What happened?'

'Nothing.'

'Not nothing.' Britt took her sister by the arm and walked her back to the cathedral entrance. 'Nobody cries about nothing.'

'Oh, sometimes people do.' Mia tried to keep her voice light, but it cracked at the end.

'Tell me,' said Britt.

'You can't order me around now.' Mia's smile was watery. 'I'm not your assistant any more.'

'No,' said Britt slowly. 'But you're my sister. And you're upset. So – why?'

They were in the central park again. Their tour bus was still waiting at the opposite side of the square, and Mia glanced at her watch.

'We'll be going shortly,' she said.

'Time to have a coffee,' said Britt. 'Pick a place.'

Mia hesitated.

'If you won't, I will,' said Britt. 'That café over there looks good.'

'Tourist trap,' said Mia.

'I don't care.'

The two of them sat down at a wrought-iron table with a mosaic top of swirling orange and red tiles. A smiling girl took their order for two American coffees with cold milk on the side.

'Well?' said Britt when the wide cups arrived. 'Tell me.'

Mia told her. About coming to Guatemala, about Alejo and about Belén. And all the time Britt's blue eyes grew harder and harder.

'The shit,' she said when Mia had finished. 'So what excuse did he give you? That she didn't understand him? Even though she'd travelled halfway around the world to be with him?'

'No.' Mia stirred her coffee slowly. 'He didn't say any of that. He told me that they'd been married for three years and that they were going through a bad patch and that coming away on this trip had been a . . . trial separation for them.'

'Oh God, not the "we were on a break" excuse!' Britt looked scornfully at her sister. 'That's pathetic.'

'I know. I know. He said they'd agreed to think about their marriage while he was away . . .'

'He did a lot of thinking!' exclaimed Britt.

'. . . and that they needed to get their feelings sorted out,' said Mia. 'But . . . but . . .' She swallowed hard as a tear escaped, and she wiped it away quickly. 'But Belén discovered that she was pregnant.'

'Oh, Mia.' Britt reached out and took hold of her hand. 'I'm sorry. I really and truly am. Why didn't you tell me any of this before? Do Mum and Dad know?'

Mia shook her head. 'I couldn't tell anyone. My heart was broken.' She smiled waterily at Britt. 'I know that sounds melodramatic, but that's how it felt. It was easier to be the stupid girl who'd got pregnant from a one-night stand than have them shower me with sympathy for being a fool.'

'You weren't a fool.'

'Of course I was.' Mia sniffed. 'I just lost my head completely. I didn't ask him any of the questions that you normally do about other girlfriends or stuff like that. It never occurred to me for a second that he might be married. I just wanted him so much that I had sex with him without even thinking about the consequences.'

'And his part in the blame is where, exactly?' demanded Britt. 'Like not telling you he was "on a break". Like not telling you he was married in the first place. Like not being the one to talk protection.'

Mia smiled faintly at her. 'The thing is – and I know you're going to be all divorce lawyer on me, but still – we did love each other. He did love me. He was stunned to see Belén. And when she told him about the baby – well, what could he do?'

'He could have told her that he'd got someone else pregnant while they were "thinking about things",' said Britt hotly.

'He didn't know I was pregnant too,' said Mia simply. 'I never got around to telling him. And afterwards, what was the point?'

'Mia McDonagh!' Britt stared at her. 'He doesn't know about Allegra? At all?'

'Why would I have told him?' asked Mia. 'His wife had just given him the news that he was going to be a father. He didn't need to hear the same story from me.'

'But . . . but . . .'

'If I'd told him then, perhaps he'd have tried to choose,' said Mia. 'How could I make him do that?'

'Did it ever occur to you for a second that he might have meant everything he said to you, and that in the end he would've chosen you? Divorced Belén and married you? So that you and he and Allegra could be a family?'

'I never realised before how keen you were on families,' said Mia.

'Don't be stupid.' Britt drained her coffee. 'You let him walk away from you and his responsibilities because this woman – with whom he was already having problems – turned up and said that she was expecting his child. But Mia, if their marriage was in trouble, having a baby might not have helped. It might have actually made things worse.'

'I thought about that,' said Mia. 'I really did. But I

didn't want to get into it all then. I thought I could wait until later and then decide what was best to do.'

'So did you?'

'After I had Allegra and we moved to Spain, I planned to get in touch with him. Sierra Bonita isn't all that far from Granada. I thought I might be able to track him down there.'

'Didn't you have an address? Email? A mobile number?'

'We both had pay-as-you-go while we were here,' said Mia. 'So we couldn't get in touch afterwards. Not a bad thing really.' She laughed harshly.

'So what did you do?'

'Nothing in the end,' she said. 'Because I saw him in Granada. In the square. He was having coffee with Belén and there was a baby in the pushchair beside them.'

'Oh, Mia.'

'So what was the point? They were clearly still together. They were laughing and joking and . . .' She sighed. 'I walked away.'

'He has a right to know,' said Britt after a short silence. 'Allegra is his daughter too.'

'No he bloody doesn't,' snapped Mia. 'He didn't have the right to make me fall in love with him. He didn't have the right to make love to me when he was supposed to be "thinking things through". He shouldn't have done that. So I hate him for it and I don't want him to have anything to do with Allegra because he doesn't have the right to know about her either.'

'But she'll want to know about him one day.'

'And I'll let her find him and meet him. When she's old enough.'

'Do you still hate him?'

Mia sighed again. 'I . . . Oh, I was crazy about him and I know he was crazy about me too, and it was just totally romantic and lovely and wonderful, and if it hadn't been for getting pregnant . . . Of course I don't hate him!' She looked shamefacedly at Britt. 'To be honest, I still sort of love him. I can't help it. And that's probably why I can't meet him or see him or tell him about Allegra. Because I'd want him to be there for her and he can't be, no matter how much I wish it was different. Or he might want to have influence over her. He might—'

'He should be paying you maintenance,' said Britt. 'He has a responsibility towards you.'

'Maybe. But I have a responsibility too. And it's not to mess up any more.'

'So if you don't want him to know about Allegra and if you don't want anything from him and if you've decided that he's now happily married to this Belén woman, then you should just forget about him,' said Britt.

'How can I,' asked Mia, 'when every single day Allegra reminds me of him?'

'Find someone else.'

Mia shrugged. 'Unmarried mum alert. It's not that simple.'

'You're still young and gorgeous,' said Britt. 'Of course it's that simple.' She shrugged quickly. 'I know, I know. Not entirely. But surely . . .'

'Thank you for saying I'm gorgeous, even though that's so not true,' Mia said. 'Oh, Britt, part of me wants to find someone. Another part of me doesn't want to mess up my family. Me and Allegra. We're good together. And another part of me . . .' She tapped her fingers on the mosaic table. 'Well, Alejo was the one, Britt. You know. The One. He might not have been the available one but he was the one for me. And when you've found the right person, then nobody else will do.'

'That's utter nonsense,' said Britt mildly. 'I've seen loads of women come through my office who all thought they'd married The One. But they wanted a divorce all the same. Sometimes The One is really The Wrong One, even though it takes time to see it. You can find someone else, Mia. You really can. Someone who won't make you sit in an ancient cathedral and cry.'

'You don't approve of me crying.' Mia gave a half-smile. 'It looks weak.'

'Hey, I've cried in the past,' said Britt. 'But you can't cry for ever.'

'You sound like some kind of relationship counsellor,' said Mia.

'I don't think so,' said Britt. 'But I've seen it all. Why people split up. Why they get divorced. I've seen them after they've tried to make a go of it and failed. And they're miserable or angry or hurt or a combination of all those things. But they have to move on, and so do you.'

'You think I haven't?' demanded Mia. 'I'm doing well.'

'You're stuck in that dead-end pueblo with Allegra and you're there because of him.'

'Not because of him,' retorted Mia. 'Because I like it, and it's not dead-end. And I like my life there.'

'You don't need a man in it?'

'I'd've thought you'd be the last person banging on about me having a man in my life,' said Mia scathingly. 'You don't believe in love and romance, after all.'

'I believe in responsibility,' retorted Britt. 'And if you can't be responsible, I believe in substituting that with hard cash. So I think you should tell Alejo about Allegra and force him to be responsible for her.'

Mia shook her head. 'I don't want to get into all that with him, I really don't. I've been thinking a lot about it since we came on this trip. I wanted to come here to see if I could make sense of it. And I think I have.'

'Closure?' Britt's voice was laced with irony.

'Sort of,' admitted Mia. 'To me, Guatemala has always been this intensely romantic period in my life. Along with the despairing stuff. But it was a special place for me. I needed to be able to put it into context.'

'And today you did?'

'A little,' said Mia. 'I went to the places we went to and suddenly I realised that they were just bars and restaurants like any other bar or restaurant and that they weren't gloriously wonderful after all.' She smiled faintly. 'I had my rose-coloured sunglasses on while I was here. Today I took them off. Central Park is just a park – a nice park, but just a park all the same. I used to think of it as this beautiful old square, full of joy and colour and movement and passion.'

'It *is* beautiful,' said Britt.

'I know. But in my head it was ultra-gorgeous and there were flowers and oranges and everything was muzzy and unfocused, like a Monet painting. None of it was real.'

'Monet had cataracts,' observed Britt. 'That's why his paintings were fuzzy.'

Mia laughed. 'Your practical nature reasserts itself.'

'Can't help myself.'

The waitress came out of the café and asked if they wanted more coffee. But Britt pointed towards the bus, which the *Aphrodite* passengers were beginning to board.

'We'd better go,' she said. 'Can we have the bill?'

She paid for the coffees and then walked across the square with Mia towards the coach.

'And when you got closure on the city, did you get closure on him too? Or do you still think he's The One?'

'I can never quite have closure on him,' admitted Mia. 'But maybe I can put him behind me.'

'And you don't think he should know about Allegra?'

'He lost all his rights when he lied to me,' Mia said. 'And that's why I don't have to tell him anything at all.'

Chapter 18

Position: at sea.
Weather: clear skies. Wind: north-easterly force 9.
Temperature: 22°. Barometric pressure: 1013.0mb.

On their final day at sea, the day of the Valentine Ball and the result of the Treasure Hunt, the passengers on board the *Aphrodite* awoke to rougher seas than they'd previously experienced. It was difficult to walk around the ship, and for their safety, the Captain had forbidden them to go on to the promenade decks. The Trident Pool had been closed off too because the pitching of the ship was making the water slosh wildly from side to side and soak the surrounding deck.

'It'll be calmer later,' said the steward who delivered Britt and Mia's breakfast. 'We're in Tehuantepec Bay and we've no protection from the winds. But that'll change in a few hours.'

'I do hope so.' Mia looked uninterestedly at the plate of banana bread and pastries that she normally demolished every morning. 'I don't think I can eat any of this, and losing my appetite is not a good thing.'

'I don't mind it.' Britt popped a strawberry into her mouth. 'In fact I quite like rolling around the place like this. Makes it seem more of a ship.'

'I know I'm the one who's supposed to like roughing it,' said Mia, whose face was pale. 'But I think I'll sit here until it calms down a little.'

'Whatever you like.' Britt ate another strawberry. 'I'm going to the cybercafé to check on my emails.'

There were fewer people out and about on the ship, many of them deciding to do like Mia and remain in their cabins until the sea calmed a little. The cybercafé, normally busy at this time of the day, was empty. Britt sat down at one of the terminals and logged on.

Meredith had sent her an email saying that she'd heard nothing but good reports from the *Aphrodite*. Steve Shaw had told Annie Highsmith that Britt's talks had been a huge success and that they'd been delighted with her presence on board the ship.

'I'm so sorry I wasn't able to be there with you,' Meredith had written. 'But clearly you didn't need me. Good news is that sales are still strong. I do hope you got inspiration for that second novel while you were lazing your way through the tropics . . .'

Britt smiled to herself as she read the last sentence. Meredith just didn't give up. She wanted another book from Britt and would keep on and on at her until she wrote it. Or until I get back and I'm very, very firm about not doing it, thought Britt as she logged out of her email program again. Funny, though, I feel better about being able to say no to her now. I don't feel as trapped by everything as I did a couple of weeks ago. I wonder why that is.

She looked up as another passenger, braving the conditions, entered the cybercafé, and then smiled in greeting at Leo.

'A bit choppy today,' she said.

'Frisky is what the Captain calls it, apparently.' Leo sat down in front of the terminal opposite her. 'D'you feel all right?'

'Perfectly,' said Britt. 'It doesn't seem to bother me at all, but poor Mia is a bit green around the gills and she's lying down in the cabin.'

'So's Pippin,' said Leo.

'Are you coming to the Valentine Ball tonight?' asked Britt. 'Always provided that we can stand up by then.'

'Everybody will be at the ball,' said Leo. 'So will I. What are your plans for dinner?'

'Well, the Captain has asked us to join him again.' Britt blushed slightly.

'How nice for you,' said Leo. 'I'm joining the Costellos.'

'Lovely,' said Britt.

'How do you rate your chances for the big prize in the Treasure Hunt?' asked Leo.

'Depends on how well everyone else did,' said Britt. 'We answered all the questions, although I know we messed up on a couple of them, and we got most of the scavenger items. I suppose there'll be someone who got everything. There always is.'

She noticed the expression on Leo's face.

'Did you? Get everything?' she asked.

'I don't know,' he replied. 'I might have thought outside the box on a couple of occasions to come up with the answers.'

She laughed. 'I know. Some of ours were a bit of a stretch too. But still, the ring is beautiful and worth a few mad guesses.'

'Yes.' The tightness had returned to his voice again.

I wish I knew, thought Britt. I wish I could find out about him. She suddenly felt awkward in his company. It was strange to sit opposite somebody and want to know all about them (to be actually making things up about them – a million possibilities about Leo and his life were chasing each other around her head). She'd never felt like that before. She suddenly did what Pippin had done and typed his name into the search engine on the web page in front of her. But she could see at a glance that none of the links was to him. She closed the window again.

'I'm finished here,' she said. 'I'll leave you to it. Have a nice day.'

'You too,' said Leo, and waited until she'd left before turning to his own emails.

'Pippin???' Mike had typed her name in capitals. 'I've seen her pix in a few of the papers. Wow, man, you've hit the jackpot there. She's a total babe. I knew you could do it. What's she like? Looks a goer.'

'She's pretty sensational all right,' Leo typed. 'And it's the Valentine Ball tonight so might give her the benefit of the top Tyler moves.' He thought his reply seemed a little tacky but he sent it anyway because, God only knew, he needed to sound a bit like a red-blooded male again and not the useless no-hoper he had been. Then he went back to his cabin, because the rolling of the ship did make it rather difficult to do anything else, and took the Rebus from the bedside locker. He'd put it to one side while he was reading *The Perfect Man*, but he wanted to finish it before they arrived in Acapulco the following day.

Steve Shaw had gone to town on the ballroom. It was swathed in silver and blue chiffon and the ceiling lighting sparkled like tiny stars. He'd festooned it with silver and blue hearts and more of the fat little Cupid cut-outs that Britt so hated. But they looked wonderful in the big room, which had been transformed into a dreamy homage to St Valentine. Each of the small round tables had a red rose in the centre and had been decorated with a scattering of tiny foil hearts, while the candle-effect table lights flickered gently and cast a mellow glow. The band, in evening dress, was playing a selection of languid love songs, and later the singer would be performing for them too.

The ship's photographer, looking very pretty in a simple white cocktail dress and bright red shoes, took photographs of each couple as they arrived for the ball. The women were wearing their best outfits of the voyage and many of the men had acquired buttonholes from the florist earlier in the day. There was a buzz and a sense of excitement on board that far exceeded any of the other nights as the women allowed themselves to think about winning the Treasure Hunt and graciously accepting the diamond ring.

'I'm glad the sea has calmed down,' said Mia, who was

wearing her (now beautifully laundered) purple chiffon again but who, at Britt's insistence, had gone to the hairdresser's and had her mass of curls arranged into a very sophisticated up-do. 'I dread to think what this would be like if we were all chucking up.'

'And I'm supposed to be the unromantic one?' Britt laughed as she followed her sister into the room, neatly sidestepping the photographer.

'You look *very* romantic,' Mia told her. 'Despite your non-Brigitte style.'

Britt too had gone to the hairdresser's but had asked that she be left curl-free for the evening, and so her hair had been styled into a chic chignon. She was wearing a plain evening dress in shimmering black silk and a Swarovski crystal necklace that glittered in the light.

'Black isn't romantic,' she told Mia. 'It's just very practical.'

'Practical?' Mia grinned at her. 'What you're wearing is so not practical, sis. It's totally sexy.'

They sat down at one of the small tables and ordered the Voluptuous Valentine, that day's cocktail, which was a delicate shade of pink and which tasted to both of them suspiciously like a Cosmopolitan.

'Cheers.' Britt raised her glass and touched it gently against Mia's. 'I know I wasn't always the easiest, but thanks for coming along and looking after me.'

'Thanks for making it a good deal easier than I expected,' Mia responded.

'Did you think it would be awful?'

Mia hesitated.

'You did! You thought I'd be terrible to work for.'

'Only because you always want everything your way,' said Mia apologetically. 'But you didn't. You were grand.'

'Not always,' admitted Britt.

'I think we did really well for two women sharing a cabin.' Mia laughed. 'There could have been hairbrushes at dawn, you know.'

Britt laughed too. 'You're probably right. And goodness knows how I would've got on with Meredith. I've travelled a lot with her but I only had to share a room with her once. So a fortnight could've been a total disaster.'

'I'm glad it all worked out,' said Mia. 'And I'm glad that you – well, you seemed to enjoy it in the end.'

'Enjoy probably isn't the word,' Britt said. 'But it was an experience. And it's always good to have new experiences.'

'Ah! Miss Martin.' Steve Shaw came up to them. 'What are the chances of having the opening dance with you?'

'I'm a hopeless dancer,' said Britt.

'Surely not,' he said gallantly.

'Listen, I don't do false modesty.' She grinned at him. 'But if you can bear to be embarrassed . . .' She allowed him to lead her on to the dance floor and put her hand on his shoulder.

'You're not bad,' said Steve as they moved to the rhythm of the music.

'You're being very generous,' Britt told him. 'I should have gone to the dance classes.'

'Too busy working on your own classes,' said Steve. 'They were very popular.'

'That was a relief,' admitted Britt. 'Thanks for all the trouble you went to.'

'No trouble at all,' said Steve. He twirled her around and she shrieked but managed to stay on her feet. She glanced towards the table, where Mia was watching her idly. I didn't do very well on the matchmaking front, she thought, as she saw Leo and Pippin sit down at a table nearby. I should have tried to get Leo and Mia together. He's a really nice guy and Mia deserves someone like him.

Leo caught her gazing in his direction and she blushed, because once again her stomach had somersaulted. This is ridiculous, she thought as she tightened her grip on Steve's hand. I don't know why I'm getting these feelings. Is it some kind of lust thing I'm feeling for Leo? The same as I felt for Ralph? Only Ralph was a disaster and I don't, I simply don't, want to jump on Leo and drag him to the nearest bed. I've just been wishing he was dating my sister, for heaven's sake!

'Thank you,' said Steve as the music faded and everyone applauded the band. 'I really enjoyed that. Now I'd better check on one or two things.'

He disappeared and Britt sat down at the table again.

'You make a lovely couple,' said Mia lightly.

Britt made a face at her, but before she had time to say anything else, one of the other officers came over to them and asked Mia to dance. Britt wondered whether Steve had asked them to make sure that the two of them weren't left on their own at the table all evening. It wouldn't be in the Valentine spirit to have them sitting around like old maids.

* * *

There was plenty of Valentine spirit among the passengers, who danced their way through the night, laughing and joking as the band upped and slowed the tempo. Britt and Mia hardly spoke to each other because both of them were occupied with dancing. When not partnered by the officers, they paired off with some of the male passengers they'd met over the last two weeks. Mia felt very honoured to be asked twice by the Captain, who was a very accomplished dancer indeed.

Steve Shaw, who had returned to the ballroom, then asked her up too, and she happily took his hand and allowed herself to be waltzed around the room to the band's Strauss selection.

'You're a better dancer than your sister,' Steve told her. 'But don't tell her I said that.'

Mia giggled. 'She knows that already. She's not really the dancing type.'

'Well she's up and at it again now.' Steve nodded towards Britt, who was being led on to the floor by Leo.

'She'll do better with this,' Mia said as the band switched to a slower pace, and the singer, who'd just come on stage, began to croon the words to the Beatles' hit 'Something'. 'She doesn't know proper steps but she's a good lurcher! Hey!' She yelped as Steve twirled her around just as he'd done with Britt. And then she smiled as he pulled her closer to him. She knew that she was a good lurcher too.

Britt, conscious that her hand was being held far too tightly for comfort by Leo, was trying to move in time to the music. All the other men she'd danced with had chatted as they swung around the ballroom. Leo didn't say anything at all.

'I've always liked this song,' she said after the singer had got halfway through and neither of them had uttered a word.

'Me too,' said Leo.

He wasn't like Ralph, Britt thought as she glanced at him. He was . . . well, what? She didn't know. She didn't have enough experience to tell how he was different. Quieter, of course. More reserved. But she trusted him. She didn't think he was acting. And she couldn't believe that she was feeling safe in his arms.

The band switched to 'Yesterday', and she saw the sudden tightening of his jaw again and the shadow pass across his face. It wasn't a bad love affair, she realised suddenly. It was more than that. Much more.

She had to know.

'Did she die?' Even as the words left her lips, Britt realised that they were horribly insensitive.

'I beg your pardon?' Leo looked at her in astonishment.

'I'm sorry,' said Britt. 'I wasn't thinking properly.'

'Did who die?' Leo's hand tightened even more on hers and she held back a gasp of pain.

'It was just . . .' She knew her face had flamed with embarrassment. 'I was thinking . . . wondering about you. I thought that maybe you'd lost someone.'

'Why would you think that?' he asked harshly.

She shrugged imperceptibly. 'No reason. Absolutely none. Please, don't mind me. I was totally out of line there. Absolutely. I'm sorry.'

His grip on her hand had tightened so much that he was really hurting her. But Britt didn't say anything. Neither did Leo. They continued to move slowly around the ballroom floor.

'Yes,' said Leo as the music ended. 'She did.'

And just then Pippin came up to him and kissed him on the cheek and told him it was time to dance with her again.

The buzz of anticipation grew throughout the night, so that by the time Steve Shaw, amid a roll of drums from the band, said that he was going to announce the winner of the Treasure Hunt prize, excitement among the passengers had gone beyond fever pitch.

'It's not that I need a diamond,' said Tamara O'Neill, who was standing beside Mia and Britt looking at her own enormous engagement ring, which sparkled beneath the lights, 'but you can never have too many, don't you think?'

'One would be good as far as I'm concerned,' said Mia cheerfully. She stretched out her hand in front of her. 'I wish I had the fingers for it, though. Mine are kinda stubby, whereas a rock like tonight's prize needs long and elegant.'

'Wasted on me too, in that case,' commented Britt. 'But I'd so love to win. Just for the achievement.'

'Hates being beaten,' Mia confided to Tamara. 'She's supercompetitive.'

'Ladies and gentlemen.' Steve stood behind the mike. He had three envelopes in his hand. 'I have here the results of the MV *Aphrodite* Valentine Cruise Treasure Hunt.'

Mia realised that she was holding her breath.

'In third place,' said Steve, 'with a fantastic ninety out of a hundred correct answers and forty-five out of fifty scavenger items – Mr and Mrs Johnson, cabin D33.'

A whoop of delight echoed from the back of the ballroom and a petite redhead, who Mia had spoken to a couple of times at the various buffets, made her way to the stage.

'Congratulations,' said Steve as he handed her the envelope and then kissed her on the cheek.

'In second place . . .' he paused dramatically and read from the card in front of him, 'with a slightly more fantastic ninety-one out of a hundred correct answers and forty-seven out of fifty scavenger items – Mr and Mrs O'Neill from cabin C82.'

'Omigod!' Tamara jumped up and down. 'That's us. Well, it's not the diamond ring, but still, we never win anything. How great.'

'And the main prize of the evening – the magnificent diamond ring from our very own jewellery collection . . .' Steve looked up, heightening the tension, 'with a truly astounding ninety-five out of a hundred correct answers and forty-nine out of fifty scavenger items . . .'

Mia realised that she was holding tightly on to Britt's arm.

'. . . the winner is Mr Leo Tyler from the Delphi suite.'

Amid some groans from disappointed passengers was an excited cheer from Pippin Costello, who was standing beside Leo and kissing him on the cheek. And then all the passengers applauded as Leo walked to the stage and Steve presented him with the diamond ring in its blue and white box.

Leo took it and looked at it. He blinked a couple of times, not knowing whether he was dazzled by the glittering diamond or whether there were tears in his eyes because seeing the ring had almost immediately brought back the sensations he'd felt when he'd bought one for Vanessa.

'Congratulations, Leo!' Pippin had followed him to the stage and blew him a kiss.

He looked down at her. She was wearing a maroon evening dress, more demure than her usual evening clothes because it had a halter neck, even though it was bare at the back. Her nut-brown hair was piled into yet another extravagant arrangement, held in place by glittering diamanté clips. Her eyes sparkled with pleasure.

'Pippin.' Leo smiled at her. 'Thanks for your help in solving clue number thirty-two. The one about the number of evening gowns that were modelled on the night of the fashion show.'

There was a ripple of laughter through the crowd.

'Thank you for cutting a lock from your hair for the "souvenir lock" they asked for from Panama.'

More laughter.

'Thank you for being a great travelling companion.'

This time they aahed sentimentally.

Leo looked at Pippin again. She was smiling up at him, her face bright and happy. It was wonderful to have someone look at him like that. As though he was the most important person in the world. It was wonderful to think that someone cared about him again. He hadn't believed it would be possible. But Pippin cared. And he cared about her too.

She was the sort of person that anyone would want to care about.

'I'd like you to have this ring,' said Leo. And then, as if realising for the first time what he was saying, he stopped. She was still smiling up at him. The most beautiful woman on board the ship. Who'd whispered earlier that she loved him. And he loved her too. How could he not? He took a deep breath. 'I'd like you to marry me,' he said.

And then the passengers erupted.

'Talk about over the top,' said Mia as, a couple of hours later, she and Britt got ready for bed. 'I mean – Leo! I never would've thought it.'

'Neither would I.' Britt was sitting at the end of the bed, unfastening her dainty high-heeled sandals. They fell to the floor and she massaged the soles of her feet. 'It was such a crazy thing for him to do.'

'I didn't think he could possibly be serious about her,' said Mia. 'I know they've been together a lot, but even so . . .'

'She did get those elegantly manicured nails into him fairly smartly,' said Britt.

'Yes, but tonight I thought . . .' Mia shook out her hair. 'You and him. The chemistry.'

Britt laughed, but she blushed too. 'You're cracked, you know that, don't you?'

'I know you think so, but when I saw you dancing with him tonight, you seemed . . . well, good together.'

'Not really.' Britt rotated her ankles round and round. 'God, but those things would ruin your legs!'

'You were looking at him as though you cared tonight,' said Mia. 'In fact you always look at him as though you care.'

'I do care,' Britt said. 'I like Leo, even though he was so rude to me at the start of the trip and even though he was tacky beyond belief tonight. I don't think he's rude or tacky deep down, so I want it to work out for him, although in all honesty, getting engaged to someone he hardly even knows – well, it doesn't bode well, does it? Still . . .' she yawned, 'what do I know? I only see people when they hate each other, not when they love each other.'

'And there was nothing between the two of you?'

'No. I really don't know why you'd think there was.'

'Sure?'

'Of course I'm sure.' This time Britt sounded irritated. 'You think there's something between me and Leo because we looked well together? Ralph and I looked great on our wedding day. It was still one of the shortest marriages in history.'

'True,' said Mia. 'But at least you can laugh about it now.'

'Not usually,' she said, a touch grimly. 'It's one of those things . . .'

'What?'

'Wrong man, wrong time, wrong place,' said Britt. 'And . . .' she'd never told anyone about the financial aspect of her divorce before, 'he left me with a huge credit-card bill. It took me years to repay it.'

'The bastard!' Mia was shocked. Britt had never shared information about the breakdown of her marriage before, and although Mia and James had often chatted about it, the idea that Ralph would have left their sister in financial difficulty had never crossed their minds.

'I resented that more than anything.' Britt looked shamefaced.

Mia looked at her curiously. 'Was it just money?' she asked.

'God, no.' Britt bit her lip.

'What then?'

'He . . . he . . .' It was harder to talk about than the money. She hadn't told anyone about this, either. But Mia was her sister. She'd understand, wouldn't she? So she told her about the role-playing and the handcuffs and the actress; and about the way that Ralph had come home and made love to her so wonderfully, then left again.

When she'd finished speaking, a huge tear rolled down Britt's cheek and plopped into her lap.

Mia leaned over and hugged her. 'You're well rid of him,' she said.

'I know.' Britt wiped her eyes with the back of her hand. 'I've always known that, and yet I've never been able to convince myself.'

'Why is that?' wondered Mia. 'Why do women always blame themselves?'

'Well, in my case people think I'm a heartless bitch. I understand that. I can be a bit cold and remote. That's how Ralph saw me too.'

'You're not at all heartless.' Mia's eyes blazed. 'And that fucker didn't deserve you.'

'Mia McDonagh!' Britt's smile was shaky.

'He bloody didn't,' said Mia. 'If I'd known . . . If any of us had known . . .'

Britt shrugged. 'Maybe some people would be into it. I wasn't. And he didn't try any of it when we were going out, so I never expected . . . But hey!' Her smile was firmer this time. 'It's in the past. We were different people and we wanted different things.'

'Hmm. Maybe,' conceded Mia. 'We were all a bit taken aback by how quickly it broke up. And then you wouldn't talk about it.'

'I couldn't,' said Britt seriously. 'I had to put it out of my head. Otherwise I wouldn't have been able to cope. Whenever I did let myself think about it, all I ever did was cry. Or rage. I couldn't possibly have talked about it.'

'You've made some progress so?'

'Thanks to you,' said Britt as she put her sandals in the wardrobe. 'What a PA you're turning out to be!'

She couldn't sleep, which surprised her. Usually it was thoughts of Ralph and her failed marriage and the total mess she'd made of it all that kept her awake. But tonight she kept thinking of Leo and Pippin and his ridiculously showy marriage proposal. She'd thought Leo was a more sensible man than that. A more thoughtful, serious man. But he'd been romancing the model all through the trip, hadn't he? So maybe he didn't want serious in his women. Maybe he just wanted big boobs and the wide-eyed look.

But it wasn't thinking about him and Pippin that was actually keeping her awake. It was thinking about the time when she'd danced with him and asked that terrible, terrible question that had clearly upset him so much. What had been going through her head then, asking him whether 'she' (the woman that Britt had known must have been in his life) had died. Even if she and Leo had formed a relationship on board, that still wouldn't have been an appropriate question to ask. And she felt bad about the fact that she'd posed it, and worried that somehow it had spurred him on to asking Pippin to marry him. She wasn't sure why she thought that might be the case, but she was.

That's so arrogant, she told herself as she pummelled her pillow and turned over in bed. You had nothing to do with it. Talking to him, saying what you said, wouldn't make him come to a decision like that. He must have planned it already.

And yet she was still awake and still thinking about it thirty minutes later, when, frustrated at her inability to empty her mind, she got up and slipped into the black silk dress again. There was something soothing about the *Aphrodite* at night, she thought as she let herself out on to the promenade deck. The sea was calm again now and the movement of the ship on the water almost imperceptible.

It was strange to be outside on her own. All during the cruise, no matter what time of day or night, there had been other passengers on deck. But tonight, their last night at sea and obviously worn out from the excitement of the Valentine Ball, everyone was now in bed. It was three in the morning, Britt conceded. Nevertheless, she was pretty sure that earlier in the cruise at three in the morning plenty of passengers had been out and about, laughing and joking so that their voices carried on the still night air.

Now, though, the only sound was the steady thud of the ship's engines as it travelled northwards towards Acapulco. Britt walked along the deck, towards the bow of the ship, in her bare feet, the ends of her dress trailing along the ground. She liked being at the front of the ship – she liked standing there feeling as though she was in some way in charge of it. She would have loved to stand at the bow rail, with nothing at all in front of her, but that part of the *Aphrodite* wasn't accessible to the passengers and the nearest she could get was the sun deck, a favourite spot for relaxing with a book during the day.

She stood at the rail, protected by the Perspex front, which sheltered her from the wind and the spray, and gazed at the still dark horizon. Then she jumped, startled, when a man's voice behind her said hello.

She whirled around. Leo Tyler was sitting on one of the loungers, the black jacket of his formal suit slung over the edge of it. His bow tie was loose around his neck and the top button of his crisp white shirt was open.

'You scared the living daylights out of me,' she said as her heart thudded in her chest.

'Sorry.'

And yet he hadn't really. Somehow she wasn't really surprised to find him here. Even though he should have been in his cabin with his brand-new fiancée.

'You're the very person I needed to talk to,' she said.

'Oh?'

'I wanted to apologise. I was thoughtless when I . . . when we were dancing.'

'About what?'

'Asking you . . . It was a private matter. I'm sorry.'

'I don't mind,' said Leo. 'It's all in the past. Don't worry about it.'

'But whoever she was . . . whatever it was – it mattered to you then.'

'I'm over it now.' His smile was crooked. 'Didn't you say that at one of your talks? That people always get over lost loves.'

'Was she a lost love?' Britt realised that she was asking questions again. She wondered if it was just her nature, if she was unable to meet anyone without wanting to know everything about them.

'She was my fiancée,' said Leo shortly. 'Actually, she was my ex-fiancée. Her name was Vanessa.'

Britt blinked as she processed the information.

'Oh,' she said.

'She was killed in a car accident with my brother, Donal.'

'Oh no.'

'With whom she was having an affair.' Leo looked straight at Britt, who had sat down on the lounger beside him. 'Dramatic enough for you? Material for your next book, perhaps?'

'Of course not.' She was horrified. 'Leo, that's awful. It must have been terrible for you.'

'Nobody knew,' he said. 'About the affair. Not even me until the day they were killed. So not really.'

'Pardon?' Her tone was disbelieving. 'That's worse.'

'No.' He shook his head although his face was expressionless. 'It was fine.'

'I doubt that,' she told him. 'How long ago?'

'Less than a year.'

'Leo!' She stared at him. 'Leo – you must have gone through hell.'

'Why do all women think that?' he demanded in irritation. 'It wasn't great, I'll admit. But I got over it. I'm not losing sleep over them.'

'I don't believe a word of that,' said Britt. 'I do hope you're getting over it, but I bet you lost oceans of sleep. I know I would've.'

'There's nothing to be gained by letting it take over your life,' said Leo. 'It happened. That's that.'

'Leo.' Britt reached out and took his hand without realising what she was doing. 'I felt like that about my marriage to Ralph. When it was over, I tried to pretend that it had never happened. But you know what? It did happen, and to tell you the truth it totally messed with my head for ages. Probably still does, if I'm honest. You can't pretend.'

'I'm sorry about your marriage,' said Leo. 'But I'm not pretending. Yes, it was difficult, but I'm over it. Over her, and over my lying, cheating brother too. And I forgive them.'

Britt's grasp on his hand tightened. 'OK, this is going to sound like the biggest cliché in the world, and I know you'll think that I write stuff like this all the time, but . . . Leo – have you forgiven yourself?'

'I don't have to forgive myself for anything,' said Leo. 'I was blameless in the whole thing. And now, just like you should be recommending, I'm moving on.'

She knew that she was meddling but she couldn't help

herself. 'You think that by getting engaged to Pippin Costello you're moving on?' She was unable to keep the tone of incredulity from her voice.

Leo jerked his hand from hers and picked up his jacket from the back of the lounger. 'It's none of your business,' he said. 'None.'

'I know.' She stood up too so that she was facing him. 'But divorces are, Leo. That's what I did before I got involved in this book stuff. I dealt with divorces every single day, and . . .' She broke off. 'I'm sorry. Again. I don't know what's happened to me on this trip. I normally don't go round dishing out unwanted, unneeded, unasked-for advice to people I hardly know. It must be the sea air or something. Please forget I said all that. I'm sure you and Pippin will be great together. She's lovely.'

'She is, isn't she?' Leo smiled slightly.

'And you know yourself much better than I do,' said Britt. 'I'm sorry for being so melodramatic. It seems I can't help myself.'

'She's good for me,' said Leo. 'She's easy to be with. She loves me. She wants to be with me for ever.' He exhaled slowly. 'She told me that. She said that she knew the minute she saw me. And I was attracted to her right away too. This was meant to be my honeymoon cruise, you know. I hadn't really intended to come. But I'm glad I did. I've met the right girl for me. Someone who thinks I matter. Someone who loves me.'

Britt said nothing.

'It's my happy ending,' said Leo. 'In real life.'

Britt was still struggling to find the words. She wanted

to say the right thing, but she couldn't help thinking that what Leo wanted to hear and what she wanted to say were very different. So in the end she just wished him all the happiness in the world.

'And I wish you good luck with your next book.'

'Thank you.'

They stood in silence for a moment, and then Britt said that she'd better get to bed, and Leo nodded and said he'd do the same in a moment too, and they looked at each other uncertainly, and then Britt leaned forward and kissed him briefly on the cheek.

'Good night,' she said.

Leo stood looking after her. At the top of the stairs she turned to him and smiled. It was a warm, generous smile from someone who had been right about how he felt. And quite suddenly, Leo felt as though a part of him had suddenly unfrozen. The sensation was almost physical, a surge of warmth inside him that caught him completely by surprise. He smiled in return. But she had already gone down to the deck below.

Britt still couldn't sleep. She kept thinking of Leo and his ex-fiancée who'd had the affair with his brother, and she wondered how he really felt about it. She wondered whether he saw Pippin as a replacement for Vanessa, as someone to prove that he was still out there, still desirable. That he could still attract gorgeous women into his life.

She wondered why the hell she cared. And she wondered

why she could still feel the warmth of his cheek on her lips as she lay staring at the ceiling.

Pippin was asleep in his cabin, curled up underneath the pink quilted sheet, her dark hair falling over her face. She'd collapsed on to the bed when they'd come back to the cabin after copious glasses of champagne with Eileen and John and the rest of the group. Captain Henderson had produced a bottle too, and Pippin had murmured that she didn't have a head for alcohol any more and that she really and truly shouldn't drink it, but in the end she had. Which was why she'd been wobbly on her feet when they'd eventually left everyone and why, in the end, he'd had to slide the beautiful dress from her exquisite body and cover her gently with the quilt.

'I'm sorry,' she'd murmured. 'I wanted to do things to you tonight that nobody has ever done before.'

'That's OK,' he said. 'There's always tomorrow.'

She'd fallen asleep straight away, but he'd remained wide awake. He'd sat on the balcony for a while and then, realising that she was in a deep, deep sleep, wandered down to the internet café, where he'd fired off an email to Mike to give him the news. Telling somebody else, somebody who hadn't been on the *Aphrodite*, suddenly made it seem very real. He'd stared at the subject line, where he'd typed 'Engaged!', and he'd wondered what had possessed him to propose to her in such a flamboyant way. Better, he thought, to have done it discreetly. But he'd proposed to Vanessa discreetly, and see where that had landed him.

After sending the email, he'd gone to the promenade

deck and talked to Britt McDonagh. He'd been annoyed with her at first for suggesting that he and Pippin weren't suited to each other. For having the nerve to imply that they were a divorce waiting to happen. She had no idea, thought Leo. No idea of what it was like to have your life ripped apart. If she had, then she wouldn't have lectured him like that.

Although not lectured, he conceded. She'd been kind really. She was a decent person. And maybe her ideas about love, as expressed in *The Perfect Man*, weren't so idealistic after all. Maybe everyone could find the right person.

He had, after all.

Chapter 19

Position: Acapulco.
Weather: fine and clear. Wind: southerly force 3.
Temperature: 29°. Barometric pressure: 1011.1mb.
Total voyage distance: 2,941 nautical miles.

B ritt, with less than four hours' sleep, was tired the
following day and out of sorts. Mia, thinking that her
sister was peeved about not having won the Treasure Hunt
(not even having come third!), didn't try to cheer her up
but just reminded her that they were going to see the cliff
divers that morning and so she'd want to get a bit of a
move on. Also, Mia said glumly, they'd have to think about
their packing too – their luggage would be collected later
that evening.

'I can't believe we're going home already,' she added.
'The time has gone really quickly and I've loved every
minute, but I'm so looking forward to seeing Allegra again.
I've missed her like crazy.'

The idea flitted through Britt's head that it would be
nice to think someone would have missed her like crazy

too. Then she told herself that she was being moody and silly and that Meredith would be happy to have her back and at her desk writing. And then she wondered why she thought that when she wasn't going to write anything ever again. Although as she'd lain in her bed the previous night, totally unable to stop thinking about the tragedy in Leo's life, the germ of an idea had come to her and she hadn't been able to help herself plotting it out. It didn't mean she was ready to write another book. She didn't have to do anything about the characters who were already forming in her head.

After watching the famous cliff divers of Quebrada (terrifying, they both agreed), the girls chilled out on the beach and swam in the bay before having beer and tortilla at one of the many restaurants along the strip. They didn't see any of their fellow passengers during the day among the hordes of people in the town. Britt said that it was nice, if a bit weird, to be suddenly plunged into a busy city again, and Mia agreed that it was good to have a bit of a buzz, but that in all honesty she preferred the quietness of Costa Rica or Guatemala. When she mentioned Guatemala, Britt looked at her anxiously and Mia told her not to worry, she wasn't going to get upset about Guatemala and Alejo, and that she definitely had closure on it now and Britt wasn't to think about it.

It occurred to Britt that she'd had the potential to upset too many people during this trip. She was still carrying guilt around about her words to Leo the previous night. She hadn't said anything to Mia about meeting him on deck later – her sister, who'd fallen asleep almost as soon as her head hit the pillow, didn't even know that she'd left the cabin. What was quietly freaking Britt out, although she wasn't saying anything about it, was the fact that she couldn't get Leo's anguished face out of her head. As far as she could see, he was still caught up in whatever had happened with his ex-fiancée and his brother and the car crash, and it seemed to Britt that until he dealt with that, any relationship he had with Pippin would be doomed to failure. And although she'd already thought that Leo and the model didn't have good long-term potential, she now felt it would be devastating for him if it didn't work. And she couldn't understand why it was that she wanted to interfere in his life so much when she'd always considered herself the sort of person who stayed detached and didn't interfere at all.

'You seem distracted,' Mia said as they sipped Coronas and gazed over the picture-perfect bay. 'I've asked you a hundred times about your plans for after the trip and you haven't answered me yet.'

'You asked twice,' said Britt mildly. 'And I haven't decided yet.'

'No major book tours planned?'

She shook her head. 'I need to meet with Meredith and discuss what I'm going to do. And then maybe meet with Jeffrey Clavin and talk about my legal career.'

'You couldn't possibly go back to law!' Mia sounded horrified. 'After all this glamour!'

'This is the exception, not the rule.' Britt laughed easily. 'Most times I'm rushing around to out-of-town bookshops in places that are hard to find, and I'm nearly always wearing totally unsuitable shoes when I'm doing it. And I suppose . . .'

she considered, 'if I actually did write something else, well then I'd just be holed up in Ringsend at my laptop, which would hardly be the height of glamour either.'

'Of course, you wrote *The Perfect Man* while you were still being lawyerly,' agreed Mia. 'You haven't embraced the cult of the reclusive writer yet. Still, you like being reclusive.'

'I guess.' Britt sounded doubtful. 'I'm just not sure I could spend all my working day at home on my own.'

Mia laughed. 'I'd've thought there was nobody better to put up with her own company.'

'True,' conceded Britt.

'Anyway, you've loads and loads of material now,' said Mia. 'You can do a shipboard romance book about the lovely Leo and the peachy Pippin.'

'A bit too unbelievable,' said Britt.

'Not when you take the aphrodisiacal qualities of the ship into account,' Mia said. 'All you need to do is scatter in a bit of on-board glamour and you're laughing.' She eyed her sister quizzically. 'Unless you still believe they're doomed to failure?'

'I don't know,' said Britt. She hesitated and then filled Mia in on Leo's story.

Her sister's eyes opened wide with astonishment. 'I never would have guessed that,' she said. 'Poor, poor Leo. Well, let's hope it all works out with Pippin so.'

'Absolutely.' Britt drained her beer. 'Come on, let's have another swim and then get some more of this lovely Mexican sun.'

*   *   *

The final dinner on board the *Aphrodite* was quieter than any of the others. Britt and Mia arrived early at the Parthenon Restaurant and found a table for two, where they gorged themselves on smoked duck salad followed by grilled mahi-mahi and a mixed berry pavlova.

'I don't think I'm ever going to eat this well again,' observed Mia when they'd finished. 'It's probably just as well the cruise is over, though. I know I'm bursting out of my clothes.'

'You'll lose the weight once you're back running after Allegra,' said Britt, and Mia laughed and said she hoped she was right.

There was no sign of the Costellos or Leo in the dining room. When Mia remarked on it, Britt said that they'd probably gone to the Calypso to celebrate the engagement – the notice of which had been printed in the ship's daily newsletter with effusive congratulations from the Captain and crew.

After dinner, they headed off to the Terrace Bar, where they ordered their final mojitos and drank them overlooking the lights of Acapulco, which, Mia said, was without doubt the most beautiful night-time location ever.

'Glad to hear you say that.' Steve Shaw, who had just arrived at the bar, smiled at her. 'We like keeping the best till last.'

'Hi, Steve.' Mia beamed in return. 'It's fabulous. We love it. We're just devastated at leaving tomorrow.'

'And I'm devastated at you going.'

Mia laughed. 'I bet you say that to all the passengers.'

'Of course I do. But with you I mean it. I'll miss you, Mia.'

Mia was taken aback by the sudden note of seriousness in Steve's usually light tone.

'I'm just going to the ladies'.' Britt stood up. 'Back in a mo.'

'I was looking for you earlier. I wanted to say goodbye to you,' Steve told Mia when Britt was out of earshot.

'You'll see me tomorrow, I'm sure,' said Mia.

'It'll be crazy tomorrow. Passengers arriving for the next cruise, passengers departing from this one. Complete mayhem. And I mightn't get the chance to say . . .'

'What?'

'That I really and truly did enjoy your company on this cruise. That you were great.'

'Thank you,' said Mia. 'You were great too.'

'No,' said Steve. 'What I mean is . . . I'd like to keep in touch with you.'

'Oh, don't be silly.' Mia felt herself blush. 'You're just being nice.'

'I'm not. Look, Mia, I know it might seem totally inappropriate and everything right now, but I . . . well, I really like you, and . . .'

'Stop before you say something you regret,' warned Mia. 'I'm sure you'll meet someone else on the next cruise, and someone who might well be able to keep in touch with you. But I can't, Steve. I'm a single mum and I don't have time to get involved with someone who spends half his life at sea, so there's really no point in saying things that you don't need to say.'

'Being a single mum doesn't stop you from being a person.'

'No, but it does stop me from getting involved in some light-hearted affair – though I have to say, if you wanted that, you really should have asked on the first night, not the last.'

'A light-hearted affair with you sounds absolutely lovely,' said Steve. 'But that wasn't what I had in mind.'

Mia stared at him. Then a gaggle of passengers walked by and one of them asked Steve about the entertainment later that night, and before they had the chance to talk again, Britt had returned and Mia was left wondering exactly what Steve Shaw might have had in mind for her.

As Steve had anticipated, the following morning was organised chaos. Britt and Mia were getting a taxi to the airport, and after breakfast, having checked that their luggage was in the right place for collection, they sat on the promenade deck and watched the new arrivals as they boarded the *Aphrodite*. The pretty photographer was on the quayside taking the embarkation photos again – although this time without the huge heart-shaped background.

'Have you seen Leo this morning?' asked Mia as an announcement was made that passengers on the midday flight to London should disembark now. 'I wanted to say goodbye to him.'

Britt shook her head. She'd wanted to say goodbye to him too, but he hadn't been around. She'd seen Eileen Costello earlier and wished her a safe journey home. Eileen had been as chatty as ever, saying that she was still in a whirl about Leo's proposal and Pippin's acceptance and the thrill of it all. Britt had told her to pass on her best wishes to Pippin and say that she'd look out for the wedding photos in the papers or in *VIP* magazine. Eileen had laughed and then said that she hoped Britt and Mia would come to the wedding, an invitation that had left Britt completely taken aback. She thanked her and said that she was sure there was a lot of planning to be done yet and that she hoped Leo and Pippin would have a long and happy marriage.

'I'm sure they will,' Eileen had said, and then headed off to buy some last-minute gifts from the souvenir shop.

Mia glanced at her watch and nudged Britt.

'The taxi is due now,' she said. 'We'd better leave.'

The two of them walked down the stairs to reception for the last time and made their way to the gangway.

'Mia!' Steve Shaw was on the quayside, looking every inch the part in his pristine white unform. 'Hang on a sec.'

The two of them waited while he came over to them. Mia felt her mouth suddenly go dry.

'Goodbye, Britt,' he said as he shook her hand. 'Thank you again for all your hard work.'

'Thank you for yours.' Britt smiled at him. 'Thank you for the hearts and Cupids and balloons and all the things I told you I didn't really like but that did actually look great. And thanks for being so nice at the times when I wasn't.'

'You're very welcome,' said Steve. 'And next time head office sends me an author, I'll tell them they have big shoes to fill.'

'Give me a break!' Britt laughed. 'I'm only a size five.'

'Goodbye, Steve,' said Mia when he turned to her. 'You made the trip a whole lot of fun.'

'It was my pleasure,' he said seriously.

'Mine too,' Mia told him.

He put his arm around her and hugged her.

'I'm sure that's against protocol,' she gasped.

'Probably,' he agreed. 'But you deserve it.' He looked into her green eyes. 'I meant what I said last night.'

'And I meant what I said too. I'm a mum. I'm not cut out for . . . well, whatever you were thinking of.'

The taxi driver tooted his horn at them.

'I was only thinking of good things,' he said.

She looked into his eyes and the taxi tooted again.

'We've got to go.' She disentangled herself from him. 'That taxi is for us. It was a great trip. I'll miss you.'

'I'll miss you too.'

'Bye, Steve.' Britt, who had been watching them curiously, now patted Steve on the back. 'Thanks for everything.'

As they walked towards the taxi, Steve called Mia's name again.

She turned towards him and he beckoned her.

'Wait here,' Mia said to Britt.

'What?' she asked as she stood in front of him again.

'I . . .' He looked at her hesitantly. 'I wanted to say that I wish I'd asked you on the first night and not the last. And that it definitely wouldn't have been a light-hearted affair.'

She stared at him. And then he kissed her rapidly on the lips.

'Steve!' She jerked away from him. 'You'll get fired or something.'

'I don't care,' said Steve.

'I do,' said Mia. She bit her lip. 'I care about you. But . . . oh Steve, don't do this to me. Not now.'

She whirled away from him and hurried towards Britt.

'What was that all about?' asked Britt.

'He was just being silly,' said Mia. 'He . . . I . . . It was silliness, that's all.'

'It didn't look silly.'

'It was. Really.' Mia shook her head. 'This isn't the time or the place . . .' She glanced back along the quayside, but Steve was now in conversation with some new passengers. She shook her head again. 'Come on, Britt, the taxi driver looks as though he's going to have a heart attack. I thought everyone here was laid-back, but it's a gene that's clearly passed him by!'

'Yes, OK.' Britt nodded and then stopped. She looked back at the gleaming white ship once more. High above her, on the promenade deck, she saw Leo Tyler leaning over the rail. He was gazing in their direction. Britt raised her hand and waved. At first she didn't think he'd seen her but then he waved in return. She knew he couldn't hear her, but she called out goodbye anyway. And then, as he waved once again, Pippin joined him. She whispered something into his ear and the two of them turned away from the rail. Britt waited for a second but he didn't reappear.

'You ready?' asked Mia, who had been watching her.

'Absolutely,' said Britt, and got into the taxi.

Chapter 20

Position: Dublin.
Weather: partly cloudy. Wind: south-easterly 2kph.
Temperature: 13°. Barometric pressure: 1001.1mb.

Back in Dublin, the sky was lowering and the temperature considerably less balmy than they'd been used to. Mia, who'd been peppering with anticipation at the thought of being reunited with her daughter again (she'd phoned twice since the plane had landed), insisted that Britt come with her to see everyone. Britt hadn't visited James and Sarah for over a year, and she'd been sure that both of them would be offhand with her because of her neglect. But when he opened the door, James enveloped her in a bear hug and said that it was great to see her, even if coming to Rathfarnham had to be a bit of a letdown what with her glamorous jet-setting life taking her to much more exotic locations. Britt had punched him gently in the stomach as she'd done when they were kids, and somehow it had all been friendly and enjoyable and not at all awkward as she'd expected.

And then Allegra had come shooting out from the living room, shrieking with joy at seeing Mia, who swept her up into her arms and smothered her with kisses and told her that she had grown tremendously in just two weeks and had turned into a big girl now, which was such a surprise.

Britt was equally surprised at how much her nephews had grown since she'd last seen them, and utterly bewitched by Allegra, who, she told Mia later, was becoming prettier by the day.

'She gets her looks from Alejo,' said her sister. 'He was – is – the most attractive man I ever knew.'

'More attractive than Steve Shaw?' asked Britt.

'A million times more,' replied Mia.

'But not a million times as nice,' returned Britt.

'You'll never be a matchmaker,' Mia told her, and Britt hadn't said anything else but had picked up her gorgeous niece and swung her round in the air, something that Allegra enjoyed and wanted more of but that left Britt herself dizzy and breathless.

Mia stayed with James and Sarah until she returned to Spain. Britt had been slightly hurt at that – she'd expected her sister to ask about staying with her – but of course Mia wouldn't have asked because it made no sense. Allegra was used to being with James and Sarah, and Britt's house wasn't geared up for kids, lacking as it did any electronic games whatsoever and being decorated almost totally in shades of white and cream. But still, Britt thought, it would have been nice to have them stay for a day or two.

She realised, after Mia had gone, that she was

unexpectedly lonely by herself. *The Perfect Man* had begun slipping down the bestseller lists, there were no more requests for interviews, and nobody was looking for her to share her views on love and romance. (Obviously a good thing from her perspective, but it was weird not to be asked.) Right now, in fact, Britt had nothing to do. She was suddenly overwhelmed by the silence of her house and began leaving the TV on no matter what programme was showing, simply because she wanted the noise.

She'd got used to the relentless activity on board the *Aphrodite* even though she'd been so bad at taking part, which made the quietness all the more unnerving. It was scary knowing that the day was stretching in front of her without any definite plan of how to fill it.

She kept asking herself if she was a sad loser to be at home alone, but then reminded herself that she liked being on her own, that being surrounded by people as she had been on the *Aphrodite* wasn't normal for her. She was an independent person who liked to do her own thing. Of course her own thing was working at Clavin & Grey. She intended to talk to Jeffrey about her return, but when she rang the office his secretary told her that he was away at a conference, after which he was taking a couple of weeks off. Britt had thanked her and replaced the receiver, knowing that there was no point in talking to anyone else at the firm. So she had to wait.

She called in to her neighbour, Harriett, a sprightly seventy-five year old who had keys to her house and generally kept an eye on things while she was away. She gave her the coffee that she'd brought her back from Costa Rica, and a silk shawl from the *Aphrodite*. Harriett said that there'd been no need to bring anything back, but Britt said that she'd loved buying bits and pieces and that the royal-blue shawl matched Harriett's dark blue eyes.

'God, you're an awful flatterer,' Harriett said. 'So, listen to me, did you find any romance on the boat yourself?'

'Not a bit of it,' Britt told her, even though she felt herself blush, and her neighbour looked at her speculatively.

A couple of weeks later she met her agent, Meredith, in the stylish Merrion Hotel, where they sat in one of the elegant public rooms and drank coffee in the alcove of a long window overlooking the courtyard garden.

'So.' Meredith put her delicate china cup on the rosewood table in front of her and looked enquiringly at Britt. 'You had a fab time on the cruise and everything went well, even though I wasn't there to look after you!' She rubbed her shoulder, which still ached from time to time. 'Now you're back and refreshed and we have to decide what you're going to do next.'

Britt sat back in the high-backed armchair and twirled the ends of her hair around her fingers.

'I've been thinking about that,' she said slowly.

'You need to do a bit more than think.' Meredith's tone was firm.

'I wrote *The Perfect Man* for me,' said Britt as though Meredith hadn't spoken. 'I didn't have a plan, I didn't think about the characters or the plot. In fact every time I gave a talk on board the *Aphrodite* and realised how wrong I'd done everything, I was astonished that it had been published at all, let alone that it ended up being so successful.'

'Sweetie, you were very successful as a lawyer,' Meredith pointed out. 'Everyone says that you're hugely ambitious. It couldn't have been that much of a shock.'

'It was,' said Britt. 'Because it was such a different thing for me. I never had any ambition to be a writer. Only to be good at my job. *The Perfect Man* was a one-off.'

'If you're totally set against writing, I won't try to persuade you any more,' said Meredith with resignation. 'It's a shame and I know Lisa-Anne will think so too, because she enjoyed editing the book with you, but there's no point in me nagging you to do something you don't want to do. Besides, if your heart isn't in it, it'll be worthless.'

'If I write another book and nobody buys it, what will happen?' Britt asked.

'Life will go on,' replied Meredith.

'But I'll have let everyone down,' said Britt. 'All expecting me to, you know, reach into people's hearts and souls, and the stuff they said about *The Perfect Man*. The thing is, I don't know how I did that, Meredith. I didn't try to do anything. It just happened. If I write something that people don't like, they'll say that I'm a failure, and I couldn't bear it.'

'So fear of failure means you won't try?'

'I didn't say that.' Britt looked at her doubtfully.

'Have you got an idea?' Meredith suddenly realised that

Britt wasn't dismissing the thought of writing another book as comprehensively as she usually did.

'It's not an idea,' said Britt uneasily. 'It's just something I've been thinking about at home on my own. It's like an itch that I have to keep scratching. But it's not *The Perfect Man* all over again.'

'Nobody's asking you to do that.' Meredith looked at her sympathetically. 'Why don't you write something? And then after I've looked at what you've done, we can chat about it.'

Britt reached into the briefcase she'd brought with her and took out a sheaf of paper. Meredith looked at her in astonishment.

'You've started already?'

'Yes,' said Britt anxiously. 'I'd been thinking and thinking about it and suddenly I had to start . . . I couldn't help myself. I was waiting to call Jeffrey at my old law firm and ask for my job back, and I started this, and now I have to finish it. It might be awful. It's probably awful because it's nothing like *The Perfect Man* and—'

'I can't wait to read it. And I'll give a copy to Lisa-Anne the minute I get back,' said Meredith excitedly. 'I'm so pleased, Britt. I really am.'

'I'm terrified,' admitted Britt.

'Don't be,' said Meredith.

'Easy for you to say,' Britt told her as she took another sip of tea.

Britt had told the truth when she'd said that she couldn't help herself starting to write again. She'd realised that all of the time she was at home on her own, characters were appearing in her head, jostling for their voices to be heard. She'd thought, at first, that she was going crazy. And then she'd sat down in front of her laptop and opened it, and quite suddenly the words had begun to flow. She'd been excited and terrified all at once, not knowing exactly what she was doing, only knowing that she had to tell the story that was by now forming in her head.

Her novel was about two brothers. William and Richard had always been competitive, with Richard, older by a year, initially outdoing his younger brother. But then William had grown taller and stronger and started competing with Richard on equal terms. At school and at college they'd fought for places on the rugby pitch, sometimes both ending up on the team, sometimes one of them being dropped. The motto they shared was: 'In defeat, malice; in victory, revenge', and while neither of them was truly malicious or vengeful, the winner always tormented the loser. After college, both of them became lawyers; both worked at family law and both specialised in high-profile divorce cases, although for competing firms.

Britt was enjoying writing about the brothers and using her knowledge of the law for the background story. Although they were both determined people, they were different in many ways, William being gentler and more subtle than Richard, who met every problem head on.

The novel centred on a divorce case they were both handling. William was representing Persia, the wife. Richard was representing Christopher, the husband. Persia was claiming that Christopher had been unfaithful to her. She was also looking for over half of his substantial wealth for herself, as well as a six-figure annual sum for the maintenance of their teenage daughter, Camille.

The case was high-profile because Christopher was currently Ireland's most flamboyant celebrity chef, with restaurants in Dublin, Cork and Galway. He also presented a weekly TV programme and was a consultant to two different hotel kitchens.

The competitive spirit in the two brothers, never far from the surface, had erupted over the case. Both of them badly wanted the kudos that getting the right settlement for their client would bring. The added complication was that William was falling for Persia, even though he knew he shouldn't get emotionally involved.

Britt had written the first hundred pages in a frenzy, trying to pin down the characters of the two men and the reasons they needed to compete with each other so much. She liked both of them – despite the constant competition they had redeeming qualities: William was gentle and considerate, Richard was thoughtful and protective. She didn't want things to turn out badly for either of them, but as she wrote, she knew that she was stirring up a storm.

Even if Meredith and Lisa-Anne hated the book, she wasn't bothered. She needed to write it. The characters had taken over her life. She wanted to know more about them and what made them tick, and she wanted to be the one to resolve the many issues that existed between Richard and William.

Right now she wasn't sure how she was going to fix it. But she knew that she would.

She wished that she could fix things for Leo Tyler the same way.

She blinked in dismay at her last thought. This was the first time since leaving the *Aphrodite* that Leo had come into her head. Well, if she excluded thinking about him when she looked at some of the photos of the trip and when she'd seen a photograph of him and Pippin in a gossip magazine. But those were incidents that had made her think about him. She hadn't allowed herself to think about him any other time.

And now she looked at the computer screen in front of her, wondering if her feuding brothers had been inspired at some subconscious level by Leo and Donal. She didn't think so. But how could she be certain? There was nothing similar in the story of William and Richard. Neither brother was going to die horribly in a car accident. Persia would come through the divorce – although whether it would be a satisfactory conclusion from her point of view, Britt wasn't certain.

Two brothers. But not the story of Leo and his brother. Not by a long chalk. So why had they made her think of Leo? She shook her head in frustration. She wanted to stop thinking about him and get back to William and Richard. Get back to fixing things for them.

Besides, Leo had fixed things for himself by proposing to Pippin. It wasn't how Britt would have done it if she had been writing his story, of course. But it was what he'd wanted to do. And there was no point in her thinking that she could or should get involved in his life (and how, she asked herself, could she anyway?), because what he did was entirely his own business and nothing to do with her, no matter how much she wanted to help him.

I don't bloody well want to help him, she muttered to herself as she gazed unseeingly at the computer screen. There's nothing to help him with. He's made his decision on how to move on and that's all there is to it. And yet no matter how often she told herself this, when she'd finished writing for the day she couldn't help thinking about him, and about Pippin and his dramatic proposal at the Valentine Ball, and wondering whether his romantic gesture was enough to last them a lifetime. Would their feelings for each other transcend the move from the super-charged romantic atmosphere on board the *Aphrodite* to the more prosaic day-to-day living routine on dry land? Did Leo see Pippin as a substitute for his ex-fiancée? Did Pippin think that snaring the attractive Leo was an achievement in itself?

She didn't know why the questions were suddenly plaguing her, but they were. She was annoyed at herself for thinking about them so much, for giving head time to people who, in all likelihood (and despite Eileen's effusive invitation to the wedding), she'd never see again in her life. But she couldn't help herself. She was thinking about Leo and Pippin in the same way as she sometimes thought about her clients. Needing to know their motivation. Needing to know what they were aiming for, what they'd be happy with and what, finally, they'd actually put up with.

She still hadn't worked out why she thought they were so ill-matched in the first place. She told herself it was because Leo seemed to be a much deeper person than Pippin, who she regarded as being superficial and a little bit silly. But she knew that she was stereotyping them. She thought all models were air-headed bimbos and so there was no reason for her to think any differently about Pippin. And as for Leo – well, she'd clearly been drawn in by the tragedy of his doomed relationship with Vanessa. She understood doomed relationships. She'd been there and bought that particular T-shirt.

And there was a part of her, which she identified late that night as she lay sleepless in her big bed, that couldn't help asking whether it was because, deep down, she thought that she and Leo had connected. Because he'd made her stomach somersault. Because he was reserved and hard to know, just like her. And yet when that thought bubbled to the surface she laughed at herself and told herself that she had also clearly been affected by the Valentine Cruise and the hearts and balloons and Cupid cut-outs on every available surface. She knew that she wasn't suited to being in a relationship with anyone. Least of all, she added to herself, a person with the emotional baggage that Leo Tyler was so very clearly hauling around with him.

She didn't need anyone. She hadn't needed anyone since her first week at school, when pint-sized Bernie Cassin had mocked her for being too tall for their class and had told her that she'd never have any friends. Bernie had somehow turned everyone, including Mary Byrne, who shared a desk with Britt, against her. That was when Britt had created Steffi, the imaginary friend who'd stayed with her for so long. The alienation of the classroom hadn't actually lasted that long (Bernie Cassin was a bully who eventually began tormenting someone else and who left before the first term was over, much to the general relief of staff and pupils alike), but it had been painful. Over time, Britt had made new friends. Nevertheless, the experience had stayed with her, and now she didn't like depending on other people. And when she'd let her guard down, when she'd allowed herself to depend on Ralph, it had all gone horribly wrong again. So even though she'd gone out with men since, she hadn't wanted to fall for any of them. She didn't think the rewards were worth the risks.

I'm right not to put myself through it all again, she told herself now. And I don't even know why I'm thinking about men in the kind of way that women do when they're wondering if they're going to end up watching weepy movies on a Saturday night with only a bottle of Chardonnay for comfort. I was never going to be that woman. I was always much better on my own.

Thinking about love now . . . thinking about me and Leo and Pippin . . . well, that's very definitely residual *Aphrodite* Romantic Rum cocktails and evenings-under-the-stars stuff. It's not real. True love isn't real. It's something we've made up. And the sooner I get over this ridiculous *thing* in my head about Leo Tyler – which, memo to self, certainly isn't love, because you can't love someone you don't really know – the better.

Besides, she reminded herself, she hadn't thought about him very much on the *Aphrodite*, when he'd been there all the time. There'd been the moments, of course, when she'd gone through the stomach-somersaulting experience, but they'd been few and far between. The truth was that he was a nice guy who'd had a bad knock but had dealt with it in the time-honoured way of men everywhere by shagging the girl with the big tits. And so, when all was said and done, he wasn't very different from any other man Britt had ever known, and it was much better not to feel connected to him in any way at all.

Chapter 21

Position: Dublin.
Weather: cloudy. Wind: easterly 5kph. Temperature: 12°.
Barometric pressure: 1021.1mb.

Leo was standing by the water cooler when Karen Kennedy walked out of one of the walnut-panelled meeting rooms. Ever since the day he'd snapped at her that Vanessa was in the past, and his colleague had looked at him as though he was a heartless sod, he hadn't been comfortable in Karen's company. He filled the small waxed cup with cold water and hoped that she'd ignore him.

'Hi, Leo,' she said, her grey eyes looking at him appraisingly. 'How are you?'

'Great, thanks,' he said.

'I heard your news. Congratulations.'

'Thanks,' said Leo again.

'It's fantastic,' said Karen. 'After everything that happened, I'm so pleased. It must have been so hard for you before.'

'It was a difficult time,' he said. He'd never been able

to talk about Vanessa's death that way before. He'd never been able to say that he'd found it hard.

'Of course it was,' said Karen. 'Everyone knew that. We really and truly sympathised with you. But it's wonderful to see you back to yourself again. And your engagement – so romantic!' She grinned at him and he smiled back. How strange, he thought as he realised he was smiling. He was having that unfreezing feeling again, as though life was slowly returning to numbed limbs.

'We must all go and celebrate,' said Karen. 'And meet your gorgeous fiancée.'

Leo nodded. Pippin had said much the same thing. A party, she'd suggested, to celebrate their engagement. Loads of people would come and they could turn it into a real media event. Leo wasn't sure that he wanted his engagement to be a media event, but Pippin's eyes were shining with excitement and he knew that he would let her have whatever kind of party she wanted, because it was good to know that he could make someone feel that way again.

'When am I going to meet her?' demanded Mike. 'You can't keep a girl like that under wraps! Not from your mates, anyway. I saw pix of you both at that party at Krystle. You looked great. And as for her – wow!'

'She's stunning, isn't she?' Leo looked pleased.

'Well, all I can say is that I told you to get out there but I didn't realise you were going to hit the jackpot!' Mike laughed. 'I'm glad the Tyler moves still work.'

'I didn't need any moves,' said Leo complacently. 'She came on to me.'

'Oh, man.' Mike looked envious. 'I don't want to know that. Makes me feel hard done by. So, what's she like?'

'You've seen the pictures,' said Leo.

'No, you fool.' Mike dug his friend in the ribs. 'What's she like, you know, as a person?'

Leo looked surprised. 'As a person?' he said jokingly. 'When did you ever care about what any girl was like as a person?'

'I wondered,' said Mike. 'What with her being a total babe and everything. Is she a dumb blonde or is she really smart?'

'For starters she's a brunette,' Leo reminded his friend. 'And she's . . . well, she's sweet.'

'Sweet?' Mike grinned.

'She is,' said Leo. 'She looks after me. She wants me to be happy. She's uncomplicated.'

Mike raised an eyebrow. 'Uncomplicated?'

'Would you stop doing that?' demanded Leo. 'Repeating everything. She's a sweet, uncomplicated person and she loves me. And she's the best-looking girl I've ever gone out with in my life. I'm totally lucky to have found her.'

'Hey, I agree with you,' said Mike. 'So does half of Ireland.'

'Good.' Leo took a draught from his pint.

'So what was the rest of the cruise like?' asked Mike. 'Did you meet any other women who might want a desperate guy in his thirties with a good sense of humour who's looking for a long-term relationship?'

Leo grinned. 'Long-term? You? You mean longer than a couple of weeks?'

'I'm not getting any younger,' said Mike plaintively. 'Time for me to think about settling down with the right girl.'

'Like I said before, it wasn't the kind of trip that was heavy on available single females,' said Leo. 'I mentioned the only others in my email to you.'

Mike took a sip from his pint. The two men had met in their favourite bar because they could watch the football there too, but so far they hadn't really seen the footie at all because Mike had been quizzing Leo about the cruise and about Pippin.

'The Romantic Slush Queen and her sister? I can't see it happening somehow. Sure there was no one else?'

'Afraid not,' said Leo. 'But the Slush Queen and her sister were interesting people.'

Mike glanced at him. 'Interesting in what way?'

'Well, they were different. And the Slush Queen wasn't all that slushy really, which is surprising when you read the book. She was actually quite chilly at first, although she did eventually thaw. I thought you'd have liked the sound of the sister.'

'A bit kooky, you said.'

'True. But fun.'

'Would it be worth an introduction?' asked Mike. 'D'you have a contact number for her?'

'The Slush Queen has a website address.' Leo spoke slowly. 'The sister has a kid . . .'

'She comes with baggage?' Mike shook his head. 'I'm hoping to find a girl who doesn't want kids, to be honest. I hate rug rats.'

'So in that case it's a strike-out for the Kook and the Slush Queen,' said Leo. 'Actually, I don't like calling them that. Mia was nice and so was Britt when you got to know her. She was . . . perceptive.'

Mike looked at him thoughtfully. 'What did she perceive?'

'She guessed,' said Leo. 'About Vanessa.'

'What!' Mike was startled.

'She asked me if my girlfriend had died.'

'OK, mate, that's creepy.'

'She didn't ask in a creepy way. She just said it.'

'She's not one of those psychic types, is she? Her book isn't about love beyond the grave or anything?'

'Of course not,' said Leo impatiently. 'It wasn't like that. And then she just seemed to . . .' His voice trailed off.

'What?'

'Oh, I dunno.' Leo shrugged. 'I've never met anyone like her before. She was never quite what you expected.'

'Well, I'm not sure either works for me,' Mike said after another mouthful of his beer. 'Single mother and scary romance queen. Nope, Leo, my friend. You bagged the only decent one of the pile. Luscious model with great chest.'

'I don't like her just for her chest,' protested Leo.

'But I bet it helps,' said Mike as he waved at the barman and ordered two more pints.

Britt turned off the water and got out of the shower, wrapping a towel around her body and another around her hair. It was six thirty in the morning and she didn't really need to be up so early, but she'd found, over the last few weeks, that she wrote best early in the morning. And she liked to be showered and dressed and sitting at the table in her small living room to do it. Writing *The Perfect Man* had been different – then she'd written at night after a day at the office, sitting up in bed with her laptop propped on her knees. But this way suited her better. It was easier to deal with the problems of her characters early in the morning. She'd forged a routine for herself: shower, break-fast listening to the news, dry hair, get dressed and then open laptop and start writing.

However – and very worryingly – for the last week, although her characters had been in her head, she hadn't been able to get them on to the paper. She was terrified that she was suffering from writer's block. She didn't know exactly what writer's block was (after all, she wasn't a real writer; she was only a lawyer faking it), but if it meant more staring blankly at the wall than progressing the story, then maybe that was what was wrong with her. Or perhaps what was wrong was the fact that William, Richard and Persia were ruining her carefully plotted book by not doing what she expected them to do.

Richard, whose own marriage was under stress because of the long hours he worked, had begun to suspect that his wife, Nanette, was having an affair. This was affecting his performance at work and his performance in bed too. He didn't want to confront her with his suspicions but he couldn't get them out of his head.

Britt had written the scenes between Richard and Nanette at a blistering pace, burning up the keyboard as she got the ideas on to the screen. But now she was stuck, unsure of what to do next, because Nanette's possible affair and an explosive row between William and Persia over her divorce settlement had come out of the blue and she didn't know what was going to happen.

Now, wearing a pair of ancient tracksuit bottoms and an equally ancient fleece, she went downstairs to start the next part of her ritual – a banana and yoghurt breakfast with a cup of extra-strong coffee from the high-tech machine she'd bought for herself – thinking about the brothers' increasingly complicated lives and wondering what to do about them.

She turned on the radio before chopping the banana, spooning yoghurt over it and taking it to the table while she waited for the coffee to filter. Her mind was still occupied by her characters as she sat down and almost immediately jumped up again. There was a pool of water on her chair and, she realised, on the floor beneath the table too. She looked upwards and saw the ominous dark shadow on the ceiling above her. And then her coffee machine emitted a loud bang and stopped with the cup half full.

'Damn and blast,' she said, and went to change out of her damp bottoms before phoning for help.

The plumber who arrived later that morning told her that the bathroom shower tray needed to be resealed. Though, quite honestly, he added, it was probably time she thought about a new one anyway. There was a small crack on the surface of the current one and it was bound to get worse, so whatever he did would probably only have a temporary effect.

The electrician turned up shortly afterwards and walked

around the house tut-tutting and shaking his head every so often, so that Britt knew that whatever the matter was it was going to be a big job to sort out.

While he continued his prowling around the electrical circuits, Britt leaned against the bathroom wall and gazed at her shower unit. It was beginning to look tired and dated and the head grimy from calcium in the water. She wondered how easy it would be to get a new one fitted.

'Simple enough,' said the plumber when she asked him. 'But why would you just do that? Seems to me that it would be a good time to give your entire bathroom a makeover.'

She was trying not to feel insulted when the electrician popped his head around the door and told her that he could solve her immediate problems but that the whole house needed rewiring sooner rather than later.

Feeling as though she was in a TV DIY horror programme, Britt told both the plumber and the electrician that she'd be in touch about getting more work done. As soon as they'd left she contemplated her bathroom and then decided to go to the store recommended by the plumber to see what might be available to drag her bathroom out of the time warp it was apparently in.

Maybe, she thought, as she closed the front door behind her, there could be a bathroom scene in my book. With lots of bubble bath and scented oils and hot fluffy towels. (She'd got into the whole hot fluffy towel scene on board the *Aphrodite*, where the towels were always warm and comforting.) But who would be in the scene? she wondered. Nanette and Richard? Nanette and the man she was thinking of having an affair with? William and Persia? Persia and Christopher – because they'd met up and had an un-expectedly flirty dinner together in Christopher's newest restaurant? What was best for them? she wondered. What was right?

They're not real people, she reminded herself sharply. I can do whatever I like with them. But she knew she couldn't. She knew that they were the ones who were calling the shots. She just hoped they knew what they were doing.

Chapter 22

Position: Sierra Bonita, Costa del Sol, Spain.
Weather: clear skies. Wind: southerly 3kph.
Temperature: 21°. Barometric pressure: 1010.2mb.

Mia was sitting on the steps of her terrace, looking down the valley towards the sea, which was just visible as a thin silver-blue line at the edge of the horizon. A gentle breeze chased dried bougainvillea petals across the tiles, and caused the shell wind chime that hung from one of the terrace's wooden beams to tinkle softly. Sunlight soaked through the canopy of climbing flowers and greenery that made up the roof of the terrace, dappling her legs and warming the back of her shoulders. The occasional bark of a dog floated on the languid mid-morning air. The dog belonged to the Ferrero family on the other side of the valley and he always barked whenever Jose Ferrero pulled into the driveway of his house. Mia waited for the sound of the jeep doors being slammed, the sudden more excited barking of Pepe and then the silence as the dog followed his master into the house.

The valley was quiet again. It was too early in the year for visitors to be at Carmen Colange's, jumping in and out of the azure pool and shrieking with laughter. It was too early for Sierra Bonita to be buzzing with life, although many of the locals, Mia included, liked it the way it was now.

And yet for some ridiculous reason she felt her eyes brim with tears. She told herself that it was because the scene in front of her – the green of the valley, the blue of the sky and the yellow of the sun – was so beautiful that it squeezed her heart. But it wasn't just that. It was that she was here in such a beautiful place and there was nobody to share it with.

Silly to be upset about that, she told herself, when she'd been delighted to drop Allegra off at the *guardería infantil* that morning and know that she would be picked up by Ana Fernandez to go to her daughter Loli's birthday party afterwards. Allegra wouldn't be home until later and Mia had been pleased to have an entire day to herself. She'd planned to drive to Malaga and do some shopping and perhaps go for something to eat near the sea front, but when she'd come back to the villa she'd suddenly realised that it was dusty and in need of a thorough cleaning. And surprised by her own sudden urge for domesticity but happy to embrace it because housework wasn't normally her favourite thing, she'd got to work with her warm water, beeswax polish and microfibre cloths and forgotten about Malaga.

Then, as she rinsed out the cloths, she'd got the call from Sergio on the town council to tell her that they wouldn't be restarting the English classes until later in the year, that they were too busy with other projects right now but that he'd give her a call at the end of the summer. He was sorry, he said, if it inconvenienced her.

She'd said that it was no problem and she'd be happy to come back in the autumn, and had hung up the phone on Sergio without letting him hear the anxiety in her voice, because she needed her job with the council. She needed to be working and to earn money, and what the hell was she going to do now?

When she'd first come to the town she'd worked in a bar, but despite what she'd told Paula at the time, it was a totally impractical job for a mother of a small child. She'd been lucky, though, because then she'd been offered a short-term job in the art gallery, where the hours had been much more suitable for her and which she'd enjoyed very much.

And although she was sure she'd get something eventually, Mia knew that she couldn't afford to be out of work for long. The rent for the villa and the insurance on her car were due the following month, and then there was the water bill and the electricity bill and . . . Why am I so bad at this? Mia asked herself. Why can't I cope better?

She rested her chin on her knees as she gazed down the valley and tried not to allow herself to panic. She'd managed in the past and she'd manage again now. There was no need for her heart to be racing nervously in her chest just because she was thinking about money. She wished now that she'd saved more of what Britt had paid her on the cruise instead of spending it on T-shirts from every port and other gifts for Allegra, but what was the point in getting money, she asked herself, if not to spend it (at least some of the time) on nice things?

She'd never needed money to be happy before. She didn't need it to be happy now, though a cash injection would certainly help her stress levels. Mia wiped the tears from her cheeks. The thing was, she admitted to herself, it wasn't all about cash. It was much more fundamental than that.

Since they'd come back from Ireland, Allegra had been asking why they didn't have a Wii and why she didn't have brothers like Luke and Barney and why her papa didn't live with them like James lived with Sarah. Mia had pointed out that not everyone's papa lived with them, and Allegra had jutted out her chin and said defiantly that they mostly did and that Luke and Barney's papa did and where was hers? Did he not love her?

How was Mia supposed to answer that question? She couldn't say anything other than of course he did, but then Allegra wanted to know why he wasn't there if he loved her. She'd become quite insistent about it. And about the bloody Wii too! Although a Wii was the least of Mia's worries.

Mia supposed that it was for times like this that Britt had insisted that Alejo should know about Allegra. How would he feel, wondered Mia, to know that she was sitting here panicking about the car insurance and next month's rent and being thankful that it was warm enough in the evenings not to need any heating now but not so warm that it was necessary to turn on the air-conditioning?

Allegra deserved more, Mia thought. She deserved a mother who could look after her properly. And perhaps she also deserved a father who knew that she existed. But for him to know about Allegra, Mia would have to cause trouble in his family. And she'd let him go because she hadn't wanted to do that.

Mia pictured Alejo. At home with Belén and their child, sitting on their terrace (a much bigger terrace) looking out over the Sierra Nevada. Mia didn't know whether they'd had a boy or a girl. It had been impossible to see the baby in the square in Granada where she'd seen Alejo and Belén laughing and joking together as Belén leaned towards the pushchair to adjust the covers over the sleeping baby. Obviously, she'd thought bitterly at the time, they'd put their problems behind them. They looked happy together. Belén's pregnancy had changed everything.

She squeezed her eyes tightly closed and wiped away the traces of tears while asking herself what exactly she was crying for. Because since coming back from the cruise, she hadn't, until now, felt the desolation that sometimes over-whelmed her when she was on her own. Whenever she felt lonely she'd thought of Steve Shaw and how he'd kissed her and how he'd suddenly made her feel alive again. And even though she didn't believe a word of what he said about caring about her and wishing that he'd told her so earlier, it was still nice to know that there were men out there who found her attractive and who wanted to kiss her and who – above all – weren't Alejo. Thinking of Steve had stopped her thinking of Alejo. But today she'd started again.

Maybe Alejo had loved her. Who knew? But it had been the wrong place and the wrong time, and now Belén was living the life that Mia had hoped to lead. (Well, not the exact life. Mia knew that Belén and Alejo were living a very different life to the one she would have expected to have with him. More things that he hid from me, she thought bitterly. More things that he didn't want his affair girl to know.)

She had originally come to Spain and Sierra Bonita to be near him. She hadn't quite figured out why she thought being near him was a good thing, since she was determined never to see him again. But it had given her some comfort to know that she was in the same country as the father of her child. It would be pointless to tell him about Allegra now, though, no matter what Britt thought. Britt was looking at things from a legal viewpoint. She didn't know what it was like to have loved someone like Mia had loved Alejo and to have had it all turn to dust in an instant. Mia frowned as that thought went through her mind, because of course Britt had seen her love life crumble too. Maybe it's us, she thought. Maybe the McDonagh girls just aren't good at hanging on to a man. She snorted. They'd be fine with the right man, of course they would. Ralph and Alejo had been wrong, that was all.

All the same, Mia wondered, if she did tell him about Allegra, would he help out, or would he be furious about her even contacting him? Would he think she had an ulterior motive in telling him about her? Would he be right?

Mia brushed a leaf from her hair and sighed. That was the problem, of course. The ulterior motive. Why would the woman he'd known for such a short period an absolute lifetime ago suddenly appear out of the woodwork and mess up his life? He would wonder what exactly she wanted from him. What her long-term goal would be. He would think she saw Allegra as a potential money-spinner, a way of tapping him for cash. She couldn't really blame him if he thought like that. If she was in his position she'd probably think the same way too.

And yet, she thought as she trapped a stray bougainvillea blossom in her hands, she didn't have the right to withhold the potential benefits that Alejo could give Allegra out of some misplaced idea about what was the right thing for his damned marriage! And was she, as Britt had told her, being selfish in never having told Alejo about her in the first place? She'd thought she was doing the right thing. But if she was, was she doing it for entirely the wrong reason?

She hadn't known, at the time she was in Guatemala, that the geology company for which Alejo was working was a subsidiary of a much bigger Spanish corporation. TierraMundo, the parent company, specialised in environmental technology, and its founder, Ernesto Ariza, was one of Spain's wealthiest men, who featured regularly in the business pages of the newspapers and sometimes in the social pages too. Everyone in Spain knew of Ernesto Ariza.

Ernesto Ariza was also Alejo's father.

She would never have guessed that Alejo, with his long hair, loose shirts and faded jeans, with his laid-back approach to life and his passion for his work, was the son of someone who was a permanent feature of Spain's Rich List. It was

Christian who'd imparted that information, a few days after Alejo and Belén had headed off to Los Angeles.

'Alejo is a great geologist and he loves what he does,' Christian had said as they shared tapas together along with Per-Henrik and Vivi at a laid-back cantina near Central Park. 'But I know that Ernesto hopes he'll eventually take on a managerial role at TierraMundo along with his brother and his sister, David and Teresa.'

'Maybe he could take over the geology company,' suggested Vivi as she glanced at Mia.

'Perhaps.' Christian shrugged. 'But it's not a cutting-edge part of the Ariza empire. Environmental technology is a growing industry and worth a lot of money. Eventually Alejo will probably move over to that side of things. After all, TierraMundo is a very green company. He'd be helping the environment, which is close to his heart anyway. Ernesto is happy to let his kids do their own thing, but eventually he draws them back in. David is on the board. Teresa is head of the research department. Alejo is the youngest, so Ernesto has indulged him the longest. But he'll be on the management team eventually. And now that Belén is having a baby . . .' Christian continued, 'well, that changes everything.'

True, Mia thought. It's changed things already.

'It was a great match,' he added as he popped an olive into his mouth. 'TierraMundo and Banco del Valle.'

'Banco del Valle?' Mia looked at him enquiringly.

'Belén's family owned it,' explained Christian. 'It was taken over by one of the big banks in Spain a few years ago, but the family are still shareholders.'

'Does that mean she's filthy rich too?'

Christian grinned. 'Filthier than Alejo will ever be. The Riveras are old money. The Arizas are just blow-ins.'

'Right,' said Mia as she realised that the ties that held Alejo and his wife together were far too strong ever to be broken by her. 'I see now.'

So if she told Alejo about their daughter, she would seem like a fortune-hunter. A nobody who'd got pregnant to gain a hold on the Ariza money. Belén's money too. She didn't want his damn money. Even for Allegra. Money wasn't everything. It didn't, in the end, buy happiness.

But it did put food on the table she thought. And it did provide education and opportunities, and she didn't have the right to keep those from Allegra if Alejo was willing to supply them. She massaged her eyes with the tips of her fingers. She wished she knew what she should do for the best.

She got up and walked inside the villa. It had been built in the 1960s and had traditional whitewashed walls, with the same plain terracotta floor tiles inside as out on the terrace. The furniture was mainly traditional too, honey-pine chairs with rattan seats and high backs, a large pine table and dresser and (non-traditionally) a deep, squishy orange sofa on which both Mia and Allegra liked to curl up in the evenings when the temperature dropped. The local newsletter was on the table. Mia had picked it up in the *panadería*, where she'd bought fresh bread after dropping Allegra off earlier. It was full of information about town activities (Sierra Bonita held lots of festivals; the locals enjoyed celebrating whenever they could, and picked the flimsiest of excuses to hold a fiesta) as well as its usual list of important phone numbers and advertisements from local businesses. Mia scanned them all, looking for something suitable. It was easier in the summer when the town was full of tourists and there was work of some sort for just about everyone who wanted it. But the season hadn't started yet, and besides, Mia still had to think about childcare for Allegra.

How do other single mums manage? she wondered as she dismissed job after job as being totally unsuitable. Am I just particularly useless? Or am I simply mad to be trying to do it all on my own, just like Mum thinks?

She read through the jobs section again later that night after she and Allegra had had their dinner together, chatting about Loli's birthday party and how much fun it had been. There had been a magician, Allegra told her with wonder in her voice, who had magicked toys for everyone. Wouldn't it be great, she said, if he would come to her brithday party too?

Mia smiled and said that it would; she hoped that by the time Allegra's birthday came round in a couple of months, she'd have forgotten about the magician. Somehow she doubted it. Allegra had a razor-sharp memory. And although she was happy that her daughter had had a good time at Loli's party, Mia wished that Ana hadn't gone down the route of hired entertainment for her. Children's birthdays in Sierra Bonita were usually simple if fun. Introducing magicians was upping the ante far too much.

She hadn't missed any jobs in the newsletter. Mia felt

the flutter of fear in her stomach again. She'd never been in the situation before where she had no prospect of a job. Every other time something had come up. But now she felt as though she was hanging from a cliff by her fingertips. And she was desperately afraid of falling.

The phone rang, reminding her that Telefonica was another bill that would be due soon.

'Hi,' said Britt. 'How're things?'

'Fine,' replied Mia, surprised at hearing from her sister. They'd only spoken once since Mia had returned to Spain, although Britt had emailed her some photos from the trip and had also forwarded her an email from Steve Shaw thanking Britt herself for being a great speaker and asking her for Mia's email address, which he didn't have. Britt hadn't given it to him straight away because she wanted to check first whether it would be OK with Mia. She'd ended her email by saying, 'Well????' but Mia had replied that she was pretty sure Steve Shaw had found himself another passenger by now and not to bother with the email.

'I was wondering if you could help me out again,' said Britt.

'Another cruise?' Mia laughed. 'Was everyone so bowled over by you that they're asking for a repeat performance?'

'Not quite,' said Britt. 'Um, this is different.'

'What then?' If it involved going away and leaving Allegra again, Mia knew that she would have to turn down whatever Britt was proposing. It didn't matter how much money was on offer, or even how much she might need it, she simply couldn't leave her daughter for a second time in a year. She didn't want to.

412

'I was wondering if . . .' Britt hesitated.

'If what?'

'You said on board the *Aphrodite* that you had a spare room,' said Britt quickly. 'I wondered if you rented it out?'

'I can't,' said Mia. 'I'm renting the house myself, and one of the clauses is that I don't sublet. I don't want to do anything to mess up the rental, because I get it for a really good rate and the owner could charge three times as much during the summer.'

'Yes, but he probably wouldn't get anything in the winter,' said Britt. 'So it evens out.'

'I know. All the same, I love it here and I don't want to cause any trouble. Who did you want me to rent it to?'

'Me,' said Britt.

Mia was silent for a moment. 'You? For how long?'

'A month or so,' said Britt. 'I've a bit of a domestic crisis on. My house needs rewiring and I'm having my bathroom done at the same time, as well as getting everything painted, so I need somewhere to stay in the meantime. I thought it would be nice to come to you.'

'You can stay with me, of course.' Mia was wondering if Britt would be any good at babysitting. Because if she could look after Allegra in the evenings, then perhaps Mia could expand her job search to include employers who would expect her to work more flexible hours. 'But don't be stupid. You don't have to rent a room, for heaven's sake. Just stay.'

'I want it to be a business deal,' said Britt. 'Like you being with me on the cruise. I'm hoping to be working and not just there for the break.'

'Working?' Mia sounded surprised. 'Here. In Spain?'

'I'm . . . well, I'm writing something again, but it's not going well.'

'You're writing? I thought you never wanted to—'

'I know, I know,' said Britt. 'I started something. I don't know why. And now I need to finish it, except that I keep getting stuck. But with everything going on in the house now, I can't see myself managing to get unstuck.'

'Come.' There was a surge of warmth in Mia's voice. 'It'll be fun to see you again. And I can't wait to read what you've written.'

'It's not fit to be read yet,' said Britt anxiously. 'I've given it to Meredith, but that's all. You can't read it.'

Mia chuckled. 'I haven't had the chance to read anything other than the paper in weeks,' she said. 'Allegra is going through one of her frantic phases. I'd love to read your book.'

'It's not a book yet,' said Britt. 'It's a jumble of paper. Quite honestly, I'm not sure if it ever will be a book.'

'I bet you thought that about *The Perfect Man*, too,' said Mia. 'Anyway, I won't read it if you don't want me to. And I'll do my best to keep Allegra out of your hair.'

'Thanks,' said Britt. 'Thanks a lot.'

'You're welcome.' Mia realised that she was looking forward to seeing Britt again, even as she wondered how she'd manage to make it appear as though she was living the perfect life in Sierra Bonita, and that she didn't have a care in the world.

Chapter 23

Position: Travelling.
Weather: partly cloudy. Wind: south-easterly 10kph.
Temperature: 16°–24°. Barometric pressure: 1015mb.

B ritt had checked in her luggage and was making her
way towards the departure gates at Dublin airport
when she heard her name being called. She recognised the
voice although she couldn't place it immediately, so when
she turned around to see Leo Tyler behind her, a look of
surprise crossed her face. Despite the verbal wedding invitation (not yet backed up by anything written), she really
hadn't expected to see him ever again. It had never occurred
to her that she might bump into him back in Dublin.

The tan he'd acquired in the Caribbean had faded, but
he looked well. Better, Britt thought, than he had at the
start of the voyage. Smiling, which he hadn't often done
on the trip. And the bags under his eyes that she'd noticed
in his magazine photo had disappeared. Clearly being
engaged to Pippin suited him after all.

She smiled in return, even as she felt her heart do that

strange jump in her chest and her stomach turn over again. A sensation only ever caused by Ralph before. And now, unnervingly, Leo.

'Hi there,' she said equably, ignoring her racing heart. 'It's good to see you.'

'How have you been?' he asked.

'Pretty good,' she said. 'Busy.'

'Giving more lectures about how men can be perfect?'

She laughed, suddenly feeling more relaxed in his company again. 'I should never have tried to come up with a man who was perfect. He's going to be the monkey on my back for the rest of my life.'

Leo grinned. 'Writing the next most-romantic-novel-in-the-world, then?'

'Writing,' she told him. 'But not romantic.'

'I bet it is,' Leo said. 'Mia asked me if *The Perfect Man* made me cry. She said it made everyone cry.'

'And did you?' she asked curiously.

'I'm the strong silent type,' he replied lightly. 'I try not to cry.'

'I see.'

'But I have to admit that Jack was a pretty romantic sort of guy, at least from a woman's perspective.'

'Not half as romantic as you,' she reminded him. 'He never proposed to someone in front of a crowd of people at a glittering social event.'

'I admit that was a little out of character for me,' he said. 'But it seemed the right thing to do.'

'You were the talk of the ship,' said Britt.

'And you didn't approve,' he reminded her.

'God, no. I mean yes. I mean – once you've met the right person, you do what you have to do.'

'Spoken like a true romantic.'

'Sorry,' she said earnestly. 'I'm not trying to be. You deserve to be happy, Leo. Even if . . . I mean . . .' She shook her head in exasperation. 'No matter how good I might be at writing it, I'm utterly useless at telling people emotional things. What I'm saying, badly, is that you've found the right person, and that's great because, you know, you're moving on. And I know I was a bit . . . dismissive, maybe, of Pippin at first, but I'm notoriously crap at being diplomatic too, and I'm sure she's exactly the right person for you after . . . after Vanessa and everything.'

'She doesn't know,' said Leo.

'What?'

'About Vanessa and Donal.'

'Leo!' Britt stared at him. 'Why on earth not? You have to tell her.'

'She knows about the accident. But not about their relationship.' Leo flinched. 'Like everyone else, she just thinks it was a big tragedy. I didn't want . . . I didn't think it was something she needed to know.'

Britt looked concerned. 'Don't you think it would be better if she did?'

'No.' Leo shook his head. 'I don't want to be forever defined as the fool who lost his fiancée to his brother. And I don't want Pippin worrying that I could still be harbouring dark thoughts about either Vanessa or Donal either.'

'Are you?'

He released a slow breath. 'Not so much now,' he said. 'I've you to thank for that.'

'Me?'

'Yes. You were the first person I told. And when I did, I felt better. Like a knot in my stomach had undone.'

'I'm glad.'

'So thanks,' he said. 'Thank you for helping.'

'You're very welcome.'

'Are you off somewhere exotic today?' he asked suddenly, a gently mocking tone in his voice. 'Lecturing people in the Far East, perhaps?'

She shook her head.

'Meeting someone?'

'No,' she said. 'I'm going to stay with Mia for a while.'

'You two are really close, aren't you?'

Britt laughed. 'A few months ago I wouldn't have said so. But we became closer on the *Aphrodite*. I'm getting some work done on my house at the moment, which means that I need to move out for a couple of weeks, so it seemed like a good plan to go to Mia and do some writing there.'

'You *are* writing the next most-romantic-novel-in-the-world, then,' he teased. 'Or at least another heart-wrencher.'

'That depends on what wrenches your heart,' she replied lightly. 'But it's not going too well at the moment, so the change of scenery might help.'

'What happens when it doesn't go well?' asked Leo.

She gave him a despairing look. 'Nothing,' she told him. 'I sit in front of the computer screen and think that I was right all along about divorce being a lot easier.'

'Oh dear,' said Leo. 'I hope things improve. Why don't

you do those exercises you set everyone on the ship? The ones that you promised would unlock our creativity?'

'Do as I say and not as I do,' replied Britt darkly. 'I think my creativity is stuck in a basement somewhere. Hopefully it'll come back eventually.'

'I hope so too,' said Leo. 'I'll buy the book when it comes out.'

'Thanks.' She smiled at him. 'So . . . when are you and Pippin tying the knot?'

'We haven't set a date yet,' said Leo. 'She's having talks with a selection of wedding planners. Or something. And her mother too, of course.'

Their eyes met and both of them laughed.

'I imagine that Eileen is very into it all,' said Britt.

'Very.'

'I'm sure it'll all work out in the end.'

'She's right for me, you know,' said Leo. 'She understands me.'

'I'm sure she does,' said Britt. 'And she's very beautiful.'

'Do you think that's the only reason I'm marrying her?' demanded Leo. 'That she's beautiful?'

'God, no,' lied Britt. 'I'm sure you're marrying her because you're madly in love with her.'

Just as I'm sure that you're making a horrible, horrible mistake and that she'll break your heart, she added silently.

'Britt?'

'Sorry.' She dragged herself back to the present. Leo was looking quizzically at her. 'I . . . um, author moment. Just thinking of something for the heart-wrencher.'

'Have you totally abandoned the idea of going back to the law?' he asked suddenly. 'Now that you're writing another book.'

'Oh, no.' She shook her head. 'This is a one-off.'

'I thought the other book was a one-off.'

'Yes. But there was a whole contractual thing, and then I had an idea that . . . Anyway, this is it. Definitely.' She spoke decisively. 'Once this book is published, I'll reclaim my career and my life and put it all down to experience. What about you?' she added brightly. 'Are you going anywhere exotic yourself?'

'I've had enough exotic this year, thanks,' he said. 'I was seeing Pippin off. She's going to Portugal for a magazine shoot.'

'Wow,' said Britt. 'That's good, isn't it?'

Leo nodded. 'It's for a property company,' he explained. 'They're selling a new condo and she's on the brochure.'

'I saw both your pictures in the papers a while ago,' Britt told him. 'At Krystle.'

'It's Pippin's favourite nightclub. She hangs out there a lot. Not really my scene, to be honest, although it can be fun from time to time.'

'Do you get jealous?' asked Britt. 'I mean, if she's at nightclubs without you or on shoots without you, or if you see someone looking at her picture – does it bother you?'

'Not really,' said Leo. 'What she does is just a job.'

Britt nodded.

'You think I'm crazy, don't you?' said Leo suddenly.

Britt blushed. 'It's not that,' she said. 'It's just that I've never met anyone like her before. You don't generally, in law.'

'You still disapprove.'

'I don't,' she said. 'I guess I thought . . . Well, it seemed you were so hurt by your brother and Vanessa, and suddenly you were with Pippin and I couldn't help feeling . . .'

'. . . that she caught me on the rebound?'

'Something like that.'

'You're wrong,' said Leo firmly. 'I love her because she's not Vanessa. And she loves me more than Vanessa ever did.'

'Do you love her more than you loved Vanessa?' asked Britt abruptly.

Leo stared at her. 'This is totally different,' he said tightly.

They stood looking at each other for what seemed to Britt at least to be for ever.

'Well.' Leo looked away from her and at his watch. 'I'd better get going. It was nice meeting you again.'

'You too.'

'Tell Mia I said hello.'

'I will.'

'I know Eileen has an address for you. You'll both get an invite to the wedding.'

'I love a good wedding.' She grinned at him. 'All us romantic types do.'

'I hope it lives up to Pippin's expectations.' Leo suddenly looked anxious, and then smiled. 'I'm sure it will. And I hope things work out for you with the book. Will it all end happily ever after?'

'Depends on what happily ever after means,' she told him as she turned towards the departure gates again.

* * *

Leo watched her until she had disappeared into the throng of people waiting to pass through security. He wondered why it was that every time he met Britt McDonagh he felt so unsettled. Whenever he talked to her he felt as though she was looking inside his head, sifting through his thoughts and making judgements about him. He thought that perhaps she found him wanting in some way, not living up to some idealised standard of male behaviour, while at the same time he couldn't help feeling as though she understood him too, and maybe pitied him a little.

He wished that he hadn't told her about Donal and Vanessa. That, he assumed, was the source of her pity. The last thing he wanted was people pitying him, which was why he hadn't told anyone else the full story. And although it had been an unexpected relief to share it with her, he felt that the knowledge diminished him in her eyes.

His mobile buzzed and he looked at it before answering.

'The flight's been delayed,' Pippin told him glumly.

'What a pain,' he said.

'Oh, it's only half an hour. But I so hate hanging around in airports.'

'Have you gone to the lounge?'

'Yes. I'm having a cappuccino.' Pippin had a pass card for the Anna Livia lounge, which meant that she could wait in a little more comfort than at the gate itself.

'At least you can chill out there,' said Leo. 'Read a magazine or something.'

'I wish I had a private jet!'

Leo laughed. 'Maybe one day. When you're totally famous.'

'Or when you land a mega deal with that bank of yours.'

'Can't see it happening with the bank,' he said cheerfully. 'I'm depending on you for my future life of luxury.'

She giggled. 'Maybe I'll come through.'

'I know you will,' he told her. 'Text me when you're boarding.'

'Sure,' she said. 'Meantime, you behave yourself while I'm away. No partying.'

'I'm planning an early night tonight,' he promised. 'I've a meeting in the morning so I need to be alert.'

'Oh, I think we both know you're always alert in the morning.' She giggled again, and Leo smiled.

'You're a witch,' he said.

'You betcha.' Pippin made a loud kissing noise down the phone and then ended the call.

Leo was still smiling as he walked out of the airport. She doesn't pity me, he thought, feeding money into the car park machine. She loves me and we have a good time together and I can be pretty certain that she's not messing with my head like Britt McDonagh. Which has to be a good thing.

Britt thought she might see Pippin at one of the gates, but there was no sign of her. She bought herself a couple of magazines and settled down to wait for her flight to be called.

There was a picture of Pippin in one of the magazines looking more stunning than ever. She was with some girlfriends at, according to the story, a charity coffee morning. She was wearing a cream shift dress that set off her endless golden legs in glossy high-heeled shoes. Her perfect white teeth dazzled in her exquisitely made-up face. She was holding a glass plaque with the logo of the charity in front of her, and her *Aphrodite* engagement ring was clearly visible on her finger.

She's absolutely amazing, thought Britt as she studied the photograph. It's no wonder he fell for her. Who could blame him really, when she looks so astonishingly perfect? Britt peered more closely at the picture. In real life Pippin had a small scar above her right eyebrow. (She'd got it, she'd said, when a girl in school had thrown a pencil case at her and she hadn't managed to get out of the way quickly enough.) The scar had been airbrushed out of the photograph. If only we could do that with the rest of our lives, thought Britt as she closed the magazine. Brush away the bad bits as though they'd never happened. How much easier everything would be.

Mia and Allegra arrived at Malaga airport just in time to see the Aer Lingus plane glide towards the runway.

'*Tía* Britt is on that plane!' cried Mia as it roared overhead. 'She's coming to stay.'

'I know.' Allegra looked at her mother patiently. 'You told me.'

'And you're to be really good because *Tía* Britt will be working. So no interrupting her all the time.'

'Except to play,' said Allegra confidently, while Mia wondered how on earth Britt expected to get any writing done when her niece wanted to claim her for every spare moment.

It was nearly half an hour later when Britt walked into the arrivals hall, to be met by Allegra running towards her and wrapping her arms around her legs. Britt laughed and picked her up.

'It's lovely to see you,' she said as she kissed the little girl on the cheek. 'And I think you've got taller.'

'She has,' confirmed Mia as she began to pull Britt's case behind her. 'Two whole centimetres since you last saw her. She's *muy alta*, no?'

'*Sí.*' Allegra nodded. 'I'm a big girl now.'

Britt followed Mia to the car park, noting that the sun was stronger and hotter than back in Dublin, and enjoying its warmth.

'Maybe not the luxury you're used to,' Mia said as she opened the doors of the jeep. 'But it gets us around, and to be honest, you need something sturdy in the mountains.'

'Whatever you say.' Britt got in and adjusted the seat belt.

'*Vámonos!*' cried Mia as she started the car. 'Let's go.'

The jeep rattled along the motorway and then Mia took the exit and began the climb into the mountains. Britt, beside her, hung on to the door as she negotiated the hairpin bends that brought them ever higher.

'It's not that far as the crow flies,' explained Mia as she urged the jeep around a particularly sharp corner. 'But it's just awkward to get to.'

'The view is great.' Britt chanced a nervous glance behind her.

'And it's superb from the house,' Mia assured her. 'You'll love it. Very much the artist's retreat.'

Britt laughed. 'I hope it works.'

'Book still stalled?'

'And some. They just won't do what I want them to,' said Britt.

'Maybe you want them to do the wrong thing,' suggested Mia as she suddenly braked hard to avoid Pepe, Jose Ferrero's dog, who was trotting across the road in the carefree way of an animal who doesn't believe in human boundaries.

'They started off doing the wrong things,' said Britt. 'I'm trying to make it right.'

'I'm sure you'll work things out for them,' said Mia as she turned the jeep down a dirt track, sending stones scattering in front of her and causing Britt to tighten her hold on the door. 'You'll give them a happy ending.'

'You're the second person today who's thought that,' said Britt as the jeep came to a halt outside Mia's villa. 'Oh, Mia! This is heaven on earth.'

'Wait till you see inside before you make snap judgements,' said Mia, but there was pleasure in her voice. 'Come on then. Welcome to the Villa Serena.'

The guest room was a long, narrow bedroom at the back of the house. The window opened out on to the garden, where all shapes and sizes of cacti thrust upwards from beds set into more terracotta tiles. Hibiscus covered the white wall at the back of the garden, its delicate scent carried towards the house on the wind. There was a small cactus topped with tiny pink flowers in a cobalt-blue pot on the bedside locker and a brightly coloured picture of a cactus on the sunburst-yellow wall, as well as on the woven rug at the foot of the bed. The room was warm but not too hot, and Britt had the unexpected sensation of stepping out of one life and into another. It was as though the chaos of her own house as well as the tension she felt over the progress of her book had suddenly been replaced by a welcome feeling of calm.

She unpacked her suitcase, hung her clothes in the pine wardrobe and put her toiletries on the small dressing table on the wall opposite. Then she went outside to the terrace where Mia and Allegra were drinking juice.

'It's lovely,' she told her sister. 'Not at all what I expected.'

'Why? What did you expect?'

'I don't know. Maybe something more tumbledown. Or perhaps something more modern! Not something so pretty, at any rate.'

'Gee, thanks.' But Mia grinned.

'I'm sorry. I sound patronising and I don't mean to be. It's just cute, that's all.'

'It is, isn't it?' Mia looked pleased. 'I love it here, and I'm so lucky that the owners are happy to have me rent it. A pool would be nice, but you can't have everything; anyway if she doesn't have a rental, Carmen, down the hillside, lets me use hers. Other times we fill Allegra's paddling pool and sit in it. But it's not quite hot enough for that yet. So.' She looked enquiringly at her sister. 'You hungry?'

'Ravenous.'

'I made some gazpacho earlier,' Mia told her. 'And I

got some lovely crusty bread from the *panadería*. I thought we could have some sizzling prawns afterwards. It's sort of traditional Andalucian.'

'Sounds excellent. Can I help?'

'Not really,' Mia told her. 'The soup is cold and the prawns only take a minute. I like home cooking, but I like it to be easy.'

'I'm crap at home cooking,' confessed Britt. 'I'd starve if it wasn't for Marks and Spencer.'

'I hope you've never let Mum hear you say that.' Mia grinned. 'She'd be devastated.'

After a meal as good, Britt told her sister, as any they'd ever had on the *Aphrodite*, washed down with a glass of local red wine, and after Allegra finally went to bed, the two sisters pulled on light fleeces and sat on the terrace looking out at the sky, which was turning a navy blue in the gathering darkness.

'I really appreciate you letting me come here,' said Britt.

'No worries.'

'I thought you might have had enough of me.'

'We've had a break.' Mia grinned. 'I'm hoping that perhaps you might repay me by doing some babysitting.'

'Of course I will. But I'm going to pay you for the room anyway.'

'I can't let you do that.' Mia shook her head.

'I can't just plonk myself here and expect you to look after me for nothing.'

'It wouldn't feel right to take your money,' said Mia.

'It wouldn't feel right to me if I didn't at least cover

my costs.' Britt opened her purse and extracted some notes, which she pushed over to Mia.

'I can't,' said Mia.

'Put it aside for Allegra,' Britt told her.

Mia needed the cash, but she didn't like taking it from her sister. And she couldn't figure out whether Britt knew she needed it.

'You'll never guess who I saw at the airport.' Britt changed the subject.

'Who?'

'Leo Tyler.' She recounted their conversation. 'And I guess, in the end, Pippin is right for him,' she said. 'So much for my instincts.' She looked at Mia. 'How are you doing these days? Have you emailed Steve yet?'

'No,' said Mia.

'Ah, Mia! Why not?'

Mia looked uncomfortable. 'In another life, Steve and I could have been a bit of fun. But I'm way past that now. I can't mess around because of Allegra.'

'He seemed to want more than just fun. I thought he was serious about you.'

'For an anti-romance person, you sure want people to rush into things,' Mia said. 'You can't fall in love in a fortnight.'

'I fell in love in a second,' said Britt. 'Fell out of it nearly as quick, but it's totally possible.'

'I think I should make it my mission to make you fall in love again,' said Mia. 'A hunky Andalucian man, perhaps.'

'I seriously doubt that,' said Britt.

'Is that a challenge?'

'God, no. But you should get in touch with Steve,' said Britt as she watched the blinking red light of a plane high in the sky above them.

'For heaven's sake, would you drop it?' demanded Mia. 'I admit he's a nice guy, but he spends months on board the *Aphrodite* and it wouldn't make for a stable relationship – even if I wanted one.'

'Don't you?' asked Britt.

'Oh, sometimes,' conceded Mia. 'But great as he was, and much as I . . . much as I liked him, I don't think it would work. And I'm really not in the business of having my heart broken again.'

'I can understand that,' agreed Britt. 'I guess I just thought it would have been so great if you'd found someone on board the ship.' She grinned suddenly. 'Just as romantic as Leo and Pippin.'

'Romance again!' Mia teased her. 'Oh dear, sis, maybe I was a bad influence on you.'

'I need to embrace it,' Britt said. 'For creative purposes.'

Mia laughed. 'Embrace away. And think of all the times you were in love.'

Britt snorted. 'The brief moment, you mean.'

'Forget the bad bits,' Mia told her. 'Remember that second when you first fall in love. Remember the elation. The feeling of being so very much alive. There's nothing to compare to it.'

'You're right about that,' said Britt as she gazed across the darkening valley.

'And then it fades.'

'Sure,' agreed Mia. 'But you have the memories for ever.'

'Perhaps.' Britt glanced at her. 'I wonder if it's half as exciting the second time around? Or has common sense kicked in by then?'

'I don't know,' replied Mia thoughtfully. 'I don't know, and I'm not sure that I ever want to find out.'

Chapter 24

Position: Sierra Bonita.
Weather: mostly sunny. Wind: southerly 4kph.
Temperature: 24°. Barometric pressure: 1011mb.

The sound of a car door closing and an engine turning over woke Britt the following morning. She had a momentary feeling of panic, forgetting where she was and disoriented by the sunlight pouring in through the chink in the light blue curtains, before she gathered her thoughts and slid out of bed.

The villa was empty and silent. There were breakfast things in the sink, but no sign of Mia or Allegra. Britt filled the kettle with water and turned it on. While she waited for it to boil, she washed the breakfast dishes and then made herself a cup of coffee. She drank it walking around the small living room, pausing to check the contents of Mia's bookshelf.

Her English-language copy of *The Perfect Man* was there, along with the Spanish translation. But most of the space was given over to books about raising children and self-help volumes. Britt flicked through *The Single Mother's Survival Guide* and *How to Succeed as a Single Parent*, as well as *You Can Heal Your Life* and *I Can Mend Your Broken Heart*. Britt had never thought of her sister as someone who needed self-help books. She'd always believed that Mia was very comfortable about her choices.

But I suppose no one's comfortable all the time, she thought, feeling a sudden surge of sympathy for her sister as she replaced the books carefully on the shelf. It's nice to have some kind of support, even if it's only out of a book. I wish I'd been more supportive myself before now.

She walked outside in her pyjamas and bare feet and finished her coffee sitting on the terrace.

Her mind was still a confusion of images; mostly, she now realised, from the dream she'd been having the night before, in which William had suddenly confessed to Persia that he was absolutely crazy about her, but Richard had then burst into the room and declared his love for her too. It had all been very disconcerting.

Britt suddenly wondered whether Persia would have books like *I Can Mend Your Broken Heart* on her bookshelf. She wouldn't have thought so; Persia was a tough cookie. Nevertheless . . . Britt frowned. Persia would have a different kind of book. Something about how to dump a man, lose ten pounds and have a fabulous life.

When Mia arrived back at the villa forty minutes later, Britt, still in her pastel-pink pyjamas, was staring at the laptop in front of her, an expression of intense concentration on her face.

'Everything OK?' asked Mia, and Britt nodded perfunctorily as she began to type.

Mia left her to it and went into the house, where she phoned Dixie's restaurant and the town's art gallery, both of which were looking for temporary staff, and made appointments to call to see them.

She realised after a while that the constant tapping of Britt's fingers on the laptop keyboard had stopped, and went outside again. Her sister was staring at the screen once more, but this time her expression was worried.

'I've done enough for the time being,' she told Mia as she looked up. 'There's a new person, Lucie. She's just muscled her way into the story and she might make a difference. But maybe not the way I thought.'

'Well I'm glad that Villa Serena seems to be inspiring you,' said Mia cheerfully, 'but you surely can't be finished for the day?'

'I need to think,' said Britt. 'I had a dream last night, and it's made me wonder about Richard and Nanette . . .'

Mia laughed. 'You're talking about them as though they're real.'

'They are to me.'

'In that case, do you want to hang around here in case the muse strikes again?' asked Mia. 'Or would you like to do something?'

'Where's Allegra?'

'At school,' explained Mia. 'The *guardería infantil*. It's like an advanced kindergarten. She loves it.' She looked at her sister with a hint of defiance. 'I send her there so that she doesn't grow up to be a solitary peasant girl.'

Britt flushed. 'I know I said that, but I was wrong,' she admitted.

'You wouldn't be if I kept her to myself all the time,' Mia said. 'She does need to mix with other kids. Luckily she's madly outgoing and she gets on well with them.' She looked at her sister speculatively. 'I was wondering, though . . .'

'What?'

'Remember I mentioned the babysitting last night?'

'Yes.'

'It would be a million times more useful to me than money,' Mia told her. 'Tonight especially. I have a job interview.'

'Oh?'

Mia explained about the restaurant and the art gallery. 'You'd be working every evening?'

Mia nodded. 'Most of them. I was lucky with the town council job because that was in the morning and it fitted in with Allegra. The truth is, though, that hardly anything else will.'

'So what will you do when I go?' asked Britt, who was trying not to look panicked at the idea of being responsible for her niece for more than one night at a time.

'Hopefully the town council will start the classes sooner rather than later,' Mia told her.

Britt leaned back in the chair. 'It's all kind of precarious, isn't it?'

'Yeah. But it usually comes right in the end. Now . . .' She looked at Britt. 'Are you going to sit around all day in your jammies, or would you like to come out and about and see what the fine town of Sierra Bonita has to offer the reclusive writer?'

Britt chuckled. 'I guess I should get dressed. I do at home, you know. I don't slope around like this all day.'

'We can go into the town and have a wander and a coffee and then pick Allegra up,' said Mia. 'They get a siesta break at twelve and go back later in the afternoon.'

'OK then. Give me a few minutes to turn into a present-able human being and I'll be with you.'

Britt went inside, had a quick shower (thinking about her new bathroom and hoping that everything was going OK back in Dublin) and then dressed in a cerise T-shirt and a pair of white Capri pants.

'Very summery,' remarked Mia as she walked back on to the terrace again. 'Thank heavens the sun is shining.'

'It's gorgeous.' Britt sniffed appreciatively. 'And the air – lovely.'

'C'mon.' Mia grinned. 'You're going all native and you've only been here a few hours.'

Britt climbed into the jeep beside her sister and then yelped as they turned out on to the road.

'I didn't realise it was such a steep drop,' she said as she looked down towards the valley.

'Chill,' said Mia. 'I drive it all the time.'

'It's not a great road, though.' Britt hung on to the door handle. 'Now I see why you were so laid-back when we were wheezing our way up and down the mountains in Costa Rica.'

'Yup. Our whitewashed Andalucian mountain villages prepare you for anything.' Mia shoved the jeep into a higher gear.

Ten minutes later she'd parked it in the car park at the

edge of the town. At the top of the hill to their left were the steps that led to the church. To their right was a row of restaurants and cafés where people were sitting having coffee.

'This is the most touristy bit,' explained Mia. 'There are cafés at the top of the village too. Let's go.'

Britt followed her up a narrow street flanked on either side by white houses with blue and green window shutters and wrought-iron balconies laden with potted plants.

'It's postcard pretty,' she said.

'I know,' said Mia. 'That's why the tourists come. During the summer you can't get down this street for people with cameras.'

'I wouldn't be keen on it myself,' admitted Britt when they stopped for coffee in the gorgeous café at the highest point in the town. 'I need my city life. But I was wrong to call it an arse-wipe town.'

'It can be,' Mia conceded. 'In the middle of winter, when it's cold and raining. Not that it happens much, I have to admit, but it's grim being on the mountainside in the rain.'

'Do you plan to stay here for ever?' asked Britt.

Mia shrugged. 'I don't know.'

Britt was about to give her sister the lecture about her future, but stopped herself just in time. Not on the first full day, she thought. And not when we're being so relaxed in each other's company.

It was at the end of the week that she put the question to Mia, and her sister looked at her in resignation. They'd gone out for dinner, to the restaurant in the square oppo-site the church where the bells pealed every quarter and made conversation temporarily impossible, although the quality of the food compensated for the clamour. Allegra had eaten dinner with them but was now playing with some other children on the steps of the church, while Mia and Britt drank *café cortados* after their meal.

'I knew you'd come out with it sooner or later,' said Mia.

'I tried hard not to. But . . . well, this is so lovely and perfect and everything, but all the same, Mia, for ever?'

'People move here to live,' Mia reminded her.

On the first day she'd shown Britt the urbanisation at the far end of the town – a development of over fifty homes that had been bought by people who wanted somewhere peaceful to retire to. Not all of them were retirees, of course, Mia had said. Some of them were working in the town (the internet café was owned by an Englishman) or at the coast, fifteen kilometres away. There was a vibrant ex-pat community, she said, and she knew some of them quite well, though she didn't want to get too involved. She preferred blending in to local life.

'But those people are usually families,' said Britt. 'And before you get all sniffy with me, I accept that you and Allie are a family. It's just—'

'Yada, yada,' said Mia. 'I don't know why you're so set on finding me a man.'

'I think it would be nice if your family was a bit bigger,' said Britt.

'And you have someone in mind?' Mia looked at her enquiringly. 'Emilio, perhaps?'

Britt laughed. Emilio was the barman at Sierra Bonita's most popular café-bar. He had a bit of a crush on Mia and would call her his *chica favorita*. Emilio was nearly seventy.

'I like Emilio,' said Britt. 'And you know me, never ageist. But perhaps he's not the one for you.'

'There's no one,' said Mia. 'That's fine by me.'

'It's just that Steve—'

'Oh God, not Steve again!' interrupted Mia.

'He was nice,' said Britt doggedly.

'We were on the Valentine Cruise,' Mia reminded her. 'He was *supposed* to be nice.'

'But don't you want—'

'Yes,' said Mia, suddenly fierce. 'Yes, I do want someone. Someday. Of course I do. But not here and not now, because here and now it's Allegra who's the most important person in my life, and I just don't have room for anyone else, and especially not Steve, because yes, he was lovely, and yes, I liked him very much, but no, no, no, I can't do it all again with someone who might not stick around. And let's face it, Britt, Steve isn't actually a sticking-around person, is he?'

Britt crumbled a cube of sugar into her coffee. 'You could give him a chance.'

'I could!' cried Mia. 'And if it was only me . . . well, I maybe would. But Allegra . . .' She swallowed hard. 'I can't be the sort of person who brings a variety of "uncles" to the house. I can't let her think that I care about a selection box of men more than I care about her.'

'We're only talking about one man,' Britt reminded her.

'I know.' Mia looked hunted. 'And I do think about

him, but it was only a fleeting friendship really. It was the setting that was romantic, that's all. And I can't afford to make a mistake.'

'Then you'll never do anything again,' said Britt. 'Everyone makes mistakes.'

'You're a right one to talk,' retorted Mia. 'You haven't gone out with anyone since your divorce!'

'That's not true.'

'Oh, did we all miss someone?'

'Not exactly,' said Britt. 'There hasn't been anyone serious. Of course I've gone out from time to time, but—'

'But you haven't had a proper relationship, have you?'

'I'm not cut out for it.'

'Hah!' Mia looked triumphant. 'That's such rubbish. The reason, my dearest sister, you haven't had a relationship is exactly the same as me – you don't want to make a mistake either. Though in your case, the only person to suffer would be you. You're afraid!'

'I am not!'

Mia held her gaze and eventually Britt gave in.

'Maybe. I don't know. My work was important. But shuffling divorce papers doesn't exactly instil confidence about the whole thing.'

'Yet you're trying to push me into something with someone I hardly know and who could only meet me a few times a year. When you find yourself a man, then I'll think about it.'

'You're being silly.'

'So are you. The thing is . . .' Mia's tone was suddenly gentler, 'when you're responsible for another person, you have to be careful about the mistakes you make. So – Allegra comes first. Always.'

Britt stirred her coffee. 'I do understand that,' she said. 'The last few nights when I've had her to myself . . .' She smiled. 'We've had a great time together.'

In fact Britt had been surprised at how much fun she'd had babysitting her niece. She'd been exhausted afterwards, answering Allegra's never-ending stream of questions, playing games with her, reading to her and (although she'd never let anyone know, because she hadn't a note in her head) singing songs with her. It had been fun, and she'd suddenly realised why people had children. (Not in her personal game plan right now, of course. But, she'd thought the previous night, not something she would rule out either.)

'Allegra is mad about you,' said Mia. 'You're her total heroine.'

'What about the day she asks about her father?' asked Britt suddenly.

Mia hesitated.

'She's asked already,' she said eventually. 'Not who he is or anything; she's too young for that. But why he doesn't live with us.'

'And what have you said?'

'Oh, at the moment she can be palmed off with that he's working far away but he'll be back one day soon.'

'Mia!'

'I told you before, I won't stop her finding him when the time is right,' Mia said. 'Though I suppose that might be a shock for him.'

'Wouldn't it be better if he knew now?'

Mia stared wordlessly in front of her for a moment. Then she turned to Britt and told her about Alejo. About TierraMundo. About Belén and Banco del Valle. About her fears for Allegra if he knew about her.

Britt was shocked. 'You mean this guy is rolling in it, literally rolling in it, and you're scraping a living on the side of a mountain? Are you nuts?'

'You bring it all down to money!' cried Mia. 'Perhaps that's how you legal eagle types think of it. But it's not money. It's more than that.'

'It's not just about money. It's about responsibilities,' said Britt. 'His to you and Allegra. Yours to him and Allegra. How the hell can he be responsible when he doesn't know about her?'

'I don't have to be responsible to him,' retorted Mia. 'He lied to me and cheated on his wife. You think that's the right sort of dad for my daughter? Regardless of how big his bank balance is.'

Britt looked at her sister unhappily. 'I don't know. I don't know what's right and what's not, but in this case I can't help thinking – well, women always bang on about how useless men are and how they leave us holding the baby, but don't you think that perhaps he'd do the right thing?'

'He didn't before,' said Mia darkly. 'And what's the right thing, exactly? I truly don't want to wreck his marriage. Besides . . .' she swallowed hard, 'if I saw him again – oh Britt, maybe I'd fall in love with him all over again. And getting over him was the hardest thing I had to do in my whole life. I'm not sure I'll ever be properly over him. He made me feel more alive than anyone I've ever known. So I can't contact him. I really can't.'

'But you could?' This time Britt looked at her shrewdly. 'If you really wanted to? You know how to get in touch with him?'

Mia looked away. 'It's not an option,' she said. 'No matter what.'

A week later, on a Friday afternoon when Britt was sitting in the garden staring into space, Mia plopped herself down on the stones beside her.

'How's it going?' she asked.

'Stuck again,' said Britt. 'I go like the clappers for ages and then seem to hit a brick wall.'

'D'you want to take a break from it?' suggested Mia. 'For the weekend?'

'And do what?'

'I thought we might take a trip to Granada. You and me and Allegra.'

'Why?'

'It's a lovely city and you should visit the Alhambra,' said Mia.

'I didn't really come here to sightsee,' said Britt doubtfully. 'Thanks for the offer, but perhaps I should just stick with the legal eagles and work out their problems.'

Mia looked at her hesitantly.

'What?' asked Britt.

'It's just . . .'

'You think I'll get inspired in Granada?'

'No,' said Mia. 'I thought that you could maybe help me with one of my problems.'

'Huh?'

'I have an address for Alejo,' she said flatly.

Britt stared at her. 'You've always had this?'

'Yes.'

'For heaven's sake! You're unbelievable. So are we going to go and accost him after all?' There was a gleam in Britt's eyes as she spoke.

Mia shook her head. 'I just want to see where he lives, that's all.'

'That's hardly solving a problem, is it?'

'Britt, please.'

'Oh, OK.' Britt bit back the words she was going to say and stood up, brushing the dust from her skirt. 'Have you booked somewhere to stay?'

'There's a small hotel I stayed in before,' said Mia. 'It's nothing much, but it's very clean and central.'

'Forget the nothing much!' Britt told her firmly. 'Let's pamper ourselves and fetch up somewhere really nice.'

'Britt—'

'My treat,' said Britt. 'And it's not a favour to you or anything. I like nice hotels.'

'But—'

'No arguments,' said Britt firmly. 'I'm your big sister and I'm in charge.'

'Fair enough so,' said Mia, and went inside to check out the availability of chic minimalist hotels in the city.

Chapter 25

Position: Granada.
Weather: clear skies. Wind: easterly 10kph. Temperature:
26°. Barometric pressure: 1012.4mb.

It was hot, and Mia had the jeep's canvas roof rolled back. Allegra sat in the rear seat singing a song she'd learned at school and that both Mia and Britt now knew off by heart too. Britt had a map open on her lap, although they didn't need it yet – Mia knew the way to the city and was driving along the busy but picturesque coastal road before turning inland towards the motorway.

'*Túnel!*' squealed Allegra with delight as they drove through the long tunnel cut through the mountains. '*Luz, Mama!*'

Mia switched on her lights, although the tunnel was brightly lit already.

'There are quite a few of them on this road,' she told Britt. 'Amazing engineering. I guess you'd appreciate that.'

'I do,' said Britt. 'Though I'm not sure how I feel about being stuck under the earth.'

'You're such a wuss!' Mia teased. 'You don't like heights, you don't like tunnels, you don't like men . . .'

'Why?' asked Allegra from the back seat. 'Why do you not like men?'

'Your mama is being silly,' said Britt. 'She's joking with me.'

They emerged into the sunlight again and Mia switched off the lights.

'You have to joke about them,' she said as she changed gear. 'Otherwise you'd go crazy.'

It was nearly two hours later when they arrived in Granada, and Britt, turning the map around in her hand, directed Mia to the underground car park that was, according to the website, less than a hundred metres from their hotel.

'City hotels rarely have car parks,' Mia had explained when Britt had wondered about it earlier. 'The cities are so old, most of the streets are way too narrow for cars.'

'Left, left!' Britt interrupted her as she spotted the car park sign. Mia turned down the steep ramp and reversed into an extremely tight space near the exit.

'Great driving,' said Britt as they got out of the jeep. 'I'd have made a mess of that reversing.'

'Lots of practice,' said Mia succinctly. 'Come along, Allie. Don't forget your bag.'

The three of them trooped along the narrow street until they arrived at their hotel. They pushed open an opaque glass door and found themselves in a cool reception area with a small indoor courtyard topped by a glass roof four storeys up. In the centre of the courtyard was a low fountain where water gurgled over smooth stones. Green plants were scattered around the reception area too, adding to the feeling of an oasis in the centre of the hot city.

'*Hola.*' Mia smiled at the receptionist and asked about their reservation.

Their room was on the top floor and overlooked the street, where they could see people sitting at tables in the shade and eating lunch. The three single beds had enormous white duvets and big fat pillows. Allegra bounced up and down on hers until Mia told her to stop.

'This is lovely,' she said as she turned to Britt. 'It's quirky and elegant and very you.'

'I'm glad you think I'm quirky and elegant,' said Britt lightly.

'Well, quirky anyway,' amended Mia, laughing.

'I'm hungry,' Allegra informed them.

'Give us a couple of minutes to put our things away,' said Mia, 'and then we'll get food.'

They ate almost directly outside the hotel in one of the pavement cafés. Both Mia and Britt treated themselves to a glass of wine to go along with their salads and crusty bread, while Allegra slurped up a plate of mussels.

'She loves them,' said Mia. 'I think they're horrible.'

'Don't do it for me either,' agreed Britt as she watched her niece pile the plate high with empty shells. 'But I'm sure they're better for her than the dreaded turkey twizzlers.'

Mia giggled. 'She's never had a turkey twizzler in her life. Another advantage of country living.'

Later that afternoon, after they'd had a siesta, and when

the temperature had dropped a little, they went for a walk around the town, finally ending up in the plaza where Mia had seen Alejo and Belén.

'In that café.' She nodded across the square. 'Playing happy families.'

'I'm so sorry,' said Britt. 'I really am.'

'Hey, I'm not!' Mia shrugged. '*Qué sera sera* and all that sort of stuff.'

'So d'you want to try and find the house?' asked Britt after they'd stopped for ice cream as demanded by Allegra. 'According to the address you have, it's outside the town a bit, so we'll have to drive.'

'I guess so.' Mia sounded half excited and half reluctant.

'What house?' asked Allegra, scooping the last of her chocolate ice cream into her mouth.

'Just one I want to see.' Mia looked at her and took a tissue out of her bag. 'How d'you manage to get so much food on your face?' she demanded as she tried to wipe it away.

'I don't.' Allegra squirmed as Mia dabbed at her chin.

'You're the messiest girl in the whole world,' said Mia.

Allegra looked mournfully at her from her dark eyes, and Britt couldn't help laughing.

'She's just like you when you were small,' she told Mia. 'You're quite scarily alike in a whole heap of ways.'

Alejo and Belén's house was a few kilometres outside the city, with a wonderful view of the mountains. It was hidden behind a long wall topped with green tiles, behind which was a hedge of tall cypresses. Only the roof of the house, further back in the garden, was visible from the road. The letterbox, set into the wall, said 'Ariza' in neat gold lettering. There was a security camera over the gates which had a no parking sign in front of them, so Mia drove further up the road.

'Well?' Britt looked at her enquiringly as she stopped the jeep. 'What d'you want to do?'

'It's huge,' said Mia. 'Really huge.'

'I've seen bigger in Dalkey,' said Britt dismissively.

'Oh, come on, Britt. It's massive.'

'All right, it's pretty impressive,' conceded Britt.

'I just can't imagine him there,' said Mia. 'He was so cool and laid-back in Guatemala. He wasn't the kind of guy who lived in a house with high walls and security. They had tents when they went looking at the volcanoes, you know.'

'Things change,' said Britt.

'Who're you telling?'

'D'you want to walk by it?'

'What if he comes out?'

'Mia, hon, you'll get plenty of warning. Those gates are electric. They'll have to whir into action.'

'OK then.'

They got out of the jeep and walked back down the road, following the wall of Alejo's house the entire way. Mia's heart was racing. He was here, she thought, a few hundred metres away. He could be sitting on the terrace or walking through the garden or swimming in his pool right this minute. Perhaps if she called out his name he'd hear her and come running to her. He would sweep her into his arms and cover her mouth with kisses and tell her that he still loved her. That he'd always loved her . . .

'Why are we here?' demanded Allegra pettishly, dragging her feet as they paused outside the gates.

'That's a really good question.' Mia picked her daughter up and hugged her fiercely, pushing all thoughts of Alejo out of her mind. 'No good reason. We're going back to our hotel now.'

'Good,' said Allegra. 'I'm tired.'

'But don't you want to—' Britt broke off as they heard the sudden purr of an engine and the electric gate began to slide slowly open.

'Oh crap!' Mia turned away. 'Come on, Britt. Let's get out of here.'

But Britt remained where she was, and so, as the black Mercedes swept out of the gate and turned on to the road, she was able to see the woman behind the wheel.

'Pretty,' she told Mia reluctantly as they walked back to the car. 'But I only got a glimpse, so I didn't see her bad points.'

'He wasn't with her?'

Britt shook her head. 'No. She was quite alone.'

'Not that it means anything.' Mia glanced back at the house. 'You know, this was an incredibly stupid thing to do.'

'Why?'

'There's no future for me or Allegra with Alejo in it.'

'What makes you so sure about that?'

450

'I was always sure really. And all that stuff about him being entitled to know about Allie . . . well, it's true up to a point. But I can't mess up his life now. Maybe when she's grown up it'll be different. As for a father figure – perhaps one day there'll be someone else.'

'Anyone in mind?' asked Britt casually.

Mia laughed. 'You're very transparent,' she said. 'Nobody actually in mind. But Steve made me realise that there could be someone else for me in the future.'

'Are you going to get in touch with him?'

'No,' said Mia. 'There's no point. But I'll always be glad that he kissed me.'

The following night, after Allegra had gone to bed and fallen asleep, Britt asked Mia if she was absolutely sure she didn't want to call Alejo. Mia, however, was adamant that seeing the house was more than enough and that there was no way she was going to subject Allegra to a life behind electric gates and security cameras. Britt tried to persuade her that she was being silly; that Allegra wouldn't want to live there and Alejo wouldn't want to take her from Mia, but Mia was insistent that even if he didn't actually try for custody of his daughter, the influence of the Ariza family would certainly be far greater than her own in Allegra's life. And she didn't want that to happen. Besides, she argued once again, Alejo had behaved abominably. What right did he have to interfere in Allegra's life?

'Maybe I'm seeing it too much from the legal rather than the moral viewpoint,' agreed Britt as they finally got into bed themselves. 'And I'm honestly not trying to influence you in any way. I'm just trying to give you all of the arguments.'

'You haven't said anything to me that I haven't thought a million times already,' Mia assured her.

But as she lay in the darkness, listening to the steady breathing of her sister and her daughter, Mia couldn't rid herself of the image of the house on the hillside, and Allegra and Alejo inside the walls.

Chapter 26

Position: Malaga.
Weather: clear skies. Wind: southerly 5kph. Temperature:
25°. Barometric pressure: 1015.9mb.

Britt was sitting on the shadiest part of the terrace,
but even so it was difficult to read the screen of the
open laptop. Which, she thought glumly, probably wasn't
a bad thing. The novel still wasn't progressing as quickly
as she'd hoped, due to the fact that it continued to veer
off in unexpected directions. The cast of characters now
included Lucie, an old flame of Richard's who'd suddenly
reappeared because she'd read about the divorce in the
papers and decided to get in touch with him. Her presence was making things even more complicated.

Britt looked at her watch. Mia would be returning to
the villa soon, having collected Allegra from the *guardería
infantil*. She had a night off tonight, so they'd have an
evening together in the quiet of the terrace with only the
sounds of the crickets to disturb them. Britt was enjoying
herself in Sierra Bonita, but she knew that she needed to

go home soon. The electrical work was done, and the tiler had phoned her to say that her bathroom and kitchen were both finished too and that he'd returned the key to her next-door neighbour as she'd asked. Britt had then phoned Harriett, who'd told her that everything looked just lovely and that she'd be really pleased with the result, but that since it had been raining in bucketfuls ever since she'd gone away, she might as well stay in Spain for a little longer.

Britt said that she was giving it another week or so (although Mia was now working afternoons and some evenings in the art gallery again, she was still searching for a job with more suitable hours, and Britt didn't want to abandon her and Allegra), but that she was looking forward to getting back.

I wonder will I be able to sort out my characters better at home? she asked herself. I can't help thinking that because it's so glorious here I want everything to work out for them. Which is daft really, because in real life things don't always work out at all. And sometimes people's reasons for acting the way they do are impossible to really discover.

Why had Vanessa left Leo?

Britt desperately wanted to know the answer to that real-life question. It still nagged at the back of her mind, and there was a part of her that felt that if it bugged her so much when she wasn't even involved in the whole tragedy, how much more difficult must it be for Leo? Always wondering, never knowing.

After he'd told her about Vanessa and Donal, she had created scenarios in her mind of how they could have reacted if the accident hadn't happened; if Leo had been able to confront his brother about it and if they'd all had to get on with their lives. Britt thought it was because he had been robbed of the opportunity to rage at Donal that Leo continually held himself as tight as a coiled spring. What he needed to do was release that passion and that anger. Although how was another matter entirely. She wished she could write a happy ending for Leo.

She snapped the laptop closed and got up from the terrace. She walked around the house until she had banished all thoughts of Leo, William and Richard from her head. She wasn't going to write any more tonight. She needed to deal with her random skittering thoughts before trying again.

She returned to the verandah and opened her computer once more, clicking on her email application. (She'd been astonished to find that the Villa Serena had Wi-Fi broadband. Mia had told her that she might be halfway up a hillside but that internet access was good. They really weren't peasants at all, she added, with a wicked grin at her sister.)

Lisa-Anne had sent a message to ask how things were coming along with the new book – she couldn't wait, she said, to find out what happened next.

James and Sarah had sent some photos of the boys and reminded Britt that she'd promised to come for dinner as soon as she got back to Ireland.

And Steve Shaw had emailed from the *Aphrodite* to say that the ship was now in the Mediterranean for the pre-summer season and would be docking at Malaga the next day. He apologised for mailing Britt, who, he said, was probably working busily in Dublin on her next novel, but he wondered whether Mia would like to meet him in Malaga. Mia hadn't given him her email address when they'd been on board the ship. But Britt's was still on his file.

'Oh, I don't know about this,' said Mia when Britt, her eyes shining, showed her Steve's email. 'It's not such a good idea.'

'It's a great idea,' said Britt forcefully. 'He likes you a lot, Mia. Look – he says he'd be thrilled to see you again.'

'Yes, but . . .'

'Mia! I know you were a bit cautious on board the ship, but don't you think he's worth a shot now? I mean, he's obviously still thinking about you, and he must care a lot!'

'You don't know what he's thinking!' cried Mia. 'You know, Britt, you *made* me go to Alejo's and now you're making me go to Malaga, and I honestly don't know how the hell you did so many divorces when all your attention these days seems to be focused on fixing me up with unsuitable men.'

'You were the one who suggested Granada. And Steve Shaw isn't necessarily unsuitable,' Britt pointed out.

'No, but . . .' Mia looked at her helplessly.

'Can't you just meet up with him anyway?' suggested Britt. 'There's no harm in it.'

'There's no point in it either,' protested Mia.

'You need to get out,' Britt told her. 'You really do. I've accepted that you're not living in an arse-wipe town, but your social life isn't exactly hopping.'

The defiance that had been in Mia's eyes suddenly faded.

'You're right,' she conceded. 'And I'll go. But only if you and Allegra come too. Let's see how chirpy your favourite cruise director is when he meets her.'

The *Aphrodite* had arrived in port early in the morning, and would be departing late that night. When they arrived in Malaga just before midday, they immediately spotted the cruise ship moored in the port, her white hull gleaming in the sunlight. Britt could make out people standing at the rails or walking around the promenade deck, and she remembered doing the same thing herself.

They'd arranged to meet Steve at one of the beachside cafés, and he was already there, sitting at an outside table, looking cool and smart in his regulation whites.

'It's hard not to find that devastatingly attractive,' murmured Britt as they approached the table.

'You do have a point,' replied Mia. 'They shouldn't really allow guys to wear uniform. It blinds you to everything else.'

'Mia! Britt!' Steve stood up and smiled at both of them, then hunkered down to Allegra's level. 'And you must be Allegra. What a lovely girl you are.'

Mia's daughter regarded him thoughtfully from her dark eyes.

'It's great to see you both again,' said Steve, straightening up. 'Can I get you something to drink? Or eat? Are you hungry?'

'Ice cream,' said Allegra promptly.

Mia and Britt both asked for orange juice.

'I was with your mum on the ship,' explained Steve to Allegra as he pointed in the direction of the *Aphrodite*.

'And how has it been since we left?' asked Britt.

'Not half as much fun,' said Steve. 'And, of course, no hearts and flowers.'

He filled them in on the cruises that had taken place over the last few weeks, making them laugh with stories of the passengers and sigh with envy at descriptions of places they hadn't been to themselves.

'And are you due any time off soon?' asked Britt.

'I took some holidays when we finished in the Caribbean,' Steve replied. 'So it's back to the grindstone for me. It'll be another four months before I have time off again.'

'Do you like it?' asked Mia. 'Being away all the time.'

'There's nothing to keep me on dry land,' said Steve lightly. 'I don't have anyone waiting for me to come home.'

The silence was broken only by the sound of Allegra's spoon scraping the glass bowl.

'Don't you have a girl in every port?' Mia, too, kept her voice light.

'Not even in one port,' he said. 'It's nice to meet one here, though. Especially when she's you.'

Mia said nothing. She realised that her heart was beating faster.

'Come on, Allie,' said Britt as Allegra licked the last of her ice cream from her spoon. 'Let's you and me walk to the beach and let your mama and Steve finish their juice together.'

'OK,' said Allegra happily as she climbed down from her chair.

'You can catch up with us,' said Britt. 'See you later.'

Mia wiped her daughter's face with a paper napkin.

'Be good,' she said.

'I bet you're always good.' Steve grinned at the little girl, who smiled back at him.

'Of course,' she said primly, which made him laugh.

'So,' he said to Mia after Britt and Allegra had disappeared from view. 'The Romance Queen lives on. Despite herself.'

Mia chuckled. 'She thinks I live in an arse-wipe town and don't get out enough. So she was thrilled to get your email.'

'I was thrilled to discover she was here too,' said Steve, which made Mia look at him in sudden surprise while a flicker of uncertainty crossed her face.

He grinned at her. 'Because I knew she'd make you come. I wasn't sure otherwise.'

'I don't know what's happened to her,' said Mia. 'Ever since she's arrived she's been immersed in writing her next book, which she says is going terribly. I think that as an aside she's trying to sort out my love life.'

'Oh?' Steve's eyes widened in mock horror. 'You mean there's more than me?'

Mia smiled. 'I have a complicated life,' she said.

'Do you?'

'Of course. I have a daughter.'

'Lots of women have daughters. That doesn't mean their lives are particularly complicated,' Steve told her.

Mia fiddled with her hair.

'I've missed you,' Steve told her.

'Don't be silly,' replied Mia. 'You barely know me.'

'You don't have to know someone for ever to miss them,' Steve said. 'And you made quite an impression on me.'

'Fleeting,' said Mia.

'Not at all.' He stretched his hand across the table and rested it on hers. 'Being with you . . .'

Mia slid her hand from beneath his. 'You weren't "with me", as you put it,' she said. 'We . . . we . . .'

'We clicked,' said Steve. 'C'mon, Mia. You've got to admit that we clicked.'

'I enjoyed your company,' she admitted with a smile.

'Jeez.' He sighed. 'You're such hard work.'

She chuckled. 'I'm not really.'

'So there's a chance?' He looked at her anxiously.

'Steve, I really like you. But you're just here for a few hours. You'll be gone by midnight. What's the point?'

'I'd like to go on a date with you,' he said. 'Not have dinner with you on a ship where everyone is watching us.'

'It's just one evening,' said Mia. 'What do you want it to lead to?'

'I don't know,' said Steve. 'Whatever you want.'

She didn't know what she wanted. Being with Steve wasn't the same as being with Alejo. With him, she'd wanted to rip the shirt off his back a few seconds after meeting him. She wasn't entertaining any fancies of ripping the shirt off Steve's back. But despite her reservations, she was enjoying being with him, enjoying the closeness of him. It was nice to be sitting in a café with a man again.

She looked at her watch. 'It's after noon now,' she said. 'What time did you plan to meet up again?'

'I have the whole day in port,' said Steve. 'I wasn't planning on letting you go.'

Mia laughed. 'You're persistent.'

'What have I got to lose?' he asked. 'I'm on a tight schedule here.'

'I can't spend the entire day in Malaga,' said Mia.

'Why not?'

'I have Allegra to think about. She has to get home . . .'

'How far away is home?'

'Forty kilometres.'

'Less than an hour.'

'Let's catch up with Britt. See what she wants to do.'

'I don't really care what she wants to do.'

Mia laughed. 'Oh, how your tune has changed. On the ship, nothing was too much trouble when it came to what she wanted.'

'That was different. Although,' he admitted, 'I do like your sister. Once you get past her barbed-wire exterior she's a pussy cat.'

Mia grinned. 'A tiger cub, more like. Anyway, I need to talk to her first.'

Britt and Allegra were at the water's edge, where Allegra had decided to dig a hole in the sand and watch it fill up with every wave that broke on the shore. Her construction work had led to her short pink and white sun-dress becoming caked with damp sand.

'Having fun?' asked Mia.

'Yes!' cried Allegra. 'I like this.'

Mia told Britt that Steve wanted to spend time with her, and Britt told her to do whatever she liked.

'What about you and Allie?'

'I'll take her for lunch and we can spend some time together at the beach, and then I'll drive us home.'

'Up the mountain?' asked Mia doubtfully. 'On your own?'

'I can manage,' Britt assured her. 'I'm used to it now.'

'OK,' said Mia.

'Do you want me to pick you up afterwards?' asked Britt.

'Don't be daft,' said Mia. 'You'd be sitting around all night waiting.'

'All night?' Britt raised an enquiring eyebrow and grinned at her sister, who suddenly laughed.

'Till late,' she amended. 'Don't worry, I'll get a cab or something.'

'Well, if you need me to come and get you, just call.'

'OK,' said Mia.

'And Mia . . .'

'Yes?'

'Have a great time.'

Mia and Steve wandered around the old part of the city because Steve told her that he'd never done a tour of it before. She brought him to the Alcabaza, the Moorish king's palace perched on the hillside, where they sat for a while in the beautiful gardens; then they visited the impressive cathedral after which Steve called time on the culture and suggested that they head to the beach again and lie out in the sun.

'I'd've thought you'd be bored with the idea of lying out in the sun,' she teased. 'You spent the winter in the

Caribbean, for God's sake. Surely you got enough heat there to last you for ages.'

'The *Aphrodite* might have been in some gorgeous locations, but to be honest with you, I was far too busy to spend time lolling around,' Steve told her. 'And so it would be lovely to do nothing for an hour or two.'

She grinned. 'Have I tired you out with the historical stuff?'

'A bit,' he admitted.

'Well it's certainly siesta time, but I don't have any beach stuff with me,' she said.

'I thought of that.' He opened the small *Aphrodite*-logoed backpack he'd been carrying over his shoulder and took out two small towels, a pair of men's shorts and a purple swimsuit.

'I had to guess the size' he told her. 'But I'm hoping it'll fit.'

'You came prepared,' she said.

'You learn that on a cruise ship.' His eyes twinkled.

'Nice colour.'

'You looked lovely in your purple dress,' said Steve. 'So I thought it might be your shade.'

'Thank you.'

She couldn't remember the last time she'd lain on a beach with a man beside her. She wasn't actually sure that she'd ever done it before. She didn't count the rare days in Ireland when she'd headed off to Brittas with whoever her boyfriend of the time had been and they'd sat on the beach debating how long they could manage to put up with the cool easterly breeze that kept the air just the wrong side of pleasant. There had been lovely days in Brittas too, but they'd usually been when Mia was smaller and they'd gone as a family: Paula and Gerry, James, Britt and herself. Paula and Gerry would sit on a huge blanket while the three children romped in the sea and sand.

It was so much easier then, she thought, as she felt a pang for the fact that – the way her life was at the moment – there wasn't any chance of Allegra ever playing on the beach with a brother or sister. Or with Mia and her father sitting watching them.

'You OK?' Steve, who was sitting on the adjacent sun lounger, glanced at her.

'Oh, fine,' she said as she lay back and tipped her base-ball cap over her eyes. 'Absolutely fine.'

Back at the villa (she'd driven slowly and carefully up the mountain, but it had still been nerve-racking and her heart had been tripping in her chest), Britt and Allegra were sitting side by side on the squishy orange sofa. Britt's laptop was perched on her knees while Allegra was quietly turning the pages of one of the English picture books that Britt had brought to Spain for her. Every so often Britt would glance at her niece, engrossed in her book, not yet able to read it but knowing the story off by heart now anyway.

As she gazed at her, Allegra closed the book and looked upwards.

'Tina Trouble was a very bold girl,' she told Britt solemnly. 'I don't think she really and truly has learned her lesson. I think she'll be in trouble again.'

'Do you?'

Allegra nodded. 'Most probably for keeping her bedroom untidy,' she said. 'That's what I get into trouble for too.'

'I should have brought a change of clothes,' Mia remarked as she and Steve left the beach. 'I've got sand in my shoes and my dress is crumpled.'

'Details,' said Steve dismissively.

'All the same,' Mia said, 'if I'd realised I'd be out all day I'd've made provision for that.'

'How long were you planning to spend with me?' asked Steve.

'I didn't think about it,' admitted Mia.

He reached out and took her by the hand. 'Well you can't go home yet,' he told her. 'I still have a few hours off and I want to spend them with you.'

At first she thought of taking her hand away. But it was nice to know that someone wanted to hold it. So she didn't.

'Some day my papa will come home.' Allegra, who was attacking a picture in her colouring book with crayons, looked at Britt, who – deprived of pre-packaged food – was rather enjoying making spaghetti bolognese for dinner.

'Will he?' Britt was startled. She'd never heard Allegra talk about her father before.

'*Pues, sí.*' Allegra's voice was confident.

'Did your mama tell you that?' asked Britt.

Allegra shook her head. 'But he will come,' she said. 'He's my papa.'

* * *

'I'm *so* seriously underdressed for this,' hissed Mia as Steve led her into a restaurant with gleaming cutlery and crisp linen tablecloths.

'You look fine to me,' he said.

'You know I don't,' she told him. 'Plus my hair is a mess from the beach.'

'And they won't let you in because of a bit of mussed hair?' He grinned as she pulled her fingers through it and then nodded as a waiter led them to a table in an alcove. 'See. They think you're as lovely as I do.'

'You don't have to keep on with the complimentary stuff,' she told him. 'It's very distracting.'

'I'm trying to romance you,' he said.

She giggled. 'I've been living with Britt for the past two weeks,' she reminded him.

He laughed. 'Does that mean that it's been heavy on the romance or not?'

'Hard to tell,' she admitted. 'She's writing her next tearjerker so. Sometimes she goes around with this totally moony expression on her face and doesn't hear a word I'm saying, while other times she's as crisp and practical as ever and giving out that her characters are far too emotional and could do with a good slap.'

'Sounds like Britt all right,' he said. 'But how about tonight we do our own romantic thing?'

'You're a desperate charmer, Steve Shaw,' she said sternly.

'And you're a gorgeous woman, Mia McDonagh,' he told her.

* * *

William and Persia. Persia and Richard. William and Lucie. Richard and Camille. Nanette and Lucie. William and Richard. Britt read over the words she'd written and frowned. None of it was what she'd expected, but perhaps it was right for them. Which was the most important thing.

I'm quite nuts, she murmured to herself as she closed the laptop. I care about them more than I've ever cared about real living people. I'm clearly some kind of emotional retard.

She slid the laptop from her knees and put it on the tiny coffee table. Allegra, asleep on the sofa beside her, instinctively found the extra space and moved her head on to Britt's lap. Britt stroked her dark hair gently. And her niece sighed with satisfaction in her sleep.

'I'd better call Britt.' Mia looked at her watch as she and Steve stood outside the restaurant.

'Leave her be,' said Steve. 'I'll see you home. We'll get a taxi.'

'Are you crazy?' she demanded. 'It's nearly an hour's drive away, and . . .'

'And what?'

'And my daughter is there, Steve, so I'm afraid that . . .'

'That there'll be no hanky-panky?' He grinned.

'Precisely.'

'Well, I have to admit that's a bit of a disappointment,' he told her. 'It's a while since I've hanky-pankied. But since I have to be back on board by eleven, it'd have to be a quickie, and that's not what I want with you.'

She felt a lurch at the bottom of her stomach. Not passion, she told herself. Just a feeling that had been buried deep within her for the last few years. A feeling that it would be nice to sleep with a man again, to feel his arms around her and his lips on hers. A feeling that it would be especially nice to be with Steve.

'You could stay here until I leave,' he suggested as he saw the hesitation in her eyes. 'We could go to a hotel and you could stay the night.'

Mia said nothing.

'You'd be home before Allegra wakes up,' he told her urgently as he slipped his arm around her waist and drew her closer to him.

She didn't stop him when his lips came down on hers. She put her arms around him and pulled him closer to her, and felt herself relax within his hold. His body was warm and she felt safe and protected in his arms. He was the first man she'd kissed since Alejo. She kissed him again. She could feel a passion inside her now, slower burning than she remembered, but sweeping through her body from her toes to her lips.

'I knew it would be like that,' he said when they stopped for breath. 'I knew that you'd have the softest lips and the warmest body and that you'd taste of smooth vanilla.'

She swallowed hard as she leaned away from him. 'It's my lip salve,' she told him.

'Mia!' His eyes crinkled. 'You're not meant to shatter my illusions quite so quickly.'

'Steve.' Her eyes were serious. 'I have to. And I have to tell you that I can't stay here, that I must be home for Allegra and that . . . I'm sorry. I really am.'

'Britt is there,' he said softly, tightening his grip around her again. 'Britt will look after her. I'm sure she can cope.'

'No.' Mia moved away more decisively this time. 'I'm sure Britt can cope too, but that's not the point. I'm sorry, Steve. I have to go home. I really do.'

She couldn't hear any frustration in Steve's voice as he told her that it would have been great.

'Maybe.' She smiled a little. 'Probably.'

'It's not just a holiday romance kind of thing with me,' he told her seriously. 'I care about you, Mia. I can't stop thinking about you.'

'Oh, come on . . .' She kept her tone as light as she could. 'I'm sure there are plenty of other women.'

'Stop saying things like that!' he cried. 'Of course there are plenty of other women! On the *Aphrodite*. In the whole world! But I'm not interested in plenty of other women, Mia McDonagh. I'm not in love with plenty of other women.'

'You're not in love with me either,' she pointed out.

'How do you know?'

'Steve . . .'

He kissed her again. And she said nothing at all.

Britt heard the sound of a car stopping at the top of the narrow road that led to Villa Serena. She sat still, listening for the noise of the creaky gates opening. Mia kept talking about oiling them but she hadn't got around to it yet. After a minute the rasp of the gates reached her and she felt her shoulders relax. It wasn't that she'd been worried about Mia exactly, but she'd been alert to the fact that she might have had to drive to Malaga to collect her. Britt had been perfectly prepared to pick Mia up even though she hadn't been looking forward to strapping a sleeping Allegra into the jeep and tackling the twisting mountain roads at night, but she was glad that her sister had made it home under her own steam. And then, as she heard the crunch of Mia's footsteps on the gravel outside the house, she wondered if she had come home alone.

'Of course I'm by myself,' Mia said when Britt had shared her thoughts with her.

'He's lovely,' said Britt. 'He really is. So how was your date?'

'If I'd realised it was supposed to be a proper date I'd've done my hair.' Mia peered at herself in the mirror over the open fireplace and scrunched up her nose in despair. 'It's a bloody haystack.'

'Didn't seem to bother him.'

'He brought me to a fantastic restaurant too,' said Mia. 'I was totally like the peasant in the city there!'

Britt laughed. 'You look fine,' she said. 'You're naturally pretty. Which is probably a relief to him after all the women on board. You know how much time they spend getting ready every night!'

'Maybe,' conceded Mia. 'Perhaps I'm his bit of rough.'

'Mia!'

She smiled. 'He said that he was in love with me.'

'Oh!'

'It was when we were in a passionate clinch, so I suppose it doesn't exactly count. I told him he was just imagining it.'

'Are you in love with him?' Britt demanded.

'Don't talk nonsense.' Mia blushed.

'Mia McDonagh! You are!'

'Get a grip,' she told her sister. 'I'm not in love with him. I . . . He's nice, that's all. And he's a good kisser.'

'Excellent.' Britt's smile was broad.

'Stop it!' cried Mia.

'But you let him go?'

'Well, he was running out of time at that point. And he knew I wasn't going to sleep with him because I'd turned down the suggestion of staying the night in Malaga.'

'Was he annoyed about you not sleeping with him?'

Mia considered the question. 'I suppose he must have been. But he was good about it.'

'He must be really keen.'

'Not to get upset about not sleeping with me?' Mia asked.

'To care enough not to push it,' said Britt.

'Oh look, let's not make this out to be more than it is,' said Mia. 'A bit of fun for him, that's all.'

'You can't believe that,' said Britt, suddenly serious. 'You really can't.'

'I can't believe anything else either,' said Mia. 'I'm not ready to believe anything else.'

'Don't let him slip through your fingers.'

'For heaven's sake!' Mia frowned. 'I'm not trying to snare him, you know. I don't care if he slips through my fingers.'

'Really?'

'He's sweet and he's lovely and he's a good kisser,' said Mia after a moment's silence. 'I like him a lot. I really do.

And maybe if I was young, free and single I'd hop into bed with him just to see what it would be like. But I can't do that, Britt. You know I can't. And the thing is . . .'

'What?'

'Yes, he makes my heart beat faster. Yes, I like being with him. Yes, he's the only decent guy I've met in the last four years. But he doesn't make the blood pound in my veins and he doesn't make me feel like I'm going to faint every time I see him, and when I'm with him I don't feel as though we're the only two people in the world.'

'And you think love should be like that?' demanded Britt.

'It was with Alejo.'

'Alejo left you.'

'That's so unfair.' Mia looked angrily at Britt. 'Circumstances . . .'

'Don't tell me you're about to try and defend him.'

'No. But . . .'

'You had an affair with a married man and he dumped you when you were pregnant,' said Britt brutally. 'Don't tell me you're going to measure every guy you meet against the yardstick of Alejo's behaviour.'

'You're twisting it.'

'No, I'm not,' said Britt.

'I loved him.'

'And like you said, it's so over.'

'I know.' Mia looked past her sister and stared at a point on the wall.

Britt's eyes were full of concern. 'You can't wait for the

same thing from every guy you meet,' she said while Mia continued to look straight ahead.

'Why not?'

'Because it's about more than passion,' said Britt. 'It's about living together for the rest of your life.'

Mia's smile was disconsolate as she turned to look at Britt again. 'So you want me to compromise?'

'No,' said Britt firmly. 'I want you to stop fantasising.'

'I'm not.'

'You are, you know,' said Britt. 'Right now I think you're so blinded by memories of the handsome prince that you can't recognise the knight in shining armour when he rides up to your door.'

Chapter 27

Position: Sierra Bonita.
Weather: partly cloudy. Wind: easterly 10kph.
Temperature: 21°. Barometric pressure: 1011.2mb.

Britt decided to go home the following weekend. She felt she had done as much as she could do to her novel in Spain and she was itching to get back to Dublin and to her own house again. The interlude with Mia had been more enjoyable than she would have thought possible a few months earlier, but she needed to regain her own life. Besides, Mia had received some good news on the job front. The morning after her date with Steve Shaw, she'd had a call from the Sierra Bonita tourist office asking if she'd be interested in some part-time work. It was a job-sharing position and the money was better than either Dixie's restaurant or Ursula's art gallery.

Morning work suited Mia down to the ground. Allegra would be at the *guardería infantil* for all but an hour while she was in the office, and Ana Fernandez had offered to look after her until Mia finished. Additionally, Ana had offered to look after Allegra during the school holidays too. Ana had three other children and, she said, one more wouldn't make any difference. Besides, she added, Allegra and Loli were best friends and were actually easier to deal with together than apart.

'It's all coming together,' Mia told her sister the day before Britt was due to leave for Dublin. 'I couldn't have imagined it would work out so perfectly, but it has.'

'I'm delighted for you,' said Britt sincerely.

She had realised shortly after arriving in Sierra Bonita that Mia was in a constant state of worry over money, and although she had tried to be as generous as she could when putting cash into the household expenses jar that Mia kept on the kitchen shelf, she knew that her sister was very touchy about the idea of accepting more than was due. She had to bite her tongue every time she thought of Alejo Ariza's house in the foothills of the Sierra Nevada and the difference that some Ariza support would make to Mia's life, although she perfectly understood her sister's reluctance to involve him. And, she thought, if things develop a bit more with Steve Shaw, who knows what might happen in Mia's future. She hoped desperately that Mia would realise what a good man Steve was and would forget about Alejo. She wished that she'd never suggested to her that it would be right for Alejo to know anything about Allegra. Sometimes, she thought, what might seem the right thing to do could end up being totally wrong. In Mia's case, she couldn't help but feel now that any contact at all with Alejo would be utterly, utterly disastrous.

'You're sure you don't want to stay a bit longer?' Mia

slipped on the light blue jacket she wore in the tourist office while at the same time checking to see that Allegra had everything she needed for the day ahead. 'Sierra Bonita has been inspirational for you. You've done loads while you've been here.'

'I know,' said Britt. 'But it will be easier to tidy it all up back in Dublin, where I won't be distracted by the scent of the orange trees and the hibiscus and where I won't think that sitting on the terrace staring into space is a perfectly valid way to spend the day.'

Mia laughed. 'OK then. See you later. Don't work too hard.'

'I won't.'

Britt waved them goodbye and returned to the terrace. It was true that she seemed to be able to spend an inordinate amount of time simply gazing over the green valley below her, letting her thoughts wander into all sorts of places. Sometimes those thoughts were about her fictional character and sometimes they were about real people. A lot of the time her thoughts were personal ones. But she didn't get stressed as she used to when she remembered her life with and after Ralph. Somehow the biggest mistake of her life didn't seem as important as it once had. Getting it so badly wrong didn't mean that she'd been made a fool of. Nobody got it right all the time. She knew that. She just wished she didn't think she was the one who was supposed to live a mistake-free life.

She knew now how impossible that was. Everybody made mistakes. She had. Mia had. So had Leo. But there were always opportunities to get over them. Leo had found

Pippin. Mia – well, Steve had come into her life, and although she wasn't really letting him be part of it, he had at least opened her eyes to the possibility of moving on. And as for me . . . Britt watched a swallow swoop across the valley as she thought about her own mistakes . . . maybe one day I'll let someone get close to me again. Maybe one day someone will actually want to. It doesn't seem hugely likely, but perhaps I'll be a little more open to it in the future. Because it would be nice . . . she blinked in the bright light of the sun . . . it would be nice to have someone who cared. Someone for whom she mattered.

That was what Leo had found. Someone to care for him. And Leo's hurt had surely run much deeper than hers. So if he could get over the things in his past, surely she could get over feeling such a fool for losing her heart to the wrong person; for being so daft as to marry him.

The sound of the car crunching along the uneven road surface surprised her. Mia wasn't due back for hours yet, and since Villa Serena was at the end of the narrow road, no unexpected visitors ever turned up. She sat up straighter in the wicker chair, wondering if someone had got lost. If so, they would need to have exceptional reversing skills to get back up the road again, or would (as sometimes happened) have to ring the bell and ask if they could turn their car in the villa's driveway.

She heard the engine being turned off and then the solid thunk of a car door being closed. There was silence for a moment, then the jangle of the brass bell at the gates. She got up from the terrace and walked to the front of the house.

The man standing outside was tall and distinguished, wearing a navy silk suit and white shirt. The only splash of colour was his bright green tie. As she walked towards him, Britt saw him smooth back his dark hair from his forehead.

'Hello,' she said. 'Can I help you?'

'*Hola.*' He frowned and his eyes narrowed as he looked at her. 'I am at the right house? I am looking for Mia.'

'Mia is at work, I'm afraid,' said Britt. 'She won't be back until two thirty.' She glanced at her watch. It was almost midday.

The man frowned again. 'And you are?'

Britt looked at him uncertainly. She had an uncomfortable feeling that he might be someone in authority, someone who was checking up on Mia, perhaps. From the Spanish Social Services. Checking to see that she was doing a good job with Allegra. Or that she was paying her taxes. Or something.

'Would you like to come back later?' she asked without answering his question. 'I'm sure that Mia would be happy to help you then.'

He brushed his hair back from his forehead again, and Britt could see that despite the fact that it was a few degrees cooler today than it had been in the last few days, perspiration was gleaming on his brow.

'Perhaps I could wait?'

Britt was startled. And nervous. She didn't want a man she didn't know hanging around Mia's house. And why did he look so anxious? What was he worried about? Her imagination kicked into overdrive and she pictured him as a manic serial killer hacking them all to death because she'd been foolish enough to unlock the gate to him.

'I'm sorry,' she said firmly. 'I don't want to be rude, but I don't know you, and Mia didn't say anything about anyone calling to the house. So it would be better if you came back later.'

At first she thought he hadn't understood her, because he said nothing.

'I am an old friend,' he said eventually. 'I haven't seen her in some time.'

Britt suddenly felt her heart beat faster. 'How old?' she asked.

'I knew her in Guatemala,' he replied.

The first thing Mia saw when she returned to the house that afternoon with Allegra in tow was the Mercedes convertible parked in the driveway. She looked at it in puzzlement, wondering fleetingly if Britt's flash agent had come to visit her. From what Mia could tell, Meredith wouldn't be the sort of woman who'd hire a bog-standard car in a foreign country. Meredith was a convertible sort of girl.

She'd almost convinced herself that she'd guessed correctly as she walked around to the back of the house and was met by Britt, who was at the bottom of the steps that led to the terrace.

'Who's your visitor?' asked Mia.

Britt glanced at Allegra, who was hopping up and down beside Mia, showing off her hand-print painting.

'I . . . It's *your* visitor,' said Britt hesitantly.

Mia looked at her sharply.

'You probably want to talk to . . . to him on your own.'

'Britt . . .'

'He's come to talk to you. From Granada.'

Mia stared wordlessly at her sister.

'Maybe I should take Allegra back into town. She likes ice cream from Limón Limón, don't you, sweetie?' Britt beamed at her niece, whose eyes widened. The ice cream parlour was very popular, but Mia rationed her visits there very strictly.

'Oh, Mama, I want an ice cream.'

'Where is this visitor?' Mia's voice was taut.

'Inside,' said Britt as she took Allegra by the hand. 'I'd stay but I know that I'd want to interfere. And that wouldn't be right. It's your life. Your choices.' And before Mia had the chance to utter another word, Britt had whisked Allegra away and left her sister standing at the bottom of the steps.

She was still standing there, staring after the disappearing jeep, when the door opened and he walked outside. She heard the footsteps on the terrace and turned around. And then, even though she had known it would be him, she had to grasp the whitewashed balustrade to stop herself from falling as her knees almost gave way beneath her.

'*¿Qué tal*, Mia?' His dark eyes regarded her solemnly.

At first she couldn't speak, and then she said his name slowly.

'Alejo.'

He said nothing, and she repeated it. 'Alejo.'

He looked at her with his dark brown eyes. She remembered how he used to look at her, how his eyes could soften and smile. They weren't soft now. They were grave.

'It's me,' he said. 'Yes.'

'What are you doing here?' She was shocked that it really was him, unable to quite believe he was standing in front of her. 'How did you know where I was? Why have you come?'

'I came to see you,' he said.

She could feel her nails digging into the palms of her hands. He was here. He'd come to see her.

But why? She could feel her legs begin to buckle again. She mounted the steps and then sat down abruptly at the terrace table.

'How did you know I was here?' she repeated. 'How did you know where to find me?'

'Were you hiding?' he asked. 'Did you not want me to find you?'

She frowned slightly. 'I'm certainly not hiding. But I never expected you to try to find me. I'm not sure I wanted you to.'

'No?' There was a puzzled tone in his voice. 'In that case, why did you come looking for me?' he asked.

'I didn't!' she cried. 'I don't know what you're talking about.'

'You were at my house,' he said. 'You and your sister and the little girl.'

Mia's heart was hammering in her chest so fast she was afraid it would, quite literally, explode. She could feel the pounding not just in her chest but in her head. How did he know she'd been at his house? How had he tracked her here? How did he know about Britt and Allegra?

'Would you perhaps like some water?'

There was a ceramic jug on the table. And some tall frosted glasses. He poured water from the jug into one of the glasses and handed it to her.

'I did not think I would ever see you again,' said Alejo as she sipped the water. 'I did not know where you were or how to get in touch with you.'

'Well, there was nothing to get in touch with me about,' she said. 'You left, after all.'

'Yes.' He poured some water for himself. 'I'm so, so sorry.'

'Sorry?' She laughed faintly. 'There's no need to be sorry. Your wife came and you left. You explained it to me very simply at the time, and it's perfectly understandable.'

'Mia, please . . .'

'Don't,' she said. 'Don't try to make excuses. It's a long time ago now and I'm over it.'

'So why did you come looking for me?' he asked.

'I didn't come looking for you,' she said. 'What makes you think I did?'

'*Pues*, it is simple. I saw you on the security camera at my house. I knew it was you straight away. You were looking at the house. You were talking to the other woman. Your sister. The little girl was holding her hand.'

'Yes,' said Mia. She didn't say anything about Allegra. She didn't want to give herself away. But she wondered frantically what Britt had told him. How much she had interfered.

'I could not believe it,' he said. 'I didn't know you were in Spain. I didn't know why you were in the city and why you were at my house. And then why you did not look for me if you knew that I lived there.'

'I was curious,' she told him. 'I'd heard about your family. I wondered about it.'

'And me?' he asked. 'Did you wonder about me?'

'I didn't need to wonder about you,' said Mia shortly. 'I knew all about you.'

She stood up quickly. 'Excuse me for a moment.' She went into the house and into her bedroom, closing the door behind her. She leaned against the yellow-painted wall. He was here. In her home. Looking even more hand-some than he had four years ago. Dressed so differently in the suit and tie. Looking self-assured. Wealthy. In control.

But still with the power to make her catch her breath and think that he was the most attractive man in the world. Still with the power to make her heart beat faster. Still able to make the passion fizz in her blood so that she had to close her eyes to contain it.

Allegra sat on a high stool at the marble counter of the ice cream parlour. Britt watched her niece as she studied the pictures of the ice creams on the card in front of her, her pink tongue jutting out of the corner of her mouth as she weighed up the possibilities. She was simply adorable, thought Britt. Over the past few weeks she'd grown to love Allegra; to laugh at her way of looking pityingly at Mia when she did something of which Allegra disapproved; to smile at her when she emerged blinking into the kitchen ready for breakfast and then snapped into wakefulness almost immediately to begin another day of questions about why the sky was blue or why water was wet or why they couldn't have a pet dog or cat or chicken. She was a bundle of questions and hopes and dreams, and Britt realised that she had been utterly captivated by her. And she understood, as she hadn't at the beginning of her stay, why Mia would be terrified of sharing her with anyone else at all.

'Banana split,' said Allegra finally.

She always picked the banana split. But she had to go through all the other possibilities first.

'Excellent choice.'

Britt ordered a banana split for her niece and a *café cortado* for herself.

'I love you, *Tía* Britt,' said Allegra as the ice cream was placed in front of her.

'I love you too,' said Britt, and kissed her on the top of her head.

'Mia. Are you all right?'

It was five minutes later when he rapped at the door.

'I'm fine,' she said. 'I'll be out in a moment.'

'OK.'

She waited until she heard his footsteps recede, and then she went into the bathroom and splashed cold water on her face and the back of her neck. She patted it dry and went outside again. He had returned to his seat at the table.

'So,' he said. 'I saw that you were at my house and I wanted to know why. I asked some people about you and it took time, but I found you here.'

'What people?' She looked at him guardedly.

'It's easy to find someone these days,' he said. 'It wasn't difficult.'

'Not for someone who is part of the TierraMundo world, I guess,' she said diffidently. 'I suppose you just snap your fingers and they do what you ask.'

'It's not like that.'

'Isn't it?'

He shook his head. 'No, Mia. Now can we talk? There are things you need to know.'

'No there aren't.'

He was a different person. He was cool and businesslike, and even though she could see traces of the old Alejo, they'd been pushed into the background by the new one. His hair, once long and unruly, was cropped short. His eyes were still dark and soulful, but now they were also firm and demanding. And as for the rest – the suit, the tie, the soft leather shoes – none of it was the Alejo she'd known and loved. But he was still the sexiest man in the whole world. She still wanted to rip the clothes off his back and make love to him.

As though he could read her thoughts, he suddenly took off his jacket and loosened the green tie, sliding it from his throat and opening the top button of his shirt.

'I hope you don't mind,' he said. 'But I never feel comfortable in a jacket and tie.'

'I never saw you wear a tie before,' she said.

'There wasn't much call for them in Guatemala.'

'I guess not.'

He was more accessible without the tie. Still not her Alejo, but not quite as forbidding as he'd been before.

'I don't want you to be here,' she said abruptly. 'I don't need you to be here.'

He flinched and rubbed the bottom of his chin.

'I don't need to see you and remember that you made a fool out of me in front of my friends. In front of everyone we knew. They were all laughing at me and feeling sorry for me. The girl you met and seduced and left. The girl you never told about your wife.'

'I tried to tell you. I wanted to explain . . .'

'After she had turned up! After I'd heard about her being pregnant! How d'you think that made me feel? You should've told me before. And then you headed off to Los Angeles and forgot about me, and that's absolutely fine, Alejo, I'm glad you did, because I don't want to know you or anything, but you have a damn nerve turning up now like this, just because I happened to walk past your house one day.'

'You didn't walk past,' he reminded her. 'You stopped and looked.'

'It's a big house,' she retorted. 'I bet a lot of people stop and stare at it. Can't blame them. It's so damn ostentatious I suppose they can't help staring. I know I couldn't. Security cameras! But, of course, you need them, seeing as you are part of a family that owns half the country. You forgot to mention that to me in Guatemala too. *Madre de dios*, Alejo, there were more things you didn't tell me than you did.'

'I know you are still upset and angry, and you have every right to be,' said Alejo. 'But can I tell you my side of the story?'

'You already did,' she replied. 'The bottom line is that you had an affair with me and your pregnant wife came to town and you left with her.'

'The circumstances . . .' said Alejo softly.

'Meant nothing!' she cried. 'I thought what we had was wonderful and special and counted for something, and the truth was that it was just a quick shag as far as you were concerned.'

'Shag?' He looked confused.

'I don't know the word,' she said. 'It's not something I thought I'd need. But you know, Alejo. Someone to sleep with and leave. That's what I was.'

'That's not true,' he said. 'It *was* wonderful and special and it did count for something. It wasn't this . . . this shag that you speak about.'

'Who cares what it was or wasn't,' she said wearily. 'You had your life – a life that you didn't tell me about – and I had mine. And it's fine. I'm happy. You're happy. Let's leave it like that.'

She could still feel the passion. That was the worst of it. Despite everything, she could feel the desire surging through her body, her need for him exactly the same as it had been four years earlier.

'I had no choice but to leave,' said Alejo.

'Actually you had,' said Mia. 'But it would have been difficult to tell your pregnant wife about your mistress, and so I guess you took the most obvious route.'

He nodded. 'I should have told you,' he said. 'I know. I was wrong.'

'You were wrong then and you're wrong now.' She

swallowed hard. 'And I was wrong to go looking at your house and make you think for a second that there was some reason we needed to talk to each other again. You'd better go, Alejo. I don't think there's anything more to say to each other.'

'Mia, please. Please understand how very sorry I am.' He traced his finger along an embroidered flower on the blue and white tablecloth before looking at her again. 'I didn't want to hurt you.'

'I loved you.' The tears that Mia hadn't wanted to shed now pooled in her eyes and overflowed down her cheeks. 'I loved you like nobody else, and you broke my heart, you faithless bastard.'

He let her cry, her face hidden behind her hands, her shoulders shaking.

Eventually he moved closer to her and put his arm around her.

'*Querida* Mia,' he said softly. 'Please do not cry.'

The touch of his fingers scorched her skin just as they'd done that first time. She caught her breath but the tears continued to slide down her cheeks even as he held her more tightly so that his expensive shirt was soaked.

'You broke my heart.'

She felt him flinch, and he pushed her gently away from him so that he was looking at her tear-stained face. 'I did not deal with it well, I know.'

'An affair is never dealt with well.'

Alejo looked at her pleadingly. 'It wasn't just an affair, Mia. I loved you.'

She rubbed her eyes and took a deep breath. 'Look,

Alejo, it was four years ago and it's in the past. We were different people then. We both did stupid things, but doesn't everyone? I'm sorry I got upset just now, but I guess it was the shock of seeing you. It's in the past now, isn't it? You have your life and I have mine and we can't go back. Besides,' she smiled faintly, 'it *was* an affair. A mad, crazy affair, but that's all. It wasn't true love. It was hot and sultry and romantic until it turned out so badly. Let's just forget about it.'

She didn't want to forget about it. She wanted to make love to him again. She was disgusted with herself.

'Belén lost the baby.'

For a second she didn't take in what he'd said. Then she looked at him in shock.

'But I saw you,' she said. 'In the plaza. With a baby.'

He stared at her in astonishment. 'When?'

'A couple of years ago. You were laughing and joking together and there was a child asleep in the pushchair beside you. I couldn't see properly but I know he – or she – was there.'

Alejo nodded slowly. 'Eduardo,' he said.

'Your child?'

He nodded again. 'Belén was very, very depressed when we lost the baby. It happened after we left Los Angeles. And then when we came home she got pregnant again.'

'I'm glad,' said Mia, even though she felt sick.

'Neither of us expected that she would get pregnant again so quickly.'

'But it all worked out.'

'Yes,' said Alejo.

'Well, I'm glad for you,' repeated Mia tersely. 'I'm not sure why you felt the need to come here to tell me all this, but it's good that your life is fine.'

'It's not fine,' said Alejo.

'Alejo, you're living in a gorgeous house with a gorgeous wife and an undoubtedly gorgeous son,' said Mia. 'It sounds pretty damn fine to me.'

'How can it be fine when those I love are not in it?' he asked.

Mia lifted the jug to pour herself some more water, but her hand was trembling so much that it splashed on to the table.

'I'll get a cloth,' she said. 'I'll be back in a minute.'

She went into the kitchen and stood in front of the sink. Alejo was here. He had come looking for her. She still didn't know why, but the point was that he had come. She gripped the edge of the sink. All she'd ever wanted was him. She still thought about him almost every single day, still felt herself shake with longing for him. At night she thought about him before she fell asleep, and sometimes she even dreamed about him. In her dreams they were together in the house in Guatemala, and she was wearing her blue dress and he was walking towards her, smiling.

She heard a sound at the kitchen door and turned around. He was standing looking at her.

'It's a nice house,' he said.

'Not quite in the same league as yours.'

He shrugged.

'Why didn't you tell me?' she asked. 'When I first met you? Why didn't you tell me that you were married and that you were part of this big conglomerate and that your family was filthy rich and that you weren't just some average geologist doing an average job.'

'Because none of that was important to me.'

'You didn't think the fact that you were married might be important either?'

He winced. 'Of course. But we were separated, Mia.'

'A temporary separation,' said Mia. 'And when she came looking for you, you went home with her.'

'Because she was pregnant.'

'So why are you here now?' asked Mia.

'Because I saw you,' said Alejo.

'Nothing has changed.'

'My marriage to Belén . . .' said Alejo. 'Well, we have . . . we have papered over the cracks, yes?'

She nodded.

'I care about her very much. But I do not love her in the way that I love you, Mia. I cannot.'

She felt sick again. Sick and excited.

'So what do you want?' she asked.

'That is what we have to talk about.'

He'd stepped into the house and now he was looking at her bookshelf. Mia suddenly felt her heart go into overdrive. Because she knew that her single-mother self-help books were there. And that he would see them. Although perhaps he'd seen them already.

'Your sister is a writer,' said Alejo. 'She told me she was working here with you.'

'Yes,' said Mia cautiously.

'You used to tell me that she was a pain in the neck.'

'She used to be.' Mia exhaled slowly. 'She's not so bad any more.'

'She told me about you both going on the cruise. That you had met someone there. A good man, she said. Perhaps the right man for you.'

Three cheers for Britt, thought Mia. At least she didn't let him think I'm a sad loser! And suddenly she thought of Steve, and the feeling of his lips on hers and the comfort of his arms around her and the slow-burning desire that had crept through her and almost made her throw caution to the winds and tell him that she would sleep with him after all. She shivered.

'I didn't expect that you were sitting waiting for me.' Alejo regarded her thoughtfully from his dark eyes. 'I don't suppose that you even like me very much. I understand that there might be other men.'

'Not that many,' said Mia. 'I don't have time for men.'

'No,' said Alejo. 'I suppose it is difficult with a little girl. Our little girl.'

She couldn't speak. She was afraid of saying the wrong thing.

Alejo was here because of Allegra.

Chapter 28

Position: Sierra Bonita.
Weather: partly cloudy. Wind: easterly 10kph.
Temperature: 21°. Barometric pressure: 1011.2mb.

'I kept things from you.' Alejo looked at Mia. 'And you kept things from me.' She held her breath as she watched him pick up the photo of Allegra in its filigree frame from the top of the TV.

'She is very pretty,' he said.

'Yes.' Mia forced the word from her lips.

'You would think,' he said as he studied it closely, 'that she was the twin of Eduardo.' He walked out to the verandah and returned with his wallet, from which he took a photograph. She took it from him and looked at Alejo's son. He was right. Eduardo had the same dark hair and mischievous eyes as Allegra.

'So?' Alejo looked at her. 'Why did you not tell me?'

'Let's go outside.' Mia felt as though the walls of the house were closing in on her. She needed some air.

She realised that she had forgotten to bring a cloth to wipe up the water she'd spilled earlier.

'Let me.' Alejo went back into the house and returned with the cloth. He mopped up the water, filled her glass, brought the cloth back into the kitchen and then returned to the verandah. Mia was sitting at the table, tapping her fingers nervously against the glass.

Alejo sat down opposite her.

'What was the point in telling you?' she asked after they had sat for almost a minute without speaking. 'What would it have achieved? You and Belén were back together. She was having your baby. You wanted to make your marriage work. Telling you that I was pregnant wouldn't have helped.'

'You went through it on your own?' asked Alejo. 'I wish . . .'

'That you could have been with me?' She looked at him scornfully. 'Give me a break.'

'I could have . . . I would have . . .'

'What?' she asked. 'What would you have done? Left Belén? You weren't prepared to do that when you heard she was pregnant. And I understood that. I really did.'

'Your daughter is my daughter too,' said Alejo. 'I don't want her thinking that I don't care. I don't want her growing up thinking another man is her father.'

'I would never let Allegra think that,' said Mia. 'I planned . . . Well, there's no other man.' She pushed from her mind the sudden image of Steve laughing with them both in Malaga.

'It's a pretty name,' said Alejo after a pause.

'She's lovely.' Mia's face lit up. 'She's the best thing that ever happened to me.'

He looked at her thoughtfully. 'Better than you and me?' he asked. 'Because the truth is, *querida* Mia, you are the best thing that ever happened to me. And I let you go.'

'Don't say that.' She felt a knot form in her stomach.

'It's true,' said Alejo. 'I made the wrong decision in Guatemala. I should never have left.'

'And if you hadn't, you'd have felt guilty for ever,' said Mia.

'Perhaps I would have got over that.'

'And perhaps I wouldn't,' said Mia. 'Because if we'd been together and I'd known about Belén and heard about her losing her baby, I'd have felt guilty, Alejo. I'd have blamed both of us.'

'It is a difficult situation,' admitted Alejo. 'No matter which way you look at it.'

'It was difficult but you made your decision, and it was the right one.'

'Then why don't I feel that way about it?' he asked. 'Why, when I saw the tape of you at the gate, did my heart beat faster?'

'I don't know,' whispered Mia.

'It's because I will always love you,' said Alejo. 'Because it wasn't just an affair, Mia.'

He was saying the words she'd always wanted to hear, the words she'd sometimes imagined him saying to her. He had looked for her and he'd found her, and he still loved her.

'What do you want, Alejo?' she asked.

'I want to take care of you,' he said. 'And our daughter.'

'It's been a long time,' she said. 'How do you know you still want me?'

'How could I not?' he asked.

He got up and walked around the table towards her. She stood up too. He put his arms around her. And then, as he had done the last time he kissed her, he tilted her face so that she was looking up at him before he brought his mouth down on top of hers and held her tightly to him.

And in that moment Mia knew that she had forgiven him for everything, because he was the only man she'd ever really loved, and it wasn't just about Allegra, it was about her too, and he still loved her just as much as ever.

'And then you came back,' said Mia as she and Britt sat on the terrace later that evening and talked about Alejo's unexpected reappearance in her life. 'Possibly jolted him into what family life with me would really be like when he saw Allie with sick all down her front and being hysterical.'

'I'm sorry about that,' Britt said. 'She wolfed down the banana split and then it all came back up again, and we had to come home.'

'Well, it put a stop to his gallop anyway.' Mia smiled wanly. 'Which I think was probably a very good thing, because I don't know what I would've done . . .'

'Do you still love him?' asked Britt.

'He was the love of my life,' said Mia slowly.

'And now that he's seen you and knows about Allegra . . .' Britt looked seriously at Mia, 'what do you want to do?'

'Run off into the sunset with him,' said Mia. 'Spend the rest of my life making love to him.'

'Mia . . .'

'He is the Handsome Prince,' Mia told her. 'He's everything I ever wanted.'

'So it's as though he never left you at all?'

Mia exhaled very slowly. 'He's changed, of course,' she said. 'The suit. The car. The rich family.'

'And you still love him?'

'I've always loved him,' said Mia. 'Oh, Britt – he's still impossibly sexy and impossibly handsome and impossibly hot! He still makes me shake with desire when I see him. Doesn't everyone want hot, sexy and handsome?'

'I guess.'

'Wasn't Ralph hot, sexy and handsome?' demanded Mia.

'And a fruitcake,' said Britt. 'Hot, sexy and handsome wasn't enough for me.'

'Are you saying it wouldn't be enough for me either?' Mia looked at her sister in exasperation. 'Hell, Britt, you were the one who convinced me to go to Granada in the first place. You were the one who talked about his responsibilities. If he's here now, it's your fault!'

Britt looked uncomfortable. 'It's not that I don't think he should face up to his responsibilities towards Allie,' she said. 'It's just that everything is moving so quickly. I don't think you should rush into anything.'

'You were perfectly prepared for me to rush into something with Steve Shaw,' countered Mia. 'In fact you were pushing me into his bloody arms!'

Britt exhaled sharply. 'Steve isn't married.'

'Maybe he is,' said Mia. 'How do you know these days?'

'I don't think he would've said the things he said to you if he was married,' Britt told her.

'I didn't think Alejo would've said the stuff he said either,' said Mia.

'Can you trust him?' asked Britt.

Mia looked at her sister angrily. 'After everything? Yes, I can. I understand why he didn't tell me about Belén in Guatemala. He should've, of course. But I know why he didn't. There's nothing in his life I don't know about now.'

'He didn't tell you about the family company either,' Britt reminded her.

'Because we were in a particular situation.' Mia defended him. 'OK, it was wrong. He knows that. But it's different now. All our cards are on the table and he wants to make it up to me and Allegra.'

'So he should,' Britt agreed. 'And it's not that he might not be your handsome prince coming to rescue you – and not that I still don't think he should take some responsibility for Allegra – but the truth is, Mia, that you're strong and determined, you're a fantastic mother and you don't need rescuing by anyone.'

Mia blinked in surprise. 'Thank you.'

'Does he live up to your memories of him?' asked Britt.

'Yes.'

'He seemed genuine enough,' said Britt neutrally.

'You didn't like him, did you?'

'I think he's the sexiest man I ever met,' admitted Britt. 'But that's entirely different to liking or loving. I didn't dislike him. I'm probably just a bit prejudiced against him.'

'That's my fault,' said Mia. 'I didn't paint him in the best light. But he's a good man.'

'And still married,' said Britt.

'What's that supposed to mean?'

'Nothing,' said Britt hastily. 'Just – well, before you do anything stupid, you need to have some assurances.'

'Anything stupid?'

'It's easy to get carried away on emotion,' said Britt. 'But you have to live with the consequences.'

'I forgot I was talking to someone who thinks that true love is horribly selfish,' said Mia. 'I forgot you'd be judgemental.'

'Oh, come on!' cried Britt. 'I'm not making judgements. I'm just saying that before you make any radical changes to your life, and before you believe every word that Alejo is telling you, you need to think about what's important to you.'

'*He's* important to me.'

'You were getting over him.'

'And maybe now I don't have to.'

'Because he'll give you everything you want?'

'All I want is him.'

'Mia! Think about it for a second,' said Britt. 'Sure, you want him. But you also want security for yourself and Allegra, and you want to be certain that he's going to provide that, which means that he's going to have to divorce Belén, and quite honestly, I think you should make sure he does that before you make any commitment at all.'

'You can be so heartless!' cried Mia.

'Not heartless,' Britt said. 'Just practical.'

'Who said love is practical?' demanded Mia.

'You have to be practical because of Allegra.'

'I won't do anything to hurt Allegra,' said Mia. 'Neither will he. But think about it, Britt. We could be a family together.'

'In Granada?'

'Who cares?'

Britt looked at her sister helplessly. 'I just don't want you getting hurt,' she said.

'I won't get hurt,' Mia promised her. 'I've done the hurt thing. I won't let it happen ever again.'

Mia and Allegra drove Britt to the airport the following day. They'd gone to dinner in Sierra Bonita the previous night, eating once again in the restaurant opposite the church, and had studiously avoided talking about Alejo, even though both of them were thinking about him.

Mia was imagining a future with him, planning her life and Allegra's, picturing them living in the big house in Granada. It was a beautiful house and a wonderful place to bring up a child. She didn't care any more about the high walls and the security gates because they'd be behind them. Safe and protected by Alejo, who loved them. Who had always loved her. Who'd said so.

If only, Mia thought, they hadn't wasted the last four years. And then she remembered that in the last four years he'd been with Belén and they'd lost one child and had another. And that for her and Allegra to live in the big house, Belén and Eduardo would have to leave. But they'd be looked after. Belén's family were wealthy. She wouldn't be living in an old house in the hills. She'd have everything she wanted.

Except Alejo, of course. But then she didn't want Alejo, did she?

Mia picked at the bread roll beside her plate. If only Belén hadn't been pregnant four years ago. If only she hadn't come to Guatemala and whisked Alejo away. Then perhaps Mia herself and Allegra would be living in the big house in Granada already. And she wouldn't have gone through the hell of the last few years, feeling angry at herself and angry at Alejo and angry at the whole damn world. She was still a bit angry at Alejo, she realised as the bread roll crumbled between her fingers. But she had forgiven him because she loved him, and that was what you did when you were in love.

Britt watched the changing emotions flicker across her sister's face. She hadn't wanted to leave Mia and Alejo alone at Villa Serena, but she'd known that this was a conversation the two of them needed to have. At the same time she'd worried that Mia would fall for him all over again. Britt had wanted Alejo to take some responsibility for his daughter. But she hadn't really expected him to want Mia and Allegra to live with him. If that was what he truly did want. Mia was excited and infatuated by him all over again. Which wouldn't matter if they both wanted the same things. But the divorce . . . Britt shuddered. Wealthy people and divorce was always a nightmare. She wasn't at all sure how Mia would cope being in the middle of it. But her sister deserved a second chance with the love of her life. And people put up with a lot of things in the name of love.

Chapter 29

Position: Dublin.
Weather: heavy showers. Wind: westerly 15kph, gusts
40kph. Temperature: 15°. Barometric pressure: 963mb.

The sky had been clear when Leo got into the car, but by the time he arrived at Donal's house the clouds had rolled in again and the rain, whipped by the wind, was cascading from the angry sky. He waited in the car for a moment but there was no sign of any easing of the deluge, and so he opened the door, hurried up the short driveway and put his key in the lock.

A musty smell greeted him. It was months since he'd visited the house. He'd been there a couple of times after the accident, but only to deal with mundane things like emptying the fridge and switching off the heating. All of Donal's post had been directed to the solicitor who had looked after his estate, and although Leo was the named executor of the will, Ferdia Grey was taking care of it. Leo didn't want to know that Donal had left him everything. What did it matter when he had taken everything from him first?

There was a pile of hand-delivered junk mail in the hallway, mostly leaflets from takeaway restaurants and garden services. Among them was a glossy brochure from an estate agency saying that they were looking for properties in the area and to contact them if planning to sell. Leo bundled them all together and put them in the green bin outside Donal's front door. He wiped the raindrops from his hair as he came inside again.

He could hear the steady tick of the clock in the kitchen. He'd never noticed the ticking of the clock before. Despite the fact that he lived alone, Donal's house had always been noisy. His brother had liked sound, and so would often have the radio and the TV on at the same time while playing on his Xbox or surfing the internet. Even when he was out he would leave something playing. The silence, more than anything, underlined the fact that Donal had gone for ever.

Leo stood in the long, narrow kitchen and remembered leaning against the table drinking from a can of lager while Donal (who prided himself on his ability to cook) chopped vegetables to stir-fry in his big wok. Bananarama's *Greatest Hits* was playing loudly on the speaker system. Leo used to tease Donal gently about his affection for the eighties girl band, but Donal would laugh and say that they were his guilty pleasure.

'You gotta learn to look after yourself, bro,' he'd said as he slid the vegetables into the wok. 'Can't expect Vanessa to do it for you. She's a party kind of girl.'

Donal had known even then that Vanessa was a party girl. Donal wasn't a party guy. So how had he stolen her away from Leo? What had he had that Leo himself hadn't? Why had Vanessa decided that Donal was the one for her? Why had they done this to him?

Leo wasn't sure whether he'd shouted the last words out loud or whether the cry was only in his head. He looked out of the kitchen door into the back garden. The grass was unkempt and uneven and the bushes were growing out of control. Perhaps he should've kept the gardening leaflets, he thought wryly. Perhaps it was seeing the garden at the front, where the grass was also overgrown, that had caused them to be pushed through the letterbox in the first place.

The living room was neat and tidy. Leo himself had cleaned up the day after Donal's funeral. He'd washed and put away the wine glasses, thrown out the gossip magazine that Vanessa had left on the sofa and plumped up its cushions. He'd done it without thinking. A few days later he'd called a cleaning company and asked them to do the house for him, from top to bottom. Every surface. He'd let them in and closed up after them, thinking that they had done a good job. Now, as he ran his finger along the mantelpiece over the flame-effect gas fire, he left a track in the dust that had settled over the last few months.

The TV was plugged in. He switched it on and the room was filled with the voice of the newsreader. Donal had been a news junkie. He would watch the same story on every channel, wanting to see what kind of slant each one would put on it. It had been work as well as pleasure, because Donal had been a political reporter for RTÉ. The news of his death had made the next day's bulletins, along with video clips of some of his reports for the station. Leo had looked at the first of them and had then changed channels so that he wouldn't see it again.

The house seemed less eerie with the noise of the television. He sat down on the sofa and looked at the news images without seeing them. The only pictures in his mind were of Donal and Vanessa and the shock on their faces when he had walked into the house.

At least they hadn't been having sex. He squeezed his eyes shut to blank out the thought. But it had been with him ever since that night: his brother and his fiancée in bed together. He wished he could let it go, forget it completely, but he couldn't. Sometimes when he was with Pippin, at dinner or in a bar or just together in his Monkstown house, the thought would come to him and he would tense beside her. Occasionally she would notice it and ask him was anything wrong, and he would shake his head and tell her that it was fine. But he knew she didn't always believe him.

He also knew he should tell her. He didn't know why he found it so hard. He had, after all, blurted it out to Britt McDonagh that last night on the *Aphrodite*, and it had been a relief to finally talk about it to someone. Britt hadn't come back with meaningless platitudes either. She'd been understanding. She'd also told him to tell Pippin. He couldn't remember what reason he'd given for not doing so, because, being totally honest with himself, he didn't really know why he was so reluctant. When he'd tried to pin it down, he'd decided that it was because Pippin was so sunny and guileless that he didn't want to bring such a horrible thing into her life. Telling her that Vanessa and Donal had been killed in a car accident had made her warm and sympathetic. Telling her about Donal's involvement with Vanessa seemed to turn it into something sleazy.

He wished Pippin was here now. He wished there was someone to put their arm around him and tell him that they loved him and that everything would be all right. He felt totally alone sitting in the empty house, hearing but not listening to the news. He hated being alone. He hated knowing that Aunt Sandra was his only living relative. It made him feel disconnected from the world. Disconnected from other people.

He wouldn't be disconnected when he married Pippin. He would have a mother-in-law, Eileen, and a father-in-law, John. And although Pippin was an only child, there were uncles and aunts and cousins . . . He would be OK with all of them. Besides, Pippin had lots of friends and contacts in the media world. He'd been socialising more since he'd come back from the cruise with her than he ever had in his life before. He'd never gone to events with Vanessa because she'd been working. But even though Pippin, too, said that social events were work, she liked him to be there. She liked showing him off, she said. She wanted people to know that she had a devastatingly handsome fiancé. When she said that, she would tuck her arm into his and smile at him in mock-adoration, which always made him smile too. So he went with her. It had been difficult at first, talking to people from a world completely different to his. But the great thing was that they didn't know him. They hadn't known Vanessa. They were terribly gossipy, but the gossip wasn't about him. He didn't actually know most of the people it *was* about, but he listened and laughed all the same. It was a very, very different life to the one he'd been leading before, but he liked it. His picture had been in the paper at least half a dozen times in the last month. Seeing the pictures made him feel as though he existed again. Being with Pippin made him feel alive.

He got up, switched off the TV and went upstairs. He hadn't been upstairs since the night – before he'd even met Vanessa – when he'd been to a party at the rugby club Donal supported and everyone had gone back to the house and Leo had stayed over because he'd been far too drunk to even consider going home. It seemed like yesterday and at the same time a lifetime away.

He pushed open the door of the bathroom.

There was a bottle of Head & Shoulders and a half-empty bottle of body wash in the shower tray. On the shelf over the basin was a tube of toothpaste, the cap replaced crookedly. There was also a canister of shaving foam, a Gillette razor and a bottle of Aramis aftershave.

He hadn't expected to see them there. He'd assumed the cleaning company would have thrown them out. But he hadn't asked them to, and he supposed it wasn't something they'd take upon themselves to do. He opened the bathroom cabinet. It contained refill razor blades, a men's moisturiser, more shaving foam, two packets of paracetamol, a packet of Imodium and an open Durex Pleasuremax Warming 24 Pack. Leo looked inside the Durex pack. There were six left.

'You bastard!' he hissed under his breath. 'You utter shit. I can't forgive you and I never will.'

He left the bathroom and stood indecisively at the top of the stairs. Then he turned and pushed open the door to Donal's bedroom.

He hadn't told the cleaners to strip the bed, and so they had made it instead, the duvet in its neutral cover placed neatly over it, the pillows carefully arranged above the duvet. Leo went around to the left-hand side of the bed, the side Vanessa slept. There was a long brown hair on the pillow.

Leo needed to sit down. He sank into the wicker chair at the end of the bed and covered his face with his hands. He started to cry. It was the first time he'd cried since the gardai had come to break the news.

Once he started, he couldn't stop. Somewhere deep inside he felt that crying was weak, and crying in Donal's house was weaker still. Somehow his brother would know that he was here, would know that the tears were streaming down his face. His brother, who'd always looked after him and protected him and who he admired more than anyone else in the world, could look down on him now and see him cry. The more he told himself that he was being foolish, the more he cried. And yet as the tears fell, he could feel something inside himself shift. Just as it had when Britt McDonagh had smiled at him and he'd felt himself unfreeze. And when he'd spoken to Karen Kennedy and felt that way too. It was as though he had been holding himself tightly together and suddenly it was all un-ravelling. And although it was uncomfortable, it was also a relief, because it had been difficult to stay wound up for so long.

He rubbed his eyes with the thumb and forefinger of his

right hand. He'd told Dr McClelland that crying would be a sign that he felt sorry for himself. But he didn't really feel sorry for himself right now. He just felt sorry. Sorry that it had happened at all. Sorry that they had died. Sorry that he would never really know why Donal had been the one Vanessa had turned to.

You always had the best women, he murmured now. You didn't need to take my fiancée. You really didn't.

And maybe one day I could've got over it.

He released his breath in a slow sigh. He was over it now, wasn't he? He was engaged again. There was no need for him to feel angry or betrayed. He'd done what they all said and moved on.

At that moment his mobile phone rang.

'Hi, babes.' Pippin's voice, clear and cheerful, came down the line.

'Hi.'

'Are you OK?' she asked. 'You sound a bit odd.'

'I'm fine,' he said. 'Will I pick you up later?'

'Where are you now?' she asked.

She knew that he'd been going to Donal's house. To sort things out, he'd said, before putting it on the market. He'd asked if she wanted to come, even though he'd hoped that she wouldn't. She'd said that the idea of going into a dead person's house was a bit creepy, and would he mind if she passed on that one.

'Just about to leave my brother's house,' he told her. 'So I can get home and change and then meet you.'

On the rare occasions he mentioned Donal, he never used his name. He always called him 'my brother'.

'That'd be perfect!' cried Pippin. 'And then we're all going for something to eat in the Clarence, which will be fabulous fun.'

'All?'

'There's a gang of us here,' she told him.

He didn't feel like going to the Clarence. He didn't feel like being with a gang of people. He didn't really want to go out at all.

'I was thinking of a night in together,' he said.

She laughed. 'Plenty of time for that when we're old and grey.'

He wanted to talk to her about it. He wanted to explain how he felt. But he knew she wouldn't understand. He wouldn't expect her to.

'Sure,' he said. 'See you later.'

Chapter 30

Position: Sierra Bonita.
Weather: partly cloudy. Wind: southerly 5kph.
Temperature: 26°. Barometric pressure: 1011.2mb.

Mia was enjoying her time at the tourist office. Her job entailed a bit of everything, although dealing with the tourists was her favourite part. They were beginning to arrive in greater numbers now, and she knew that the streets would soon be thronged with holidaymakers lured by the thought of a fortnight in a traditional white Andalucian village. Sierra Bonita was one of the prettiest in the region, and the challenge for the town council was retaining its charm while benefiting from the money that the tourists had to spend.

She handed some leaflets to an English couple who had asked for information on nearby restaurants, pointing out both the cheapest and the most expensive and mentioning the one she liked best herself. The tourists left, happy with her insights, just as Candice, the girl who did the afternoon shift, arrived. Mia smiled at her, brought her up to date on some things that needed to be done and then waved goodbye. She could feel the strength of the sun outside. In the last few weeks it had picked up in intensity so that people were starting to seek out the shade during the day.

Mia had arranged to go to lunch with Ramira Cortez, one of the teachers at the school. Mia and Ramira had become friendly since Allegra had started at the *guardería infantil*. Ramira had lived and worked in Dublin for a few years before returning to Sierra Bonita, and had good memories of her time in the city. She was older than Mia, with a fourteen-year-old daughter, and had taken the Irish girl under her wing when she'd turned up in the Spanish town.

'It's lovely here,' said Ramira enthusiastically as they sat down at a table on the wide outside terrace. 'Good menu too.'

They ordered off the *menu del día*, deciding that the restaurant was a real find and that the tourists would love it.

'I think they do already.' Mia looked around. It had filled up while they had been sitting there and was now bustling and busy.

'So you will recommend it?'

Mia nodded. 'To be honest, there's hardly anywhere in the town that I don't,' she said. 'I want to be totally objective, but the truth is, I like all of our restaurants!' She patted her stomach. 'A bit too much, maybe.'

Ramira laughed and then looked at her a little more seriously. 'But you've lost weight recently, no?'

'Not that I know of.'

'You have.' Ramira was definite. 'I can see it in your face too. Is everything OK for you?'

'Absolutely fine,' said Mia.

'The job is not too difficult? Taking too much time?'

'Of course not,' replied Mia. 'It's ideal. The hours suit me and Allegra, don't they, *chiquita*?'

Allegra, busy with the colouring books that the waitress had brought over when the adults ordered coffee, ignored her.

Ramira grinned. 'She's good, that one. So well behaved.'

'She has her moments.'

'I have some news for you,' Ramira told Mia.

'Oh?'

'Alfonso has moved back.'

'Oh!' Mia was startled. 'What happened?'

Ramira and her husband Alfonso had split up a few weeks earlier, after he'd confessed to a brief fling with one of his colleagues. Ramira (who hadn't suspected the affair and who half wished that he'd kept quiet about it instead of throwing himself on her mercy) had chucked him out and had come to Mia in tears. The two of them had shared a bottle of wine and agreed that all men were bastards. Mia, although devastated for Ramira, had felt good to be the one offering comfort and advice about men for a change.

'You know he has been living with his mama since?'

Mia nodded.

'She meant nothing to him, that *puta*. She turned his head, made him feel good. But only for a short time. Then he felt nothing but guilt. So I forgave him.'

513

'That was . . . very good of you,' said Mia.

'*Pues, nada.* Alfonso is a man. A stupid man who thinks that the grass is greener elsewhere.'

'But it wasn't. He came back to you.'

'I know. I do not think he will stray from me again.'

'Can you trust him?' asked Mia.

Ramira shrugged. 'Who knows?' she asked. 'I am trusting him now. He has come to me many times begging me to forgive him. And in the end – well, I thought perhaps it was the right thing. For me, for him and for the family.'

'All the same . . .'

'. . . it would have been better if this hadn't happened,' said Ramira. 'It would have been better if he had behaved as he should. But that's not always the way in life, is it? People do not always do what they should. And these girls . . .' She snorted. 'They know a man is married and they try to take him away from his wife, and this is not right!'

Mia nodded wordlessly.

'And so I say to him that he can come back and we will try again but that there is no more chance after this. If he does the wrong thing again, he can live for ever with his mama and see how he likes it!'

'Why did he do it?' asked Mia.

'He wants the excitement,' Ramira told her. 'He wants the affair and the secrets and the meeting in different places. I understand that. I want excitement too. But in the end he realises that it is not excitement for ever. That you cannot live always on the edge.'

'I guess not,' said Mia.

'Actually, I feel a little bit sorry for her,' Ramira said. 'She thought he would leave me for her. I knew he would not. I let him get this fling out of his system. I think he will behave for the future.'

Mia looked at her friend's grim expression.

'I'm sure he will,' she said.

Later that afternoon, as Mia swept the terrace, Allegra came up to her and said that she wanted to talk about something important.

'Yes?' Mia smiled at the seriousness in her daughter's face. To Allegra, everything was important.

'If Eva's papa can come home, why can't mine?' she asked.

Eva was Ramira's daughter. Mia hadn't realised that Allegra, engrossed in her colouring, had been listening to their conversation.

'Your papa lives a long way away,' she said eventually.

'So does *Tía* Britt. But she came to stay.'

'It's more difficult for your papa.'

'Why?'

Britt had warned her that Allegra would ask these questions. But Mia had expected it to happen sometime in the future. Sometime when she'd be able to have a mature discussion with her daughter about life and love and how it all went horribly wrong.

'It's not easy for him to come to us.'

'He could come to the airport. Like *Tía* Britt.' Allegra looked mutinous.

'It's hard for him to find a plane.'

Allegra grasped a lock of Mia's hair and began twirling it rapidly around in her fingers, something she did whenever she was upset.

'But maybe he will find one,' said Mia, pulling her closer.

'And he could come for my birthday?' Allegra sounded hopeful.

'Well, I don't know about that,' said Mia. 'But I'm sure he'll send you a present.'

'Does my papa love me?'

Mia thought her heart was going to break.

'Of course he does,' she said as she kissed the top of her daughter's head. 'Of course he does.'

Mia sat on the squishy orange sofa with the laptop on her knees. It was nearly midnight and Allegra was in her room asleep. But Mia knew that there wasn't a chance of her being able to sleep herself that night. All she could think of was Allegra's question about her father. And the conversation she'd had with Alejo earlier that evening.

She had called him on his mobile (he'd given her his card before he'd left) and he'd sounded pleased to hear her voice. He said that he had been doing nothing but thinking of her and that they had to meet up soon, only this time, perhaps, somewhere they wouldn't be disturbed so that they could get to know each other all over again.

'I need to think,' she told him.

'About what exactly?' he asked.

'About everything you said.'

'What part of that do you need to think about?'

'It was a shock to see you again,' she told him. 'I wasn't prepared for it.'

'I thought you'd be pleased.'

'I was,' she said. 'But I'm confused, too.'

'Why confused?'

'About how things will work out. About what you plan to do.'

'I plan to love you,' he said. 'Like I did before.'

Her grip tightened on the receiver. 'Alejo, what do you want from me?'

'I want you to love me again,' he said simply.

'And Allegra?'

'She is my daughter.' His voice was firm. 'I want to know her and I want her to know me. I have responsibilities.'

'You don't have to feel responsible . . .'

'Mia! Of course I do.'

'I need to think,' she repeated. 'I need to do the right thing.'

'I thought I was doing the right thing when I left Guatemala,' said Alejo. 'But it wasn't the right thing at all.'

'But you are still with Belén, and you have a child . . .'

'Yes,' said Alejo. 'I love my son. I will love my daughter too.'

'And Belén?' asked Mia. 'When I saw you in Granada, you were laughing.'

'We do not hate each other,' said Alejo. 'We have a long history together. But we don't have the passion that you and I have.'

'Do you love her?'

'I will never love anyone the way I love you,' said Alejo.

Mia felt a tear roll down her cheek. He was saying the words she had always wanted him to say. He still loved her. And she still loved him. How could she not? She grabbed a tissue from the box on the nearby shelf and rubbed her eyes.

Allegra deserved a father. She deserved Alejo's support.

'Mia?'

'I was thinking,' she said as she balled the tissue and threw it at the waste-paper basket.

'What about?'

'Allegra,' she said.

'I was thinking too,' said Alejo. 'Of the last time we were together in Guatemala. Of how wonderful it was.'

'She was conceived the first time,' said Mia. 'When we were careless.'

'Do you wish that she hadn't been?' he asked.

'No.' Mia felt herself smile. 'No. She's the best thing in my life.'

'Because she was conceived out of love,' said Alejo. 'You've got to remember that.'

'Yes,' said Mia. 'I do.'

'So perhaps next week you will come and visit me?' he suggested. 'Stay with me in the house.'

'In your house!' Mia exclaimed. 'We can't come to your house. What about Belén?'

'She will be in Madrid next week.'

'All week?'

'Yes.'

'It's her house,' said Mia uncomfortably. 'I don't think . . .'

'It's *my* house,' Alejo corrected her. 'An Ariza house. It always has been.'

'But you live there together.'

'She spends a lot of time in Madrid. With her family.'

'Let me think about it.'

'I would like to see you again,' he said. 'It would be better maybe if you could come alone.'

'I can't leave Allegra.'

'I understand. But you and I have things we need to talk about.'

'I know. I'll call you,' she said. 'I can't make a mistake about this. I've got to get it right.'

'*Claro*,' said Alejo. 'Call me. Let me know.'

'Thank you,' she said.

Mia remembered the conversation word for word. She had replayed it in her head, over and over, trying to extract every ounce of meaning from Alejo's words. She was exhausted with the effort. She put the laptop to one side and stood up. From the bookshelf she selected the copy of *The Perfect Man* that Britt had signed for her. Why couldn't they all be like Jack Hayes? she wondered glumly. Why couldn't you have them strong and forceful but soft and sensitive too? Why couldn't you depend on them not to break your heart? Why couldn't you be sure that they'd do the right thing?

Because life would be very boring, she muttered as she returned the book to the shelf. Perfection is overrated. My affair with Alejo might not have been as perfect as I imagine. My life with him in the future might not be perfect either. But would that matter? If we love each other, if we care about each other – that's what matters. Things will go wrong. They always do. It's how you react that counts. And he's been great so far. He drove all the way up here, and he was kind and understanding and as perfect as anyone could be.

I can't help loving him, thought Mia. I've always wanted to be with him for ever. Now I have that chance.

The laptop pinged and startled her. She turned to it, seeing the flashing icon that told her she had email. She clicked on the program and opened it.

'Hi from Corsica,' wrote Steve Shaw. 'Our guest speaker on this trip is a politician who spent a year in prison because of an expenses fraud he cooked up. I hate to say it but he's a very nice guy. I like to think of my fraudsters as mean and nasty. We also have a total diva singer this time round. She actually did ask about M&Ms with the blue ones taken out. We told her that we didn't do M&Ms at all except by special request. And that we weren't sure whether there were blue ones in them any more anyway. We'll be in Malaga again in a couple of weeks. What are the chances of meeting up? I miss you. Steve.' He'd put two little xs beside his name.

Mia rested her chin on her hands and reread the mail. She could hear Steve's voice, warm and cheerful, as she read. Uncomplicated Steve who'd said that he loved her. Who had been an unexpectedly expert kisser. Who'd made her feel safe and comfortable in his arms but who had also made her think that she was ready to make love to a man again. She hadn't for one second imagined she'd want to sleep with Steve. But on the night of their date together, when he'd kissed her, she'd wanted to do just that. And it had shocked her. It had seemed like a betrayal of Alejo and everything they'd once had. A betrayal of their hot, sultry sex. A betrayal of herself.

After Alejo, she'd thought about other men from time to time, but knowing that she was in the same country, knowing that he was less than two hours away, knowing that she could always turn up on his doorstep, had stopped her from letting those thoughts go any further (anyway, there hadn't really been available men; mostly it had been fantasy on her part). She had, she realised, been saving herself for him. For the day when he came back to her.

And now he had.

She sat staring into space for nearly ten minutes. Then she logged out of her email and closed her laptop.

It was the following day before she picked up the phone and dialled the number on the business card again.

'Ariza, *dígame*.'

She took a deep breath. 'Alejo, it's Mia,' she said. 'I'll come to your house.'

Chapter 31

Position: Dublin.
Weather: heavy rain. Wind: southerly 15kph.
Temperature: 18°. Barometric pressure: 1001.5mb.

The foyer of the Four Seasons Hotel was thronged with people dressed up for a night out. Half of them were there for a party to celebrate an award-winning advertising campaign for a range of hair-care products; the other half were guests of Dagger Press, a sister company of Britt's publishers, Trevallion. Dagger Press was holding a party too – in its case to celebrate its successful thriller writers, who had taken the top three spots in the bestseller list for two weeks in a row. Dagger, Trevallion and their other sister company, Trefoil, had invited all their authors as well as lots of booksellers to the event, which was taking place in a function room decorated with posters of the top-selling books.

Britt, not immediately recognising anyone in the foyer, checked in the beige raincoat that she'd worn over her black cocktail dress and made her way towards the function room where the publishing party was taking place. It, too, was fairly crowded, and her eyes scanned the room for someone she knew. She spotted Lisa-Anne, her editor, sipping a glass of white wine and talking to Chesney Price, a well-known feminist writer who was usually described as powerful and provocative. Britt was wondering whether she should join them when Lisa-Anne looked up, saw her and waved.

'Hello,' she said as Britt approached. 'It's lovely to see you.'

'You too,' said Britt. 'Hi, Chesney.'

Chesney looked at her curiously.

'Britt McDonagh,' said Britt. 'Brigitte Martin.'

Chesney looked blank, although she'd met Britt on two previous occasions when they were both taking part in radio programmes.

'*The Perfect Man*,' said Lisa-Anne helpfully. 'Britt's bestseller.'

'Oh, yes,' said Chesney eventually. 'I haven't read it, of course. Naturally wouldn't with a title like that. Setting back the feminist agenda by decades.'

'That's a bit harsh,' said Britt.

'Feeding women's heads with the notion that they get a man and everything will be OK.' Chesney snorted.

'My book doesn't do that.' Britt was mildly irritated by Chesney's attitude. 'And it's no worse than telling women they can have it all and making them feel inadequate when they realise that's totally impossible.'

'I never said that,' said Chesney. 'My view is that we should leave men out of the equation altogether.'

'Don't you think life would be dull if we did that?' asked Britt.

'Not in the slightest. But it doesn't matter. In a few decades they'll all be redundant anyway.' Chesney drained her glass. 'I'm going to get a refill. Excuse me.'

Lisa-Anne turned to Britt. 'I'm sorry,' she said. 'Chesney isn't known for her tact.'

'Ah, she's not the worst. I think she's a bit of a caricature of herself these days. And that's sad, because a lot of the feminist stuff is right. Sadly, too many girls now think that being featured in *Heat* is a career choice. All those years when we fought to get an education and opportunities, and it's wasted by people who dye their hair blond, get a boob job and smile at photographers.'

Lisa-Anne grinned. 'Quite the feminist yourself.'

'I believe in women being financially independent,' said Britt. 'Though not through flashing their tits. Mind you,' she glanced down at her own cleavage, 'this dress is a bit lower cut than I realised.'

'You look sensational,' Lisa-Anne assured her.

'I don't know whether I should be upset at that or not.' Britt grinned. 'Since I've clearly sold out to some kind of anti-feminist dark side. I even waxed my legs last night in anticipation.'

Lisa-Anne laughed. 'Like the hair, too.'

Britt had gone to the hairdresser's that morning and had it done in a softer version of her Brigitte curls. She'd felt that she should show up in her Brigitte persona, but liked the less fussy look the stylist had achieved and was thinking that she'd stick with this for her glammed-up image in future.

'I bet Chesney would have a fit if she knew it had taken me nearly two hours to get it done,' she said. 'I got my colour touched up as well. She's right, you know. We can be shockingly superficial sometimes.'

'It's a party,' said Lisa-Anne. 'You're allowed to be superficial. Now come on and let's mingle.'

The party was, as far as Britt was concerned, surprisingly good fun. In the past she had always struggled at industry events, feeling that she was an outsider who didn't really have any right to be there. She would listen to other authors talking confidently about their books and their writing and she'd keep her own mouth firmly closed, because she didn't really know anything about the subject. When real writers complained about how difficult it was to meet deadlines, she said nothing. She hadn't written to a deadline; the words had simply tumbled on to the page, and she felt bad about the fact that she hadn't had to struggle to finish it by a specific date.

But now, with the experience of the *Aphrodite* behind her, she felt more confident about talking to other people.

She had a long and interesting chat with one of the crime writers, as well as a discussion with a well-known literary novelist, who was much warmer than his public persona and who confessed to enjoying sci-fi when he wasn't writing himself.

'Goodness,' she said. 'I thought all you literary types only read books that need the assistance of a dictionary beside them.'

Hugh O'Driscoll grinned. 'I admit that we can some-times be overly convinced about our superior word power, but I like stuff that fires your imagination. And sci-fi has to because it's dealing with the future and things we've no idea about.'

'I have the *Star Trek* series at home,' confessed Britt.

'From the original TV shows?' asked Hugh.

'Yes.' She looked shamefaced.

'Brilliant,' he declared. 'Loved 'em all.'

They spent the next thirty minutes comparing the characters of Captain James T. Kirk, Jean-Luc Picard and Kathryn Janeway. (Britt liked Janeway best, although she did admit that Jean-Luc had a very sexy voice.)

'Enjoying yourself?' asked Meredith, who joined her just as Hugh was nabbed by a photographer. 'I'm sorry I couldn't be with you for the dinner but I didn't have any say in the layout. Were you OK?'

'Fine,' said Britt. 'Chatting to other novelists.'

Meredith beamed suddenly.

'What?' asked Britt.

'I think that's the first time you've ever called yourself a novelist,' she said. 'Until now it's always been a lawyer.'

'Oh.' Britt looked surprised.

'Does this mean that you've changed your mind about your future career?' asked Meredith.

'I don't know.' Britt was still surprised at herself.

'Of course there's the lecture circuit too.' Meredith looked wickedly at her. 'You can carve out a new career encouraging fledgling writers.'

Britt looked at her in puzzlement.

'I received three chapters and a synopsis of a book the other day from a woman named Eileen Costello, who said that she'd been at your workshops on board the *Aphrodite* and that you'd been great at them, and she was very confident that what she was sending me was right up there with the best.'

'Eileen was a confident woman all right,' agreed Britt. 'Gosh, but she was quick off the mark, wasn't she? What was the novel like?'

'It was very melodramatic,' confided Meredith. 'Full of steamy affairs and secret marriages and God knows what else, all before page fifty. It opened with a bang – quite literally: the two main characters were shagging each other senseless on a cruise ship that was hit by a stray torpedo – and continued at that frantic speed.'

'Oh my God.' Britt couldn't help giggling.

'There was an additional bonus,' Meredith continued. 'An outline of a plot about a model who takes the world by storm despite her tragic childhood of abuse and deprivation. That was sent to me by her daughter.'

Britt's eyes opened wide. 'Pippin Costello?' she asked.

'Yes. You certainly brought out the creative streak in that family.'

'Is it any good?' she asked.

'It's only an outline,' said Meredith. 'And she actually suggested that what would work best would be a ghost to write it for her, while she provided them with the inspiration. She said that she was far too busy to write it herself.'

'Oh.'

Meredith grinned at her. 'She suggested you.'

'Me!' squeaked Britt. 'Why would she think . . . ?'

'She said that you seemed like a competent person and *The Perfect Man* was a good book.'

'Right.' Britt looked bemused.

'She suggested that her fame and your skill as a writer would make it an excellent deal.'

'And would it?'

'She's not famous enough,' said Meredith. 'I've never heard of her. And I've heard of everyone! Besides, I'm not sure that you're cut out to be a ghost.'

'I'm glad you said that. I wouldn't want to write someone else's book,' said Britt. 'Anyway, I think she wants to get on to *Celebrity Something-or-other*.'

'Well if she does, and if she wins, then perhaps someone would be willing to think about a book deal with her,' agreed Meredith. 'But until then, she's whistling in the wind.'

'What are you going to do?'

'Send her back a letter telling her to actually write something.'

'And Eileen?'

'Her bonkbuster doesn't work for me, though I am intrigued to know where she's going with the story.'

'I'm kind of glad,' said Britt somewhat shamefacedly. 'I know it sounds stupid, but I don't want to share you with the Costello family.'

Meredith smiled and then hugged her. 'You're sharing me with one of the crime writers.'

'That's totally different. And I love his stuff. Will you introduce me to him?'

'Sure,' said Meredith. 'Let's go.'

* * *

It was after midnight when Britt looked at her watch. She was surprised at how late it had become. She'd had a good time at the party, enjoying the company of Meredith's crime writer and spending some time talking to Corinne Doherty, the author of a popular series featuring a model turned detective. Corinne confessed to having excruciating bouts of nerves about every book she wrote and to having gone through a total block for her fourth novel, which had, eventually, become her biggest seller.

'It's bloody terrifying,' she admitted. 'I'm so afraid that people will be disappointed with the book I've just done that it takes me ages to get everything right, and then I invariably meet someone who's written a five-hundred-page novel in three weeks, which makes me feel like a total slacker.'

Britt chuckled. 'And on the other hand, there're the people who take ten years to produce anything.'

'I know.' Corinne nodded. 'You'd kind of think you were trying too hard at that point. Anyway,' she glanced at her watch, 'I'd better go. I'm heading down to Waterford tomorrow for a friend's wedding and I need some zzzs so that I don't look totally haggard. It's ages since I've been to a wedding. I'm thinking there might be some good plot material there: you know, groom found strangled in the vestry or something . . .' There was a sudden faraway look in her eye as her voice trailed off.

'I'll probably head myself,' observed Britt. 'It's way past my beauty-sleep time.'

She finished the last of the sparkling water she'd been drinking and made her way over to Lisa-Anne and Meredith to say good night. Then she went to the cloakroom to get her coat.

The hotel foyer was as busy as it had been earlier in the evening. People from the hair-product campaign were clustered together, laughing and joking. The women's hair gleamed underneath the bright lights, and Britt wondered whether the products would give her hair that luxurious glossy sheen too. Although, she reflected, she'd have to turn brunette for that. Blonde might be the colour that many women wanted to be, but brunette (in her view) was infinitely more sophisticated.

Then she saw Pippin Costello, with the most extravagant hair-do of them all, looking utterly sensational in a gold evening dress and stunning gold jewellery that gleamed softly against her smooth spray-tanned skin. Pippin was laughing and joking with a group of people while a middle-aged man stood behind her with his hand proprietorially on her back. As Britt watched them, the man whispered something into Pippin's ear, and she turned and beamed at him and allowed him to usher her through the crowd almost to the very spot where Britt was standing.

Pippin's eyes opened wide in surprise, and then she shrieked and wrapped her arms around Britt, hugging her fiercely.

'I don't believe it!' she cried. 'It's so lovely to see you. What are you doing here?'

'Book thing,' said Britt as she disentangled herself from Pippin's hold.

'And I'm doing a hair thing!' exclaimed Pippin. 'This is Gerry O'Shea, he's the CEO of Sleek and Sheer.'

'Hi,' said Britt as the man held out his hand and she shook it. 'They must be great products. Everyone's hair looks wonderful.'

'They are,' said Pippin. 'I totally recommend them.' She beamed at Gerry and then at Britt. 'We're heading off for something to eat,' she said. 'Poor Gerry is starving. I keep telling him that I'll just be nibbling on a bean sprout, but he doesn't believe me.'

'I don't want you to fade away,' said Gerry.

'Don't worry. I won't,' Pippin assured him. 'Would you like to join us?' She turned back to Britt.

'It's very kind of you to ask,' Britt replied. 'But I'm heading home. I'm not really a late-night person.'

'You're probably going to work,' said Pippin knowingly. 'I can just visualise you tapping away at the keyboard in the small hours.'

'Not tonight,' said Britt. 'I'm just going to fall into bed. I clearly don't have your stamina.'

Pippin giggled. 'I can keep going till dawn,' she agreed. 'In fact, if I don't see dawn I'm a bit disappointed.'

'Not every night, surely,' said Britt.

'Only when I'm out and about,' Pippin said. 'But I'm out and about a lot.'

'And how does Leo like that?' Britt wished she hadn't spoken, but the words were out of her mouth before she could stop them.

'Well, of course Leo understands how important my career is,' said Pippin. 'And he comes to some of the events with me. Not midweek, though, because he has to be in work the next day and he says he needs a clear head for

531

that. And not tonight, because he was out with some clients of his own. He was a bit disappointed that I couldn't come with him, because Sleek and Sheer is my big, big promotion.' She glanced over at Gerry O'Shea, who'd left them to talk to each other. 'It's very lucrative for me.'

'I'm glad it's all working out so well,' said Britt.

'Brilliantly.' Pippin rearranged the tiara in her hair with her left hand so that Britt couldn't help but notice the glittering light of her engagement ring. 'My career is going from strength to strength, and Leo is a poppet.'

'Tell him I said hello,' said Britt.

'I will.' Pippin smiled. 'I'm sure he'll be glad to hear I met you. He has a soft spot for you, you know.'

Britt felt herself blush. 'No. I didn't.'

Pippin looked at her archly. 'Oh, come on. There was a time on board the *Aphrodite* when I thought that you and he . . .' She shrugged. 'But happily for me, it didn't turn out that way.'

'I'm sure you and Leo will be great together,' said Britt.

'I'm great at everything I do,' Pippin told her. 'So I'm sure we will too.' She beamed. 'I believe you'll be coming to the wedding.'

'If you invite me,' said Britt.

'Oh, everyone wants to invite you.' Pippin looked at her archly again. 'You were such a hit with my family.'

'Have you set a date yet?' asked Britt.

'No,' replied Pippin. 'But we're thinking Winter Wonderland in December, maybe. Somewhere in the country. We'll do it up with fake snow and everything.'

'Sounds fun,' said Britt.

'It will be fabulous,' Pippin assured her. 'The most romantic wedding ever. I'm sure it'll inspire you to even greater heights. Coming, sweetie,' she added as Gerry called to her. 'Gotta go,' she told Britt. 'See you around.'

'Yes,' said Britt. 'See you.'

Pippin didn't mention meeting Britt to Leo until a couple of days later, when they were having a drink in the Cantina bar in Dun Laoghaire. Leo's friend Mike was going to join them later.

'Dublin is such a village,' Pippin concluded. 'You meet everyone everywhere. You wouldn't want to be trying to keep a secret.'

'No,' agreed Leo. He thought about whether Donal and Vanessa had gone out together or whether they had only met in secret at Donal's house. He'd never really thought about that before. Had they visited restaurants, eaten meals in tucked-away corners, worried about being seen? Or would that even have bothered them? Would they have been able to make it all seem innocent and above board? The brother and the fiancée out for a bite to eat together. Nothing to worry about. All very friendly.

Will I ever be able to stop asking myself these questions? Leo wondered. Will I ever be able to let it go?

He wanted to believe that he had. Meeting Pippin had made him feel good about himself again. Having someone who loved him as much as she loved him, who looked up to him in the way she did, had been balm to his wounded pride as well as his broken heart. She admired him, she told him, because he was smart and intelligent and could do the hard sudoku in fifteen minutes whereas she'd yet to figure out the easy one. He'd liked appearing smart and intelligent to her, although as time went on, he realised that she was probably a good deal smarter than him. She knew what she wanted and she went for it with a single-minded determination.

Most women were infinitely smarter than men, he thought as he watched Pippin sip on her soda water while her eyes scanned the bar in case she saw someone she knew. They fooled you into thinking that they were air-headed and superficial, but they weren't. They were sharper and they were stronger and they had a power over you that you simply didn't realise until it was too damn late.

'Leo!'

He blinked and turned to his fiancée, who was clicking her fingers beside him.

'I've been trying to get your attention for ages,' she said. 'You keep doing that, you know.'

'What?'

'Drifting off into some dream world.'

'Sorry.'

'That's OK. I was asking if this weekend would be a good time to drop into Brown Thomas about our wedding list. We want to give people plenty of time.'

'Wedding list?'

'Presents, you dope!' She shoved him gently. 'Everyone does lists now.'

Of course. He knew that. He'd had a list with Vanessa. It had been at Brown Thomas too.

'Not there.' His voice was strangled.

'Oh, but Leo, it's the best place!' Pippin's eyes widened.

'I don't care.' He knew that he sounded harsh. 'Anywhere else.'

'There *is* nowhere else!' she cried.

'Don't be stupid,' he snapped. 'There are loads of shops in Dublin and you know all of them.'

'Leo . . .' Pippin had never heard him sound so determined before.

'I mean it,' he said. 'I really do.'

'We'll talk about it another time.' Pippin put her empty glass on the table in front of her.

'There's nothing to talk about,' said Leo tersely.

Pippin stared at him.

'There's Mike.' Leo spotted his friend with relief and waved his hand in his direction.

Mike threaded his way through the tables to join them.

'Mike Doorley, this is Pippin Costello,' said Leo. Mike looked appreciatively at his friend's fiancée. He'd been away for their engagement party and so hadn't met her before now.

Pippin had gone for a casual look that evening. Her make-up was light and natural. She was wearing a black waistcoat over a plain white T-shirt and Kate Moss skinny jeans, and her burnished hair fell loosely around her face.

'Wow,' said Mike. 'Great to finally meet you.'

'You too,' Pippin told him. 'Leo's told me lots about you. I'm so sorry we didn't get to meet before now.'

Leo went to the bar and got them some drinks while Pippin flirted coyly with Mike. By the time he returned, they were laughing and joking like old friends. Leo hadn't seen Pippin so relaxed in ages. With him, she seemed to hold herself in check somehow. She didn't giggle the same way she did with Mike.

He frowned. She was probably just acting this way because she was annoyed with him over the wedding list. He knew he must seem unreasonable. He'd have to work on her, make her realise that the list could be somewhere else. Not even for Pippin could he consider having it at Brown Thomas.

It was an hour later when she told them she had to go because she was appearing on *Ireland AM* the following morning and couldn't afford to have bags under her eyes. Leo, who'd known she'd be leaving early, asked if she was sure she wanted to head off on her own, and she reminded him that she lived less than ten minutes away and that she'd be fine. Her tone when she spoke to him was still slightly chilly, but she kissed him on the lips before kissing Mike on the cheek, and then walked out of the bar leaving them enveloped in a haze of Vera Wang Princess.

After she'd gone, Mike leaned back in his seat and looked enviously at Leo.

'What a total babe,' he said. 'You lucky son of a bitch.'

Leo felt the familiar self-satisfaction about his fiancée envelop him. 'She's fairly gorgeous, isn't she?'

'Man, she's just – amazing. I love her. I really do.'

'You've never said that about any of my girlfriends before. But maybe that's because none of them were six-foot stunners.'

'It's not just her looks,' said Mike. 'It's the whole package. She's cute and funny and I . . .' He broke off as he saw Leo looking at him curiously. 'Sorry, pal,' he said. 'Getting a bit carried away.'

'Indeed,' said Leo. 'I'd better remind you that she's *my* fiancée.'

'Yeah, well, if it ever goes pear-shaped . . .' He broke off again and hit his forehead with his hand. 'Sorry. Foot in mouth. Not thinking.'

'It's OK,' said Leo. 'She has that effect on people.'

'I hope you two will be ecstatically happy together,' said Mike as he raised his glass. 'You deserve it.'

'Thanks.' Leo clinked his own glass against Mike's. 'I know we do.'

Chapter 32

Position: Granada.
Weather: clear skies. Wind: southerly 5kph. Temperature:
24°. Barometric pressure: 1011.5mb.

'I want to go with you.' Allegra looked at Mia mutinously and stamped her tiny foot in its bright pink jelly sandal.

'Get out of the jeep and stop your nonsense,' said Mia as she opened the door. 'Loli is your best friend. You like playing with her.'

'She doesn't have a pool.'

Mia sighed. She knew she shouldn't have got the plastic paddling pool out of the shed the evening before. But the weather was getting hotter, the afternoons on the verandah were becoming stifling and the pool had seemed like a good idea. (Actually, it *had* been a good idea. She'd sat in it with Allegra, skimming through her copy of ¡*Hola!* magazine while her daughter taught her selection of Bratz dolls how to swim. It had been peaceful and relaxing and Mia couldn't think of a better way to pass the time.)

'When we get home, you can play in your pool,' said Mia.

'Want to play now.'

'I'm sure Loli has nice things to play with.' Mia tried not to let her exasperation show. 'Come on, *palomita*. Please.'

'Oh all right,' grumbled Allegra as she climbed out of the jeep.

Mia bit her lip to stop herself smiling. She always found Allegra's bouts of temper funny, even though she tried hard not to let her daughter know.

'You can take *Tía* Britt's CDs with you,' she told her as she took a selection out of the glove compartment.

Britt had bought Allegra a heap of storybook CDs in Malaga, narrated in both English and Spanish, and the little girl loved them all.

'Don't forget *Lima's Red-Hot Chilli*,' Allegra told her, naming her favourite CD and one she knew off by heart in both languages.

Mia made sure that she included it as Allegra rang the bell.

'*Hola, chica!*' cried Ana. 'How are you today? Loli is in the garden. D'you want to go through?'

Allegra had already run past her while Mia looked apologetic and handed Ana the CDs.

'She was a bit moody earlier,' she told her friend. 'Hopefully she'll behave.'

'She's always a little angel,' said Ana. 'Don't worry. And have a nice time today.'

Mia blushed. She'd told Ana that she was meeting a

man. Ana didn't know the history of Mia and Alejo, but she was constantly encouraging Mia to socialise more and find herself someone.

'I won't be late,' she promised.

'Be as long as it takes to have fun,' said Ana.

Mia smiled at her and got back into the jeep. She slid a music CD into the player, and the air was filled with the energetic beat of Rodrigo and Gabriela, whose funky Latin guitar-playing was perfect for driving through the mountains.

An hour and a half later she turned on to the long, tree-lined street and pulled the jeep to a halt outside the gates of Alejo's house. Her mouth was suddenly dry and her heart was beating nervously. What if Belén was still here? What if she hadn't gone to Madrid after all? What would Mia say? What would she do?

Don't be silly, she told herself sternly as she leaned out and pressed the intercom button. He would have contacted you if there was a problem. There's no need to worry.

The gates swung open slowly. She put the jeep into gear and drove carefully up the long, curving driveway.

Alejo's house was recently built in traditional Andalucian style. It was two storeys high, with whitewashed walls and terracotta roof tiles. There were two windows either side of the main door and six windows above, all with wrought-iron balconies on which hung baskets of colourful flowers. The house was set in large gardens dotted with palm trees and hibiscus, and Mia knew, from the scent that lingered in the air, that there were orange and lemon trees somewhere too. It was serene and peaceful and very, very beautiful.

The front door opened and Alejo stepped outside. He was wearing a white T-shirt and stone-washed jeans. His feet were bare.

'*Hola, Mia*,' he said as she cut the engine and got out of the jeep. 'I'm so happy that you came.'

'*Hola, Alejo*.' She kissed him on each cheek and he smiled at the formality. He put his hand on the small of her back.

'Come along,' he said, leading her through the cool hallway and into a large living room with patio doors that opened on to a terrace easily three times the size of the Villa Serena's. Mia glanced around the living room, looking for any signs of Belén and Eduardo, but it was an impersonal room although elegantly decorated. Out on the terrace was a long marble dining table surrounded by high-backed chairs, as well as a couple of well-upholstered loungers. Wide steps led down to a large swimming pool. The water glittered enticingly in the sun.

'Oh my God, Alejo,' she said. 'This is stunning.'

'Isn't it?' he agreed. 'Would you like to swim?'

'I didn't bring my things,' she said.

'Who needs them?' He grinned at her and she felt herself blush, which made him laugh. 'I have seen you naked before,' he reminded her. 'Many times. You were very beautiful.'

'You might think a bit differently now,' she said. 'Stretch marks and baby flab aren't beautiful.'

'Of course they are,' he said.

She felt herself blush. 'Maybe later.'

'OK,' he said. 'Would you like something to eat? It's a little early, but I have made us some lunch.'

'Food would be great,' said Mia. 'I'm famished.'

Although, she thought, when Alejo had gone into the house again and returned with Spanish omelette, mixed salad and freshly baked bread, I very much doubt I can eat anything at all.

He poured her a glass of red wine, despite the fact that she said she was driving and so couldn't drink.

'One glass,' he said. 'It will relax you. And you don't have to drive back for hours yet.'

'I can't leave Allegra with Ana for too long,' she told him. 'She's very good to me and I don't want to impose on her.'

'And you?' he asked as he pushed a bowl of enormous green olives towards her. 'Do you look after her little girl too?'

'Of course,' said Mia. 'We have a network.'

'So it is a mutual thing. You are scratching her back and she is scratching yours.'

Mia laughed at the way Alejo came out with the phrase.

'But yes,' he said. 'Am I not right?'

She was still laughing as she agreed with him.

'It is good to see you smile,' he said. 'It is my favourite thing about you.'

'My smile?' She looked at him with mock severity. 'I always thought there was a good deal more that you liked about me than my smile.'

'Oh yes,' said Alejo. 'For sure.'

Mia suddenly felt herself blush again, and so she turned away from Alejo and looked out over the gardens towards the Alhambra.

'Wonderful,' agreed Alejo as she commented on the view. 'Although that is one thing you do have at your house.'

'Yes.' She smiled. 'I love looking out over the valley.'

'Me too.'

She wondered whether she'd ever be able to talk to him without the sudden flashes of awkwardness that seemed to engulf her. I slept with this man, she reminded herself. I kissed his naked body and I made love to him and I carried his child. I never felt as alive as I did when I was with him.

She remembered the last time. Before she knew she was pregnant. Before he went on his volcano trip. Before Belén showed up. He'd brought her to his hotel. He didn't do that very often, didn't want to get a reputation around town, he said. She'd laughed at that and said that it was OK for her reputation to be trashed, was it, what with him coming to her place every day?

He'd protested that it was different, and she'd said that it wasn't one little bit, but then he'd silenced her with a kiss, pushing her on to the bed and undoing the buttons on her polka-dot blouse before sliding his hands along her sides and behind her back, releasing her bra strap with practised ease. She'd been almost dizzy with desire then, revelling in the featherlight touch of his fingers, wanting more from him, impatiently pulling him down on to her and then, suddenly, swinging herself on top of him so that she was in control.

He'd laughed, and she'd laughed in return. Then she'd positioned herself above him so that he slid into her smoothly and easily, and she'd thought at that moment that they were like one person, completely at ease together, knowing everything about each other, caught up in their love for each other.

And then she'd met Belén. And discovered that none of it was real.

'More olives?' Alejo broke into her thoughts. 'Or perhaps some oil to go with the bread?'

She took a slice of the baguette and dipped it in the luscious green olive oil, even though she really wasn't hungry at all any more.

'It's from our own olives,' said Alejo.

Mia looked around the garden. She could see the orange and lemon trees she'd caught the scent of earlier, further down the garden behind the pool. But she didn't see any olives.

'My father's olives,' Alejo amended. 'He has a *cortijo* outside the city.'

'It's lovely oil,' agreed Mia. 'Are the olives themselves from your farm too?'

Alejo shook his head. 'These I got in the market. But you should see the *cortijo*. It's very pretty.'

'Does anyone live there?' asked Mia.

'Not full time,' replied Alejo. 'But my parents like to spend weekends there when they can. They like to be out of the city.'

Mia nodded.

There was a sudden buzz of the intercom, which startled them. Mia caught her breath. Alejo frowned.

'I'm not expecting anyone,' he said. 'Wait a moment.'

He went inside and Mia held her hand out in front of her. It was shaking. Oh God, she thought, please let this not be Belén. Or anyone important.

Alejo stepped back out on to the terrace.

'My assistant, Paz,' he said. 'She has come to get me to sign some papers. It will only take a few moments.'

A moment later a tall, elegant woman who was, Mia guessed, about the same age as her walked out to join them. She was dressed in a pale grey linen trouser suit and a white cotton blouse. Oversized sunglasses were perched on her streaked blond hair, which was pulled back into a ponytail. She smiled briefly at Mia, who felt suddenly frumpy in her blue cotton vest-top and biscuit-coloured shorts.

'I'm sorry if you have company.' Paz allowed her eyes to slide from Alejo to Mia and back again. 'But these only arrived today.'

'No problem.' He took the manila folder from her, glanced through the papers and began to sign them rapidly.

'D'you mind if I have a drink of water?' asked Paz as she pulled out one of the chairs and sat down, crossing one ankle elegantly in front of the other. 'It's very hot today.'

'Of course not,' said Alejo. He picked up the crystal jug and poured some for her. Paz sipped it slowly while Mia observed her from behind her fringe. She was very beautiful, she thought. And she was looking at Alejo in a very proprietorial way. Mia poured herself some water. I need to get a grip, she thought. I can't suddenly become jealous over his PA! I'm not married to him, after all.

'The pool looks very inviting,' said Paz, glancing between

Alejo, who was still signing the papers, and Mia, who had tipped her own sunglasses over her eyes again.

'You don't have time to go swimming.' Alejo gathered the papers up, replaced them in the folder and handed them to her. 'Can you make four copies of them all and send them to the people marked on the cover sheet?'

'Of course.' Paz stood up. 'I will see you in the office . . . later or tomorrow?'

'Tomorrow,' said Alejo.

Paz nodded and took the folder from him. She kissed him rapidly on each cheek and then walked back through the house.

'I'm sorry,' said Alejo. 'I'm afraid that happens these days. I am the director of one of the divisions in the company, and it doesn't matter what day it is, I have to work.'

'So does your assistant.'

'She gets very well paid.'

Mia couldn't help herself. 'She's very pretty.'

Alejo laughed. 'Compared to you, she is nothing. She is very pretty, yes, and very efficient. But she does not have the same fire in her veins.'

'And you know that how?'

'I can tell,' said Alejo dismissively.

'How does she get on with Belén?'

'Pardon?' Alejo looked startled.

'Belén. Do they know each other?'

'*Pues, sí.* But they are not friends. They speak on the phone sometimes. And . . .' he looked shamefaced, 'Paz buys flowers from me for Belén.'

'Why do you send her flowers?'

'When I am late at the office.'

'Does that happen often?'

'*De vez en cuando*. From time to time. Mia, this is a silly conversation. These are not important things for us to talk about. I want to talk about us.'

He stood behind her and massaged the tops of her shoulders with his fingers. Mia winced as he found the knots in her muscles.

'You are very tense,' he said.

'I know.' She leaned back and looked up at him. 'It's been a tense time for me.'

'But you should not be tense now,' he said, his fingers moving around so that they were touching the sides of her breasts. 'You are here with me and everything will be perfect.'

She felt herself begin to tremble and she moved back in the seat so that he was now cupping her breasts in his hands. He leaned down towards her and kissed her, upside down, on the lips.

She couldn't stop herself. She got up from the chair and turned to him, and he was pulling the T-shirt over her head and she was unbuttoning the belt of his jeans and it was all coming back to her now: the fire and the passion and the belief that they were meant to be together, that there was nobody else in the world for her, only him, and that she loved him more than she had ever loved anyone in her life before.

'Mia.' His voice was low and urgent and she was stepping out of her shorts and naked in front of him, not worried now about her stretch marks and her less than perfect stomach but only thinking that she had to have him here and now.

He lifted her up so that she was sitting on the low balustrade of the terrace and then he pulled her to him and she wrapped her legs around him while he pushed himself into her with a throaty gasp. She tightened her hold on him, pulling him closer and deeper while she closed her eyes and allowed the pleasure to envelop her as it always had with him, and as it always would.

And then she cried out and he found her mouth with his and smothered her in kisses and she felt herself tense and relax and then quiver as the waves subsided.

'Oh my God, Mia,' he said after a moment. 'It was everything I remember and more.'

'Yes,' she whispered as she released her hold on him. 'It was perfect.'

'Come on!' He was still holding her as he walked rapidly across the terrace and down towards the pool.

'What are you doing?' she asked.

'Going for a swim!'

He jumped into the water, Mia in his arms, and the sudden cold made her gasp as she broke the sùrface and shook her wet hair out of her face.

'You're crazy.'

'Of course!'

'But I love you.'

'And I love you too,' said Alejo as he swam towards her and dragged her beneath the water with him.

* * *

'I have to go,' she said after they got out of the pool and she'd wrapped herself in one of the brightly coloured towels that had been on the loungers.

'Why? You have only been here a couple of hours.'

'Yes, and it will take me the same to get home. I can't leave Allegra with my friend any longer.'

'Can you not phone her?' asked Alejo. 'Tell her that you are here with the most wonderful man, who will not let you go?'

Mia wrung some more water out of her hair. 'I'd love to,' she said. 'But I can't.'

'You mean you will leave me here in this big house all alone?' he said plaintively.

'I'm sure you're used to it.'

She padded to the terrace and began to gather her things.

'Once more,' said Alejo, who had followed her. 'Once more before you go.'

'I can't, Alejo,' she said. 'I'm late enough as it is.'

He kissed the back of her neck. 'Tell me you don't want to and I'll let you go.'

'I can't tell you that.' She squirmed away from him. 'You know I do. But I must go, Alejo. I really must.' She picked up her bag. 'And I need to use the bathroom before I leave.'

'It seems to me a waste of time that you are here and we are not making love for every single minute of it,' said Alejo.

'There will be other times,' she said.

'Promise?'

'Of course.'

He pulled the towel from her and kissed her on the throat. Then he moved down her body, covering it with kisses, while her breath quickened yet again. And then he was inside her once more and she held him tight, and she knew that nobody would ever be better for her than Alejo Ariza.

'OK, this time I really, really have to go.' Once again she began to gather her things. 'Bathroom?'

'Through the lounge and to the left,' said Alejo. 'That was sensational, by the way.'

'I know,' she said as she slipped her feet into her espadrilles. 'I'm always sensational.'

The sound of Alejo's laughter followed her as she made her way to the bathroom, where she pulled on her clothes, splashed water on her face and pulled a comb through the tangle of her curls.

She looked at herself in the mirror. There was a sparkle in her eyes that hadn't been there for a long time, and her cheeks were tinged with a colour that had nothing to do with the sun. Her lips were gently swollen.

I needed that, she thought, leaning back against the tiled wall. I needed it so much and I needed him so much too. She opened her bag and sprayed herself with her favourite Carolina Herrera perfume. I feel like a person again, she told herself. He's the only one who could do that for me.

She let herself out of the bathroom and stood for a moment in the large hallway. It was the most amazing house, she thought. The furniture in the hallway alone (a couple of chaises longues and a long walnut table) was probably worth more than all of the furniture in the Villa Serena. Alejo lived in a different world to her. But he wanted her to be part of it.

She could hear his voice from the terrace, speaking quick-fire Spanish on the telephone. She hesitated for a moment and then, instead of walking through the lounge, she went past it and into the room next door.

It was a bright and airy kitchen. It too had patio doors to the terrace, but these doors were closed. It was clearly a working kitchen – there were pots on the gas range and stainless-steel utensil holders crammed with various cooking implements. At the end of the room was a huge American-style fridge with an ice dispenser. The fridge was covered in photographs, held in place by novelty magnets. Mia walked over to it.

They were photos of Eduardo, Alejo and Belén's son.

In one, Belén was holding him. She looked different to how she had looked in Guatemala. Her hair was longer and fell softly around her face. There were huge diamond earrings in her ears and a gold chain around her neck. And she was smiling in a way she hadn't been the last time Mia had seen her.

She stared at the wife of the man she had just made love to. On the terrace of her home. Where she probably sat with Eduardo in the afternoons looking at the pool where a girl she'd met once had swum with her husband.

Mia felt sick.

Alejo hadn't had any right to make love to her in Guatemala when he'd said nothing about being married. But she hadn't had any right to make love to him in Granada when she knew that he *was* married. Even if their marriage wasn't happy. Even if they were thinking about divorce.

Of course he hadn't actually said that yet. He'd talked about Mia being part of his life, but he hadn't said anything about Belén and Eduardo. But he would divorce her. He'd been going to divorce her before Guatemala. Nothing had changed.

Except that they now had a son.

And she had a daughter. Mia took a deep breath. Alejo's daughter. Conceived with a passion she had never felt before or since, until once again today. Conceived by mistake, when Alejo was already married to the mother of his son. There had been no mistakes today. They'd both known better.

She felt sick again.

'Mia, *querida*!'

She hurried out of the kitchen to the lounge. Alejo was standing at the patio doors, snapping closed his clamshell mobile.

'I thought you had got lost,' he said.

She shook her head.

'Are you all right?'

This time she nodded.

'Sure?'

'Yes. Sure. It's just that I'm late and I have to go.'

'I know.' He put his arms around her and drew her close. 'When can you come again?'

'I . . .'

'Or I can come to you? When?'

'I'll call you, Alejo.'

'I will call you,' he said. 'It's easier that way.'

'Sure. Yes. You can call me.'

He kissed her and she leaned her head on his shoulder.

'I love you,' said Alejo.

She didn't reply.

'Do you love me?' he asked.

'You're the father of my child,' she said. 'How can I not love the father of my child?'

Chapter 33

Position: Dublin.
Weather: partly cloudy: Wind: south-westerly 3kph.
Temperature: 20°. Barometric pressure: 1002.5mb.

Position: Sierra Bonita.
Weather: clear skies. Wind: southerly 3kph. Temperature:
26°. Barometric pressure: 1008.5mb.

B ritt sat in front of her laptop and stared at the open document in front of her. She scrolled through the words, not needing to read them because she now knew her story so well. The names whizzed by her in a blur: William, Richard, Persia, Lucie, Christopher, Camille, Nanette; their lives hopelessly intertwined, the tension between the brothers stronger since Persia's divorce, which had seen William win a much bigger settlement for her than Richard had been angling for. William had sent Richard a bottle of champagne afterwards, suggesting that he might like to drown his sorrows.

The story was all about the competition between the

brothers each needing to feel that he was better, stronger, cleverer, more successful than the other. Their parents had always pushed them, thinking that success was important. But, Britt thought as she stared at the words on the page, it wasn't. Not as important as having people in your life who cared about you and who supported you. Not as important as being relaxed in your own skin, happy with who you were. Success was lovely. But it wasn't everything. Both Richard and William needed to learn that. She hadn't yet got to that part of the story, though. She was at a part where they had both attended a function at which Richard had suggested to William – who was now going out with Persia – that he'd been trapped by an attention-seeking man-hunter who would soon leave him out to dry just like her former husband. But then, he'd said, William had always gone for other people's cast-offs. Hadn't he once dated a girl Richard himself had dumped?

Richard had left the party after saying this, and William, hesitating only briefly, had rushed after his brother. Richard was standing at the edge of the kerb. William's anger was still boiling inside him, but common sense told him that he would be better off hailing a cab and just going home. A yellow taxi sign caught his eye and he stuck out his arm to stop it. Richard had seen it too. Both of them tried to get into the cab, neither giving way to the other.

They argued loudly, pushing and shoving each other, and then, as Richard tried to get into the taxi, William grabbed him by the collar of his jacket. 'I'm going to fucking kill you!' he yelled. 'I really am.'

Was it too strong, wondered Britt, William actually saying

that he wanted to kill Richard? It was a phrase people used in anger but very seldom meant. It was a way of releasing the pent-up emotions.

She kept speed-reading until she reached the very end. It was a darker book than *The Perfect Man*. It didn't offer the solutions that Jack Hayes had offered. But she was satisfied. She hadn't thought she'd ever write another novel, but she had and she was proud of it. She was proud of how, after the fight, the brothers had finally reconciled with each other. It was right for them, although she knew that two women wouldn't have solved their differences with an unedifying scuffle at the side of the road that left one with a black eye and the other with a swollen lip.

She paused with her fingers over the keyboard and then typed the words THE END underneath the final paragraph. She sat in front of the laptop for ten minutes staring into space, feeling suddenly alone.

But when she went to bed a few minutes later, she fell into a deep, untroubled sleep.

Mia and Allegra were sitting in the paddling pool when Allegra asked about her father again.

'He would like this pool,' she said as she dunked her Bratz doll beneath the water. 'He could play swimming with me.'

Mia pictured the big pool in the house in Granada. Allegra would love it, she thought. But would she ever get the chance to swim in it? And why should she? It was, after all, the pool in Belén and Eduardo's home. If Alejo got a divorce, he would probably be the one to leave.

But even in his phone call to her the day after she'd

visited him he said nothing about divorce. He talked to her about making love, telling her that it had been better than he remembered, saying that just thinking about it was exciting and asking her did she feel the same way.

She did.

And she didn't.

She was feeling too guilty to be excited. Because whenever she thought of the house in Granada, all she could really see was the picture of Belén and Eduardo stuck to the American fridge.

How could she? she asked herself. How could she go into another woman's home and make love to another woman's husband there? Having sex with Alejo in Guatemala or, indeed, anywhere else in the world was one thing; doing it with him in his house had been . . . disrespectful. The word had seeped into her consciousness and she hadn't been sure about it at first, but now she was certain. It wasn't that she cared about Belén (at least not very much), but it had been wrong to do what she'd done in her house. Mia knew that if she and Alejo had been living in Villa Serena together and Belén had made love to him there, she'd feel humiliated.

She told herself that it didn't really matter, that Belén would never even know, but she felt badly about it all the same. And so when Alejo called her and spoke to her as he'd done a few times since then, she hadn't been able to feel anything other than guilty. And when he phoned, she wondered where he was because the idea of him calling her from the house, no matter whether Belén was there or not, made her feel guilty too.

He usually phoned at seven o'clock. Mia didn't tell him that seven was when she had dinner – early by the standards of most of the inhabitants of Sierra Bonita, but because – unlike her neighbours – she was in bed most evenings before midnight, it was a good time for her. However, since Alejo had started calling, she was eating later and later and sometimes, after talking to him, she didn't feel hungry at all.

The day he didn't call she was like a cat on a hot tin roof. So that when the telephone did ring, at nearly a quarter past seven the following evening, she leaped on it and answered it immediately.

'That was quick,' said the voice. 'I'd like to think you were waiting to hear from me, but I guess that'd be asking too much.'

'Steve?' Her voice echoed her surprise.

'Your friendly naval officer,' he said. 'Calling to let you know that we'll be in Malaga again in a few days.'

'Why didn't you just email?' she asked. Steve had sent her emails every couple of days. Light-hearted, jokey emails that always brought a smile to her face. Sometimes she sent him a jokey reply. Sometimes she didn't send anything at all.

'Because I wanted to hear your voice.'

'Oh. I didn't think you were due here for another couple of weeks.'

'Slight change in plan,' he told her cheerfully. 'Happens sometimes. Lucky for me, though, because I get the opportunity to see you. If you want to see me too, of course.'

She hesitated.

'If you're busy, I quite understand.' There was no change in the tone of Steve's voice.

'No. No. It's not that.' She felt her hand tighten around the receiver. 'It's . . .'

'Is everything OK?' asked Steve.

'Fine,' she replied. She took a deep breath. 'Allegra's father has showed up.'

'Oh.'

'He's not living with us or anything,' Mia said hastily. 'It's not like that. It's just . . .'

'What do you want to do? Have a relationship with him again?' This time she could hear a slight edge in Steve's voice.

'I want to do what's right. But I'm not sure what's right any more. He's Allegra's dad. It's important that I keep in touch with him. I thought that because he was her father I should love him too.'

'He'll always be her father,' said Steve. 'He doesn't always have to be a man you love.'

But she had always loved Alejo. Not because of Allegra but because he was The One.

'Well, look – if you're in a bit of a state about this guy, there's no point in us meeting up,' said Steve. 'I don't want to mess with your head. Other parts of you, maybe,' he added wryly. 'But not your head.'

'You're a really nice man, Steve Shaw,' she told him. 'Far too nice for me.'

'You deserve the best,' said Steve. 'Someone who thinks you're the most important person in the world.'

'Allegra already thinks that,' she joked.

'I think you're pretty damn important too,' Steve said.

'Do you?'

'You know I do.'

She closed her eyes and pictured him in his uniform, the *Aphrodite* behind him, telling her that he wouldn't have had a fling with her. Alejo isn't having a fling with me either, she told herself. He loves me.

'If you're too busy to hook up, that's fine,' said Steve. 'I just thought it would be fun.'

'I'd like to see you,' Mia said suddenly. 'I just don't want you to have a disappointing day.'

He laughed. 'Meet me. And if it's a disappointment to both of us, then I'll sail off into the sunset and leave you in peace.'

'OK,' said Mia.

'See you soon.'

'Yes. See you soon.'

It was Vanessa's birthday. Leo had remembered it at the beginning of the week but pushed the thought to the back of his mind. Sitting at his desk, though, with the interactive calendar on his computer showing the date in the top corner of the screen, he couldn't help recalling the previous year and how he'd taken her for a meal at Patrick Gilbaud's and given her the silver chain with the gold locket into which he'd already put a small photo of each of them. I was so arrogant, he thought. Arrogant and confident, because I never thought for a second that she would betray me. I was sure of her and sure of us and I was completely and utterly wrong, and how do I know that I'll ever get it right again?

The thought caught him by surprise. Obviously he was getting it right again. He was getting married, wasn't he? Hadn't he gone to Debenhams with Pippin to discuss their wedding list?

She was still sore at him about the Brown Thomas list. He knew she couldn't understand his utter implacability over it. She'd argued vehemently with him, but in the end she'd given in.

It was the first time he'd ever put his foot down about anything in their relationship.

It was another thought that shocked him. It hadn't been like that with Vanessa. He'd often argued with her about things. He hadn't let her walk all over him in the way he'd allowed Pippin to. Until now.

But was it because he'd rowed with Vanessa sometimes that she'd turned to Donal? If he argued with Pippin, would she turn away from him too?

She hasn't yet, he reminded himself. She still loves me. Despite the list.

Chapter 34

Position: Dublin.
Weather: clear skies. Wind: south-westerly 3kph.
Temperature: 26°. Barometric pressure: 1008.5mb.

There was a launch party on the hottest day of the year to celebrate the publication of Britt's second book, *The Wrong Husband*. It was held in a fashionable restaurant in Temple Bar, where the air-conditioning had to work overtime to keep the temperature of the room at a comfortable level. The restaurant had been decorated with posters of the book cover (a similar style to that of *The Perfect Man*, but this time showing the silhouette of a man and a woman, their heads close together) and a variety of blue and white balloons to match the jacket colour.

'Reminds me a bit of giving those workshops on the *Aphrodite*,' murmured Britt to Mia as they walked into the room.

Her sister laughed. 'Only no Steve Shaw for you to complain to,' she said. And as she said his name, she felt a slight shiver along her spine and she remembered seeing him at Malaga and him lifting her off her feet after he'd reached her and twirling her around in the air as though she was Allegra before kissing her softly on the lips. (Allegra had spent the day with Loli. Mia had felt terrible about leaving her with Ana Fernandez again, but her friend told her not to be crazy; that it was great that she was seeing a man! And Mia said, not the same man, which made Ana open her eyes very wide and call her a dark horse before telling her to have loads of fun.)

They'd spent another carefree morning in the city, and then Mia had asked him if he'd like to see Sierra Bonita, and so he'd come to the town with her and walked through its steep cobbled streets and exclaimed, as Britt had done, about the prettiness of the hanging baskets and the indolence of the cats sunning themselves on the whitewashed walls. It had been a totally relaxing couple of hours. Then she'd brought him back to the Villa Serena, where they'd sat on the terrace looking down towards the thin silver-blue line of the sea. And then Steve had kissed her and she'd kissed him back, and suddenly he'd lifted her up in his arms and carried her into the house, and although she hadn't intended it to happen, he'd made love to her on the big double bed where nobody had made love to her before.

It had been nothing like making love to Alejo. It had been slower and more gentle and utterly, utterly different, but she'd sighed with pleasure afterwards even though, almost immediately, she'd asked herself what sort of person was she that she could make love to Steve after having hot sex with Alejo. And then she'd wondered at her own phrasing, because she had been emotionally involved with making love to Steve, whereas with Alejo . . . She couldn't quite believe she was thinking that it had been more physical than anything else, because she'd always, always believed that Alejo was the love of her life, and that nobody could match up. Only Steve had. And she'd felt very confused as she'd lain in the bed beside him, drifting into half-sleep and glad that he'd been confident enough to bring condoms with him.

She'd been dozing in the crook of his arm when the phone had rung and she'd picked it up, thinking that it would be Ana but instead hearing the unmistakable voice of Alejo. She'd sat bolt upright in the bed, stark naked, and pulled the white sheet across her body as though he could see her.

He'd been away on business for a few days, he said. He hadn't been able to call. He was sorry. He couldn't wait to see her again. Belén would be going back to Madrid the day after tomorrow. Would she come to him? And this time stay the night?

'I'll call you back,' she said, replacing the phone and lying back on the bed, staring up at the ceiling.

Steve had guessed. He hadn't said anything, but he had slid out of the bed and into his clothes – not his white *Aphrodite* uniform but a pair of faded denim jeans and a short-sleeved shirt that had caused Mia not to recognise him straight away but that looked just as good on him as his uniform. He was, she'd realised, a very attractive man.

'Don't go,' she'd said as she watched him do up the buttons of his shirt.

'Why?' he asked.

She hadn't been sure of the answer.

Steve looked at her silently, then slipped on his worn deck shoes and walked out of the room.

'You're in a daze,' Britt told her now as they stood in the centre of the room.

'Um, *Aphrodite* flashback,' she lied. She took a glass of champagne from one of the waiters. 'It's fab, isn't it?'

'Yes.' Britt nodded enthusiastically and then waved happily as Corinne Doherty walked through the door. Britt and Corinne had stayed in touch following the Trevallion party, having discovered that they had a lot in common. Corinne would joke that people expected her to be broody and mysterious just because she wrote crime, while Britt shared her black thoughts about supposedly being a romance expert. The two of them had hit it off, and although they'd only met up once since the party, they'd exchanged regular emails. Corinne was off to take part in a literary festival in the States shortly and had promised to give Britt the lowdown on her talk about the perfect female detective.

'The good thing about being a crime writer is that you get diehard fans,' she told Britt. 'Some of them know far more about your characters than you do yourself. Which can be a bit of a problem when they ask searching questions to which you don't know the answers. That's when they look at you as though you're a big, big disappointment and you realise that they're going to switch to someone else.'

Britt grinned. 'You'll be a huge hit, I'm sure.'

'You sound like my agent,' said Corinne mischievously. 'But you know quite well that the whole tour business is hit and miss.'

Today's launch was a hit, though: lots of booksellers as well as Britt's family and her friends from Clavin & Grey had turned up and were now happily drinking iced cocktails.

'I do so envy you,' said Janice Brampton, who worked in corporate law. 'No rat race for you any more. How wonderful.'

'It is rather,' said Britt, who wanted to talk to Jeffrey Clavin about her future career. Not tonight, obviously. But she wanted to set up a meeting with him. Jeffrey, however, was in deep conversation with Frances O'Malley, another Trevallion author.

'Glad you didn't invite Chesney along,' Britt told Lisa-Anne, who came up to her and kissed her on both cheeks. 'She'd hate it, it's all far too girlie for her.'

'Probably,' agreed Lisa-Anne. 'Though that's a pity. It's lovely.'

'If a bit hot!' Meredith, looking stunning in a bright red dress with killer red shoes, fanned at her face with a napkin. 'I'm melting.'

'Have a Long Island Iced Tea,' suggested Britt. 'They're perfect for a day like today.'

'A whole week of this is forecast,' said Meredith despairingly. 'I like heat, but not this sweltering humid stuff.'

'You're just in the wrong place for it,' said Britt. 'We still haven't got to grips with hot weather in Dublin. We're better at central heating than air-con.'

A waiter walked by with a tray of cocktails and the three

women took one each. Then Lisa-Anne left Meredith and Britt together while she had a word with the Trevallion marketing director, who was standing on the other side of the room.

'They want you to write another two books,' murmured Meredith. 'They've already made an offer.'

'Really?' Britt's eyes widened. 'Without having seen sales figures yet?'

'They're happy with sales so far,' said Meredith confidently. 'And the offer reflects that.'

Britt blinked. 'What if . . .'

'. . . you can't do it? What if it's terrible?' teased Meredith, and Britt blushed. 'You've got to realise that you're good at this,' Meredith told her. 'You mightn't have thought so, but you are.'

'I'm still afraid . . .'

'. . . of failing,' said Meredith. 'You won't. And even if you do – so what? Better to have tried and failed than never to have tried at all.'

'Aren't you adapting that somewhat?' asked Britt in amusement.

'Still applies,' said Meredith. 'Look, we'll meet up tomorrow and go through the deal. I have to tell you, it's a good one.' She grinned. 'Will keep me in high heels and designer bags for another few months anyway.'

'I didn't think they'd make another offer. Not yet,' said Britt.

'Ah, don't worry.' Meredith grinned again. 'When you've lost it completely, they'll fling you on the scrapheap and throw their largesse at the next bright new thing.'

'I'm so glad you're cynical,' said Britt.

'Only when I need to be,' Meredith said cheerfully.

'I didn't realise this book was being published so soon,' Britt's mother said after Lisa-Anne had made a speech saying that *The Wrong Husband* was a wonderful read. 'You certainly didn't let on the last time we spoke. I thought it'd be ages yet.'

'It wasn't scheduled until next year,' Britt confided. 'But I finished it more quickly than I expected, and apparently there was a slot they could fit it into and the marketing and publicity people wanted to go with it . . . I'm in shock really, because I feel as though I've only just printed it off! It took much longer to get *The Perfect Man* on the shelves.'

'And this one is flying off them, according to your agent.'

'I hope so.' Britt looked relieved.

Paula grinned. 'I like to see you happy,' she said. 'I'm glad you've found your sparkle again.'

Britt smiled at her and then went over to talk to Harriett, who'd just arrived looking trim and elegant and, as Britt told her, not a day over fifty.

Allegra, Barney and Luke were having fun sampling the canapés and accepting glasses of Coke from the impeccably styled waiters, while Mia and Sarah chatted about the stresses of bringing up kids and James shared DIY stories with his father. Paula, meanwhile, was chatting to Meredith again and telling her that she had a whole heap of stories about running a guesthouse that would make a brilliant book, but that so far Britt had been reluctant to use a single one of them and Meredith would have to persuade her to turn them into what was bound to be a mega-seller.

The children were getting a little cranky before the party eventually broke up. Britt, her parents, Mia and the Trevallion people all went for something to eat in the Tea Rooms. James and Sarah brought the boys and Allegra home. Mia was staying over with Britt while Paula and Gerry, taking a night off from looking after people themselves, had booked a room in the Clarence and were looking forward to a bit of pampering.

It was almost midnight before they all went their separate ways. Mia and Britt, having said good night to the Trevallion people (who were now talking about going clubbing) got the next available taxi back to Britt's house.

'Oh, it's really different!' exclaimed Mia when she stepped inside the hallway. 'Much brighter than before. I love those purple lampshades.'

'I was trying to get away from the neutral look,' Britt told her. 'C'mon, I'll show you the guest bedroom.'

After it had been repainted, Britt had refurnished it too, in shades of gold and burnt orange that Mia told her reminded her of Villa Serena.

'I know,' said Britt. 'I borrowed the colour scheme from your guest room and adapted it for Dublin. I hope you don't mind. I felt comforted and secure in that room.'

'Did you?' Mia looked pleased.

'In the whole house, to be honest,' said Britt. 'There was something very peaceful about it.'

'I know,' said Mia, who was opening the window to let some air into the room. 'That's why I love living there.'

'Is that why you're still there?' asked Britt. 'Despite Alejo?'

'Oh no,' said Mia. 'It's nothing to do with Alejo. It's because Sierra Bonita is my home.'

'Not Granada?'

Mia took a deep breath.

'I slept with Steve,' she said.

Britt stared at her.

'You what!'

'I think you heard me.'

Mia told her about Steve's unexpected return to Malaga.

'Hot, sultry sex?' asked Britt.

'Not quite. But . . .'

'You're some kind of vixen, aren't you?' demanded Britt. 'Men falling all over you.'

'Don't joke,' begged Mia. 'I'm in such a terrible mess, I don't know what to do.'

'Why?'

'I slept with Alejo too. Twice.'

Britt's eyes darkened.

'I went to Granada,' said Mia.

She told him about her trip, and about seeing the photo of Belén and Eduardo, and of her guilt.

'And has he talked about divorcing Belén?' asked Britt.

Mia gazed into the distance. She was remembering the conversation. Truth was, she couldn't forget it. She replayed it in her head every single day.

Alejo had come to Sierra Bonita. They'd gone for coffee together in the café near the square where the red-hot geraniums spilled out of the window boxes against the white walls and everything seemed picture-postcard perfect.

'So,' Alejo said. 'We need to decide things, Mia, you and I.'

She nodded.

'I will say this again. I love you. I have always loved you. I will always love you. And I have a responsibility towards you and towards my daughter.'

She nodded again. The bells from the church tower pealed the hour and Alejo jumped, which made her smile.

'I have thought a lot about this,' he said when the clamour of the bells stopped. 'I need to do what is right for everyone. I have spoken to my legal advisers about it.'

She frowned.

'Belén and I . . .' He hesitated. 'We lead lives that are sometimes separate. But not always. I have known her a long time. She is the mother of my son.'

It was the way he said it that made her suddenly stiffen. The mother of my son. As though being the mother of a son trumped being the mother of a daughter.

'After losing our first child, Belén went through a very difficult time,' continued Alejo. 'I know that women lose babies and they recover, and of course Belén has recovered – she has Eduardo. But she is a fragile person.'

More fragile than me? wondered Mia, brushing non-existent crumbs from the starched white tablecloth.

'There is also a lot of money involved,' said Alejo.

It would cost him a lot of money to divorce Belén, Mia knew. Would he lose the beautiful house in Granada after all?

'I cannot divorce Belén,' he said. 'Not now. Not at this

time. I know this may seem silly and old-fashioned to you, but the family is very important.'

She fiddled with the wrapped tube of sugar on her saucer, splitting it open and spilling brown granules across the cloth.

'I wanted to divorce her four years ago,' Alejo said. 'I would have divorced her four years ago. But it is different now.'

'Because of Eduardo?' Mia suddenly found her voice.

'Yes.'

'But what about Allegra? You said that she was important. You said—'

'She is,' said Alejo simply. 'And I utterly and completely accept her as my daughter. I will make arrangements for her. And I will make arrangements for you too, Mia.'

'What sort of arrangements?' Mia's eyes narrowed.

'I am buying an apartment,' he told her. 'In a very exclusive area of the city. A private block with its own security. It has wonderful gardens, a pool – everything you could want. This apartment is for you.'

Mia stared at him.

'I will also give you a monthly allowance for Allegra. I will visit you in the apartment—'

'Hold on!' she cried. 'You're putting us up in an apartment in the city and you'll call out whenever you feel like it? Is that it?'

'But I will be there a lot,' he said. 'Because I will want to be there. I want to be with you. There is nobody for me like you, and—'

'Alejo!' She interrupted him again. 'You're turning me into your mistress! You want me to leave my home here and take Allegra from a place she loves so that we can sit around waiting for you to call! And what about Belén? When she finds out – and she *will* find out – what then?'

'That is for me to worry about,' said Alejo. 'I can deal with that part of my life.'

'And I'll be just another part of your life to deal with!' cried Mia.

'It's not like that,' said Alejo, a hurt expression on his face. 'It's not like that at all.'

'But of course it was,' Mia told Britt. 'Being in that apartment . . . waiting for him . . . just to sleep with him . . . that's not what I want from him. That's not what I want from my life.'

Britt put her arm around her sister's shoulders. 'I'm so sorry,' she said.

'I thought he was The One, and he was, but he was The One who was great at having sex with me. He's not The One who wants to leave his wife for me. I first saw him in a cathedral, and after I found out about Belén, I supposed that he was wrestling with his conscience about their relationship, and I was moved by that. I thought because he'd stayed with her that he'd done a really honourable thing. But now I think it was easier for him to stay than to leave. And it's still easier for him to do that. So maybe he hasn't stopped loving her either.'

'If someone showed they loved me by shagging someone else . . .'

'Y'see, that's just it!' cried Mia. 'He had sex with me but he went home to her. And he didn't mind that I came

573

to their house, and it was all a bit awful really and not what I would've expected. I had this memory of him doing the right thing, but he's not doing the right thing now. Either by me or Belén. Or by Allegra or Eduardo.' Mia took a tissue from the box on the table beside her and blew her nose. 'I love him and I do truly think that he loves me too, but . . . but not enough, Britt. Not enough to change his life and give up everything. What he wants is for me to give up my life for him. He kept telling me that it was a good offer and he couldn't understand why I . . .' She blew her nose again.

'Clavin and Grey have an excellent contact in Malaga,' Britt told her. 'The company does a lot of work for people who are buying property abroad, but they have a family law department too. I think you need to talk to someone so that you know exactly where you stand. To be on the safe side. So that you've covered all the bases.'

'I know.' Mia nodded. 'All the same, I think he will step up to the plate as far as Allegra is concerned. He really does want to do what's right for her – even if she is a girl.' Mia snorted. 'I don't know how things will eventually pan out. He'll have to tell Belén and that won't be very pleasant, although I think . . .' She looked pensive. 'Well, it seems to me that Belén is a tough cookie herself and not one bit fragile like he says. If they're leading semi-detached lives, she can't possibly believe that Alejo is behaving like a saint. Which I guess he probably hasn't been. So it won't be entirely unexpected.'

'And what about Steve?'

'Steve walked out because Alejo phoned while he was

there,' said Mia. 'He probably thinks I'm a total slut, and to tell you the truth I wouldn't blame him. Anyway,' she added. 'Sweet and nice and . . . well, great though he was in bed, he spends half his life on the ship and it was never really going to work.'

'So what are you going to do now?' asked Britt.

'Move house,' said Mia.

Britt looked at her in surprise.

'To a place in the town,' she said. 'Nearer the tourist office. They've offered me a full-time job there. Moving makes it easier with the childcare, and it means Allegra is closer to her friends too. She's missed the company since coming back from Ireland. Plus it's a really nice house. I'm going to rent for a year and then I have the option to buy it. Which, on the salary I'll be getting, might just be possible.'

'That's great,' said Britt.

'It's a start.'

'I'm sorry it didn't work out with Alejo,' said Britt.

'No you're not,' Mia told her. 'You didn't like him.'

'That wouldn't have made any difference if he'd been the right person for you.'

Mia sighed. 'One day,' she said. 'One day I'll meet someone who isn't married and who works on dry land and who might be good in bed too!'

'Emilio,' Britt reminded her. 'He's a great barman, and he confided in me that he's pretty frisky still, even if he is seventy.'

'Fool,' said Mia as the two of them laughed together.

Chapter 35

Position: Sierra Bonita.
Weather: cloudy. Wind: southerly 15kph.
Temperature: 23°. Barometric pressure: 1002.4mb.

Position: Dublin.
Weather: clear skies. Wind: southerly 5kph.
Temperature: 27°. Barometric pressure: 1009.2mb.

The Aer Lingus plane rattled through the unexpectedly dark clouds before finally touching down at Malaga airport. Mia and Allegra collected their luggage and walked out to the arrivals hall, which was darker than usual because of the heavy rain that had started to fall.

They tried to dodge the raindrops on the way to the car park but they were both wet by the time they got to the jeep. Allegra immediately insisted on listening to her storybook CD, and Mia silently cursed Britt for buying them, because she was sick of every single one.

Back at Villa Serena, Mia got soaked once again as she unlocked the gates, and when both she and Allegra finally got into the house, she immediately turned on the immersion heater so that they could have a shower. They stood in the stall together, singing 'Incy Wincy Spider' as the warm water sluiced off them. And then they got into their pyjamas even though it was only seven o'clock in the evening, and watched TV together.

'I love you, Mama,' said Allegra as she snuggled beside Mia.

'And I love you too,' said Mia. 'More than anyone else in the whole wide world.'

After Allegra had gone to bed, she poured herself a glass of red wine and thought about her future. She was looking forward to moving house and to working full time in the tourist office. The fact that she now had a full-time job had lifted a burden from her. And she knew that another burden had been lifted from her too. The burden of thinking that Alejo was the only man in her life. She couldn't help the fact that she'd fallen in love with him, but she had realised that she didn't love him enough to be set up in an apartment so that he could visit her any time he wanted hot, sultry sex. Some people might be able to live like that, she knew. But she couldn't. And so she was ready to live her life without him. Ready to stop thinking about him.

He wasn't The One after all, she told herself. The One has to be about more than passion. The One has to be there for the long haul too.

Two weeks later she was sitting in Sierra Bonita's town square again. It was late evening. The geraniums were still in bloom, the air was balmy from yet another beautiful day and the children – Allegra among them – were once again playing on the steps outside the church.

Mia watched as they chanted their rhyming game together and then burst into fits of giggles. Allegra was happy here, she thought. Happy in the new house. Happy to be closer to her friends. Happy, Mia hoped, with her life.

Earlier in the week, Mia had met Alejo again. It had been for lunch, in a small restaurant in the centre of Granada. The meeting had been formal and a little stilted.

'Love isn't enough, Alejo,' she told him. 'There's more to it than that. There's honesty and togetherness and being part of something. Which wouldn't happen with me in an apartment and Belén in your home. I think you and she have something that you and I will never have.'

Alejo had said that she was hurting him, and she told him that she'd never meant to. In the same way, she added, that he'd never meant to hurt her. But there had been hurt nonetheless. And there would be more in the future when Belén learned about Allegra. But, Mia said, she didn't think Belén would leave him over it. She knew, from the flicker that crossed Alejo's face, that she was right.

'I want you to be there as Allegra's father,' she told him. 'I think you'll be a good father to her. We will work out how that will be. But you and I – that won't work.'

He'd tried to make her change her mind, but both of them knew that he was wasting his time. And so when they'd finished lunch and they parted outside the restaurant, he kissed her lightly on each cheek and told her that arrangements were already in place for support payments for Allegra.

'It was never about the money,' she told him.

'And when I came to see you, it wasn't just to find out about my daughter,' he said.

She nodded. 'I know.' She looked at her watch. 'I have to go. I have to pick her up from Ana's.'

'*Hasta luego*, Mia,' said Alejo.

'*Adios*,' she said in return, and walked down the street without looking back.

Now she drained her coffee cup and replaced it carefully on the saucer. The first of what were monthly payments for Allegra had landed in her bank account, and the feeling of terror that she usually had when checking her balance had gone. Alejo was being more generous than he needed to be. He was, thought Mia, a good man. Not, perhaps, the most faithful of men. But not bad either.

But not for her. Never for her. Always a great passion in her life. Not one to regret. But not one to carry into the future either. Because she had changed. She wanted passion, of course she did. But she wanted other things more.

She reached down and opened her bag. She took out the copy of the email she had printed out the previous day. It was from Steve Shaw.

'I'm sorry I left like that,' he'd written. 'I should've stayed around and talked to you. But I was suddenly terribly jealous about a guy I'd never met. I want you to know that I loved being with you and making love to you. And

579

that if you ever want to contact me – well, you know where I am. That's the thing about being on a ship . . . I can't escape you. Thing is, Mia – I don't think I want to.'

Mia smoothed the paper and reread the words. Then she closed her eyes and pictured Steve: friendly and warm when she'd first come to him and talked about Britt's workshops; holding her in his arms at the Valentine Ball; kissing her the day they'd left the *Aphrodite*; giving her a purple swimsuit on the beach at Malaga. She pictured his smile and the colour of his eyes. And she remembered how very, very good it had been making love to him in the Villa Serena. She thought she'd ruined it that day by taking Alejo's call. She knew that Steve had been very hurt and she hated that she had been the one to hurt him.

She folded the paper and traced her finger along the edges, lost in thought. Then she glanced up and caught Allegra looking at her.

'Come on, *chica*,' she called. 'Time to go home.'

'Can't I stay . . . ?'

'No,' said Mia.

'Please?'

Mia shook her head. 'I'm sorry, Allegra. I have to go and send an email.'

'But . . .'

'It's important,' said Mia. 'An important email to an important person.'

Allegra sighed deeply and waved goodbye to her friends as she ran over to her mother. Then, hand in hand, she and Mia walked down the cobbled street to their new home.

* * *

Dublin continued to be stiflingly hot. The city pavements were warm underfoot and the heated air shimmered as it rose. Women wore strappy tops and light skirts, and any man who absolutely didn't have to wear a business suit was dressed in a T-shirt and shorts. Those who couldn't dress down carried their jackets over their shoulders and opened their shirts at the neck. At lunchtime the office workers poured out into the parks and along the canals and returned to their desks with a pink glow. Sales of sunblock soared. So did sales of cold drinks and ice cream.

Britt thought enviously of the cooler breezes in Sierra Bonita and, longingly, of Allegra's paddling pool. She was thinking of getting one herself to put in her back yard. She was hot and she was tired and the idea of sitting in a pool of cold water was very appealing right now.

She'd spent the last couple of weeks doing publicity for *The Wrong Husband*, which was selling well, although it hadn't dominated the charts like *The Perfect Man*. She'd been worried about that at first (she still worried about it every so often), but Meredith had pointed out that the sales figures were very strong and that Trevallion were really happy. Then she told her that the film company which would soon be starting work on *The Perfect Man* was also interested in *The Wrong Husband*. So, she assured her, no need to panic.

'I think panic might be my default setting,' Britt told her. 'I can't help myself.'

'Certainly no need to panic after that offer from Trevallion for the next two books,' Meredith said. 'Always provided that you're going to sign.'

She hadn't signed yet. She knew that both Meredith and Trevallion were anxious. But she also knew that she had to do the right thing. After today, she'd have decided on her future.

She stood in front of her open wardrobe and looked at the clothes on the hangers. Then she picked out a white cotton blouse and a cerise skirt. She'd bought the skirt for an interview she'd done with a women's magazine a few months ago but hadn't worn it since. It was a tailored skirt that came to just above the knee. For the magazine photo-shoot she'd worn it with a waist-cinching belt, but it was too hot to be constrained by a belt today. She selected the pair of peep-toe shoes she'd bought at the same time as the skirt (cerise with white piping) and pulled a bag from the top shelf. It was an ordinary beige bag that she'd had for years. Unlike many women, Britt wasn't really into bags. She often felt that she should be, but she never quite managed it.

Harriett was cleaning her windows when Britt stepped outside.

'You shouldn't be doing that in this heat,' she scolded her neighbour.

'Ah, it's no bother. I like clean windows.' Harriett put down her chamois leather and regarded Britt with interest. 'And where are you off to looking so pretty?'

Britt grinned at her. 'My old law firm,' she said. 'I'm meeting the senior partner.'

'You're going back?' Harriett looked horrified. 'You can't do that! What'll I do for reading if you stop writing?'

'Did you try that crime novelist I suggested?' asked Britt. 'Corinne Doherty?'

'Yes, I did. And I enjoyed the stories. But there's no romance in them,' said Harriett.

'There wasn't any romance in *The Wrong Husband* either,' Britt told her.

'Ah, get away with you!' Harriett snorted. 'That William . . . I'm in love with him myself.'

Britt laughed.

'Seriously,' said Harriett. 'If he was real, I'd run away with him.'

'I'm glad you enjoyed it,' said Britt.

'I hope you're not going to stop writing,' Harriett warned her. 'I'll have you tormented if you do.'

'We'll see,' said Britt as she readjusted her bag on her shoulder. 'I'd better go or I'll be late. And you know I hate being late.'

'Off you go so.' Harriett picked up the chamois again. 'But even if you do go back to the law . . .' She paused as she weighed up her words. 'Well, even if you do, you should keep dressing like that. It's much, much nicer on you than that dull aul black ever was.'

The offices of Clavin & Grey were on Fitzwilliam Square. The magnificent Georgian building had been completely refurbished inside and an entire new modern wing had been added to the back. It was glass and steel, and Britt had enjoyed working in it, even on rainy days, because it was so light and airy.

Jeffrey's office was in the old part of the building. It was quiet and muted with a pale blue carpet, cream walls and a large chandelier suspended from the high ceiling.

Jeffrey's certificates, in plain gold frames, hung on the walls.

Britt had sat in this office hundreds of times, talking to Jeffrey about various clients, bouncing ideas off him and having his ideas run by her in return. She had always liked and respected Jeffrey, and even when they argued she knew that the disagreement was professional, not personal. The only time it had become personal was when he'd asked her to take leave because her writing was interfering with the business.

'Well now,' he said after they'd finished talking. 'I'd forgotten how much I enjoyed sparring with you.'

'Missed me?' Her voice was teasing.

'Yes,' he admitted. 'You were in a league of your own when it came to divorces. Ireland's answer to Fiona Shackleton.'

Britt laughed. 'At least I didn't have any angry opponents dumping jugs of water over me,' she said.

'Nobody realises what a dangerous business the law can be.' Jeffrey stood up.

'The restaurant is booked for one. Shall we?'

She nodded. 'I need to freshen up first. I'll see you in reception.'

'Great.'

She walked through the old building and into the newer annexe where the washrooms were located. She stood in front of the big mirrors and pulled her wide-toothed brush through her hair. The loose curls bounced around her shoulders. Then she re-applied her minty lip gloss, sprayed some DKNY behind her ears and on her wrists and readjusted the simple pendant she wore around her neck.

I look different, she accepted as she gazed at her reflection. Before when I looked at myself in this mirror I always knew who was going to look back. I thought it was a stronger version of myself, but now I'm not sure. Black and white and a severe hairstyle didn't make me strong. It was my cold heart that did it. Yet now . . . she frowned slightly . . . I'm in pink and white and my heart – well, it's not warm and gloopy, but maybe it's a bit more open.

Not that being open means anything, she told herself as she scooped her lip gloss and brush into her bag. Not that there's anyone for me to be open towards. She hesitated for a second as she slung the bag over her shoulder. If I'd been more open with Ralph, would it all have worked out? She laughed at herself in the mirror. Of course not! The foundation of their relationship had been all wrong.

There was passion between us at the start, she thought, but it wasn't enough to keep us going. And besides, I might be passionate, but my needs and desires were very different from Ralph's.

But, Britt realised as she stepped out into the corridor again, she did want someone, someday. Maybe not the polar opposite of Ralph; certainly not someone as perfect as Jack Hayes either. But someone to share her life with. Someone who could perhaps be romantic from time to time, because, after all, romance was the icing on a cake. It was nice occasionally, but too sugary to sustain you. Nevertheless, even a little icing went a long way.

She took the long way back to reception so that she passed by her old office. There was no name plate on the door, which was slightly ajar. She wavered for a moment and then pushed it open. She'd always tried to keep her desk tidy. Having a tidy desk helped to keep her mind focused too. Some of her colleagues liked to have files and folders piled high beside them. But she had always allowed only one file on her desk at any given time.

There was only one file on it now, and it was open, even though nobody from Clavin & Grey was behind the desk. But, she realised as she glanced inside the room and stood quite still, the client was there. Her intake of breath sounded loud in her own ears. It was certainly loud enough to make him turn and look at her.

'Britt?' His face showed his surprise. 'What are you doing here?'

'This is where I used to work,' she said. 'I came to have a meeting with the senior partner.'

'Why?' asked Leo Tyler. 'Somebody suing you over your latest book?'

'Not that I know of,' she said. 'What has you here?'

'I had a meeting too,' he told her. 'With the solicitor who's looking after Donal's affairs.'

'Who?' she asked.

'Ferdia Grey.'

She nodded slowly. Ferdia was the other senior partner, specialising in different areas of law from Jeffrey.

'And where is he now?' she asked.

'Oh, he's gone to find some piece of paper or other.' Leo glanced at his watch. 'He's been gone five minutes. I wonder, does that push me into a new billable hours slot?'

Britt smiled. 'We're not that sharp-practising at Clavin and Grey,' she told him.

'We?' He looked at her quizzically. 'Are you coming back to the firm?'

She shook her head. 'No. I thought long and hard about it. Especially when after the first couple of weeks, sales of *The Wrong Husband* were down on *The Perfect Man*. I thought I was a loser and that Trevallion would drop me like a hot potato. But it's still selling and it's doing quite well and they're happy.' She smiled faintly. 'They've offered me a new contract and I thought . . . Well, I've had this idea rattling around in my head ever since I finished *The Wrong Husband* and I don't think it's going to go away. So . . .'

He smiled at her then, and the slightly stern expression that had clouded his face lifted. 'I think it's your destiny,' he told her. 'And better than being a lawyer, surely?'

'It might depend on how good a lawyer you were.' She grinned. 'I was a hotshot legal eagle. No divorce too big or too small, that was my motto.'

'Was it really?'

'Well, no,' she admitted. 'But I was good at it. And I was never scared by it.' She looked rueful. 'Every time I put pen to paper I'm terrified. But I can't seem to stop myself.'

'It was a wonderful book,' said Leo.

'Everyone said so,' agreed Britt. 'And I guess when I was writing it I could let myself go because I never thought anyone would read it. But then when it was published and there was such a fuss . . . it was very scary.'

'Not *The Perfect Man*,' said Leo. '*The Wrong Husband*.'

'Oh.' She felt her cheeks turn pink. 'You read it?'

'Of course,' he said. 'How could I not? You're the only real live author I know. And I wanted to see if you'd put all those tips from the writing classes into practice.'

'Probably not,' she said.

'I couldn't tell,' said Leo. 'I was too caught up in the story to notice.'

'About the story . . .' she said doubtfully.

'It was an interesting subject. Particularly for me. I don't think many people have written about brothers like that.'

Britt looked uncomfortable. 'I think I have to apologise to you. Because after talking to you I couldn't stop thinking about brothers. Especially competitive brothers.'

'You think Donal and I were competitive?'

'I don't know,' replied Britt. 'I don't know a thing about your relationship and I don't want to know. It was just that when we spoke, it sparked something in my head.'

'Occupational hazard, I guess,' said Leo.

'Kind of.'

'I read it in a day,' said Leo. 'And I cried at the end.'

Britt swallowed hard. 'Sorry.'

'For them,' he said. 'Naturally. There was so much they needed to say to each other. I was glad they got the opportunity.'

'I thought it important,' she said.

He nodded. 'I would have liked that myself.'

'Oh Leo, I never meant to upset you.' Britt looked at him in contrition. 'I'm sorry if I did.'

'You didn't,' he said. 'I cried because I envied them.'

'You did?'

'I loved the fight scene,' said Leo. 'I loved where William

got Richard by the throat. I wanted to do that myself. I wanted Donal to be alive so that I could beat the shit out of him. I wanted to hurt him in the same way that William hurt Richard.'

'I don't think he should have been violent,' said Britt, 'but it turned out that way.'

'He was right,' objected Leo. 'Because of all that stuff there was in their past. All the times Richard had pulled one over on him. I loved how it came out in the end, because all the way through I kept wondering why they were forever competing against each other. But at the end I understood it. It was very satisfying.'

'It truly wasn't about you and Donal,' Britt said. 'Everyone thought my first book was somehow about Ralph and me but it wasn't. It *so* wasn't!' She smiled. 'But I suppose when I meet people who interest me I can't help the fact that they set me thinking in a certain way.'

'I understand that,' said Leo. 'When I started reading *The Wrong Husband* I wasn't thinking of Donal and me. But at the end I was. I wondered whether if we could have beaten the shit out of each other it would have helped.' He grinned. 'Obviously not, though. I'm a crap fighter. He would've taken me to the cleaners – he always did!'

'Are you OK about it?' she asked. 'You don't seem . . . you don't seem so tight.'

'You were the first person I ever told the truth to,' he said. 'And afterwards I felt as though part of me had suddenly thawed out. Later I was talking to someone else and another part of me thawed. When I read the book, when I felt the things that William felt – well, then the rest of me unfroze too. It was extraordinary. I suddenly stopped being the Leo I'd become and returned to being the Leo I'd been before. It was like stepping back into my old life.'

'Really?' Britt looked at him anxiously.

'Totally and utterly,' said Leo. 'Ever since the accident I've felt as though I was living in a bubble. I was the only one who knew the truth about them. I had to pretend that everything was OK, and every time I pretended, it was like someone sticking a knife into my back. I'll always have to pretend that everything was OK. But now . . .' he shrugged slightly, 'now it's different. It was . . . would have been Vanessa's birthday a few weeks ago. Her mum organised a service of thanksgiving for her life. She asked me to come. I wouldn't have been able to before. Or if I had, I would've got blindingly drunk and then I'd've been afraid of what I'd say or do. But I went and it was OK. Not pleasant. But OK. Somehow it didn't seem to hurt as much any more.'

'I'm glad if you think the book helped,' said Britt. 'But the truth is that it's probably Pippin. A new relationship, a new perspective . . . It takes time, but eventually you work it all out.'

Leo looked at her steadily. 'Pippin and I aren't together any more,' he said.

It took a few moments before Britt realised exactly what he'd said, and then she stared at him in surprise. 'What?'

'We broke up,' he told her.

'Why?'

'Because I realised that it was a mistake,' he said.

'Not because of the book?' She looked horrified. 'Not because William and Persia break up?'

Leo grinned. 'Give me some credit,' he said. 'I don't live my life according to a book, thanks very much.' He shook his head. 'We split up because I realised that I'd asked her to marry me for all the wrong reasons and she wanted to marry me for all the wrong reasons and the truth was that she was right for me for a few weeks but not for ever.'

He'd known it all along, of course. Even as he'd asked her to marry him, he'd known that he was making a mistake, only he'd pushed that thought to the back of his mind because at that moment he'd known that the most beautiful girl on the *Aphrodite* could be his and he'd wanted to have her. As he'd slid the ring on to her finger, he'd sent a mental message to Donal telling him that he was welcome to Vanessa because he, Leo, had got a much greater prize. A more beautiful girl. Who loved him.

It had been wrong, he knew. He'd tried to convince himself over the next few months that it was right. But somehow he'd always known. And the truth was that Pippin had probably always known too.

'Hey, it was great while it lasted,' she told him when they'd had the 'we need to talk' conversation. 'All those pictures of us together made a super couple. And now the gossip columnists will be on to me about my broken heart. I'll get loads of coverage.'

He'd asked her if her heart was broken, and she'd grinned and told him that it took more than two broken engagements to do that. He'd frowned and she'd told him that she'd been engaged before. A childhood sweetheart, she'd said. It only lasted a few months because he hadn't been able to hack it when she'd become famous.

She'd kept secrets from him. He'd thought that he was the one keeping secrets from her. Later that night, alone in his Monkstown house, he'd wondered about the fact that everyone kept secrets. Even from those they were closest to.

'And she's OK about it?' Britt's question brought him back to the present.

'Absolutely,' he replied. 'She was fine about it, actually. She sees it as a career move.' He looked at Britt enquiringly. 'I thought you might have read about it in one of the gossip magazines.'

'Well, I know it marks me out as someone not in touch with real life,' said Britt. 'But I only read them when I'm in the hairdresser's. Or the dentist's. And I haven't been to either recently. If you'd split up when I was doing publicity for *The Wrong Husband* I might have known about it because I was constantly getting my hair done then.'

Leo laughed. 'I should've timed it better.'

'Keep that in mind in future,' said Britt. 'I suppose Eileen is devastated.'

'She was at first,' Leo said. 'But I think she's over it now. Anyway, Pippin's seeing someone else.'

'Not Gerry?'

'Who?' He looked astonished.

'I met them together one night. At the launch of a hair-care product range. I think he was the CEO of the company.'

'Oh him,' said Leo dismissively. 'No, not him. Closer to home as far as I'm concerned.'

Britt frowned.

'She's currently going out with my best friend. According to Mike, it's the real deal. He's crazy about her and he loves doing the media stuff with her.'

'Oh my God, Leo.' Britt was horrified. 'First your brother, now your friend! That's not exactly good news. And you're all right with this?'

'It doesn't sound great when you put it like that,' he agreed. 'But the truth is that Donal and Vanessa probably were always better suited to each other. It was just that I met her first. I used to think it was great that they hit it off so well, but obviously I was just fooling myself. I would've been fooling myself if Pippin and I had got married too. You can't make someone love you. If something goes wrong you can't force them to stay.'

'True,' said Britt. 'Though I do sometimes think my divorce clients don't try hard enough.'

'If Vanessa and I been married, perhaps it would've been a different story,' said Leo. 'But we weren't. And she fell in love with my brother and I still hate that fact and hate that I can't punch him in the face, but I've accepted it.'

'You seem very different,' acknowledged Britt. 'Much more together.'

'Oh, only about some things,' Leo told her. 'There are others where I'm not together at all. Other times that I've thought about doing something but haven't had the confidence. I think that's the legacy Donal left me with. Being unsure.'

'You've no need to be unsure,' Britt told him firmly. 'You're a good catch, Leo Tyler.'

He smiled ruefully. 'I'm hoping that some day the right woman thinks that.'

'Of course she will.' Britt felt the thud of her heart as her stomach went into somersault mode. She wanted Leo to find someone. He deserved some happiness. She just wished . . . She closed her eyes and then opened them again. She just wished she wasn't suddenly having silly, irrational thoughts about him. She wished the butterflies in her stomach would be still and her heart would stop tripping in her chest.

'I've thought about it for some time,' Leo continued. 'And I'm hoping that it'll be third time lucky for me.'

'I hope so too,' she said. 'I hope you meet the girl you want to ask out and that she's everything you've ever dreamed of and that it all works out for you and that you both live happily ever after.'

'I've already met her,' said Leo.

Britt felt the thud of her heart as her stomach sank.

'That's great,' she told him brightly. 'And how's it going?'

'Not that well, actually,' said Leo. 'I've known her for a while but I haven't had the nerve to ring her up and ask her out. I pick up the phone but my nerve goes at the last minute. I'm afraid that she'll think I'm a serial dumpee and a sad loser.'

'That's ridiculous,' said Britt. 'Nobody would think that about you, Leo. I told you – you're a great guy. And you're not a serial anything. I agree that the situation with Vanessa and Donal was a real tragedy, but I admire how you've dealt with it. It's OK that it took time. You lost two people you were really close to. So of course it was going to be difficult. As for Pippin – well, everyone's allowed a fling, even though not everyone is daft enough to get engaged during it. But still . . .' She broke off, astonished to find that she was welling up. She swallowed hard before she was able to continue. 'It's not like the girl is going to know everything about you from the get-go. She'll just think that you're a good-looking man with a decent job. A good catch!'

'This girl does know,' said Leo. 'This girl is smart and clever in her own right, and although she might sympathise, I don't know if she would want anything more from me. And that's why I'm so afraid to ask. Because for as long as I don't – for as long as I pick up the phone and put it back without dialling her number – I can always imagine that she might say yes. I don't have to face the fact that it could be no.'

Britt nodded. 'It's like my old clients,' she told him. 'The women who suspect their husbands of cheating on them. They want to find out but they're afraid that they'll be right. And so they wait and hope. Sooner or later, though, they have to face it. Sooner or later, so do you.'

'You're right,' he said. 'I was going to phone her tonight. It would have been my third attempt this week. But . . .'

'Do,' said Britt fiercely. 'Phone her and ask her, and Leo, if she says no, then it doesn't really matter. If she says no, she's not worth it.'

'I think she's worth it anyway,' said Leo. 'No matter what she says.'

'Well you'll never find out until you ask,' said Britt.

Suddenly she needed to get out of the office. She needed to be away from Leo and away from the feelings she was having as they discussed his love life.

'I've got to go,' she said abruptly. 'Jeffrey will be wondering what on earth has happened to me.'

'Before you do . . .' Leo reached out and touched her arm. Britt felt herself stiffen involuntarily. 'Before you do,' he continued. 'Since you're actually here and it means I don't have to phone, are you free for dinner this evening?'

Britt stared at him. And then she realised what he had said. 'Me? You're asking me out?'

'Well who else do I know?' he asked. 'Who else do I know who could put me into the total loser category? Who else knows everything there is to know about me? Who else do I know who's smart and sassy and who I'd like to ask to dinner?'

Britt's stomach wasn't somersaulting any more. But her heart was on a rollercoaster.

Leo looked suddenly anxious. 'Was it all bullshit?' he asked. 'Do you really think I'm a sad loser after all? Do you think that I'm not such a great guy now that I've actually asked?'

'No,' said Britt slowly. 'No. I always thought you were great.'

'Even when I was pouring out my heart to you in a pathetic sort of way?'

'You weren't pathetic,' she said. 'It took courage to tell me that stuff.'

'But does it make me the sort of person you want to

596

go out with?' he asked. 'Or am I . . .' His voice trailed off and he continued to look at her with an anxious expression in his eyes.

'I told you what you were,' said Britt. 'I'm not going to keep telling you. That would get this relationship off to a terrible start.'

'Relationship?'

It was Britt's turn to look anxious. 'Sorry. Much too heavy a word to use.'

'But maybe the right one,' said Leo. 'Under the circumstances.'

She laughed suddenly. 'Whether it's just dinner or whether it ends up being something else, I'm looking forward to finding out,' she told him. 'And meeting you here today was . . . was . . .'

'Romantic?' he suggested.

'I was going to say lucky.' She smiled.

'I prefer romantic,' said Leo.

'You know how I feel about that!'

'I know how you feel in theory,' said Leo. 'But I'm kind of thinking that in practice it might be different.'

'How?' she asked.

He put his arms around her and pulled her close to him. Her blue eyes locked on to his. She began to smile.

'You don't smile for romance,' said Leo sternly, although he was smiling himself. 'You . . . you surrender yourself to it.'

She laughed. She couldn't help it.

But she stopped when he kissed her. Because his kiss was no laughing matter at all. It was the most serious thing that had happened to her in years.

She didn't hear the door to the office open again. She didn't hear Ferdia Grey cough apologetically. She didn't even hear Jeffrey Clavin, who'd given up waiting in reception and come looking for her, beside him.

She was lost in Leo's kiss.

The best kiss she'd ever had in her whole life.

And by far the most romantic.

SHEILA O'FLANAGAN

Someone Special

Romy Kilkenny loves her life in Australia. Her social diary is always full, her career is about to get a boost and she's happy sharing a house with Keith. But when she gets a call to say she's needed back in Ireland, Romy's world is turned upside down.

Romy's glamorous mother Veronica has never understood her younger daughter. Romy can't help feeling a poor second to her half-siblings: Darragh – happily married to perfect Giselle – and Kathryn, with her glitzy New York lifestyle. Romy feels like more of an outsider than ever. And she really wishes she hadn't tried to kiss Keith goodbye at the airport. He's her best friend, not her lover!

Sheila O'Flanagan's compelling new novel explores the tensions and the joys of being part of a family – and shows that you never know when someone special is just around the corner . . .

Praise for Sheila O'Flanagan

'Guaranteed to put O'Flanagan on the bestsellers list – yet again' *Irish Independent Review*

'The appeal is obvious . . . a romantic, feel-good factor, they're funny and she doesn't shy away from emotional issues' *Irish Post*

'Hugely enjoyable' *Best*

978 0 7553 3221 2

headline
review

SHEILA O'FLANAGAN

Bad Behaviour

Darcey has it all: a high-flying career, an apartment in the centre of Dublin and a wardrobe bursting with designer labels. OK, so she doesn't have Mr Right in her life at the moment, but she's not short of admirers. So why does an unexpected wedding invitation send shivers down her spine? Because the groom, Aidan, dumped her . . . for her ex-best friend.

Nieve's now living across the Atlantic but she's coming home to get married. It's going to be the event of the year and Nieve wants *all* her friends to be there. Especially Darcey. Isn't now the time to put the past behind them?

But can Darcey really forgive her oldest friend nd allow Nieve's wedding to go without a hitch? Or is it possible that Aidan was meant to be hers after all?

Praise for Sheila O'Flanagan's bestsellers

'A must-read' *Woman's Own*

'Hugely enjoyable' *Best*

'A big, comfortable, absorbing book . . . guaranteed to put O'Flanagan on the bestsellers list – yet again' *Irish Independent Review*

978 0 7553 3218 2

headline
review

SHEILA O'FLANAGAN

Connections

'A journey of intrigue and romance' *Irish Examiner*

Welcome to the Caribbean resort of White Sands, where the sparkling turquoise sea laps against the glittering shore, lush green palms sway gently in the breeze, and everyone has a story to tell.

Jennifer is here to marry the man of her dreams, but could an unexpected wedding guest turn her perfect day into a nightmare? Sahndhi, disillusioned winner of Pop Princess, has come to escape the media glare. Or so she thinks. Grainne and Aidan celebrate their twenty-fifth wedding anniversary, while secretly wondering if it's all a sham. Divorced dad Rudy arrives for a rare holiday with his beloved little boy – though his ex-wife may not see it in the same light. And thriller-writer Corinne observes all from the sidelines, as she battles with writer's block and self-doubt. Is the inspiration she needs closer than she thinks?

Join these and many other holidaymakers for a journey of intrigue and romance, as intertwining tales unfold from beach to bedroom to bar. Together they create a delightful collection of stories, the ideal escape to pure paradise . . .

Praise for Sheila O'Flanagan's bestsellers:

'The perfect book to bring on a flight' *Evening Herald*

'Vastly entertaining' *Ireland on Sunday*

'The Sheila O'Flanagan guarantee is a pretty powerful one' *Irish Independent*

978 0 7553 2345 6

headline
review

Now you can buy any of these other bestselling books by **Sheila O'Flanagan** from your bookshop or *direct from her publisher*.

FREE P&P AND UK DELIVERY
(Overseas and Ireland £3.50 per book)

Someone Special	£6.99
Bad Behaviour	£7.99
Yours, Faithfully	£7.99
Connections	£7.99
How Will I Know?	£7.99
Anyone But Him	£7.99
Dreaming of a Stranger	£7.99
Destinations	£7.99
Too Good To Be True	£7.99
Caroline's Sister	£7.99
Isobel's Wedding	£7.99
He's Got To Go	£7.99
My Favourite Goodbye	£7.99
Far From Over	£7.99
Suddenly Single	£7.99

TO ORDER SIMPLY CALL THIS NUMBER

01235 400 414

or visit our website: www.headline.co.uk

Prices and availability subject to change without notice.